Driven by ambition, divided by greed, the Stockwells' bitter rivalries threaten the very foundation of their dynasty . . .

"Let me guess. Your wife doesn't understand you." Patrice could feel her face growing redder. Her nervousness made her joke, but she also felt a thrill of pleasure sitting next to him. God, how she wanted him! Remember, she cautioned herself. Remember what happened last time.

"My wife has other interests. 'Extramarital,' I think is the proper description." Jack looked into her eyes in a way calculated to melt any resistance Patrice might have had.

It was a one-night stand, that's all it was. He said it wasn't, but it was. And then he ditched me for Buffy. Remember, Patrice! Remember how that hurt! Don't do this to yourself. Get up and walk out before it's too late. Instead she caught her breath sharply as Jack moved closer and took her hand.

She couldn't help herself. She was too attracted to him to resist. And since their affair, she had not seen any other man. She had immersed herself in business.

Jack leaned in and kissed her, just as Patrice had known all along he would. She responded, first tentatively, then fiercely. Had there ever been any doubt that she would? Her common sense and her memory had always taken second place to her desire for Jack.

RIVERVIEW

THE LION'S SHARE

KATHLEEN FULLER

IVY BOOKS • NEW YORK

The author of this work is a member of the
National Writers Union.

Ivy Books
Published by Ballantine Books
Copyright © 1988 by Butterfield Press, Inc.

Produced by Butterfield Press, Inc.
133 Fifth Avenue
New York, New York 10003

Library of Congress Catalog Card Number: 87-91000

ISBN 0-8041-0020-9

Manufactured in the United States of America

First Edition: February 1988

For my daughter, Julie Coakley,
Peace and Love

The Stockwells

Governor Matthew Adams Stockwell: Patriarch of the family, deceased

Mary Linstone Stockwell: His first wife, and mother of his children, deceased

Brenda "Buffy" Cabot Stockwell: His second wife

Jack Houston: Buffy Stockwell's present husband

James Linstone Stockwell: Governor's eldest son, widowed

Patrice Stockwell O'Keefe: His eldest child, divorced

Matthew Sykes Stockwell: His eldest son

Michael Stockwell: His youngest son

Lisa Stockwell: His youngest child

Alice Stockwell Lewis: Governor's eldest daughter

David Lewis: Alice's husband

Jonathan Charles Stockwell: Governor's youngest son

Ellen Smith Stockwell: His wife

Peter Stockwell: Jonathan and Ellen's only child

Terry Stockwell: Governor's daughter, deceased

Holly Stockwell Meyerling: Her daughter, divorced from first husband, Christopher Millwood, married to Zelig Meyerling

Nicholas Millwood: Holly's only child

Susan Stockwell Wells Gray: Governor's youngest child, widowed

Decatur "Deke" Wells: Susan's child

The Tylers

Sarah Stockwell Tyler: Governor Stockwell's eldest sister

Beth and Carrie Tyler: Sarah Tyler's great-granddaughters

Max Tyler: Sarah Tyler's grandson

Diana Tyler: Sarah Tyler's granddaughter, Max's younger sister

Louise Tyler Papatestus: Sarah Tyler's granddaughter, Max's youngest sister, married to Spiro Papatestus

THE LION'S SHARE

BOOK ONE

1

WAITING FOR THE wedding to begin, the four-year-old boy moved through a Sunday-afternoon forest of adult legs. His Eton suit with its lavender cummerbund, matching bowtie and boutoniere the same shade as the gowns of the bridesmaids, was a miniature version of the formal afternoon wear of the ushers. The outfit attested to his importance as a member of the wedding. He would be the ring bearer.

His name was Nicholas, and his mother, Holly Stockwell, was the bride. The wedding was taking place at the bride's family home, the three-thousand-acre estate, Riverview, situated in New York's Hudson Valley. The legs Nicholas wandered among were elite—Tory patrician and senatorial, plutocratic and congressional, talented and gubernatorial, athletically endowed and bureaucratically entrenched, blessed with genius and born to power, self-made and bred to wealth.

"Don't wander off now." Nicholas's great-uncle James, who would give the bride away, bent from the waist in his pearl-gray cutaway and peered benevolently into the little boy's face. He was a tall, lean man, and when he stooped over Nicholas the effect was not unlike a beach chair unfolding vertically. "The ceremony will start soon."

"I won't, Uncle James." Nicholas was concerned with his responsibility as ring bearer. At the same time, he wished the wedding to be over so that he could go outside and play in the autumn woods. He was bored; the fragments of conversation floating over his head were incomprehensible to him. There were too many guests and too much confusion. Weddings were no fun at all.

This particular wedding was neither private, nor intimate, nor small. Those were the adjectives the bride and groom had used when they first discussed their nuptial plans, but in their hearts, even then, they had to have known better. When a daughter of the socially and politically prominent Stockwell family marries a personage of the stature of Zelig Meyerling in a ceremony at a great Hudson River Valley estate as renowned as Riverview, neither privacy, intimacy, nor smallness is really possible. Indeed, the combined catering personnel and security force was larger than the original guest list. Holly and Zelig were pragmatic, so midway through the process of enlarging the list they had thrown up their hands, laughed, and bowed to the inevitable. What with family, social, political, and business considerations, the luminaries invited totaled well over a thousand people.

Holly Stockwell, the bride, was the favorite granddaughter of the late Matthew Adams Stockwell, a governor of New York who had once come within a hairbreadth of being president of the United States. Her uncles, James Linstone Stockwell, the governor's eldest son, and David Lewis, married to the governor's daughter Alice, were pillars of the international financial community. Along with her cousins, Holly was an heiress to one of America's great fortunes. Although she was by nature retiring, by heritage the thirty-one-year-old Holly was and would always be socially prominent.

Her bridegroom, Zelig Meyerling, was a former secretary of state and head of the Stockwell Institute, one of the nation's most influential political think tanks. Along with Henry Kissinger and Zbigniew Brzinski, although younger at forty-three than both men, he was considered

2

one of the country's leading foreign policy experts. Swiss born and a protégé of the moderate Republican Governor Stockwell, Zelig Meyerling was possessed of a diplomatic knack so fine-tuned that his reputation flourished with conservatives and Kennedy Democrats alike.

The union between Zelig Meyerling and Holly Stockwell had been touted for months as America's wedding of the decade. The pairing of Washington's most eligible bachelor and New York's "fairest heiress," as the media dubbed Holly, was an event eclipsed only by the wedding three months earlier of Britain's Prince Charles and Lady Diana Spenser.

"Everybody who is anybody will be at the fabulous Riverview estate on the Hudson," quipped one irreverent society columnist, "when the elite meet to mate."

"Vulgar," had been Holly's emphatic reaction.

"The times we live in." Zelig had been more philosophical. "Still, she might have modified it to 'when the elite meet to marry.' As I recall, the elite have not been in evidence on any of the occasions when we have met to mate."

"You're supposed to be a diplomat," Holly had teased. "You're not supposed to kiss and tell."

"My lips are sealed," he had assured her. "Only you and I and, of course, the joint chiefs shall know."

"In that case, I'll tell the National Security Council that you talk in your sleep."

"But in code." Zelig, as always, had been unflappable. "Only in code."

As Nicholas continued to wander knee high among the notables while waiting impatiently for the wedding to begin, the groom's own impatience had just been assuaged by a discreet gesture from the Reverend Malcolm Darrow Cabot, who would officiate at the ceremony. Now Reverend Cabot moved to tell the organist to give them perhaps two or three more moments and then to strike up the opening chords, before continuing toward the doorway to the anteroom, where Zelig and his best man would join him.

At the initial swell of organ music the multitude of

guests began their procession toward the large downstairs ballroom, which had been a part of the original main house of Riverview before the addition of the east and west wings, the turreted tower that contained the library, and the third story with its new ballroom that was twice the size of the older room, which on this occasion would serve as a wedding chapel. The seating for the guests extended beyond the opened sliding doors into Riverview's main entry hall. While those in back wouldn't see much of the ceremony, they would have an excellent view of the bridal party as they came down the sweeping, circular staircase of dark polished oak.

As the organ music resumed, the distinguished guests began seating themselves. A few were gently shown to their places by one or another of Zelig's eight ushers, a roster of well-known foreign service names. When this was done, the ushers spaced themselves with military precision along the aisle down which the bridal party would proceed. As the organ music built to a gentle crescendo, an expectant silence fell over the audience.

The organist took a three-beat and then launched into the groom's entry music. Preceded by the Reverend Cabot and flanked by the one-time member of the Carter cabinet who was his best man, Zelig Meyerling moved toward the altar as if he had been born to grace a bridegroom's formal frock coat.

The three men arranged themselves under a canopy of calla lilies. Opening his Bible, the Reverend Cabot laid it on the lectern, and the organist struck up the march for the two flower girls. Seven years old—one a dark-haired Cabot from Boston, the other a golden-haired Pickett from Georgia—they moved down the white carpet from the top of the stairs, through the entry hall, and into the ballroom at a slow and stately pace, strewing white and lavender flower petals to mark the path of those who followed. Finally they solemnly took their places to the rear of either side of the canopy. For the first time, reacting to the oohs and ahs of the audience, they dared to smile faintly at each other.

Now came Nicholas's big moment. Urged by his great-uncle James, he had scampered up the stairs at the first sign of the audience seating itself. Here, behind the six-teenth-century Belgian tapestry to one side of the head of the broad oak staircase, he had received a last straightening of his lavender necktie and a quick kiss from his mother. Now a pat on his small bottom started him on his journey.

Both his mother and his great-uncle had impressed on the little boy what a very important role that of ring bearer was. Elbows at his side, he supported the plum-colored cushion across both arms held in front of him as he walked down the stairs with carefully measured pace. His eyes lowered, making sure that the opened black velvet ring holder did not slip from the cushion, he moved through the hallway and into the ballroom turned wedding chapel. His gaze on the gold circlet that was his responsibility was almost hypnotic.

Oblivious to the indulgent and approving smiles that followed his progress, Nicholas marched to a point exactly two feet to the right of the best man and halted. For the first time he dared to raise his cornflower-blue eyes, and Zelig's gaze met his. Gravely, Zelig winked. Satisfied that he had done well, Nicholas looked back down at the ring again. Soon the ceremony would be over, and then he could go outside and play.

Now the organist played the bridesmaids' entrance music. In their lavender taffeta gowns, each of them smiling above the bouquet of violets clutched in both hands, they truly did look young and virginal. They assumed their positions between the ushers. To build suspense, the organist took a four-beat pause this time. Then she launched into the bridal march. At the top of the stairs, concealed by the tapestry, Holly surprised herself by feeling suddenly weak and nervous. She sagged against the oak wall.

"Don't lean," cautioned Patrice, Holly's cousin and matron-of-honor. "You'll wrinkle the silk."

The bridal gown had been specially designed for Holly by Carolina Herrera, who had performed similar services for Kennedys and Vanderbilts, Windsors, and even an exiled Romanoff. Although white would have been quite suitable for remarriage, Holly had chosen periwinkle blue

5

as the color of her wedding dress. She was more comfortable with it for her second trip to the altar, and the shade matched her eyes, complementing the bride's flawless translucent pearl complexion and flaxen hair. She had agreed with the designer that since it was to be an afternoon wedding at Riverview rather than in a church, a ballet-length gown with a gently flared skirt would be appropriate. They had chosen a beautiful watered silk, and, exulting over Holly's tall, willowy figure and delicate blond beauty, Carolina Herrera had decreed an off-the-shoulder style to complement the bride's creamy white shoulders, a dropped fitted waist to hug her hips and emphasize the curves of her slenderness. The skirt, flaring out gently at midthigh, ended in a swirl of material a few inches above her ankles. A designer friend in Milan had airmail-expressed a selection of silk stockings in a dozen different shades of white, from which Holly was able exactly to match the shade of her blue-and-white satin shoes with their antique bejeweled clasps. Instead of wearing a veil, she had opted for a matching hat that she had found in a Madison Avenue boutique. A lustrous thirty-six-inch rope of perfectly matched pearls with a sapphire clasp left to Holly by her grandmother, Mary Linstone Stockwell, was her only jewelry.

Now, with one last appraisal of the state of the bride's gown, Patrice started down the staircase with her matron-of-honor smile firmly in place. A small, lithe figure topped by wavy chestnut hair and large soft brown eyes, she both led the way and set the pace for the bridal party. Those who knew Patrice smiled at the satin bow overlaying the bodice of her dress. All her life, no matter what she wore, business suit or ball gown, cocktail dress or blouse to match designer jeans, Patrice was rarely without her identifying bow. Holly, appreciative of her usually practical cousin's lifelong act of whimsy, had insisted that her matron-of-honor's gown be designed complete with bow.

"It's time." As Patrice reached the bottom landing of the sweeping circular oak staircase, Holly's uncle James offered the bride his arm. Tall and distinguished-looking with gray hair to match the cutaway revealing the knife-edge crease of pinstripe trousers, his innate dignity and poise steadied Holly. Holly had never known her own father, and her mother had died when she was a child. Raised by her grandparents, who had both passed away the previous year, she had gratefully discovered a paternal figure in her uncle James, Patrice's father.

Holly linked his arm and returned his warm smile. At the head of the staircase she took a long, deep breath, sensing rather than seeing that all heads were craned, all eyes fastened on whatever section of the staircase would first reveal the bride's descent to them. Squaring her slender shoulders, Holly raised her head, tilting her chin at a brave angle. Once again her blue eyes met her uncle James's gaze. She smiled ever so faintly and nodded slightly. They began their descent to the organ's measured strains of "Here Comes the Bride."

When they reached the halfway point of the staircase, an audible gasp escaped the lips of those who could see the bride. The landing, graced by a stained-glass window that in the nineteenth century had adorned a Dresden church, before it had caught the eye of Amanda Stockwell, the governor's mother, and had been acquired for Riverview, served as a radiant backdrop for the bride's delicate beauty.

When the sun was shining, as it was now, the Dresden window bathed the landing in striated and rainbowed light. As Holly and her uncle James paused on the landing, the light poured over Holly as if with a promise of happiness from heaven itself. All brides are lovely, all weddings hopeful, but truly, for this brief instant, Holly was framed by a shimmering and ethereal aura that transcended the homily.

As they continued down the stairs, the aura clung to the bride as they passed the Italian Renaissance statuary set in the spaced alcoves lining the staircase and the hallway. Their step was measured by a hand-carved grandfather clock to the right of the staircase, which had once ticked off the hours of the wedding night of a Scottish queen in her groom's Highland castle.

As the bride glided slowly down the aisle on the arm of her uncle and approached the altar, her groom watched her with an expression that was uncharacteristically open.

It was an expression of undisguised love, an expression unconcerned with who discerned his emotions. In its way, Zelig Meyerling's expression was almost as beautiful as the bride herself.

Holly's loveliness impressed itself on all of those present, and particularly on her son, Nicholas. The little boy, the ring bearer, was filled with pride for his lovely mother. Mommy had never looked so beautiful!

When they reached the altar, Uncle James stepped aside gracefully and gave his niece into the custody of her husband-to-be. The bride and groom crossed their wrists and clasped their four hands. Reverend Malcolm Darrow Cabot smiled and nodded as they knelt and read a passage selected by the couple themselves from a thin volume of Kahlil Gibran.

Conscientiously, Nicholas tried hard not to move a muscle, not even to scratch an itch all through it. Still, the words were hard to follow, and the room was warm; he was very bored. All he could see of his beautiful mother now was her slender back as she knelt side by side in front of the altar presided over by Reverend Cabot.

"And, as *The Prophet* advises," intoned the Reverend Cabot, " 'Let there be spaces in your togetherness. Be joined as the branches of the tree are joined, and yet separate as they are separate. Share the sun, but take care to stand not in each other's shadow . . .' "

With heroic effort, Nicholas stifled a yawn. He wished he didn't have to stand here anymore with this velvet pillow with the gold ring on it. His elbows hurt. He wished the wedding would hurry up and be over.

" 'And please now to look into each other's eyes and to see your own reflection and to recognize the love with which it comes back to you while at the same time recognizing that it is but a reflection and not the whole and to know that therein lie the limitations of blissful marriage, and . . .' "

His mother had promised him that when it was over there would be wedding cake. He could have two pieces. The little boy sighed. He wouldn't have to stand here anymore listening to the minister speaking words Nicholas didn't really understand. When it was over he could take his two pieces of wedding cake outside to the woods. Maybe he would even take them down to the dock alongside the Riverview boathouse and eat them there.

"And just, dearly beloved, as we are gathered here in the presence of . . ." The Reverend Cabot made the transition smoothly from Gibran to the more traditional service.

Of course Nicholas wasn't supposed to go down to the dock unless there was an adult with him. His mother said it was too dangerous at this time of year when the river was up and the pier was slippery. The Hudson could be treacherous in November.

"And do you, Zelig, take this woman, Holly, to be your lawful wedded wife, to have and . . ."

Mommy was so silly. She still thought he was a baby. It was fun sliding on the dock, and he knew enough not to fall in the river. He was a big boy, and he could take care of himself.

"And do you, Holly, take this man, Zelig, to love, honor, and cherish . . ."

Yes, if it would only be over, he would take his wedding cake down to the dock to eat it. After all, this was a very special day, and on special days rules didn't always apply. Anyway, that's what Mommy had said when she told him he could take two pieces of cake instead of only one. On special days, it seemed, it was all right to risk a bellyache. So on special days, a boy who wasn't a baby and would be five in just a few more weeks, could surely eat his wedding cake on the dock and, if he was careful, even go sliding there.

"And now, if we may please have the ring . . ." At this cue from the minister, the best man took the box with the ring from the velvet pillow Nicholas was holding, extracted the ring, and passed it to Zelig so that the groom might place it on the hand of his bride.

"And so, by the power vested in me by the laws of the sovereign state of New York, I now pronounce you . . ."

He would go down to the dock with his wedding cake just as soon as Mommy and her new husband stopped kissing each other because, Nicholas understood, then the wedding would be over.

2

THE CEREMONY WAS followed by a reception in the third-floor ballroom. After a brief moment by themselves, the bride and groom proceeded up the stairs to greet their guests. It was a room that Holly could never enter without thinking of her grandfather, the governor, who had died only a little more than a year ago.

Governor Matthew Adams Stockwell had added the third-floor ballroom to Riverview shortly after Holly was born. He had never felt quite at home in the governor's mansion in Albany and much preferred to do his entertaining at Riverview. The ballroom covered the entire third floor of the mansion—exclusive of the east and west wings—an area that on the floor just below it encompassed some twelve bedrooms, each with its own private bathroom, and six with sitting rooms as well.

The room had also been designed to house the governor's thirty-million-dollar collection of abstract art, which included some of the best-known paintings of the post–World War II New York school. To display this collection, the artificial skylight provided indirect lighting. Klines and de Koonings and Pollocks, as well as early Warhols, four late Dubuffets, and three early Klees, were spaced around the vast ballroom together with prestigious lesser works.

The paintings had come down a few years later when the governor had married his second wife—a marriage growing out of a scandalous adulterous affair that most political observers believed had destroyed his well-founded and only recently announced hopes of becoming president of the United States. A renowned society beauty

10

originally from the South, Mrs. Brenda Stockwell—known as "Buffy"—did not like modern art. She had no head for abstractions, she had informed her new husband, and her eye rebelled at abstract painting. Later, when relations between the governor and Buffy had deteriorated, the collection had been rehung. It was in place now, for Holly and Zelig's wedding reception. Indeed, Buffy was herself standing between a late Picasso and a Léger. Her classic beauty stole their thunder as the bride and groom paused to exchange pleasantries with her and Jack Houston, Buffy's new husband.

In a setting filled with chic and famous beauties, Buffy at fifty nevertheless compelled notice. Her floor-length gown, flesh-colored silk with black leaf appliqué, clung to her tall, mature, voluptuous figure. The deep square cut of the neckline displayed her large, creamy bosom and a fabulous emerald-and-pearl choker, with a five-carat flawless emerald dropping down to nestle invitingly in her cleavage. Her violet eyes were darkened by the black gown, and a pile of jet-black curls cascaded over one shoulder. Buffy basked in the attention.

She had declined Holly's invitation to be a bridesmaid. "Bridesmaids should be young and virginal," she had said, "and it has been some time since I was either." Holly—who had asked her more out of respect than friendship—suspected that her real reason was that she wouldn't be caught dead wearing the same gown as six other women, no matter what the occasion. And it certainly wasn't the bridesmaids, most of them much younger than Buffy, who were drawing the stares now.

As Holly and Zelig moved on, Buffy regarded the couple cynically. Rolling her long-lashed violet eyes at her husband, she hummed the thirty-year-old song that had parodied the royal wedding of Prince Rainier of Monaco and socialite-movie actress Grace Kelly. "I'm up to here with the wedding of the year."

"Why so cynical?" Jack inquired. "After all, you like Holly."

Buffy's husband, Jack, was seventeen years younger, a handsome, virile man and a good friend of Holly's.

"She's all right," Buffy commented noncommittally.

11

"Is it Zelig, then?"

"He's better than all right." Buffy's voice was husky with memory.

"You've slept with him," her husband realized as the expression on his chiseled, handsome face reflected the hurt such knowledge inflicted on him.

"I was forty-nine years old when you married me, darling, and I had not spent the years since puberty in a nunnery. You knew that," Buffy reminded him. "Nor," she added, "were you functioning under vows of chastity yourself, as I recall."

"Sorry." Jack's apology did not clear the hurt from his blue eyes.

"Nor need you fear comparisons, my sweet. Zelig may once have been the preeminent bachelor stud of Washington society, and I'll grant his performance did not reflect disappointingly on his reputation, but he is not, my love, in the same league with you."

"Poor Jack," Zelig was remarking to Holly as they continued to pass among their wedding guests. "Buffy is a handful."

Before she could reply, the bride and groom's progress was intercepted by two male guests, one in a dress uniform with three stars on each shoulder, the other an undersecretary of state whose field of expertise was Balkan affairs. Holly sensed immediately that the polite congratulations they offered disguised their real intent. Confirming this, their next words were for Zelig alone.

"Greece," said the undersecretary in a tone that lent the single syllable a Delphic weight.

"Crucial." With matching portentousness, the general was one syllable up.

"We are relieved that you will undertake this mission for the president," murmured the undersecretary.

"You are just the man for the job," the general added.

"I would remind you, gentlemen," Zelig responded graciously, "that I am going to Greece on my honeymoon."

The general ignored the mild protest. "Greece must be

kept in NATO," he insisted. "That must be your primary mission."

"But not at the sacrifice of stability in the region." The undersecretary took issue with the general. "Nineteen eighty-two will be a crucial year for Greece. There must be an accommodation with Papandreou, even if he does lean farther left than we might like. That must be Zelig's primary mission."

"My honeymoon is my primary mission," Zelig demurred.

Holly's eyes wandered. Her gaze drifted past her cousin Patrice chatting with Governor Carey's new wife, Evangeline. She noticed the secretary of state and the secretary of defense engaged in polite conversation. Alexander and Caspar were, no matter their differences, civilized men. To their left Senator Kennedy and Edward Teller were politely disagreeing, while theatrical impresario Joseph Papp had an uncomfortable-looking Mayor Koch backed into a corner.

These little subgroups were flanked by phalanxes of Hudson River Valley gentry and their ladies—Roosevelts and Rockefellers, Harrimans and Vanderbilts, Deweys and Whitneys. Interspersed were celebrities from other walks of life: the presidents of Columbia and Harvard and Princeton and Yale, three divas and two tenors of the New York Metropolitan Opera, Zubin Mehta chatting with Leonard Bernstein—the hands of both men looking unweaponed without their batons—George Steinbrenner talking to Donald Trump. Indeed, the movers and the shakers of the world were all in attendance. And my husband is, of course, one of them, Holly reminded herself.

It was flattering, Holly supposed, but the price was that her bridegroom had been sandbagged by a general and an undersecretary bent on defining foreign policy at her wedding reception. When Zelig had first told her that the Reagan administration wanted him to undertake a delicate and unofficial mission to Greece in combination with their honeymoon, she had not balked. It was important, and patriotically, Holly had consented. Now, however, with this intrusion on her wedding reception, she was having second thoughts.

They showed in her face. Her cousin Michael Stockwell, Uncle James's youngest son, noticed from across the room. Tall like his father and boyishly handsome, he ambled over to Holly's side with a grin. "Never marry a politician," he advised.

"Too late," Holly replied, accepting Michael's wedding kiss. "Anyway, Zelig's a statesman. You're the politician."

"That I am." At age twenty-six, Michael was not yet halfway through his first term in Congress.

"Westchester Tory republicanism's hope for the future."

"Not so loud. I'm trying to cultivate a moderate image." Michael ran his fingers through curly dark blond hair.

"Be careful," Holly told him, not quite able to hide her true feelings toward her cousin. "Fence straddlers have been known to go sliding right down the razor blade of policy."

"I'm always careful." Michael smiled the smile that had gotten him elected with more than the Reagan coattail vote. "By the way," he added, "did you know that I'm going along on your honeymoon?"

"What do you mean?"

"A congressional fact-finding junket. The administration isn't alone in its concern about Greece, you know. Congress is worried, too. And so I'll see you at Louise's."

Louise Papatestus, wife of Greek shipping and munitions magnate Spiro Papatestus, had been born Louise Tyler, a distant cousin to both Holly and Michael. The Tylers were descendants of the governor's elder sister, Sarah, and he had maintained close supervision over the children of the family, largely due to the fact that Sarah had run out on her children when they were infants. Louise was Sarah's granddaughter. Close to each other in age, Holly and Louise had known each other all through their childhood.

"You'll be at Louise's," Holly echoed. Michael had guessed right, of course. She and Zelig were planning to spend part of their honeymoon as guests at the lavish Papatestus villa on Crete. Zelig had gladly accepted the invitation because he didn't want Holly to be alone while he left her to attend to his diplomatic mission.

"Sure. And my sister Lisa's over there, too. She's traveling with a friend of hers so the four of us can play tennis doubles while Zelig is off mending Reagan's Greek fences."

"How did you know about that, anyway? It's supposed to be confidential."

"Your husband's a very important man on the international scene, Holly. Did you think the administration would miss the opportunity to leak the news that an ex-secretary of state has signed on to back-channel for them in Greece?"

"But if it's known publicly, it will make Zelig's negotiations that much harder."

"Sure. And the long-term picture is that if he fails, it will be his failure, not the administration's. But if he succeeds, they'll get the credit. While in the short term, the renowned Zelig Meyerling, who has publicly disagreed with the Reagan hard-line foreign policy, has nevertheless come on board." Michael patted Holly's cheek and this time did walk away. "Do you still think," he inquired with a smiling backward glance, "that statesmanship is so very different from politics?"

He was right, Holly sighed. It was a real-politik world. For instance, her uncle James, along with his brother-in-law, David Lewis, and Peter Stockwell, Holly's cousin, were deep in conversation with President Reagan's budget director, David Stockman. Holly cynically observed that they were most probably *not* discussing the nuptials. Stockman was considered by the financial community to be the architect and prime mover of supply side economics. Holly knew that based on this conversation, there might well be major shiftings in the Stockwell portfolio when the market opened the next morning. Uncle James, Uncle David, and cousin Peter were expert at reading the tea leaves of casual conversation.

Only a short while ago the three men had constituted a troika with sole control over the vast Stockwell fortune. But since the passing of the governor, followed closely by the death of his first wife, Mary Linstone Stockwell, there had been a rather nasty and drawn-out battle over the estate, which had ended with a tenuous solution of extending control to a six-person board of trustees. Buffy had sought to break the will, which had left her with only a small piece of the pie. But it was the surprise appearance of Sarah Stockwell Tyler—long presumed dead—at the trial that had necessitated the more equitable disposition of the Stockwell fortune. In addition to James Stockwell, David Lewis, and Peter Stockwell, the new board consisted of the governor's second wife, Buffy, Holly's cousin Max Tyler, grandson of Sarah Stockwell Tyler, the deceased governor's eighty-seven-year-old sister, and her representative, a California lawyer named Halsey De Vilbiss. A truce had been negotiated, but the battle had worsened the tenuous relationship between various family members.

Now, from behind her, Holly felt Zelig's arm circle her waist. "I think they're ready to start serving," he whispered, kissing her neck.

Berkley, the Riverview butler, was putting the finishing touches to the banquet tables the caterers had set up horseshoe fashion around the perimeter of the vast ballroom. His careful eye appraised the arrangements of tuberose, freesia, and gladiolus from the Stockwell gardens and greenhouse mingled with more exotic blooms flown in from the Caribbean for the occasion. He adjusted a piece here and there of the original, signed-in-the-stone Spode china and the Baccarat crystal. He carefully moved a fork a fraction of an inch and then a spoon of the two-hundred-year-old family silver it had taken six scullery maids three hours to polish to his satisfaction the previous evening. He smoothed a hand-crocheted Irish linen tablecloth and rearranged a pair of matching napkins. Then he nodded to Holly. It was time for the wedding supper to begin.

As she and Zelig proceeded to the head table, Holly inquired if he had seen Nicholas.

"The last I saw of him was coming out of the kitchen with a piece of wedding cake in each hand and heading out the French doors."

"And we haven't even officially cut it yet." Holly

smiled. "Oh, well. It is a special day. I just hope he doesn't give himself a bellyache."

Once the bridal pair had seated themselves, the other guests found their places. Jack sat down next to his wife, Buffy, who was turned away from him, talking to the man on her other side—Jimbo Grebbs, majority stockholder and chairman of the board of one of the largest oil refineries in Texas. Grebbs was at the wedding reception because Buffy had asked Holly to invite him. It had something to do, Jack knew, with the eight hundred and forty thousand barrels of crude oil taken out of the ground of western New York State every year. Stockwell Industries held hundred-year leases on the petroleum fields. Because their Arab competitors were paying bonus fees to have their oil refined before the high prices per barrel set by OPEC began to plummet, Stockwell's crude was sitting in the tanks, unrefined and unmarketable. It was a dilemma that was already depressing the economies of Texas and Oklahoma. And if the Stockwells couldn't find a solution, before very long it would have repercussions throughout New York State. Jimbo Grebbs and his refinery were a possible solution.

Jack did not like Grebbs. A professional Texan, playing the role to the hilt, with a beefy and overfriendly arm that never recognized the reluctance of the shoulders it encircled, Grebbs stood a head taller than Jack, who was himself over six feet. Barrel-chested with a substantial belly laced with muscle rather than fat, Grebbs had one of those permanently sun-chapped faces so common in Texas. His ears, nose, and jaw were all large, aggressive. His teeth, too, were big and long and permanently bared in an expression that was either a smile or a snarl. He gave off good humor the way a fetid swamp exudes effuvia.

Although Jimbo Grebbs looked about Buffy's age, he was actually closer to Jack's. He lusted after Buffy openly, making a joke of it. "But don't you trouble yourself, young feller," he told Jack. "Ain't nothing but an old man's pipe dream." And he grinned his toothy Texas grin.

Jack was not amused. That Buffy could even play the flirting game with Grebbs upset him. He had almost browbeaten her into marriage, and her offhand manner did not assuage his doubts concerning Buffy's voracious nature. Now he picked at his food and watched them from the corner of his eye.

Buffy was doing what her husband thought of as her "southern belle number." Batting her long eyelashes at Grebbs, her words chided him for being too forward, while her expression continued to encourage him. Irritated, Jack shifted position. The movement pushed the tablecloth off Buffy's legs, and for a brief instant Jack had a clear view of his wife holding Jimbo Grebbs's hand in her lap. Although Buffy held the hand within the bounds of decency, she made no move to banish it.

"Buffy!" Jack all but snarled.

She ignored him.

"Buffy!" His voice was loud, sharp. A few heads at the banquet table turned.

Only a slight stiffening of her shoulders betrayed her annoyance at his tone. Still she ignored him.

Jack stood up. "Buffy," he said loudly, "may I speak to you privately a minute?"

More heads turned. Finally, Buffy's was one of them. Voices died down as the guests watched, curious as to the outcome. One of those startled into staring was Holly.

"Later, darling," Buffy said, her voice loud but clear. "I'm in the middle of a conversation with Mr. Grebbs." She turned a cool shoulder to her husband.

Jack took a deep breath. On the verge of exploding, his eyes met Holly's. This was her wedding. She was his good friend, and he didn't want to embarrass her. Controlling his anger, Jack excused himself and left the table.

He needed fresh air to walk off his anger. Exiting the Stockwell mansion by the French doors, he headed for the woods. He strode briskly, not paying attention to where he was going. His fury had still not abated when he came out of the woods by the Riverview boathouse on the shores of the Hudson. Emotionally drained, he walked out to the end of the dock. Brooding over Buffy's behavior, he stared blindly at the sun-dulled pewter-gray sky. After a long time, he lowered his eyes to the water.

"What?" He blinked, coming alert. There was something . . . a splash of color foreign to the river . . . bobbing beside a piling . . . lavender . . . rising and then sinking from sight . . . lavender . . . familiar . . . lavender . . .

Nicholas! The realization exploded in Jack Houston's brain. Jesus! He flung off his coat and kicked away his shoes with the same motion. Jack dived into the water. The sudden cold was excruciating. It penetrated to the bone. The momentum of his plunge carried him through the black depths toward the unseen piling and the spot of lavender that had vanished from sight an instant before he leaped.

Jack plummeted, captive to the icy water. He forced his eyes open. There was nothing but blackness. No sight of lavender, neither ring bearer's cummerbund nor bowtie. He forced himself farther down, and then farther still. Down . . . down . . . down . . . Down through the icy cold and the impenetrable blackness. . . .

3

RISING FROM THE depths, the warm water of the Libyan Sea became warmer still on the upturned face of Louise Papatestus approaching the juncture of surface and sun. Breaking through, she turned on her back and gasped, naked breasts rising as she sucked air gratefully. She floated there a moment, letting the current turn her until she was no longer looking at the expanse of ocean, but at the southwestern shore of Crete.

In the distance were mountains shadowing valleys lushly green with citrus groves and olive trees and backed by taller mountains, which were in turn loomed over by peaks white with November snow. Closer at hand were scraggly-weeded buttes rising straight from the beach to a small hillside chapel, above which was the potholed dirt road on which Louise had parked her 450 SL Mercedes sports coupe. To the east were higher cliffs knifing out into the ocean, unvegetated and smooth to the eye, although marked by a few hidden caves.

To the west was the site of Kommos, an important archaeological excavation set off by a barbed wire fence. The ruins of a four-thousand-year-old Minoan settlement were presided over by the pillars and part of the infrastructure of a recognizably Greek temple from the fourth century B.C. Like many digs on Crete and in the Peloponnesus, the remains of one ancient civilization overlaid those of another still more ancient.

The beach, not well known even in the area, was called Komo. It was not visible from the north or from the dig, which was accessible from only the west, although the ruins could be seen by Louise from beyond where the surf broke. The beach was shielded from the east by the cliff jetty. On the other side of the jetty was Matala. Here, overlooking a cove, the far side of the cliff was very steep and pocked with caves. These caves had been used as hiding places by the early Christian martyrs, who had hewn them out to provide altars, stone benches, and hidden niches to store their possessions.

During World War II, Greek partisans had hidden in the caves of Matala and used them as a base from which to attack the German army. In the 1960s, hippies from the United States, England, and Western Europe had occupied them and practiced their alternate life-styles until the regime of the Greek colonels had run them out of Matala. Now, in 1981, their heirs were back, living in the caves, drugged out, uncommitted, and sunbathing nude in defiance of gawking tourists. Their presence was the reason Louise went to the trouble of negotiating the mud road to Komo rather than bathing at Matala, where the cove was sheltered and the water calmer. Louise had nothing against the residents, but she was by nature an extremely private person, and she liked to swim nude—but by herself.

As Louise swam for the shore now, she was secure in her isolation. She emerged from the surf dripping, a tall young woman darkly tanned, her naked body sculpted to the perfection of the bronze Athena found at Delphi. Long, wet, sea-darkened red-gold hair splayed out over her bare shoulders as she turned her visage to the sun— no longer Athena now, but rather a mythic siren from the deep risen to visit the world of mortals.

Her face was not unknown. Once it had graced the covers of magazines published in New York and London, Paris and Rome. Before her marriage to Spiro Papatestus, one of the richest men in the world, Louise Tyler had been a debutante turned model. After her marriage, the papparazzi had made her one of the three most recognizable women in the world, the other two being Jackie Kennedy and Elizabeth Taylor.

Louise was not only beautiful—as many women are— but she was one of the very few who are truly unique. And while this uniqueness was due partly to her breathtaking beauty, it was also some indefinable quality that Louise possessed and which the world responded to without really being able to perceive. What the world did perceive was her physical beauty, and so assumed that this was the source of her appeal.

It was a natural assumption. Louise's body was voluptuous, the proportions perfect, her bosom deeply cleft with uptilted breasts. Her hips swelled sweetly from a narrow waist and her long, slender legs, and she dressed—whether in a bikini or a formal evening gown— in a way that incorporated her clothes into her uniqueness.

She had always been one to set style, rather than ape it. Through changing fashion, her mass of heavy apricot hair remained long and loose, her trademark, periodically copied by other women. It did not become many of them because they lacked Louise's classically aquiline face with its almond-shaped eyes, high, haughty cheekbones and strong, slightly rounded, cleft chin. Nor was she, despite the wealth that came along with being the wife of Spiro Papatestus, particularly concerned with clothes. Right now, the denim skirt and nondescript tank top that she pulled on over her panties were faded and worn. Her hazel eyes—deep set, intelligent—adapted to the shades as

21

they did to whatever colors Louise wore. Such simple garb was typical of her. For Louise, absolute contentment was an absence of friction. The sea and the sun lulled her. Serenity was an end in itself—and she had achieved it. It had not always been so. For most of her life—since puberty, in fact—peace had eluded Louise. It was only with her marriage that she had found it.

She had bloomed early. From the age of twelve, Louise had seen the challenge of her beauty and her sensuality reflected in the eyes of the boys and men who clamored to get her attention. She had never felt that any of them wanted Louise Tyler. Instead, she had felt like a prize to be won, a barrier to be overcome, a river to be forded.

The challenge Louise represented was not merely sexual, although sex was a part of it. Males were in awe of her, and this infuriated some of them. For some reason they felt they had to conquer her or face their fear of failure. Even in high school, simple conversations always took place in an arena demarcated by her beauty. Even then she had recognized the hostility behind the stammering, the fury behind the blushes.

Louise became afraid, and fear made her remote. "A cold bitch!" Once, when she was sixteen, she had overheard a boy describing her that way to his circle of friends. It had hurt.

It was no better with women. Girls her age had resented the attention she drew. While they were coping with acne and adolescent gropings in the backs of cars, Louise was building a wall to isolate herself from the threat of hostile contacts her beauty provoked. A few times she had attempted to come out from behind that wall. When she was seventeen, fortified by Scotch and stirred by determined caresses, Louise opened herself to the passion of Greg, a boy a year older than she was. He took her tenderly, and she felt soft and melting, not passionate but tender. But then he had made these noises—animal noises, gruntings—and she had opened her eyes and looked up into his red face, straining with a victory that defined her own defeat.

Subsequently, she had refused Greg, and, rejected and angry, he had publicized their lovemaking throughout the

22

school. After that, every boy Louise found herself alone with seem impelled to go all the way. Consequently, Louise's last year in high school was mostly a dateless nightmare.

In college the word was that she was a virgin. She eagerly encouraged the misconception, but it didn't help. Virginity was an even greater challenge. Jocks and grinds alike seemed to believe that her chastity and her genuine beauty marked her as fair game in open season. Occasionally Louise had succumbed, but like her first, her subsequent forays into lovemaking proved more than disappointing. They left Louise feeling sickened and heartsore. What was the matter with her? Women were supposed to have desires. They were supposed to feel aroused. But Louise felt nothing. So she admitted a few carefully chosen candidates to her bed. But she always felt strangely remote, more like a spectator than a participant.

Marriage hadn't changed her feelings about passion and sex, but it had reintroduced feelings of tenderness. Spiro Papatestus, thirty years her senior, was the only man she had ever met who had the wit and experience to lavish tenderness on her while holding his desire in abeyance. Since he was not merely wealthy, but also extremely powerful, he felt no need to conquer, only a strong desire to coexist in harmony with this gorgeous creature. It had taken Louise a long time to truly believe this, but when she finally had, she was his completely.

Theirs was no ordinary marriage. Spiro made no demands on her. All he wanted was for her to feel secure. In the warmest sense, she was like some highly valued work of art he had acquired: a crystalline sculpture to be admired and treasured, but never defiled by the print of unwanted fingers, never to be put at risk of shattering by even the most loving handling. He saw Louise in all of her true delicacy and vulnerability, and he would not touch her—not so much as clasp her hand or pat her cheek—if he sensed her reluctance toward such actions. Some women might have shriveled under such hothouse care, but Louise thrived. She came to trust her husband absolutely, and this trust was truly—if unconventionally— a kind of love.

One day after their marriage she had confessed to him, "When I am touched by men, I tense up. I can't help it."

"I know." His eyes had searched hers inquiringly.

"But you're my husband. It's not fair to you that I should be like that."

"I have no complaint."

"I"— She swallowed hard. "It's not the physical thing itself so much as the intimacy of contact that I can't stand."

"It is all right, Louise. It's enough for me to look at you. I want only that you should be at ease. I am content."

"But sex—I mean, the urge—I mean, men—" Louise had found herself stammering like a schoolgirl.

"Men, Louise. That's what I am. A man. Not a boy. A man knows that sex can be as complex as life itself. I would rather just look at you than sleep with any other woman in the world."

"Oh, I love you!" There was both truth and anguish in Louise's voice. "If there is anything at all that I can—"

"All right, then." Spiro's smile crisscrossed his strong, craggy, Macedonian face with deep lines like the imprints of lightning bolts. "Would you please stand in front of the window in the sunlight."

Puzzled, Louise had complied with his request.

"Turn around."

She had turned around.

"More slowly, please."

Pivoting more slowly, she felt the sun on her body. She was wearing a sundress of thin, yellow cotton, which was to a marked degree transparent. Conscious of pleasing him, she first let her model's training dictate her movements, and then her instinct as a woman. Her tall and perfect body, swiveling in the sun, became purposefully more provocative.

Spiro was sitting in an armchair. Watching her, eyelids half-lowered, his breathing quickened as his sturdy, muscular legs separated. She noticed his arousal.

"Thank you, Louise," he said. "That's enough."

"Are you sure?"

"I'm sure."

"But you haven't—I mean—"

"Anticipation, my dear. Prolonged anticipation. As in other areas of life, the satisfactions of sex are in direct proportion to the patience exercised in attainment."

That had been the first time. Despite what Spiro had said about anticipation, the similarly nontactile episodes that followed had evolved to provide him with more complete erotic satisfaction. Content to gratify him at so little cost to herself, Louise recognized that if their sex play was strictly voyeuristic, perhaps even perverse, it was nevertheless as painless as it was dispassionate.

Spiro was in his study now as Louise pulled the Mercedes up in back of their mountain villa and left it there for the chauffeur to garage. "Did you have a nice swim?" he inquired as she entered.

"Lovely."

"In the buff?" Spiro delighted in using American idioms.

"Of course."

"Aren't you concerned that someone might see you?" Louise shrugged. "It's very secluded at Komo."

"Someday, perhaps, I will follow you myself."

"Why would you do that?" she asked.

"To watch you naked in the sun."

"But you can see me naked whenever you like."

"Whenever I like?" Spiro's wise dark eyes approved his young wife's sea-perfumed flesh.

"Of course."

"Right now?"

"If you like." Louise moved to the window and closed the geometrically patterned Corinthian draperies. Standing in the shadows, she slowly removed her faded tank top, moving her shoulders deliberately so that her breasts swayed.

Spiro sighed. He squinted slightly, peering at her in the shadows.

"Can't you see?" Louise's voice was teasing. She unbuttoned the denim skirt and let it fall to the Venetian tile floor bordering the antique Minoan-style carpet. She rose

25

up on her toes, the muscles of her thighs defining the perfect line of her long legs.

"Enough." Spiro's voice was hoarse. "I can see enough."

Louise heard the sound of his zipper being opened.

Turning, wriggling—but not vulgarly—she removed her panties. Slowly she pirouetted as she lightly touched herself—her breasts, her buttocks, the warm insides of her thighs. Stroking herself intimately, she felt nothing, and yet she derived pleasure from the sound of her husband's quickened breathing.

Emerging from the shadows a little, into the light, her deep, serious hazel eyes met his. Her tongue peeped out from between her naturally red lips. She rubbed her thighs together and then separated them. Gauging his breathing, his movement, with a soft, calculated moan, she exposed herself to him completely.

The picture Louise presented at the moment seared itself into Spiro's brain and triggered the release that was Louise's reward—her only reward.

4

QUITE A DIFFERENT picture was etched into Holly's brain. It was a vision not of love, but of terror. It was the sight that wiped out all the other images of her wedding day at Riverview.

She had come downstairs from the wedding dinner and gone looking for her son, Nicholas. With her new husband's arm around her shoulders, chatting and laughing, they had passed through Riverview's formal gardens and were approaching the edge of the wooded slope leading down to the river when they heard Jack Houston's screams for assistance. A moment later he emerged up the hillside with the small, still, white form in his arms. The late-afternoon sun caught the lavender cummerbund, and Holly screamed.

What followed was a nightmare. Jack, relinquishing the little boy to Holly and Zelig, raced ahead of them back into the mansion, seeking a doctor among the wedding guests. The physician who responded was an old family friend who had gone to prep school with Holly's uncle James. Taking Nicholas from Zelig as they came through the French doors, he laid the child down on the couch. Peeling back the sopping frilled shirt the little boy was wearing, the doctor laid his ear against the thin bare chest.

"I gave him mouth-to-mouth." Jack was himself drenched and shivering with cold, and it was difficult for him to speak. "Some fluid came up, but—"

"He's not breathing," Holly sobbed. "He's blue. He's—he's—"

"Your son is alive." The doctor's tone was reassuring but grave. "There is a pulse and there is respiration, but it is faint." As he spoke, the doctor stripped off his jacket and covered Nicholas with it. He sent a servant scampering for blankets and in the meantime accepted Zelig's jacket and put that also over Nicholas's unmoving form. "He's suffering from hypothermia." The doctor went to call for an ambulance.

Zelig followed him. "Is he just unconscious?" he asked. "Or—?"

"He's in a coma." Compassion in his gaze, the doctor regarded the man whose wedding he had come to celebrate.

Zelig's face was ashen, his hooded eyes filled with anguish. "Will Nicholas live?" His voice was harsh with the effort it took to ask the question.

"I don't know." The doctor would have liked to answer more positively, but he was wary of the greater cruelty of offering false hope. "Only time can answer that."

The long-drawn-out period of anxious waiting began for Holly with the ambulance ride to the hospital. Holding her little boy's hand, so cold and still, she tried to will his eyes to open above the oxygen mask covering his mouth.

Zelig rode with her, his arm around her shoulder, silently conveying to Holly his love and his concern.

He stood by her all through that long night, their shattered wedding night, when the odds were against Nicholas surviving. At dawn, when the doctor—still cautious and far from optimistic—told them that the little boy's vital signs were showing marked improvement, Zelig gently coaxed Holly down to the hospital cafeteria for some hot coffee. He even managed to get her to eat half a slice of toast.

On the way back, they passed the hospital chapel. "I'd like to go in a moment," Holly said.

"I'll come with you."

"You don't have to."

"I want to." Holding her to him, Zelig choked on the words. "I want to pray for our son."

Our son. Holly had cried then for the first time since Jack had handed her the small, still body of her little boy.

It was touch and go for the next two weeks. Nicholas remained in a coma. There had, the doctors said, been a terrible blow to his system. Improvement in his condition was incremental and subject to the sorts of setbacks that medicine neither understood nor could control. The doctor phrased it as gently as he was able, but Holly had to be prepared. Nicholas might still slip away from them at any time.

Throughout this period, Zelig was constantly by Holly's side. Calls came in from Washington reminding him that he had other duties, but his response was terse and unyielding: "My wife needs me." After the first few days, he neither took the calls nor returned them. They spent their days and nights in the hospital.

One afternoon, Holly, who had been getting very little sleep, dozed off in an armchair beside Nicholas's hospital bed. Beside her, Zelig was thumbing through a copy of *Foreign Affairs*. Casually, he looked up from the page. His heavy eyebrows shot up in surprise. Nicholas was looking back at him. His eyes were open and focusing.

"Mommy," he said weakly.

Gently, Zelig shook Holly awake. "What—?" she responded.

"Mommy."

"Thank God!" Holly knelt beside the bed and kissed Nicholas. Her hand groped for the hand of her husband. "Oh, Zelig, thank God!"

"Mommy, did you save me another piece of wedding cake?"

The corner had been turned.

A week later Nicholas came home to Riverview. It would be a long convalescence, the doctor told Holly, but he was definitely on the road to recovery. "TLC." The doctor had smiled. "Chicken soup and mother love, and he'll get his strength back. For the time being, though, he'd best stay in bed."

That night, after Nicholas was asleep, Holly and Zelig finally had their long-delayed wedding night. Holly had been too distraught to even think about sex before, and Zelig had been patient and considerate. Now Holly came to him with a new appreciation born of the depths of compassion and love he had shown her throughout the ordeal.

She found an even deeper ecstasy in their lovemaking than heretofore. In Zelig's arms at last, she surrendered to the most delicious sensations building to the wonder of release. Slick with perspiration, her body rose to the thrusting demands of a penetration that filled her more fully and deeply than she had thought possible before the first time Zelig made love to her.

Finally they rolled apart, panting. Wordlessly they lay side by side, content with the closeness of mutual silence. Outside, a November wind set the needles of the tall Riverview pines to whispering. Autumn leaves, robbed of their color by the starless night, rustled an answer. These were Hudson River Valley sounds. They were the product of a history that no doubt disapproved of the abandonment in the small studio bedroom above the two-story library of the octagonally turreted north end of the Riverview mansion.

The studio and its bedroom had once been the living quarters of Holly's artist mother. When Holly had returned to Riverview after leaving her first husband, she had occupied the studio herself. Now she and Zelig were utilizing it for their lovemaking because of the privacy it provided.

"I've missed this." In the aftermath, Holly snuggled. "I love you so much."

"I love you, too." Zelig sighed, his hands caught in her tousled hair.

Holly noticed the sigh. "What is it?"

He pulled her closer to him, enveloping her in his big, strong body. "I spoke with Washington today. Up until now I've been avoiding their calls, but with Nicholas out of danger—"

"Oh, Zelig." Holly sensed what was coming.

Zelig held her tighter, not allowing her to break away. "I have to go to Europe. I should have left a week ago. The Greek situation grows more shaky by the day. I've put them off, but now with Nicholas back home I really can't delay any longer."

"I can't leave him, Zelig. It's too soon. The doctor says it will be at least six to eight weeks before he's well enough to travel."

"I know." Again Zelig sighed. "I'm going to have to go without you, Holly. It can't be helped."

"Damn! I'll miss you so much. And so," Holly added, "will Nicholas."

"I'll be counting the days until he's recovered enough for you to join me. I don't relish honeymooning in Greece all by myself."

"Just remember that you're not Washington's most eligible bachelor anymore." Holly was teasing him, but at the same time she had always been a little uneasy with Zelig's reputation as an international roué. "Stay away from those Greek Aphrodites."

As he pulled her chin up with his hand, his warm brown eyes met hers. "I adore my wife. I would never look at another woman." From their first meeting, Zelig had sensed that Holly was all he wanted in a woman. She was intelligent, compassionate, beautiful. He had no desire for any more casual affairs. The passion their bodies

30

sparked when they were together was—he was certain—strong enough to sustain him, despite time or distance.

"I'll miss you terribly." Holly reached low and touched him firmly, intimately, and with new desire. "You have turned me into a sensual glutton."

"That is my proudest accomplishment," Zelig murmured as he and Holly started to make love a second time.

5

"SECONDS, ANYONE?" PATRICE O'Keefe, Holly's cousin, raised the coffee carafe high above the ubiquitous bow of her high-necked blouse and looked around questioningly.

Her father, James Linstone Stockwell, nodded and passed his cup and saucer. His brother-in-law, David Lewis, also opted for a refill. The others present—Buffy, Patrice's cousins Peter Stockwell and Max Tyler, and the totally unrelated Halsey De Vilbiss—all refused more coffee.

The conference room of Stockwell Enterprises, on the twenty-seventh floor of the Stockwell Building in lower Manhattan, was the present site for the governing board meeting, at which Patrice's father had requested her presence. The round maple table at which they sat, a colonial antique predating Wall Street's New York Stock Exchange, was patinated with the dull, gray, early-winter afternoon light focused by the wheelhouse window looking down over the harbor. The bowsprit jut and wraparound design of the window endowed the office with a sweeping harbor view encompassing the twin towers of the World Trade Center, the Statue of Liberty, and—most impressive of all—the interwebbed Brooklyn Bridge.

Much prized, the building's location—one of the most

valuable pieces of real estate in New York City—was as much a part of the Stockwell heritage as the three-thousand-acre Riverview estate. Riverview, Wall Street, history, legend, and one of the great mercantile fortunes of America—these were the elements comprising the Stockwell family tradition. Politics played a part in that tradition as well, and so, it had to be admitted, did scandal. But always the centrifugal principle holding the tradition together was profit.

It was this principle that had drawn the group to the Stockwell Enterprises conference room. With the exception of Patrice, the group constituted the governing board of Stockwell Industries and controlled all other subsidiary and charitable aspects of the Stockwell estate as well. James, although only fifty-three years old and in excellent health, had made it clear to the others that he was contemplating eventual retirement and—quite soon—an extended vacation. He intended to designate his daughter, Patrice, the thirty-one-year-old head of the prestigious Bartleby & Hatch Advertising Agency, as his replacement on the board.

There was some question in the minds of the others as to James's right to do that. During the vicious battle over the estate that had followed the governor's death and shortly after that of his first wife, Mary Linstone Stockwell, all six of those now on the board—as well as many other family members—had been at each other's throats. The board was itself a compromise dictated by a probate judge who had pointed out that Stockwell Industries and all other Stockwell interests could be put in escrow and immobilized for years if the contesting parties did not agree to work together.

The six-man board was a less-than-perfect solution, but it was a solution. If it kept them all jockeying for position during their meetings together, it also kept them from allowing open warfare to tear apart the empire that generations of Stockwells had created. The arrangement decreed a balance of power as tenuous as Metternich's Europe, but so far it had at least staved off anarchy.

By mutual agreement, the chairmanship of their meetings rotated. Today it fell to James to preside. "The most pressing matter is our petroleum problem," he declared, once the matter of seconds for coffee had been settled. "I'd suggest we focus on that."

There was no objection.

"David." James addressed his brother-in-law. "Would you bring us up-to-date."

"No real change since our last meeting a month ago—which is to say that we are presently losing money on our New York State oil operation. Storage costs for our crude are mounting. Florida, Texas, and California refineries are not only not accommodating us, but are indicating that we will have to stand on line behind their home-state producers."

"But we're still pumping."

"Yes. We've cut back, but it will still come to over seven hundred thousand barrels this year. Even if we could peddle that oil tomorrow, OPEC might force the price down on us just to keep control of the international market."

"Your recommendation?" James asked.

"Cap the wells. Cut and run."

"Comments?" James opened the subject to discussion.

"If we cap the wells," Max Tyler asked, "what does that do to the labor force?"

"Puts them back on the market." Peter Stockwell answered, his tone indicating that the fate of labor was no concern of theirs. Although only in his thirties, his was probably the most ambitious and profit-oriented voice on the board. His father, Jonathon Stockwell, was James's younger brother. But Jonathon had inherited none of the Stockwell financial acumen, and Peter had long ago stepped into his shoes.

"How many people will be out of work?" Max wanted to know.

"Forty thousand, give or take," David Lewis told him.

"That will put quite a dent in the New York State economy, won't it?" Max addressed the question directly to James.

"Yes," James answered. "The state will feel it, and so will the market. It could cost Stockwell more in public relations terms—our generally positive employer image, our concern for the state in which we are based, the competence of our management, and the firmness of the Stockwell Industries infrastructure generally—than we might save by closing down."

"I'm against capping the wells, then," Max declared. "Not just for the reasons you cite, James, but also for humanitarian concerns."

"Hell, Max," Peter sneered at him, "can't be more than ten percent of the workers in the oil fields swing acey-deucey."

Max looked at Peter steadily for a long moment. Then he spoke. "I'm gay, Peter. I find the masculine sex organ attractive. Except for you, Peter. You're one cute little prick I don't like."

"Nothing as bitchy as an over-the-hill drag queen," Peter snapped back.

"That will be enough." James spoke loudly and firmly. "This is a business meeting, not a gutter name-calling contest." His tone commanded silence. When he had it, he continued. "Anything more concrete to support your position, Max?" he inquired.

"Not really. I'd just like to remind everybody that I don't speak only for myself. I'm on this board representing all of the Tylers except my grandmother, who is represented by Mr. De Vilbiss. Together he and I represent a one-third control of the estate. I expect to be treated accordingly."

"Of course, Max." James's tone was soothing. "I agree."

Peter Stockwell snorted.

"You will be treated, Max, with respect by all." James gazed at Peter balefully until his nephew dropped his eyes.

David Lewis, however, erupted. "How about those Tylers you represent?" he asked Max. "How about those twins, Beth and Carrie? They are an ongoing embarrassment and a threat to the family. Because they are relatives and identified with the Stockwell name, their actions for Greenpeace and their peacenik and environmentalist statements compromise us. Their last caper made us a laughingstock. Something has to be done. Let's discuss that."

"You can put it on the agenda for the next meeting," James suggested. "You're chairing it, David," he reminded him, "so you can make sure it's discussed to your satisfaction. But right now we're talking about Stockwell crude. Can we please just get on with it?"

David Lewis subsided. Halsey De Vilbiss raised a hand, and James nodded for him to speak.

Disparate as the group was, Halsey DeVilbiss more than any of the others was its sore thumb. In a boardroom of pinstripe and gray flannel, he alone glowed in watered silk. Green-and-yellow octopi scampered over his necktie, challenging subdued, old-school stripings. His very suntan—a buttery, paprika shade—was a rebuke to the eastern establishment pallors predominating around the table. And De Vilbiss's brashness of manner indicated that southern California's place in the sun gave it the right to cast very large shadows indeed over the entrenched power brokers of New York.

"The problem is refining our crude," he said now. "But before we decide to cap the wells and take our losses, there is one solution we have not considered."

"Which is?" James inquired. He detested Halsey De Vilbiss, and his usual courtesy did not quite hide the feeling.

"Libya."

All heads turned to stare at Halsey. He had their attention. Buffy was the first to speak. "Interesting," she said. "But why not Russia?" she added, deadpan.

Equally straightfaced, Halsey told her why not. "Because Russia does not have oil refineries operating at half their capacity. Libya does."

"They are operating at half their capacity because the Reagan administration has declared it illegal for American oil producers to ship their crude to Libya for refining," Buffy pointed out.

"That hasn't stopped Shell or the American subsidiaries of British Petroleum."

"They co-own those refineries with the Qaddafi government. They're exempt from the order."

"How very fortunate for Shell and BP." De Vilbiss's "very" was a faint mimicry of the Ivy League accents of the other men. "But then why shouldn't Stockwell be equally lucky?"

"Are you spinning smoke, or do you have something firm to suggest?" Peter asked.

"And they say Westerners are blunt while Easterners have all the finesse." De Vilbiss was enjoying himself. Self-made and a very successful California corporate lawyer with a rare reputation for successful litigation, he liked nothing better than—as he himself put it—"sticking it to those Harvard types." In that spirit, he continued. "I have put out certain feelers," he said.

"Nobody authorized you to!" David Lewis's round face turned red with outrage.

"No commitments have been made." De Vilbiss cut off the older man's umbrage. "The contacts have been strictly unofficial. A go-between—"

"What go-between?" Buffy was sarcastic. "You haven't gone and involved yourself with Billy-boy Carter, I hope. It's not Billy-boy of Billygate, is it, Halsey?"

"It's not Billy Carter," he reassured her. "I don't traffic with fraternal regime topplers. The go-between to whom I referred is Ezzadine al Mabrouk, the Libyan minister of petroleum. The indications are of a certain willingness on the part of the Libyans to accommodate us in refining our crude. Quite simply, Qaddafi would like the stability of some American dollars to bolster his country's economy."

"It's against the law." James was firm. "Our law. American law."

"The law can be bent. It can be waived. It has been before, and it will be again. And the Stockwell family does have access to the pertinent administration ears," Halsey De Vilbiss pointed out.

"He's right, you know." Peter was intrigued. "Now that Zelig is a member of the family—"

"He would not lend himself to such an endeavor." James was emphatic. "Zelig has been behind one Stockwell Institute position paper after another, nailing down

36

the national interest in opposition to trafficking with Qaddafi."

"That was before he married one of the major stockholders in Stockwell Petroleum," De Vilbiss pointed out.

"I love it." Buffy laughed aloud. "But it won't wash, Halsey. It's true that Zelig is no more principled than the rest of us, but it's also true that like the rest of us he is very selective regarding his chicanery. Some people even call that principle."

How like Buffy! Patrice, who had been observing silently in keeping with her unofficial presence at the meeting, was struck by the consistency of Buffy's amorality. Whether it was marriage or love, business or finance, Buffy could always be depended upon to rationalize self-interest. Fingering the silk bow at her throat, Patrice reflected on some of the victims of Buffy's philosophy. There had been the first husband Buffy publicly cuckolded at the climax of her scandalous affair with Patrice's grandfather, the governor. Buffy was responsible for the painful blow to Patrice's grandmother, whom the governor had divorced after almost thirty years of marriage in order to wed the younger beauty. And Buffy had cost the governor, a front-runner at the time, any chance he might have had to become president.

More recently, following the governor's death, Buffy had all too casually—in Patrice's view—slipped into marriage with Jack Houston. If Patrice was more bitter than fair regarding Buffy's third marriage, it was perhaps understandable. Her own affair with Jack had ended, as she perceived it, when Buffy had blithely snapped her fingers. Patrice had been—and still was—deeply infatuated—in love, she thought—with Jack. She hated Buffy for taking him from her; and she hated Buffy for making Jack so unhappy now with her extramarital diversions.

Turning her attention back to the meeting, Patrice heard her father countering Buffy's cynicism. "Regardless of how we might get around the presidential directive," James declared, "I would not myself feel comfortable dealing with Qaddafi."

There was general agreement with this attitude. Halsey De Vilbiss's scheme to ship Stockwell crude to Libyan refineries was shelved. Still, he wasn't willing to let it go at that.

"Is there some other way we can salvage our petroleum operation?" he demanded.

"There might be." It was Buffy who answered.

She's too casual. Patrice twisted the bow. Buffy sounded like a woman bemused by a secret all her own. What's she up to now?

"Thanks to OPEC, there's a worldwide shortage of oil," Buffy continued, recapping. "In our own country the price of gasoline at the pump is over two dollars a gallon. If we could refine the crude we're storing, we would make a killing. It's a seller's market and it's a once-in-a-lifetime opportunity. Now there are two problems. One—having the crude refined—we've discussed. The other is shipping, getting the oil to the refinery and then delivering it to customers after it's refined. Putting aside the first problem for the moment, I'd like to discuss the second one. If refining facilities were made available to us, just how would we transport?"

"To where?" James asked succinctly.

"East Texas, for instance."

"Jimbo Grebbs," Peter guessed.

I'll be damned. Now Patrice crumpled the bow beyond repair. What a slut she really is!

Buffy shrugged noncommittally.

"The problems would be solvable," James told her. "There are traditional lines of cooperation."

"Railroad?"

James nodded.

"And enough tank cars would be made available?" Buffy inquired.

"Vanderbilt." The name banished the problem.

"How about clearing the tracks for quick shipment in and out? There would have to be rescheduling, shuttling at the switchyards."

"Harriman."

"And how much advance notice would be needed?" Buffy asked.

"The more the better."

Buffy smiled. "Gentlemen," she said, "I think that I can solve our problem."

Now Patrice read the faces of the other board members with increased bitterness and cynicism; their expressions signaled to Patrice that if Buffy could indeed pull this off, her status on the board would be greatly enhanced. In the next rescrambling there would be no shortage of allies for her. Oh, yes, Patrice realized, if Buffy could deliver, control of the board of Stockwell Industries might be within her grasp.

The question was: Could she really deliver? Peter, a new respect for Buffy in his voice, asked it respectfully. "Has Grebbs agreed to refine our oil?" he inquired.

Buffy smiled. "Not yet."

"Will he?" Peter asked the next obvious question.

"I believe he will."

"You *believe* it?" David Lewis's tone was only slightly less diplomatic. "Or you are sure of it?"

"I am as sure as a woman can be."

Silently, Patrice gritted her teeth. The accent had been on precisely this right two-syllable word. Whatever the doubts of the men present, Patrice was sure that Buffy would deliver.

6

SPIRO PAPATESTUS HAD left Crete for Malta and a meeting with OPEC minister Ezzadine al Mabrouk of Libya. Bored in her husband's absence, Louise took the forty-minute commercial flight from Crete to Athens, rented a car, and drove to Delphi. Here, in the shadow of Mount Parnassus, she indulged the one Greek vice she had acquired—a willing surrender to the sensuality of antiquity. Over the years, at the Sacred Spring of Corinth, inside the Tholos Tomb of Klytemnestra at Mycenae, among the tragic echoes of the vast theater at Epidaurus, before the Parthenon itself in Athens, and—most of all—at Delphi's Sanctuary of the Pythian Apollo from which the Oracles decreed the fates of kings, Louise surrendered secretly to that which is most basic to all the temples of Greece: the passion with which the gods bless mortals.

"I'm badly educated," she had told Spiro when they were first married. "I really don't know anything about Greece except that it was the greatest of the ancient civilizations. I'm ashamed of myself. I'll have to get some books and study."

"Don't," he advised. "Visit the ruins. Visit the digs. Visit the museums. See Greece for yourself, don't read about it. Breathe it in. That's the only way to really learn about Greece."

Louise had followed her new husband's advice, and she had become deeply embroiled in the legends and the history of the country. In a sense, she had become addicted to Greece, and, slowly she had become aware of the large part an awakening sensuality deep inside her played in the addiction.

"It just thrills me," she confessed to Spiro. "For the first time I begin to understand the meaning of culture."

"Culture?" He restrained his amusement. "Is that all?" Spiro was a Macedonian with his toes still curled to the fertile soil of the north. He knew that the gods, the mythic figures who filled the ruins and the museums of Greece, were an uninhibited and bawdy lot.

"Of course that's all." Louise sounded bewildered, but why was she blushing? "What else could there be?"

Spiro had merely smiled.

His answer was patent now as Louise stood inside the museum at Delphi and regarded the two statues of the Kouroi—two superbly built young men from Argos—dating back to the fifth century B.C. The statues were boldly nude. Part of the firm, young man's penis had crumbled away from one of them. the other was intact.

Louise stared at the undamaged Kouroi for a long time. It was stone, not flesh. Intellectually, she knew that. Her eyes drifted to a frieze depicting naked gods and goddesses locked in Olympian battle. Her eyes picked out the naked breasts of the goddesses and the sex organs of the gods. Their proximity in the heat of battle made her catch her breath sharply. She looked back at the two Kouroi. Her hand trembling, she reached out and touched the stone phallus of the undamaged statue. The heat rose from Louise's core and flushed her face.

"It feel pleasing, yes?"

Startled, she snatched her hand away. Cheeks burning, she stared mutely at the smiling face of the young man who had spoken. He kept smiling—not a smirk, but with genuine friendliness. His companion was also smiling. The one who had spoken was obviously Greek, but the other, a black man, Louise knew to be an American.

She had run into them two or three times that morning while climbing the slopes of Delphi. From the conversations she had not been able to help overhearing, she had gathered they were graduate students, although their talk did not reveal from which university. They looked older than the average student, but in their faded jeans and beat-up leather jackets they certainly had that rumpled campus look of young men who didn't work for a living. The Greek was trying to teach the American his language, but evidently with little success. Garbled as his English was, it was light-years ahead of his companion's Greek. Twice on the slopes they had moved toward Louise with the obvious intention of striking up a conversation. Each time she had twisted skillfully through the maze of the ruins dotting the hillside to successfully avoid them. They hadn't seemed to push it, and yet now here they were again.

Their interest surprised Louise. When she traveled, she took some pains to downplay those facets of her appearance that attracted men. She dressed herself, purposely, in the drab and deceptive Turkish-style garb favored by the old peasant women in the farming valleys of Crete. Flat, square-tipped, and utilitarian black shoes, coarse black wool stockings rolled to her knees, an ankle-length, shapeless, skirt, and black pullover sweater was her disguise. To hide her long red-gold hair, she tucked it up under the traditional Kriti female head covering, a sort of bandanna, also black in color, which reached from just above the eyebrows to just below the neck. In keeping with her costume, Louise had cultivated the Kriti peasant woman's walk. By folding her arms palm to elbow, hunching her shoulders, using her heels to push her bent upper body forward against the air as if penetrating some obstacle, she transformed the magnificence of her body into something far less pleasing to the eye. And she kept her chin tucked under against her neck and her eyes always on the ground in front of her. She had mastered the Kriti woman's traditional arrogance of humility.

Nearly always, the outfit worked. Foreigners assumed she was a Greek peasant woman. Greeks, who knew that even on Crete only the older women still dressed in this fashion while the younger ones bartered with their souls for American jeans, assumed that Louise was Italian or perhaps Yugoslavian. Thus it was all the more surprising that the young Greek had addressed her in English.

Muttering the few Italian words she knew, she scampered away. Furtively looking back, she was uneasy about both men's laughing eyes. Obviously her deception hadn't worked.

Louise returned to her hotel, packed, paid her bill, and stowed her suitcase in the trunk of her rental car. With a last, fond backward glance at the breathtaking gorge and the Bay of Corinth in the distance, she pointed the car toward Piraeus. Driving in the warm November sunlight of early afternoon, her mind turned again to the statues of the Kouroi. She pictured their muscled stone thighs and high, firm buttocks. She thought of the smooth alabaster of their flat waists and broad chests. Her memory focused on the individual stone curls of hair hanging to their shoulders, and then on their young, sensual faces. Abruptly, it was not the face of either Kouroi, but rather that of the smiling Greek student that was dancing in front of her windshield as she followed the mountain road winding down toward Athens and Piraeus.

"It feel pleasing, yes?" The friendly voice whispered its broken English in her ear along with the wind from the half-opened car window. She saw his face. Then the Kouroi, the crumbled phallus and the one that was intact.

Her fingertips tingled with the memory of how the cold, hard stone had felt. Her thighs clenched with the echo: "It feel pleasing, yes?"

Louise called the rental agency and told them she was leaving the car for them in the dockside parking lot at Piraeus. She had decided she would take the ferry back to Crete. It was an overnight trip, twelve hours, but she was in no hurry. Louise hated flying, and she was always at ease on the water.

She boarded the boat at four, although it was not scheduled to leave until seven-thirty. Her first-class cabin allowed privacy as well as her own bathroom. After bathing, she took a nap and did not emerge from her cabin until she felt the first rumbles of the ship's engines. Then she went up on deck to enjoy the sight of the lights of Piraeus receding down the shoreline as the ship sailed past the lesser luminosities of one small coastal village after another before turning toward the open sea.

The wind in her face, it took Louise a moment to realize that the voice calling from the deck below was addressing her. She looked over the rail. On the deck outside the tourist-class lounge, the two young men she had last encountered in the museum at Delphi were craning their necks to look up at her. It was the American who had spoken. "Hey, lady," he had called. "Like they say, it's sure enough a small world."

When she looked down, the young Greek man spoke. "Buòna nòtte, signorina." He greeted her in Italian, a teasing note in his voice.

"Ciao." Louise turned on her heel and quickly made her way back to her cabin.

Not wanting to chance another encounter with the young men, she tipped a steward to bring her dinner on a tray. Not that the likes of those two would have access to the first-class dining lounge, Louise thought. She was acting paranoid, she supposed, but somehow she felt threatened by them—particularly the Greek.

After dinner, she got into bed and read for a while. Her book was a satire on the Greek gods by an Englishwoman named Maureen O'Sullivan. She perused a chapter and then turned out the light and went to sleep.

43

Louise dreamed of the naked Kouroi at Delphi and of touching the intact phallus and of the heavy, sculpted face with its pronounced features—the hawklike nose, the jutting anvil jaw—of the young Greek man. *"Buòna nòtte,"* he said in her dream, his large black eyes limpid and softly friendly. *"Buòna nòtte."* And he ran his fingers through his too long, curly hair and smiled approval as Louise made a fist around the stone phallus.

The next morning Louise was up and dressed and out on deck as the ferry sailed into the spectacular sunrise irradiating the harbor of Iraklion. Consciously avoiding the two young men, she was the first one off the boat when it docked. She hailed an early-morning taxi and had it take her to the airport parking lot, where she had left her Mercedes coupe. It was still early when she pulled onto the mountain road that would take her to the Papatestus villa overlooking the southern shore of Crete.

It would have been a two-hour drive if she hadn't gotten a flat tire halfway there. As much as she hated falling into the stereotype of the unmechanical woman, Louise was really not very good at dealing with emergencies like changing tires. She had a positive knack for turning the lug wrench the wrong way for too long before she realized her mistake. The damn lugs defied her strength, too. There was always one that refused to budge. She scraped her knees, banged her elbows, and smeared dirt from the tire all over her forehead. A task that should have taken twenty minutes took Louise more than an hour and a half.

Just as she was finishing, the express bus from Iraklion to Ag Galini and Matala came around the curb, honking to warn of its approach. Louise flattened herself against the cliffside behind the car, holding the tire she had just removed in front of her. The bus slowed down, but not enough to keep from depositing a cloud of dust over both Louise and the Mercedes.

In its wake she recognized a familiar voice. *"Signorina! Signorina!"*

"Hey, missy, bad luck." The second voice was right behind it.

They waved at her like old friends, two faces, one black, one white, peering out of the back of the bus until it rounded the next curve. Louise did not wave back. She was frightened. They were probably going to Matala, she thought. They would fit right in with the hippie life-style there, Louise was sure. But she was left feeling vaguely threatened. They had met in Delphi, aboard ship, and now by the side of the road. The Matala area was intimate. Undoubtedly they would meet again. Yes, even if she tried to avoid them, she would see them again. She scowled to herself at the prospect.

Serenity, to Louise, was solitude.

7

SOLITUDE, HOLLY REFLECTED, was an unnatural state for a bride. Still, she had no choice. Zelig had left for Greece, and so, on this cold December afternoon in her studio at Riverview, Holly opened her files and took out the two batches of research papers on which she was currently working.

The first stack, chronologically arranged in a folder, was made up of documents relating to the Stockwell family during colonial times and the early 1800s. Taken from the private family archives of the Charles Stockwell Memorial Foundation, these documents were the raw data on which official histories of the Stockwells during that period were based. All chroniclers of the socially and politically prominent clan relied heavily on this material.

But it was the second pile, a manuscript really, that had claimed Holly's attention for the past year. On paper brittle with age and charred around the edges, the painstakingly penned pages constituted a satiric novel written in the 1830s by George Cortlandt Stockwell, an ancestor of Holly's. It was a bitter work, amateurish, yet there was an unmistakable ring of truth about it. George Cortlandt

Stockwell had changed the names, but the incidents and characters in his "fiction" were all members of his own family. Everything in his book jibed with the official records. Little in the work, however, was flattering to the early American Stockwells of whom he wrote.

Together, the two piles of papers constituted a project on which Holly had been working for over two years. It had begun when she had returned to Riverview after leaving a very unhappy marriage. She had been morose, anguished over the bitter truths she had discovered about her husband and her marriage, and her grandmother Mary had suggested that she write a history of Riverview in order to pull herself out of the doldrums. Holly's grandfather, the governor, had arranged for her to have access to all the archives of the Charles Stockwell Memorial Foundation. When the governor died, he left her a separate trust in his will to continue her research.

Holly did not approach the task as a dilettante. She had majored in American history at Bryn Mawr, and she had been captivated by the history of the Hudson River Valley since she was a little girl. She had kept up this interest when she married and moved to England, traveling to Cornwall and Yorkshire to go through old archives that revealed the backgrounds of the Stockwells. She had spent countless hours in the reading room of the British Museum in London, familiarizing herself with the details of life during the period her family had been part of the colonization of the New World.

Research was a joy to her. Ferreting out details, piecing them together, watching characters who had once really lived take shape, and seeing patterns of lives emerge—Holly could and did lose herself in this. She threw herself into the project of gathering material for a history of Riverview wholeheartedly. Even so, it had been a plodding sort of job—searching and cataloging and taking notes, arranging and rearranging—until the day she'd stumbled on the George Cortlandt Stockwell manuscript. There had been references to the work here and there in the annals of the foundation, but all of them indicated that the manuscript had been completely destroyed in the 1838 conflagration that burned the original Riverview manor house to the ground. It was only by chance that Holly learned otherwise.

Going through the research material concerning the fire, Holly had learned that while George Cortlandt Stockwell and his father, Horace Fenton Stockwell, had perished in the blaze, George's siblings had survived it. George's younger brother, Charles, had rebuilt Riverview, and it was he who had gathered together the papers that had survived from the colonial period and seen to it that they were preserved for posterity. These were the official documents with which most biographers of the family, or chroniclers of the Hudson River Valley, contented themselves.

But George and Charles had also had a sister, Elizabeth. Marrying a southerner named Thomas Cole, she had taken up residence on a tobacco plantation in the Carolinas. As far as the Riverview records were concerned, Elizabeth and any descendants she might have had simply vanished from view upon crossing the Mason-Dixon line.

Holly was a thorough researcher, however, and Elizabeth represented a gap in the Stockwell genealogy. Through careful research and many inquiries, Holly determined where the Cole family had lived in South Carolina. She paid a visit to the county courthouse there to see what she could find out from the records. She was able to trace the Cole family as far as a descendant born in the early 1900s. There was a marriage certificate for the descendant, a woman, but no record of her having given birth to any children and no death certificate. Seemingly, the trail had petered out to a dead end.

On a hunch, however, Holly asked to see the property tax assessment records for the county. She looked up the Cole plantation and found nothing after the late 1860s. In the wake of the Civil War it had been sold. Much later it had been subdivided into tracts for an upper-class suburban housing development.

Disappointed, Holly leafed idly through the tax records for the development. Suddenly her eye was caught by a name—Mrs. Richard Peckinpaugh. Peckinpaugh was the surname of the man whom the descendant of Elizabeth Stockwell Cole had married.

Holly copied down the name and the address underneath it. She looked up Mrs. Richard Peckinpaugh in a local telephone book and called to explain who she was and what she wanted. A trembly and aging but not unfriendly woman's voice assured her it would be just fine to come on out and "chat family."

Mrs. Richard Peckinpaugh—"Mildred," she had told Holly to call her—was a spry woman in her late seventies. She had been a widow for almost thirty years. She had never had any children. When Holly told her about her researches, Mildred's reaction was enthusiastic.

"Mama had a trunk," she said, "Came down to her from her mother, who got it from her mother. It's filled with all kinds of papers."

"Where is it?" Holly had asked eagerly.

"Guess." Mildred's smile was impish.

"The attic?"

"Nope. But close. It's in the basement."

The top layers of the trunk had been filled with all sorts of Cole family memorabilia. High school albums and diplomas, wedding pictures and courtship letters, birth certificates and obituary notices—all the evidences of lives lived and milestones passed were there. Beneath these items a hand-crocheted tablecloth had been neatly folded to separate the material at the bottom of the trunk from the keepsakes above it.

"My mother told me that Elizabeth Stockwell Cole crocheted that tablecloth herself," Mildred told Holly.

Under the tablecloth were various papers relating to the life of Elizabeth Stockwell before she became Mrs. Thomas Cole. There was an obituary notice from the mid-1830s reporting her mother's death and an extensive newspaper account of the fire that had razed Riverview. Along with reporting the deaths of Elizabeth's father and brother, the article cataloged the loss of art treasures in the fire, described the jewelry and tapestries and one-of-a-kind pieces of furniture destroyed, and mentioned the destruction of the only copy of a completed but unpublished novel by George Cortlandt Stockwell.

A large pewter safebox fastened with a rusted padlock was the last item in the trunk. When, with Mildred's consent, Holly forced the lock and opened the safebox, she had found the manuscript of George Cortlandt Stockwell's novel.

That it had indeed been in the fire was attested to by the charred edges of the pages. But why had Elizabeth Stockwell Cole spirited it away after the blaze, hidden it, and allowed the world to believe it had been destroyed? With four words and a twinkle in her eye, Mildred, who before that day had not known of the manuscript's existence, had answered the question: "Skeletons in the closet."

Fortunately for Holly, Mildred didn't mind the skeletons coming out of the closet. "He wrote it almost a hundred and fifty years ago," she said. "Whatever it was my great-grandmother wanted to hide, I'm sure nobody cares anymore." And so she had allowed Holly to take the manuscript with her. "If it's spicy"—Mildred's parting words were spoken with a wink—"you be sure to let me know now."

Holly had promised she would, and she had kept the promise. The manuscript was indeed spicy. It was also devastating toward the relatives George Cortlandt Stockwell had written about. Intended to be satirical, it was really more malicious than funny.

Most important, it dovetailed with the other material on the Stockwells that was already in print. The picture that emerged was—depending on one's viewpoint—both scandalous and all too human. From the first, it seemed, the Stockwells had lived to the hilt. They had been loving and violent, hypocritical and hot-blooded, opportunistic and fascinating.

Now, in her tower study above the estate library, Holly extracted those papers relating to the first Stockwells of Riverview. She placed them alongside the George Cortlandt Stockwell manuscript. Painstakingly, Holly began comparing the documents with the manuscript of the novel and making notes to prove or disprove the satiric version. Starting with the end of the American Revolution when the Stockwells had first come to Riverview, Holly felt the thrill of events falling into place and of a story developing. . . .

8

ON APRIL 30, 1789, Colonel Roger Stockwell stood just behind the portieres shielding the balcony of Federal Hall on Wall Street in New York City. Inside the room, to the rear of the tight-packed other guests, clustered the family of his older brother, Everett Stockwell. Besides Everett was his wife, Margaret Adams Stockwell, a distant relative of John Adams, and their three children, fourteen-year-old Marcy, Horace, age eleven, and Deborah, just five.

Outside, on the balcony, in full view of the great crowd below, General George Washington was being sworn in as the first president of the newly formed United States of America by Chancellor Livingston. As the administration of the oath concluded, a mighty roar of approval went up from the crowd gathered on the cobblestoned street below. Washington bowed stiffly several times and finally backed off the balcony and into the chamber. Wiping his brow, he spied Colonel Stockwell beside the draperies.

"And so it is done, Roger." The merest shadow of a smile curled the corners of Washington's thin lips.

"Done and well done, sir."

"And now for the Congress." Washington's posture was always ramrod straight; nevertheless, Roger had the brief impression that he was squaring his shoulders as if to do battle.

"They will fall to you, sir, as did the sword of Cornwallis," Colonel Stockwell assured him. Washington had already shown him the inaugural address, and Roger Stockwell was sincere in his high opinion of the speech.

"And so, armed with your faith, dear Colonel, I advance into the lion's den." Washington gave Stockwell a brisk, military pat on the shoulder and strode toward the door leading into the hall, where the Congress awaited him.

Those in the room moved to follow. Colonel Stockwell fell in beside his brother, Everett. Despite their relationship, the two men were very different both as to looks and character. Everett, the older, was a sparrow-faced man with thinning hair and pale, lackluster gray eyes. He was as sparse of flesh as he was tight of purse. A mercantile man, a merchant and banker, more at home with columns of figures than in battles or ballrooms, nobody could remember ever having seen Everett laugh, and if his wife, Margaret, could recall his having smiled, it was only because such occasions were so rare.

Everett's younger brother, Roger, was more sensitive and, until recently, had always displayed a more energetic nature. Before the war, Roger had smiled easily and laughed heartily and enjoyed pitting his muscularity against whatever challenge came his way. His joie de vivre had defined his nature, if not the depth of his character. His outdoorsman's physique and rough-hewn, sun-leathered visage with its aggressive nose tilted from some long-forgotten brawl had lent him the sort of appeal that attracted women as well as men. At first glance a lanky "country boy" sort of man with flaxen hair and a scraggly mustache, Roger was found on closer acquaintance to have depth, emotional perception, and a loving heart.

The war had muted these qualities. A personal tragedy that Roger had never been able to bring himself to discuss with anyone had built a wall around him that made him as inaccessible to emotion as his brother. Only the anguish in Roger's deep gray eyes with their soft greenish cast reflected his deep and hidden loss.

Alienated as he was, Roger still was not oblivious to the emotionalism of the occasion that had brought them to Wall Street on this historic day. "It will be something for the children to remember," Roger remarked to Everett

51

now as they followed the others in to hear George Washington's first inaugural address. "To be present on the occasion when the first president of our country first addresses its territorial representatives."

Everett Stockwell nodded absentmindedly and, passing a hallway window, pointed to an elongated stretch of overgrown weeds between the Trinity Church and Fraunces Tavern. "Do you know what they're asking for that tract?"

Roger's eyes met those of Everett's wife, Margaret. She was a tidy woman in her thirties, bosomy and rounded, but not stout. Her waist was narrow, and her round face had a habitual flush that perhaps betrayed a certain vivaciousness denied by the twin tight coils of her pale blond hair and her rather formal demeanor. She gave a small, fatalistic shrug at her husband's blindness to the historical moment that he and their children were about to witness. Roger sensed rather than saw the conspiratorial smile that joined them in exasperation at Everett's single-minded pursuit of fortune.

"I'm not even sure it's up for sale," Roger said in answer to his brother's question.

"Of course it is." Everett was impatient with his brother's lack of foresight. "When the harbor expands, the port expands. Three piers added in the last year. That means more storage space will be needed close at hand. But that tract was farmland before the big fire. The owners aren't developers. You can be sure they have an asking price and a selling price, too. And, just between us, I am interested in buying. That strip will never do anything but increase in value."

"Everett, George Washington is about to address the Congress for the first time. It is an historic moment. A nation is being born. It is no time to talk business."

"Business, dear brother, is just what this nation will be all about."

In their wake, Everett's eleven-year-old son, Horace, yawned. He was bored. In years to come, he would recall very little of the historic occasion. The one thing that would stick in his memory was the sentence his father had just spoken.

Posterity, however, would remember George Washington's words, and so would Colonel Roger Stockwell. He was moved by the occasion to an extent that he had allowed nothing else to touch him since the end of the war. His brother's wife, Margaret, noticed this but did not comment on it.

When the ceremonies were concluded, there was a coach waiting to take the Stockwells home. It would be a journey of several hours from the tip of Manhattan Island to the Hudson River Valley, where their home, the three-thousand-acre plantation "Riverview," was located.

The plantation belonged to Colonel Roger Stockwell. The original owners, a Dutch patroon family sympathetic to the Tory cause, had fled to Canada toward the end of the war. The colonial army had confiscated the property, and subsequently General Washington had successfully petitioned the Continental Congress to award it to Colonel Stockwell in recognition of his continued service and valor during the struggle. Some members of the Congress had looked at it as settlement for the years of back pay the colonel had never received.

It was a sorry gift as far as the colonel was concerned. He knew the estate well, and it could never be anything but a painful reminder of tragedy to him. Here he had once known love, and here he had watched horrified as it was irretrievably taken from him. But the colonel did not speak to anyone of that.

Roger Stockwell, a single man with little use of such a lavish estate, had invited his brother and his family to come live with him in the Hudson River Valley. His brother, Everett, who lived and worked in the city, had children and a wife eager for a country home.

Now, under the starlight of a cloudless springtime evening, the Stockwells' carriage approached the residence from the access road below. It loomed up white and proud, one of the great mansions of the region, already over eighty years old. Margaret Adams Stockwell was filled with a quiet pride as she looked at it and knew that she was mistress of such a great house. How odd, she thought as they passed through the massive iron gates and traveled up the hill to the manor house, that the one visible proof of worldly success that truly gave her joy should have come to her not from her husband's constant pursuit of wealth, but from her brother-in-law's service in battle to establish their new country. Margaret banished the mean thought from her mind as the coach halted in front of the white-pillared verandah, and she roused the sleeping children.

Everett did not help. He had some business to attend to, he said, and went straightaway to his study. Roger started out helping her, but when servants materialized, he, too, faded away. With the children finally put to bed, Margaret went to the sitting room. The servants had laid a fire there, and it was quite cozy on the claw-legged House of Orange divan in front of it. Margaret sat there, staight-backed and prim, but comfortable with the posture, and worked on her needlepoint. After a while Everett came in to bid her good night, saying that it had been a long day and he was going to bed.

Margaret continued sewing until the close work in dim light made her eyes began to tear. Then she set the needlepoint aside and simply sat there staring into the fire. She had no wish to retire until she was sure that Everett was quite soundly asleep. Otherwise he might call upon her to submit to his husbandly demands. Most nights Margaret didn't really mind that too much, but this evening, after all the excitement of the day, the prospect of his weight pinning her to the mattress was truly oppressive.

She was not sure how long she sat there. Stiff-backed as her position was, still she may have dozed. She was not dozing when first she heard the sound, however. She was just picking up the candle to light her way to bed. It was a strange sound, and Margaret could not readily identify it. At first she thought it was one of the children having a nightmare. But these were not the sounds a child made crying in its sleep. These were the sounds of an adult in great and wrenching pain. Heart was Margaret's weakness, anguish ever a magnet to her. She moved instinctively toward the sounds of suffering.

9

Beside the sea, Louise Papatestus gazed at the sensual sight that would lead to her undoing. Even now it was unraveling all her carefully contrived defenses. And yet she stood rooted to the shore, unable to avert her eyes.

They were focused on two young men, stark naked and wrestling. Not aware that they were being observed, their movements were completely uninhibited. As they struggled, laughing, the sweat glistened on their muscular young bodies—one bronze, the other ebony—as the surprisingly hot December sun of southern Crete warmed their straining flesh.

Their frolic compounded Louise's problem. As was her custom, she had come that afternoon to Komo beach to swim. As usual, when she arrived, it was deserted. She had stripped off her clothes, left them in a pile behind a sand dune, and dived naked into the tranquil Libyan Sea. She had swum a long time, possessed of an energy she needed to work off, wanting to push her muscles to the point of genuine weariness. That accomplished, Louise intended to stretch out in the sun and capture the sleep that so often eluded her at night. But when she emerged naked from the water, there was a barrier to her plans.

Louise had come ashore near the cliffs at the other end of Komo beach from her clothes. Starting to walk toward them, she had halted abruptly. There was a man swimming about ten yards off shore between her and her clothing. He was wearing a face mask and holding a speargun over his head in one hand.

Startled, Louise retreated to the shelter of a cave at the base of the jetty cliff. From her place of concealment, she squinted at the surf to see where the scuba diver was now. She couldn't spot him. Instead, she saw a sight that had somehow escaped her notice before.

Another man, lighter-skinned, was lying on his back naked near the shoreline where the other man had been

55

diving. He seemed to be asleep. He had a full-blown erection.

Louise caught her breath. A thrill coursed through her at this visible evidence of masculine arousal. She looked at the sleeper's face and recognized him immediately. It was the young Greek she had seen with his black companion first at Delphi, and then on the boat to Iraklion, and finally on the Matala road.

Probably they had taken over one of the caves on the Matala side of the cliff and were living there along with all the other would-be hippie students. Nude bathing and sunning in the buff were common on the Matala side. The young people who gathered there weren't overly burdened with modesty. Still, the scuba diving might be more interesting here at Komo.

As Louise's mind was racing with these thoughts, and with the problem of how to get to her clothes, the scuba diver emerged from the water. Except for his flippers and snorkel tube and mask, he was as naked as his Greek friend. He took off his equipment, looked at his friend, saw the erection, and laughed aloud.

The young black man picked up a handful of sand and dribbled it over his friend's groin. The Greek came awake with a start. Cursing, but laughing, too, he leaped to his feet and chased after his friend, who was backing away rapidly.

That's when the wrestling match had started. Now, watching from the seclusion of the cave at the base of the cliff jetty, Louise was enthralled. Her erotic reaction had seized her by surprise. She was as incapable of resisting it as she had been of resisting the impulse to touch the phallus of the Kouroi that day in the museum at Delphi. Her eyes were riveted, her breathing heavy, her body tense.

Hands on each other's shoulders, the two naked young men were straining mightily to attain some advantage. The muscles of their necks and shoulders and chests rippled even as their laughing faces turned upward to the smiling sun. The black man's slightly taller and more slender body gleamed with salt beads of water from his swim. There were grains of sand still clinging to the pronounced, sinewy buttocks of the more muscular and broader-shouldered Greek.

As they struggled, the penises and testicles of both men swung violently this way and that. They were not shy with each other's bodies, but neither, Louise knew instinctively, were they gay. There was nothing carnal in their impromptu wrestling match. Yet somehow that very lack made it all the more sensually arousing.

Huddled in the mouth of the cave, her hungry hazel eyes watched the play of sunlight on their flesh, light and dark, as they locked thighs in an effort to push each other off balance. The maneuver sent their sex organs slashing like swords, moving through their tufts of pubic hair like scythes through fields of wheat. It was like some side skirmish in the battle, a phallic combat that stabbed directly to the heart of Louise's libido.

Suddenly weak and a little faint, Louise slumped to her knees in the mouth of the cave. The sun beat down on her. It had dried her skin, and now she was perspiring heavily.

The men were locked together now in a new grip, laughing, belly to belly, bottoms grinding with their efforts, sex organs crushed and mingled in the fray. . . .

Louise was dizzy. Her eyes were staring so intently that they teared. Her nipples were swollen and very painful. She felt the wetness seeping between her legs.

Then, suddenly, the Greek got the advantage. He toppled the black man and pinned him, knees planted firmly on his shoulders. Demanding his surrender, his penis swung violently back and forth, the sac below bouncing wildly.

Fragmented colors blotted the scene from Louise's gaze. An impossible heat rose up to claim her spinning brain, and her hands were clenching the rock in front of her. She had not touched herself, and yet . . . and yet . . .

Her climax was ferocious.

10

SEX AND SCANDAL culminating in tragedy were the heritage of Riverview, Holly realized as she put aside the papers on her desk. The pattern was repeated over and over again. It had preceded the Stockwells to the estate, and it had marked their first days there following the American Revolution.

Holly perceived this from having skipped ahead in her research. The time when she had to look in on her convalescing young son, Nicholas, had crept up on her, so it had been necessary to leave off her reading at the point where Margaret Adams Stockwell had gone to investigate the sounds of sobbing. But Holly had flipped through the following pages enough to recognize romance, and lust, and—inevitably—tragedy.

This was all in the back of Holly's mind as she left her west tower studio to Nicholas's bedroom. It came to the forefront again later, when she left her son's room and started for the staircase. En route she passed the door to the sitting room adjoining the bedroom shared by Buffy and Jack Houston. The door was ajar. Holly had not intended to look into the room; it just naturally fell within her field of vision. But what she saw so startled her that she was momentarily stopped in her tracks.

Buffy and Jimbo Grebbs were standing just inside the room embracing. Their mouths were clinging together in a long, deep kiss. One of Grebbs's hands was tangled in the silk of Buffy's dress over her squirming left buttock.

Buffy removed the hand firmly as the kiss ended. "I'm a married woman," she reminded Grebbs coyly, fluttering dark lashes, the gleam in her violet eyes belying the words. "And there are boundaries."

"Sure there are, honey," he drawled, reaching for her again.

Buffy slipped away from him deftly. "My husband is due home any minute," she said. "And you and I are supposed to be discussing the refining of Stockwell crude.''

"Always a pleasure to talk business with you, ma'am." Jimbo Grebbs slipped into Texas irony. "Always a pleasure to meet up with your husband, too. A fine man, Jackie Houston, even if he is a mite touchy about his wife. Seeing as you're expecting him, maybe it would be best if I just saddled up and rode off into the night."

"You are outrageous!" Buffy laughed at his exaggerated cowboy manner.

"One last kiss to give me strength against coyotes and jealous husbands." Jimbo reached for her firmly, and this time Buffy didn't evade his grasp.

Embarrassed, Holly moved quickly on down the hall. As she reached the top of the staircase, she saw Jack Houston below, entering by the front door. "Hi, Holly," he called up to her. "How's Nicholas?"

"Hello, Jack." Holly responded, her voice deliberately loud. "Nicholas is fine. So fine," she babbled, "that I'm going to have a drink to celebrate." She came down the stairs to him. "Keep me company, won't you?"

"Soon as I look in on Buffy." He started to move around her.

"Oh, don't be so husbandly." Holly grabbed his arm with uncharacteristic insistence. "She won't care if we have a friendly drink first." She pulled Jack into the sitting room and over to the bar.

Jack's back was to the staircase when Jimbo Grebbs came down and silently let himself out. A moment later Buffy joined them. "Caught you," she said, patting Holly's cheek and blowing Jack a kiss. "Martini-ing behind my back. Aren't you two ashamed of yourselves?"

It was obvious to Holly that Buffy herself felt no shame at all.

11

FOLLOWING LOUISE'S SEXUAL reaction to the men wrestling naked on the beach, Louise had felt guilty, dirty, and ashamed. But it didn't last. Intellectually, at least, she was sophisticated enough not to blame herself for an unintended orgasm. The cause of her orgasm, however, was not so easily dispelled.

She had to see the Greek again. It was a foolish obsession, she knew, but Louise couldn't help herself. Those two naked bodies, one white, one black, sculpted with muscles straining like the larger-than-life statues of the naked warriors at Delphi—the memory had been seared into her mind not with shame, but with a burning sensual brand.

Louise resisted the memory. For a week she lay awake nights with hands clenched to keep from touching herself, her blood on fire, her body stiff as a board with her resistance. Days she made herself stay at the villa. She did not go to Komo beach. She did not want to risk a repetition of what had happened. By seeking out their young, lascivious, forbidden flesh, she knew that she would risk another betrayal by her own body.

For one whole week her resistance prevailed. And then one morning, showering, a stray drop caromed off her nipple in a way that seemed to sear it with an erotic kiss— and Louise's resistance snapped like the brittle twig it was. She toweled herself quickly, pulled on shorts and a halter, and drove to Komo.

Despite the impetuosity that brought her here, Louise was nevertheless cautious. Pulling her car off the rutted dirt road, she parked it between a copse of trees and the church, where it couldn't be seen from either the road or the beach. Then she scrambled down the steep east slope of the hillside so that she would come out on the beach from the cover of the underbrush near the cliff jetty with its sheltering caves.

From the vantage point of one of the caves, she searched the beach with her eyes. There was no one in sight. She studied the surf, devoid of swimmers. The young men were nowhere to be seen. Louise waited for about an hour, but they did not come. Disappointed, she sheltered from the wind by the jetty, but the sun beat down mercilessly on her skin. Finally, with a sigh, she decided to go in for a swim to cool off.

Her body was weary with the tension of sleepless nights spent fending off her desires. The warm Libyan Sea both relaxed and energized her. She swam the length of the beach and back again, not straining, but not sparing her muscles, either. When she emerged, the sun was behind the clouds, and one of those sudden mists common to the southern coast of Crete had rolled in off the water. The dunes were lost in it; the vista was unreal, wreathed in a sort of fog; the beach had been transformed into the smoke-wrapped coastal moors of Minoan legend.

On impulse, Louise plunged into the mist. She ran, more grim than happy, pitting herself against some unformed challenge she didn't even try to understand. As she ran in the mist, the vision of the two young men, naked and wrestling, formed before her eyes. It was an illusion with soft edges. Nevertheless, her breath came more quickly with it, and her heart beat faster.

Finally, panting, she stopped running and sank to her knees. She sat back on her haunches until her naked buttocks rested on a rise of sand. Stretching her long, shapely legs out in front of her, she tossed her mane of apricot hair back over her shoulders, its tendrils tickling her bare skin. Face raised to the sky, she could see nothing but fog. She glanced around her. The mist was a wall surrounding her, protecting her. In no direction could she see more than a foot or two.

Rarely had Louise felt so completely alone. And with this solitary feeling came one of utter privacy. She closed her eyes and pictured the young men wrestling: how their muscles had strained against the shiny skins of their black and bronze bodies; how their biceps had bulged, their buttocks strained, their pectorals rippled; how their phalluses had lashed out with their movements; how the tight

61

sacs containing their testicles had rolled over their perspiring thighs.

Louise remembered the young Greek lying naked and asleep in the sand with an erection. The mist was like a shroud covering her body, rendering her invisible. There was no way to see her naked and squeezed in her fantasy between the two naked male bodies, the lighter one straining with lust. Inside the shelter, it was safe for her to touch the tips of her breasts with her fingertips, to stroke them so that the heat spread quickly downward to her belly. It was safe to follow the path of the heat with one hand, to slide over her smooth, firm belly, to let her fingertips tangle in the fine red-gold pubic hair, to allow her quivering thighs to part.

Quite deliberately, then, Louise touched herself. Her thighs separated more widely. As she touched herself with her middle finger and moaned low in her throat, she felt the warmth and wetness. She rubbed rhythmically. . . .

Suddenly the wind shifted, and the mist dissipated. Louise looked up to see a darker shadow where once there had been only haze. Clutching herself, not wanting to lose the exquisite sensation that was growing at her core, she blinked and peered through the thinning vapors at the shadow. And then—

Was it a dream? No. He was really there. Realizing this, Louise was too startled to move, too immobilized to release herself. And thus exposed, she stared up, her hazel eyes pleading as the young Greek approached her. Like herself, he was naked, his flesh shiny and wet. He had been striding through the mist, on his way back from his swim to where he had left his towel and clothes.

He stopped short when he saw Louise, recognizing immediately what she had been doing. Humanly, he reacted to the realization. His phallus crawled up his belly.

Louise moaned aloud at his reaction. Their eyes met.

Quickly erect, he took three long steps and reached her. He bent down and hooked his hands underneath her waist, lifting her up.

Reflexively, Louise's hands locked around his neck. Her legs clenched his waist just above his hips. His entry was fierce, her reception violent. They twirled in a mad circle, and Louise came and came again until the young man fell to the sand atop her and with a wild and triumphant cry exploded deep inside her.

Thirty-three years old, it was the first time in her life that the world-renowned beauty Louise Papatestus had ever truly known sexual pleasure with a man.

BOOK TWO

12

THE PROMISE OF Christmas took the edge off the harsh winter ice covering the bare branches of the Riverview oaks. It was a season of hope in a time that was otherwise bleak for Holly. Separated from her new husband, tied down by her five-year-old son's protracted convalescence, she could nevertheless find a familiar warmth and reassurance in the yule season. It made her feel like a child again, rosy-cheeked with the Hudson River Valley cold, secure in the love of her family. The delicious anticipation of getting and of giving came flooding back to her. This year in particular she was eager to see the joy on Nicholas's face come Christmas morning when he opened his gifts. What better medicine could there be for him?

Holly's spirits were lifted by the visible signs of Christmas as she descended the spiral staircase—twined with sparkling holiday garlands—to the two-story-tall library with its trompe l'oeil ceiling. Exiting the tower through its outdoor entrance, the huge carved iron door looking not so grim as usual with its red-ribboned holiday wreath, she walked along the path—its pine trees festive with white Christmas lights—that paralleled the east wing of the mansion. Another wreath greeted her as she reentered Riverview by the front entrance. A twenty-foot Christmas tree decorated with hand-carved wooden angels, medieval magi, and an eleventh-century crèche from Saxony filled the center hallway as Holly went up the sweeping staircase to Nicholas's room.

Nicholas, still recovering from the shock his system had received from his icy plunge into the Hudson, was weak but impatient to be out of bed, up and going. The imminence of Christmas only increased his impatience and made him irritable.

"How about a game of Go Fish?" Holly greeted him.

"Okay." Nicholas scowled. He was glad to relieve the boredom, sulky with the need to do so.

Always patient with him, Holly dealt the cards. Without making it obvious, she allowed him to win. After about ten minutes he commented on the play.

"Zelig plays better than you," he said. "I wish he was here for Christmas."

"So do I, Nicky. I really miss him."

"I wish we could have gone to Greece with him like cousin Michael did."

"We'll join him there just as soon as you're well enough." Holly played a card. "And," she added as an afterthought, "Zelig didn't go to Greece with Michael. They went separately. Zelig's on Crete at the Papatestus villa. They're relatives of ours. And Michael's in Athens. Michael's a congressman, and he went on a fact-finding tour. Do you know what that is, Nicky?"

"A congressman is a politician." Nicholas giggled. "And a politician is a . . . arse. That's what Great-Grandpa used to say before he went and died."

"Yes." Holly smiled wanly. "I remember. He was quoting some humorist, I'm not sure who. Still, cousin Michael has always been nice to you, and I don't think you should tell him that. He might be insulted."

"I won't." Nicholas took a trick and squeezed the cards triumphantly.

"Anyway, I meant do you know what a fact-finding tour is, not a politician."

"Sure I do." His blond head bobbed up and down. "Cousin Michael explained it to me. It's when a bunch of congressmen go somewhere together and study something so they can come back and make laws about it.''

"That's right.'' Holly was proud of him. He was so young to grasp it so clearly.

"Only I'll bet they don't pay for the trip themselves,'' Nicholas added.

"I'll bet they don't,'' Holly agreed.

"Is Zelig on a fact-finding tour, too?'' asked the little boy.

"Not really. He's on what you could call a confidential mission for the government.''

"I'm going to be just like Zelig when I grow up. That's better than being a arse. I'll go on confidential missions, too.''

They played cards for half an hour longer until Nicholas's eyelids began to droop. Holly suggested a nap, and for once he didn't balk. She sat by his bedside until he drifted off to sleep. Then she moved to a chair beside the window and stared out, smiling at the vista spread before her.

It really did look like one of those old-fashioned Christmas cards. Atop a small hill in the distance was the cottage—really a four-bedroom house—in which Holly's grandmother Mary had lived between the time of her divorce from the governor and her death. The family of Riverview servants that now occupied the cottage had lit a fire, and there was smoke coming from the chimney on the snow-topped roof. With its holiday decorations and the white-and-green wooded background behind it, the vision of the cottage renewed Holly's Christmas spirit.

A sudden outcry shattered the peace. Holly turned from the window toward her son's bed. The noise had not disturbed him; Nicholas was still sleeping soundly.

The sound had been dulled by the long hallways and the thick walls between the Riverview rooms. Now, the noises that followed the initial outcry were more violent than loud. They would not wake Nicholas, but they were nevertheless alarming.

When they continued, Holly went to investigate. Carefully, she closed the door to Nicholas's room behind her. As she strode from the east wing to the central area of the second floor, she heard loud voices and sounds of struggle. These were followed by a howl of pain, or rage, or a combination of the two.

Rounding the corner to the second-story center hall, Holly stumbled onto an extraordinary scene: Jimbo Grebbs was holding on to the railing overlooking the main foyer and bleeding from his prominent nose onto the priceless sixteenth-century Belgian tapestry. Jack Houston was staggering against the oak-paneled wall across from him with a gash on his cheek and a genuine Etruscan vase in shards at his feet. Buffy stood in the doorway leading to her bedroom suite wearing a peignoir and high-heeled slippers and screaming incoherently.

Holly went to Buffy and put an arm around her to try to calm her down. "What is it?" she asked. "What's happening?"

"I was having a business meeting with Mr. Grebbs in my sitting room when Jack came bursting in and—and—" Buffy waved her hand helplessly toward the two men, who were once again grappling.

A business meeting? Holly's thoughts were interrupted as Jack aimed a karate chop at Grebbs's shoulder. Grebbs half deflected it so that the edge of Jack's hand broke the frame of a portrait of Everett Stockwell by Gilbert Stuart. Then Grebbs picked up a fourteenth-century jardiniere that had once graced the petit palace at Versailles and tried to bash in the side of Jack's head with it.

"Stop it! Stop it right now!" Holly protested—in vain. The men ignored her as the fight continued.

Jack evaded the jardiniere. Ducking under Grebbs's arm, he butted the taller man in his prominent Adam's apple with the top of his head. Rage filled Grebbs's small brown eyes. The blood rose from his fleshy, tomato-red cheeks to the tips of his large ears. Catching Jack in a bear hug, he flung him halfway down the polished oak staircase. Then he jumped after him and tried to stomp Jack's more slender, athlete's body into the fourth-century Chinese runner covering the treads.

The noise of the brawl had attracted the servants. Half a dozen of them now huddled together in the passageway leading from the belowstairs kitchen and pantry. Three young housemaids peered over the third-floor banister with linens over their arms and frightened looks on their white faces. Just as Jack escaped Grebbs's kicks by quickly rolling down a few more steps, Berkley, the Riverview butler, materialized beside Holly.

"Shall I call the police, Miss Holly?" the butler asked her in a low voice.

Holly looked at Buffy, rumpled, still in her peignoir. A man in her boudoir. A violently jealous husband. If the police were called, the press would soon follow. The Stockwell family did not need any more scandals.

The two men weren't armed. They were evenly matched. Grebbs's grunt of pain decided Holly. Jack was holding his own. Nobody was going to get killed. The two men were simply engaged in a schoolyard brawl in one of the world's most expensive playgrounds. "No," she answered Berkley. "That won't be necessary. Don't call the police."

"Very well, Miss Holly." Imperturbable as always, Berkley started to walk away.

Below, on the staircase, Grebbs landed a punch that sent Jack spinning into the Dresden stained-glass window on the landing and caused a large crack.

"Oh, Berkley." Holly stayed his leavetaking. "Would you see that the servants get back to their duties, please. This spectacle is not being staged for their entertainment."

"Of course, Miss Holly."

"Barbarians!" Now Buffy had reached the landing and was surveying the damage with her hands on her hips and outrage on her face. She picked up a jagged piece of the jardiniere. "Philistines!" No connoisseur of art, she was nevertheless furious at the destruction.

Her disgust was to no avail. Halfway between the landing and the foyer at the bottom of the stairs, Jack removed a sculptured plaque of enameled terra cotta by Luca della Robbia from a niche in the wall and broke it over Jimbo Grebbs's large, square head. Blood trickling into his eyes, Grebbs tried to grab a Verrocchio marble bust of Lorenzo from another alcove, intending to go on the attack with it, but fortunately it proved too bulky.

69

Jack scampered to the foot of the staircase, next to a suit of armor dating back to Richard the Lion-Hearted. Jack deprived it of its cudgel and turned to meet the swearing, charging Grebbs as he descended.

Seeing his opponent brandishing the medieval weapon slowed Grebbs down. Holly took advantage of the pause to move down the staircase to try to reason with Jack. "This isn't going to solve anything," she told him.

"I'm not trying to solve anything. I'm trying to total this Texas tub of lard. I found him in my wife's bedroom making love to her."

"That's not true!" Buffy wailed from above. "We were in my sitting room, fully clothed."

Holly looked up at her in her peignoir, cut to expose cleavage and gaping to reveal one long, classically shapely leg. Well, she supposed, it could be called fully clothed if you weren't married to Buffy and didn't know her very well and still believed in the tooth fairy.

"Wrapped around each other like Greek wrestlers!" Jack brandished the cudgel at Grebbs as the Texan came cautiously down the stairs toward him, jockeying for position.

"I was demonstrating how to pin a steer for branding at roundup time." Grebbs kept coming, blood in the one small brown eye that was still open.

"He was telling me about what it was like when he was a cowboy," Buffy confirmed, "and I asked him to show me."

"He showed you," Jack snarled. "Now I'm showing him."

"I get through with you, you're dogmeat, boy," Grebbs told him.

"How about declaring a truce?" Holly suggested.

Grebbs's answer was a sudden rush that sent him and Jack crashing into the Scottish grandfather clock. Struggling to get leverage, Jack put his elbow through the glass behind which hung the clock's carved silver metronome. Muscles bulging, the two men toppled to the floor. Locked and rolling, with first one on top and then the other, they progressed from the foyer to the formal Riverview dining room. Here Jack bent Grebbs's leg backward until he had forced it into the ornate Gothic fretwork of the oak paneling framing the huge black marble fireplace. The paneling, like the fireplace itself, had once stood in the main hall of the mansion built by Henry Plantagenet, king of England, for his mistress, fair Rosamund Clifford. Now it splintered and gave way under Grebbs's frantic defensive kicking.

Countering, Grebbs sank his large teeth into the bicep of Jack's left arm. Holding on like a bulldog, he managed to get the leverage he needed to send Jack swinging into the Hepplewhite cabinet against the wall perpendicular to the fireplace. Revere tankards went flying while Waterford crystal shattered heartbreakingly and Meissen china was ground underfoot.

Floundering, Jack grabbed up a vibrantly colored Ming dynasty silk cushion from one of the heavily carved armchairs and shoved it against Grebbs's nose. Cutting off the air forced the Texan to relinquish the hold his fangs had on Jack's upper arm. As his face came up, Jack sliced at it with a karate chop that left one side of Grebbs's lantern jaw unhinged.

Roaring with pain and rage, Grebbs started to grab the El Greco from the wall over the fireplace, and Holly moaned. An El Greco! It was too much. She tried in vain to force her way between the two men. "You really have to end this!" she declared.

"End it, ma'am?" Grebbs regarded his opponent, who was still on his feet, but reeling. "All right." And he unleashed a roundhouse right that caught Jack on the point of the jaw, lifted him from his feet, and deposited him smack in the middle of the precolonial mahogany dining room table. Jack lay there, unconscious, at the precise halfway point where Berkley customarily arranged the fresh floral centerpiece. "I've ended it, ma'am." Supporting his injured jaw with the heel of his hand, Grebbs walked over to Buffy. "Now just where-all were we before we were interrupted?" he said, reaching out for her with his free hand.

"Don't touch me!" Genuinely upset, Buffy brushed past Grebbs and went to Jack.

"He'll be all right." Holly had gotten to Jack before her. "He's coming around."

"Sure he will," Grebbs agreed. "Now why don't we just go and finish our conversation?" he added to Buffy.

"Because I have nothing to say to you, you gorilla!" Buffy snapped back. She bent over Jack and cradled his head against her breast as he struggled back to consciousness. "Now get out of my house!"

Strictly speaking, it wasn't Buffy's house, but Holly approved the attitude and so said nothing. Leaving Jack in Buffy's arms, she started for the kitchen to ask Berkley for the emergency kit to dress his wounds. Behind her, Grebbs spoke again.

"All right, lady. I'll get out of your house. Didn't get what I came for, but probably it wouldn't of been worth it anyway. Any case, you won't be getting what you wanted, either. I promise you Stockwell crude will rot in the storage tanks before any Texas refinery will touch it."

"Get out!" Buffy screamed. "I never want to see you again!"

As the front door slammed behind Jimbo Grebbs, his elbow hit the button activating the musical door chimes. They had been reprogrammed for the season and sounded out the chords of "Peace on Earth, Good Will to Men."

At least something remained, Holly thought ruefully, of the Christmas spirit.

13

IT WAS ONLY two days off, but it did not seem like Christmas in Crete. The climate was balmy, the weather without bite. Besides, Zelig Meyerling, on his way to the Iraklion airport where he was going to catch the shuttle flight to Athens, had other things on his mind. It is a truism with many great men that "peace on earth, good will to men," and even Christmas itself, must sometimes be shelved while attention is turned to more worldly concerns. So it was now with Zelig.

These concerns, too, were banished, however, as he backed up the Jaguar he had borrowed from Spiro Papatestus to where the woman was standing by the side of the dusty Cretan road. Zelig peered out the window at her. "Don't I know you?" he inquired.

Initially he had passed her by. Zelig did not usually pick up hitchhikers. This time, though, he had changed his mind and backed up for her. It wasn't just that the way she jerked her thumb was so unmistakably American, it was also the flash of recognition between them during the brief instant their eyes met as he'd driven past.

"I don't know." Responding to Zelig's question, the hitchhiker opened the door and sat down in the cordovan leather bucket seat. She moved in such a way that material gaped between buttons, and Zelig caught a glimpse of surprisingly firm and rounded bosom. "But I know you."

"You recognized me?" Zelig was used to being identified by strangers. It was the price he paid as a celebrity whose face over the years had graced three covers of *Time* and one of *Newsweek*, not to mention his frequent television appearances.

"Why not? We've met."

Both the instinct that had made him reverse to pick her up and the way she said it told Zelig it was true. The woman was familiar. They had met. He was sure of it. But where? When? Under what circumstances? "You have the advantage of me," he told her.

"How delicious." She cocked her head so that the tight, rather unattractive knot of her mouse-brown hair grazed the shoulder of her faded khaki shirt. "To have the advantage of Zelig Meyerling. Not many women have known that pleasure, I'll wager."

Zelig took his eyes from the road to look at her more closely. Was she flirting with him? He didn't find her compellingly attractive, although she was certainly better looking close up than she had seemed standing on the road with her face free of makeup and pale with dust and her figure undiscernible in bush shirt and shapeless culottes. And there had been that flash of firmly molded breast. "Then you know my name," he said politely. "But what is yours?"

"Vanessa Brewster. We met at the funeral of Governor Stockwell," she reminded him.

With that the light broke over Zelig's features. Now he placed her quite specifically. She was the young woman who, according to the scandal sheets, had been with the governor *en flagrante* when he'd suffered the coronary that killed him. And she was also the woman who had so upset the Stockwell family by subsequently having an affair with James Linstone Stockwell, the governor's fifty-two-year-old widowed son. Zelig remembered Holly telling him how concerned her cousin Patrice had been about her father's involvement with "that Brewster woman."

"Of course," Zelig said now. "I remember. But what are you doing in Greece?"

"I've been doing some research at the dig at Kommos."

"Are you an archaeologist?"

"No. An anthropologist. But it's archaeology that comes up with the evidence for people like me." She crossed her legs, and the culottes rode well up, displaying an expanse of quite shapely thigh.

As with the glimpse before of her breast, this sudden erotic flash was unexpected and not in keeping with Zelig's original impression. Initially he had misperceived her, as did many men upon first meeting Vanessa Brewster. Later, the luckiest among them wondered how they could have so misjudged her at first glance.

Vanessa did not dress to enhance her appearance. She was thirty-four years old, had never been married, and wasn't bothered enough by her single status to go out of her way to attract men. She had a Ph.D in anthropology from Columbia and a master's in art history from the University of Florence. Her rumpled appearance, lack of makeup, and slightly frumpy clothes seemed to fit in with her preoccupied, erudite personality.

Nevertheless, Vanessa had known her share of lovers.

74

Those affairs that lasted longest usually involved men much older than she was. Frequently these older men shared one of two things in common: they were renowned or powerful. "In my experience," she had told James Linstone Stockwell once in a moment of confidence, "the movers and shakers of the world are the only ones who can really make it move and shake during sex."

"It takes two," James had answered gallantly. "And I suspect it's your libido that provokes the moving and shaking."

There was truth in that. Contrary to her public persona, in private Vanessa was a woman who lustily enjoyed sex and was not at all shy about indulging her appetites. Once her practical, safaristyle, one-size-too-large outer garments were removed, she proved to have a shapely body with large breasts, wide hips, and full buttocks. Shaken loose, her brown hair turned into a ticklish mantle behind which her half-dollar-sized nipples played hide-and-seek. Devoid of her usually drab-colored clothing—washed-out greens, cloudy grays, muted tans—her flesh proved quite healthily flushed and openly moist with desire.

Alone with a man to whom she was attracted, Vanessa shed the lackluster outer skin of her garments and unloosed a personality as sensually irresistible as that of Circe. Her emerald eyes compelled her lover's response. Her body enveloped him in ways that completely shattered the initial perception of a rather dowdy, mid-thirtyish, studious, and possibly overweight woman.

Zelig sensed some of this potential now as he guided the Jaguar up the winding mountain road that crossed Crete. He was not an unperceptive man, and he was certainly not inexperienced with women. Even so, the sharp-breaking curves and hairpin turns occupied his attention more than Vanessa Brewster did.

The demanding drive made Zelig sorry now that he had turned down Spiro Papatestus's offer of a chauffered limousine. Still, he had not wanted to attract undue attention to himself. It was bizarre enough that he was enjoying Spiro and Louise's hospitality on what was supposed to have been his honeymoon all by himself.

Spiro had accepted without question Zelig's story of having to get away from the pressures of the Stockwell Institute even though his bride would not join him on their honeymoon trip until later. Of course, Spiro and Louise knew better, and Zelig knew that they knew better. Spiro in particular would have believed the rumors leaked to the media that he was in Greece on some mission for the United States government. Indeed, with only a little thought, the Greek tycoon probably would have figured out the major purposes of Zelig's mission. Nevertheless, in their circle it was good form to politely accept the fiction.

Composed, as was her nature, Vanessa fell in with the silence between them as they drove. She could see that the tricky road required concentration, and even when she was attracted to a man, she was not one to try to make an impression on him with conversation or, indeed, in any other way. Vanessa's style was more laid back. She trusted her desirability to creep up on a man. From experience she had faith that he would discover her assets for himself.

Besides, while she was not unattracted to Zelig—a slightly older man and a man of power—her heart lay elsewhere. Although circumstance had distanced them, she was still in love with James Stockwell. That didn't mean she would not deny herself a casual fling if one came her way, but neither was she looking for a relationship to replace the one she had with James. It was not her way to deny her erotic needs for long periods of time, but she didn't want to trade what she and James had for instant gratification. What it came down to—and Vanessa smiled to herself with the thought—was discretion. Zelig Meyerling looked as if he would know the meaning of the word.

"Why are you going to Iraklion?" Zelig broke the silence.

"A seminar. A four-person panel. A historian, an archaeologist, an expert in deciphering linear one, and an anthropologist. I'm the anthropologist."

"What's the topic?"

"The Kommos Tablets. Their effects on the shifting

perceptions between legend and history." Vanessa turned her remarkable emerald eyes on him more fully. "Are you going to Athens to meet your wife?" she inquired.

"No. Business." Skillfully, Zelig tilted the conversation away from just what the business might be. "How did you know I was married?" he asked.

"When Riverview and Foggy Bottom unite, that's news. Even the *International Herald-Tribune* covered it. Not to mention the English-language *Athens News*." The sparkle of her green eyes hinted that his marriage just might be irrelevant. "I saw your wife a year ago at the governor's funeral, but I didn't actually meet her. She's very attractive."

"She is indeed." Zelig smiled.

"Very stylish, too. Her taste in clothes, I mean. Didn't *Vogue* once run an article on her wardrobe?"

"*Vanity Fair*." Frowning, Zelig corrected her.

"Yes, well—"

"But there really is more to Holly than that." How had it happened, Zelig wondered, that he felt just a tad on the defensive?

"Oh, I'm sure there is." Vanessa's smile was the one she used to reassure students who were shaky in their understanding of her lectures.

"She's not just a socialite."

"Of course not."

"No, I mean it." Zelig was mildly irritated, didn't know why, but nevertheless took the trouble to squelch the feeling. "Holly is an historian. For the past two years she's been involved in doing research on an extensive project about Riverview and the Stockwells."

Vanessa Brewster smiled and did not reply. Riverview and the Stockwells. Well, well. Just the project to keep a new bride's mind off her absent bridegroom. . . .

14

CHRISTMAS HAD COME and gone, and now Holly, facing the prospect of New Year's Eve alone at Riverview, was indeed spending her nights buried in her historical researches. Nicholas was having an early evening nap in anticipation of being allowed to stay up until midnight to watch the dropping of the ball at Times Square on the TV set at the foot of his bed. Except for Berkley and one or two other older servants, those with whom Holly shared residence at Riverview were out.

Holly's uncle James was having dinner with Patrice in Manhattan. Her cousin Peter was also in Manhattan at some party, while his parents were spending the evening with her uncle David Lewis and his family at their Manhattan townhouse. Buffy and Jack, who had scarcely spoken since Jack's outrageously destructive fistfight with Jimbo Grebbs, had gone their separate ways.

And so Holly, alone with her convalescing child, missing Zelig but determined not to focus on her loneliness, was losing herself in the history of the first Stockwells of Riverview. . . .

Holding the silver Revere candlestick in one hand and shielding the flame with the other, Margaret Adams Stockwell, still tingling inside her full-length flannel nightgown, glided furtively down the hall from the bedroom of her brother-in-law, Roger Stockwell. Entering her own room, she silently set the candle on the floral-carved maple nightstand. Then, moving very carefully, she slipped under the patchwork quilt of the maple bed she shared with her husband.

Everett's breathing was heavy, not quite snoring, but verging on it. His thin, birdlike nose twitched, pale against the cold air. Other than that, Everett did not stir as his wife settled beside him in the four-poster. Margaret, too, lay very still. The last thing she wanted was to wake her husband, to spark any lust in his sparrowlike eyes. Fulfilled, she preferred to dwell on the delicious experience just concluded.

She smiled with the memory. The tenderness of Roger's touch, his lips, warm and loving on hers, his strong, capable hands on her body—caressing, guiding, arousing—his naked masculine strength and passion, his possession of her—total and dizzying and so marvelously satisfying. After fifteen years of a dull marriage and the birthing of three children, Margaret felt reborn. That a round and placid middle-aged woman—for this was how Margaret saw herself—should give herself up uninhibitedly to the joys of the two-humped beast Satan creates of man and woman in sin was nothing less than amazing! If eternal hell was the price of such ecstasy, then so be it. No flames of Hades could burn so hotly as those that consumed her as she lay in the arms of her husband's younger brother: No retribution could quench the memory of the blaze that leaped at the pinnacle of their lovemaking.

Remembering, Margaret closed her eyes. She saw Roger's face straining above hers in the moment of his climax. She recalled the night on which the affair between her and her brother-in-law had started. . . .

That night at Riverview, Margaret had followed the heartrending sounds of weeping from her hearth to Colonel Roger Stockwell's study. She'd found the door closed and her knock had gone unanswered, but the sobbing had continued. Margaret had turned the brass knob and entered.

Her brother-in-law was sprawled out in a brocaded chair with maplewood arms. His anguished face was buried in his hands. On one of the chair arms stood an earthenware jug smelling sweetly and pungently of rum.

"Colonel Stockwell, sir?" Margaret addressed him formally, as she did her own husband. Custom dictated the formality.

He sobbed chokingly but did not reply.

"Roger?" Touched by his suffering, Margaret tried to reach him with familiarity.

He raised his head. "I'm sorry." He acknowledged Margaret's presence.

"What is it, Roger?"

The depth of sympathy in her voice focused his deep gray eyes, and he saw the maternal concern in her round face. He realized that the worry deepening the red of her apple cheeks under the tight-coiled pale blond hair was for him. Still, he could only manage to repeat what he had said before.

"I'm sorry." Roger's gesture of futility knocked the jug from the chair arm to the braided rug.

The jug overturned without spilling. It was empty. A quart measure, Roger had drained it dry, which explained his drunken condition.

Her brother-in-law, Margaret knew, was neither a patron of taverns nor a solitary sot. Something must have set him off tonight. "Perhaps some strong tea," she said. She went to fetch it.

She returned with a tray bearing a tea cozy and two hand-painted Spofford cups and saucers. They were part of a set that had been a wedding gift from her relatives, the John Adamses of Boston. Lost in bitter thought, Roger did not notice that he was being served with what Margaret called her "company china."

"What is it?" she asked after he had sipped off half a cup of tea. She reached out and touched his hand—a gesture of concern. Her blue eyes trapped his gaze and held it, urging him to confide in her. Margaret waited.

"It's over," he said finally. "I saw that today when General Washington spoke. The war is really over."

"But the war has been over for some time."

"I know that." Roger's face was haggard, and there was a burning now in his gray eyes. "But you see, the construction of a nation, a ruling government on the heels of it—that kept the purpose alive. It required energy. It held despair at bay. Losing yourself in some purpose—war, its aftermath, that's how to deceive yourself that you may really have some reason left to live. But when that's finished—and somehow today General Washington's inaugural address finished it for me—then all that's left is despair."

80

"But why are you so despairing?"

"I am alone." Roger spread his hands. "I have no one. I am no one."

"You are Colonel Roger Stockwell of the colonial army. You are a national hero. You have been an aide to General Washington, who is now president of our new country. You are a landowner of considerable prestige and some wealth. How can you say that you are no one?"

"I am alone," Roger repeated dully. "I have nobody."

"You needn't be. You could have your pick of the local maidens. Many of them are quite fair. Any family in the Hudson River Valley would be honored to have you take an interest in their daughter. And you are not unattractive to the ladies themselves."

"Thank you. But I am not interested."

"Do you think so lightly of my sex, then?"

"No. Not at all. Once—" Roger broke off abruptly.

"Yes?"

"Never mind."

"Once there was a woman," Margaret guessed. "What happened to her?"

"She's dead."

"I'm sorry." Margaret looked at her brother-in-law with her customarily round eyes quite narrowed. "You were in love with her."

"Yes."

"Who was she?" Margaret asked gently.

"Her name was Ursula van Bronckel. She was the daughter of the Dutch patroon who once owned this plantation."

"Riverview? But then they must have been Tories," Margaret realized. The Dutch estate owners in the valley were all beholden to the Crown. "But how did you come to fall in love with a Loyalist maiden?"

"Not a maiden. She was married. She was forced to be married." Roger's voice was very low and deeply unhappy. "We were lovers." He paused, searching for the words to explain. "It was not the way it sounds," he continued finally. "Not tawdry. Ursula loved me. I loved her." Roger's eyes clouded with pain. "I love her still," he said. "I always shall."

"How did she die?" Margaret asked after a moment.

"Of powder and shot fired from the pistol of her husband. He discovered us, and he killed her. Not me. I couldn't save her, but I saved myself." Roger's eyes were tragic with the memory. "It was just before the end of the war."

"That was a long time ago," Margaret pointed out gently. "The most deep-held grief must abate. The healing process must be given a chance."

"The healing process!" Roger laughed harshly. "You don't understand. I love her still. She was my life. It is over. Over!" Like a saucer striking brick, his composure shattered. His moan could not be contained.

Margaret was shaken by the depth of his pain. She moved to him, sympathy overcoming decorum. Unmindful of propriety, she put her small soft hands on his sharp-boned cheeks and pressed his anguished face to her plump bosom.

The contact released Roger's grief. The mourning so long bottled up inside him surfaced with a rush. Once loosed, it was not to be controlled. His arms locked around Margaret's waist. His face pushed into the deep valley between her breasts as if trying to rip away the layers of clothing covering them. His tears flooded the space between her stays, and the flesh of her bosom became warm and wet with them.

Margaret was extremely affected. Sudden emotion confused her. It could only be likened to what she had felt once or twice with each of her children while nursing them. The man's face at her breast was as dependent as that in its misery.

"There, there," she whispered weakly. "Let it come out, then." Her short, competent fingers tangled in the disarray of his long, straight, flaxen hair. "There, there, my poor Roger."

Roger's grip around her waist remained firm, tight. His nuzzling face, come home at last to sympathy and warmth, pressed down the bodice of her gown. The stays cut into her flesh cruelly, but Margaret made no complaint as his cheek now pressed against the bared upper rise of her breasts.

It hurt, but Margaret felt a stirring as well. It was a feeling of utter tenderness, a feeling she had never felt under the weight of her husband, not even on those occasions when each of their three children was conceived. Margaret's heart pounded, her thighs clenched. After a moment, afraid, she tried gently to disengage herself from Roger's overwhelming embrace.

He looked up at her, his face desolate. There was no lust in the look, no desire, yet it was filled with a yearning so bottomless, so needful of human contact, that Margaret could not stand it. Now it was she who moaned, a small sound barely escaping her suddenly dry and fevered lips. "Roger." She spoke his name, that was all.

And then she was in his arms. They were tearing at the fastenings of their clothing. Their mouths met. Fiercely, their burning flesh was joined, locked. And there was a wrenching release of grief, a dizzying acceptance of passion.

Almost immediately, and without words, they made love a second time—slowly now, intimately, savoring the experience. Margaret could tell, in the relative calmness of their lovemaking, that while Roger's first love had not been laid to rest, a demon of memory had perhaps been exorcised. Indeed, when that second time was over, he had put it into word.

"I am at peace," Roger said, his voice filled with wonder. "I am at peace."

That was how it had started. He needed Margaret as Everett never had. Satisfying that need, Margaret herself became a prisoner of a desire that was insatiable. It had driven her to Roger's room this night and kept her awake now beside her husband in their marital bed. It was responsible for the smile of anticipation on her round and placid face, a Cheshire expression savoring in advance a saucer of rich Jersey cream.

The expression came and went during the next few days as Margaret's anticipation heightened. Roger had gone into the city on business and would not be back until the following Friday. During that time, Margaret followed her normal routine. Sometimes, though, the anticipation affected her wifely and motherly functions.

"You have turned back one cuff, but not the other," Everett complained, holding up a ruffled shirt-sleeve. "Wifely woolgathering can lead to witchery, my dear. I believe it was the Reverend Cotton Mather who first pointed that out."

"I am sorry." Margaret took the shirt from him and immediately began to mend the other cuff. Like many an adulterous wife to follow, guilt pushed her toward wifely superefficiency.

At the same time, preoccupation with her affair affected Margaret's maternal role. Daydreaming while combing her fourteen-year-old daughter's hair, she yanked at a tangle so painfully that Mercy yowled with pain.

"Mama, you forgot to heat up my oatmeal," complained her youngest daughter, five-year-old Deborah.

More guilt. Margaret heated the cereal.

The guilt was most deeply felt when Margaret found herself neglecting her son, Horace. The boy was very like his father, and Margaret, who did not love her son's father, felt bad when her fantasies of Roger caused her to shortchange Horace. On such occasions she would try to make up for it by hugging her eleven-year-old son to her, telling him how much she loved him.

Horace was not impressed. He would pull away and regard her skeptically. "If you care so much about me," he would inquire, "then how is it you have misplaced my toy dragoon? Why do I ask you something three times and you don't hear me? Why is my cocoa cold and my warming pan too hot? Whatever you're thinking of all the time, Mother, it surely isn't me."

Ah, well. At least Horace had his father. The boy adored that cold and formal man. He patterned himself after him, and in doing so, the attitude of Horace toward his mother was similarly cold and formal.

Margaret cared. Rejection by a son is not easy to accept. But she didn't care enough. In all honesty, she knew that. She was consumed by her passion for Roger, and everything else took second place—while Horace possibly took third place—to their affair. Between meetings, Margaret was ever poised, waiting for their passion to renew itself.

It did the Friday Roger returned. Absence had made him as eager for her as she was for him. When he came on her alone changing the linens in Horace's bedroom, Roger did not hesitate to express his eagerness.

"The children!" she gasped, feeling his hands infiltrating her bodice from behind.

"They won't bother us," he assured her. "The girls are with Everett. I passed them on the road. He was on his way to Peekskill to see about some carriage horses."

"Both Mercy and Deborah?" Even as she inquired, Margaret was turning, unloosening her stays, freeing her breasts.

"Yes." Roger pulled off his boots. His shirt and breeches followed.

"And Horace?" Margaret was stepping free of one petticoat after another, puddling the floor of the room with them.

"Shooting imaginary Indians with his bow and arrows from his treehouse down by the river." Roger picked her up in his arms and carried her to the bed. He looked down at her.

Naked, Margaret's body was more supple and slimmer than it looked clothed. Only the bubble breasts maintained their red-tipped impression of plumpness. Her belly was rounded, but not fleshy. Her waist was small and her legs far sleeker than one would have guessed.

He kissed her and caressed her skin. Soon her hands were wandering as freely as his. Their breathing quickened. The first time after an absence of a few days was always an impatient time for both of them. They could not wait to be joined, to sink into the emotions that always accompanied their coupling. As Roger mounted Margaret and entered her, she rose to him freely, gasping, then squeezing her eyes shut and savoring the sensations of his movements deep inside her. Quickly her passion mounted. Soon she felt as if she could contain it no longer. Intending to ask if he, too, was ready, tensing, holding back for the answer, she opened her eyes.

And there, staring down at Margaret Adams Stockwell over her lover's shoulder, was her eleven-year-old son, Horace, his mouth agape, his pale eyes staring accusingly, his face a mask of unalterably damning judgment.

15

DAVID LEWIS WAS presiding as once again the administrative board of the Stockwell estate was sitting. This time the meeting was taking place in what had once been the governor's third-floor conference room in the west wing of Riverview. Convening here had saved David Lewis, who lived nearby, and Peter, Buffy, and James Stockwell the trip into Manhattan, although it had required Max Tyler and Halsey De Vilbiss as well as James's daughter, Patrice, to come up from the city. With snow blanketing Riverview in the business lull following New Year's Day, the view was well worth the trip.

David had acceded to Peter Stockwell's request to put insurance at the top of the agenda in the belief that the topic could be disposed of quickly. Peter, however, had just made it clear that he had other intentions.

"In my judgment, insurance shows the greatest growth potential of any of our enterprises. I will explain. How many of you are familiar with the acronym FAIR?"

With one exception there were blank looks all around. Max Tyler knew about FAIR because he headed his own insurance company, which served the gay community. FAIR had interested him because it offered the kind of opportunity to combine sound business practices with social accountability in a way that he knew would be attractive to the family members whose interests he represented. For that very reason, he would have thought FAIR would be anathema to Peter.

"The initials," Peter was explaining now, "stand for Fair Access to Insurance Requirements. To give you a little background, it's a program of pool insurance that was mandated by the federal government after the urban riots of the sixties and seventies caused prudent insurers to refuse to write policies in high-risk inner-city areas. The idea was that if five in-state insurance companies turned down a property owner for insurance, the high-risk pool could provide it at a higher premium with the blessing of the federal government."

"Except"—Max interrupted—"that the programs are administered locally, and at that level it's a simple matter for a broker to arrange for five turndowns so that the pool insurer can move in and sell the insurer at a higher rate."

"True, but not germane." Peter picked up the ball smoothly. "What is germane is the reason why the insurers find these high-risk premiums so desirable to write. Would you like to explain that, Max?" he asked sarcastically.

"It's the nature of the insurance business." Scowling, Max did explain. "With very few exceptions, insurance companies do not make profits from the sale of policies. Indeed, premiums barely cover payouts and operating expenses."

"What do you mean?" Patrice, who had gone to a great deal of trouble to make herself knowledgeable regarding the ins and outs of the financial world, was confused. "No field is better represented among the *Fortune* five hundred than insurance."

"True. But the profits aren't from sales. They're from investments." It was James who explained this to his daughter. "Premiums add up to millions of dollars available for investment. When interest rates are low, insurance companies are cautious. They avoid writing high-risk policies. That was the case when FAIR was initially set up. But when rates are high—"

"Not just high," Peter pointed out smoothly. "Today interest rates are at an all-time peak. And," he continued, "they're going up every day. What this means is that—regardless of risk—the more insurance a company can write, the more capital will be at its disposal to invest for unprecedented returns. And that brings us back to FAIR."

"But Stockwell insurance companies have already been writing their share of policies for FAIR," David Lewis pointed out. "We were in at the beginning."

"True," Peter granted. "We did it as a matter of public obligation." His tone was ironic. "Now let's do it for profit. Let's enlarge our operation and pinpoint specific target areas which are ripe for exploitation."

"Just what areas do you mean?" Buffy inquired.

"The South Bronx, Bed-Sty in Brooklyn, South Jamaica, for starters."

"Is this to be an exclusively New York City operation, then?" Halsey De Vilbiss arched an eyebrow.

"Oh, no." Peter was firm. His smile to Halsey was almost conspiratorial. He wanted the lawyer on his side in this. "I envision expanding to inner-city areas in cities across the country."

"Slum areas," Max pointed out. "High-arson areas."

"Of course." Peter was impatient. "Where else could you sell high premiums except in high-risk areas?"

"Some people think the insurance encourages the arson," Max told them.

"Even if that were true," David Lewis replied, perceiving the opportunity and abruptly switching to support Peter, "it would be no reason to penalize honest property owners by withholding protection from them."

"It sounds to me as if we're in agreement," Buffy said. "There are no holes that I can see in Peter's proposal. We sell more high-risk insurance at high premiums, and we invest the premiums at the highest interest rates in history. That leaves only one question. Just how great is the risk to us of a loss through arson?"

"If we had to pay out on thirty percent of our policies—an unheard-of outlay," Peter told her, "we would still recognize a handsome profit on the interest from our invested premiums."

"Then let's do it."

After some more discussion the decision carried easily, with Max Tyler alone still voicing reservations.

"There is another aspect of this I want to discuss,"

Peter then told them. "One that is international in scope and more far-reaching in its profit potential. I'm talking about the reinsurance market."

"Clarify, please," Buffy requested.

"Come back to FAIR for a moment," Peter explained. "Originally, under the federal mandate, the major insurance companies merged a certain minuscule percentage of their assets to form a pool to absorb the high-risk policies without any one firm having to take on too much of the burden. When interest rates began rising, however, smaller companies eager for capital began buying into these pools. There was nothing in the law to stop them. Pretty soon, bending the regulations here and there, a whole new group of high-risk carriers was selling insurance in inner-city areas. Now, even with the interest rates going up, riskwise some of these operations have overextended themselves."

"Chickens come home to roost." Max Tyler snorted. "Arson has been on the rise. In New York the municipal tax abatement policy made redevelopment the most profitable real estate game in town. Slum landlords embarked on a policy of having their own properties torched in order to cash in on the profits available through redevelopment."

"True enough." For once Peter agreed with Max. "And so the insurance risks became just too great, even with the high investment returns for those small companies. And that's where reinsurance comes in."

"I'm confused," Buffy said.

Halsey De Vilbiss wasn't. "Think of it," he told her, "like a bookie who finds himself top heavy with bets on the Superbowl favorite. Nothing's a hundred percent sure thing, and if there's an upset, he'd be out of business. So he has to protect himself. How he does this is, he lays off the bets with other bookies. That way his tail is covered."

"Graphic," Buffy granted. "But I get the picture. Still, just who does our high-risk insurer lay off his gamble with?"

"Other insurance companies. Banks. Investment houses." It was Peter who answered. "Lloyd's of London is one of the biggest insurance firms absorbing the high-risk layoffs. They've made billions doing it. And that's why I think Stockwell should get into it in a big way."

"But if the risks are so high . . ." Buffy still had doubts.

"Lag time." With the mention of Lloyd's, it had all clicked into place for David Lewis. He looked at Peter with new respect. "The time between when a high risk is assumed and the payout. During that time, the insurer has the use of the money, insuring the earning of interest on the premiums paid. And for *re*insurers, the lag time is still greater and the turnover higher. All it takes is a telephone and a reputation that says when it's time to pay, the reinsurer will live up to his obligation."

"Can it really be that simple?" Buffy asked.

"Oh, it's complicated enough," Peter assured her. "The profit lies in the movement of money. The vaster the sums moved, the vaster the dividends earned. You can generate tremendous capital with very little investment and practically no overhead. And any given transaction may have as many as ten or fifteen middlemen realizing a profit on investing the capital involved."

"You mean they're all selling the same insurance policies to one another?" Experienced as she was in the ways of the financial world, Patrice was startled.

"Exactly. A building insured against fire in the South Bronx may be reinsured as many as ten or fifteen times. The original insurer lays the policy off on a reinsurer, who in turn lays it off in groups of ten such policies on another reinsurer, who repeats the process, only perhaps in groups of hundreds. Then someone like Lloyd's steps in and buys up perhaps twenty million dollars' worth of such policies without concern for the risk because the interest generated by the money they've been paid—the collective premiums, that is—will more than cover it. But before it reaches somebody the size of Lloyd's, the policy may pass through reinsurers from New York to Florida to Costa Rica to Buenos Aires to Hong Kong to Delhi to Cairo to Munich and—finally—to London. And each of those reinsurers will essentially be reinvesting that same insurance premium money."

The discussion continued a while longer, but basically the decision had been made. Stockwell Industries was about to take a new direction. It was going to plunge heavily into the reinsurance business.

Only Max Tyler, concerned with the effects on low-income renters, opposed the decision. His opposition was viewed as part of a pattern by the chair. "I am getting damn tired," David Lewis declared, "of having radical viewpoints voted on this board in contradiction to its free enterprise purpose of seeking profits."

Max kept his calm. "My sister and my cousin," he said, "are committed to certain humanitarian positions. Some of them—if not all—I agree with. But whether I agree or not, I am obliged to vote in accordance with their wishes."

"A leftover Woodstock hippie and a pair of adolescent twins all starry-eyed with peacenik propaganda and antinuke nonsense and harebrained schemes to save the seals. Why don't we just let Greenpeace run Stockwell Industries?" David Lewis suggested sarcastically.

"Uncle David is right," Peter chimed in, eager to follow through on the respect his hardheaded uncle was starting to show him before the rest of the board. "Letting the twins dictate Stockwell policy is like letting the inmates run the asylum. Just look how they embarrassed the family with that Greenpeace action off the shore of Crete."

"And not just the Stockwell family," Halsey De Vilbiss pointed out. "It also compromised Spiro Papatestus, who is, after all, married to their cousin Louise."

"Louise is my sister," Max reminded him. "I represent her interests on this board as well as the twins. Like our other sister, Diana, she subscribes to a certain morality in the conduct of Stockwell Industries' business."

"This is not getting us anywhere." James made an effort to defuse the discussion. "Let's get back to business."

"Beth and Carrie Tyler are business," Peter insisted. "Media coverage of their ridiculous stunts is hurting us."

"That's right." David Lewis once again agreed with his nephew. "Now just what the hell are we going to do about those goddam Tyler twins?"

16

EIGHTEEN YEARS OLD, the Tyler twins basked in the Aegean sun like Minoan nymphs, throwbacks to a time when the temples of Knossos were staffed by sacred, bare-breasted courtesans dedicated to the erotic relaxation of seafarers and tradesmen in transit via the crossroads of the ancient world. Beth and Carrie lay side by side on the deck of the Greenpeace sailing ship barely within sight of the horizon merge of the azure noontime sky with the Levka Ori (White Mountains) of Crete. Their usually fair skin turned dusky with layers of suntan, they were nodding, half-asleep in the warmth of the Africa-spawned breeze. A male voice shouting from the returning dinghy roused them.

They reacted according to their natures. Beth reached for her T-shirt and slipped it over her head to cover her naked breasts. Carrie stood up and stretched toward the sky, her berry-tipped bosom arching impudently, well aware of the stares of the men in the rowboat.

They were identical twins. Even people who had known them all their lives had difficulty telling them apart, but inside they were as different as night and day. Beth was by nature thoughtful and restrained, Carrie impulsive and devil-may-care. Beth was burdened with a sense of responsibility and conscience, Carrie atingle with curiosity and lust. Whereas Beth was truly concerned with people, society, the world, Carrie worried mostly about herself, that she might miss something, that if she didn't grab quickly and hard, some titillation might slip through her eager fingers. In short, Beth was very serious, while Carrie was a hedonist.

Their lives reflected their different natures. Beth had outraged her prominent family by getting herself arrested in various political protest demonstrations, and Carrie had drawn down their wrath by appearing nude in a vulgar top-selling skin magazine. Beth had embraced causes in opposition to the family's extensive business interests; Carrie had compromised them with her cocaine habit. Both had left home, but, at least for now, it was Beth's rebellion that prevailed. Strung out from drugs and sex, Carrie had persuaded her twin to let her come along when Beth had joined the Greenpeace antinuke and environmentalist campaign in the waters off southern Europe.

The fact that Beth's boyfriend, Deke Wells, was also going with Beth had not been irrelevant to Carrie's decision. It wasn't just that Carrie found Deke with his boy-next-door face and curly brown hair and rangy athlete's body attractive. It was also that ever since they were infants, Carrie had always had an overwhelming need to take whatever Beth had and make it her own.

That hadn't happened with Deke Wells yet. In time, though . . . Carrie smiled to herself. Where men were concerned, she never lacked confidence.

Now, climbing on board the sailing ship, Deke carefully averted his gaze from Carrie's bare bosom. Not so the other men from the dinghy, who looked at Carrie with appreciative eyes.

Men had looked at Carrie that way, and at Beth, too, for that matter, since the twins had reached puberty. Physically they had developed early, and now, in their nineteenth year, they were both slender, sleek, and rounded, at once coltish and mature. Although of average height, the twins had long, sinuous legs; they were long-waisted and slim-hipped, their bodies as athletic as Olympic performance divers. Their necks were long and graceful, but nervous, swanlike in their movements as well as their poise.

Like all the Tylers, from their eighty-six-year-old grandmother, Sarah Stockwell Tyler, down to their cousins Max, Diana, and Louise Tyler Papatestus, the twins were blessed with a distinctive shade of red-gold hair and almond-shaped, hazel eyes. Although they lacked the height, the stature, and the aura of mystery that made Louise one of the world's reigning beauties, in their own milieu their fresh loveliness had always stood out.

Slowly now, her movements brazen and provocative as if to point up the silliness of the conventions, Carrie slipped on her T-shirt and covered her breasts. From the corner of her eyes she observed Deke. He was talking to Beth, smiling at her, paying no attention to Carrie. His attitude both irritated and intrigued Carrie. She wasn't used to being ignored. She wasn't accustomed to being upstaged by her quiet twin sister.

Carrie really didn't understand Deke Wells. He was an enigma to her. With his background he should have been a swinger. His mother, Susan Wells, was the youngest child of Governor Stockwell. An actress, she was still a top Hollywood sex symbol who looked much younger than her years. The scandals she had racked up over the last twenty-five years would have made a book and a half guaranteed to be a best-seller. Deke had been a star athlete in college. After graduation he had gone straight to a triple-A American League farm team, where his pitching arm had brought him to the attention of top management by the end of his very first year. The next year the Boston Red Sox management had brought him up to the majors, and after his first few preseason exhibition games, the sports columnists were already referring to him as "the rookie pitching sensation of the year." Carrie well knew that professional athletes attracted nubile groupies like honey draws bees. Deke should have needed a pogo stick to keep up with the available bed-hopping opportunities.

True, he had gone through a bad time. A ligament pulled in spring training had developed into permanent muscle damage. Deke had twisted in the wind for over four months before the Red Sox management had finally dropped him. Even the farm team didn't want him, and at the age of twenty-four, Deke Wells's promising baseball career was over. He was a has-been.

During those four months he had become involved with Beth Tyler, and after the Red Sox dropped him, they had become lovers. As far as Carrie could tell, Deke was absolutely faithful to her twin sister. A one-woman man: Now how could you figure an anachronism like that?

Deliberately, Carrie now intruded on the low-voiced, intimate conversation between Deke and her sister. "What's the word from Mother?" she inquired.

"Mother" was what they called the large Greenpeace

ship that supplied their sloop and other Greenpeace small craft in the area. It also served as a sort of headquarters ship where strategies were discussed and actions decided upon. Besides picking up rations, the purpose behind Deke's visit to the mother ship had been to participate in such a discussion.

"Scuttlebutt is there'll be something for us soon," Deke answered Carrie. "Family's involved again, too." Deke was more directly tied into the Stockwell family than the Tyler twins, who—despite their status as heiresses—were actually distant cousins several times removed. "Stockwells and Papatestus," he added.

"What's happening?" Carrie wanted to know.

"Greenpeace has learned that a meeting is being set up in Malta between Papatestus and the Libyan minister of petroleum, Ezzadine al Mabrouk."

"He's Qaddafi's minister of petroleum," Beth remembered. "One of the few people Qaddafi really trusts."

"What does it mean?" Carrie asked.

"The Libyan economy is in a shambles." Deke explained. "Qaddafi needs Eurodollars for his country to recover. Besides his own vast wealth, Papatestus has access to other Eurodollars. One of his major sources is Stockwell Industries."

"But what has Qaddafi got to offer in return?" Carrie asked. "Libya's chief asset is oil. But there's an oil glut on the world market now. It can't be that."

"We tossed that back and forth for a long time," Deke replied. "And finally we realized that Libya has one other asset that's in demand. They have refineries that are nowhere near operating at capacity. And outside of OPEC, oil producers everywhere are sitting on their crude unable to get it to the market while the prices soar."

"Including Stockwell Industries!" Carrie realized.

"That's right. Now we're not sure, but our suspicion is that Papatestus will broker a deal to transport Stockwell crude in his tankers past Crete through the Libyan Sea and into the Gulf of Sirte right through Qaddafi's so-called line of death. His tankers will deliver the Stockwell crude to the refineries, and then they'll pick up the refined petroleum and transport it to wherever Stockwell's buyers are, which is probably somewhere in Western Europe.''

''Just a minute.'' Beth's eyes narrowed as she remembered. ''Isn't that the scenario of the Stockwell board discussion that Max wrote us about? Didn't he say that De Vilbiss suggested a Libyan connection to get the oil refined? Didn't the board turn it down because it's illegal?''

''Right on all counts,'' Deke said. ''But Papatestus is going to Malta to meet with Mabrouk. And here's the clincher. On his way back from Malta, Papatestus is scheduled to meet with Halsey De Vilbiss in Athens. De Vilbiss has reservations to fly in and out of Athens from New York just for a two-hour meeting with Papatestus.''

''You're saying De Vilbiss is going ahead on his own behind the board's back,'' Beth realized.

''It sure looks that way.''

''And Louise's husband is in collaboration with him.''

''Well, in fairness, he may not know De Vilbiss is acting without the approval of the other Stockwell board members.''

''That's not the point for Greenpeace, or for us, is it?'' Beth, as was her custom, went to the heart of the matter. ''The point is that once again Papatestus will be moving large cargoes of oil off the coastlines of southern Europe. Whenever they do that—inevitably—there are spills. And those spills poison the coastal waters, kill the fish, and pollute their breeding grounds, which cuts down on the food supply from Portugal to Bulgaria. They destroy the beaches and turn the surf into unswimmable muck. And just like with the South African uranium, Stockwell Industries will be involved in this up to their nostrils.''

The South African uranium to which Beth referred had been shipped past Crete in a Papatestus freighter, its eventual destination nuclear plants in the United States operated by Stockwell Industries. It had never reached that destination, however, because the freighter had been maneuvered into ramming a small Greenpeace sailing ship operated by a crew of eight, which included Deke Wells and Beth and Carrie Tyler. Their exploit had focused world attention on the uranium shipment from the pariah state of South Africa to Stockwell and on the daredevil efforts of three young heirs to the Stockwell estate in thwarting that shipment. Subsequently, Stockwell had backed out of the deal, and Beth, Carrie, and Deke had become assets to Greenpeace beyond their actual efforts because of the attention their family connection focused on the antiwar environmentalist organization. It was understood that if there was another action against Stockwell, they would be in the forefront of it. Now, it seemed, such an action might be in the offing.

"You're right, Beth." Deke smiled approval of her summation. "It looks like we're going to have to upset the family applecart one more time."

Carrie regarded Beth's answering smile as a simper. She herself grimaced as Deke drew Beth to her feet and the two of them went below to the tiny cabin they shared with Carrie. Left by herself up on deck, Carrie sulked. They're probably getting it on, she fumed. The idea both made Carrie jealous and titillated her.

After a while she went below to the galley. It was her turn to do the veggies for supper. Aboard Greenpeace vessels, the labor was shared. Scraping carrots was not Carrie's idea of how to preserve the ecosystem. Still, she had yet to figure a way out of doing her share of the chores.

Deke and Beth surfaced for dinner, which the crew ate out on deck—the only place there was room enough for all of them to gather. After dinner two of the men did the clean-up, and Beth became involved in a discussion with the other woman member of the crew about women's roles, consciousness raising, and the subliminal chauvinism in the movement—perhaps even in Greenpeace.

The more intense the discussion between Beth and the other woman became, the more Carrie was bored by it. Looking over at Deke, she saw him yawn. Maybe he was bored, too. Even if he wasn't, he was certainly left out. His gender excluded him.

"Can't be one of the girls, huh?" Carrie walked over to him and teased him in a low voice.

"Just tired." He yawned again. He waited for a break in the conversation, then he bent over, kissed Beth good night, and announced that he was turning in.

Carrie listened to the conversation a while longer, but there was no way she could be a part of it. She just wasn't interested. Now, bored and restless, she went below to the head. Leaning with her back against the door to be sure she wasn't interrupted, she dug deep in the pocket of her jeans and came up with a small, carefully folded packet. She unfolded it, extracted the white powder within, and arranged it in two careful lines on the ledge of the washbasin. From her other pocket she extracted a painstakingly preserved straw.

Taking her time, Carrie sniffed up the first line of cocaine. Then, switching nostrils and inhaling deeply, she did the second line. She checked the tip of her nose in the mirror, spied a fleck of powder, picked it up on her fingertip, and breathed it deeply up her nose. Waste not, want not, she told herself, feeling the buzz and then the spreading glow.

Drugs were strictly forbidden on Greenpeace vessels, and doing coke was the quickest way to get yourself thrown out of the organization. Carrie knew this. But all her life she had acted on the conviction that rules were made for other people, never for her. And while she gave lip service to world peace and the ecology, Carrie had never really believed that her move from Park Avenue hedonism to social activism should interfere with her fun.

Cocaine ranked high on Carrie's list of pleasures. Sex ranked even higher. But aboard ship, with squares more focused on whales than whoopee, she had been going through a long dry spell. Perhaps it was time, Carrie thought, aglow with coke, to do something about that.

She went down to the cabin she occupied with Deke and her twin sister. Deke was asleep in the bunk he and Beth shared. Beth wasn't there. Still on deck exalting her consciousness, Carrie guessed.

Carrie kicked off her sandals and pulled off her sweatshirt. She wriggled free of her jeans and panties. Then, naked, she slipped between the sheets beside Deke.

"Bethie," he murmured, half-waking.

"Umm," Carrie answered. Her tongue flitted out to lick his ear.

He yawned. "I was sound asleep."

"Uh-huh." Carrie ran her hands over his hard athlete's body intimately.

"You want to fool around?" He yawned again, still mistaking Carrie for her twin.

"Mmm." Carrie pressed her warm, naked breast against his rib cage. She slid one long, sinuous leg over his.

"Whoo-ee, Beth." Deke chuckled. Then a sudden thought stayed his hand on Carrie's squirming buttocks. "Suppose Carrie walks in on us?"

"Eh." Carrie was noncommittal, afraid to talk. She kissed him, her sly and active tongue blotting out Deke's fears.

"What's got into you, Beth?" Deke asked. "You sure are turned on."

Carrie's answer was to straddle him, capture his penis in her hand, and impale herself.

"Can this by my shy baby?" Deke marveled.

Carrie began to move with small, grinding movements, rising and descending. They made love then and didn't talk anymore. And in the distance, atop the mountains in the clouds over Crete, the ancient gods, ironic and bawdy, laughed at the games mortals play. . . .

17

PERHAPS THE GODS were laughing still a few weeks later as the sun broke through those clouds to stripe the naked bodies of Louise Papatestus and her Greek lover as they entwined on the sand-smoothed floor of the cave at Matala. The striating effect was due to the way the light was filtered past the outcroppings of volcanic rock as it descended from the opening of the vault of the cave high above the couple. The "now you see it now you don't" scene it illuminated was surely one to tease the gods to risibility.

The cave had been claimed by Louise's lover and his friend, the American, as their home away from home in Matala. It was not an unusual homesteading. There were fifty or sixty such caves on the Matala side of the cliffs occupied by young people of both sexes from all over Europe and America.

They were hippies without hope, the disappointed and disappointing heirs to the liberations of the sixties. Beautiful to look at, casual in their nudity, and uninhibited in their behavior, they were living the ultimate "be-in." It wasn't just their life-style; it was their whole life. Causeless rebels, they had dropped out and turned on to thumb their noses at their elders by spending the next forty or fifty years nodding out in the Cretan sunlight.

So they had seemed to Louise, anyway, before she had actually come to one of their caves to pursue her own abandonment. Now, her hazel eyes following a whirlpool rainbow to the source of its light high over her head as her flesh strained greedily to rise with her gaze, she was not so sure. Her lover did not fit the image she had formed of the Matala hippies.

"I have name," he had told Louise in his broken English on the first occasion of their lovemaking on the other side of the cliffs at Komo. "Xanthos Konstantin."

They had met and made love regularly after that first time. Louise gorged herself on sex with Xanthos and was unashamed. This, however, was the first time she had gone with him to his Matala lair. The American friend with whom Xanthos shared it, whose name was Clint Davenport, had considerately absented himself.

"Clint is snatching ride to Iraklion," Xanthos had told Louise, "to view cinema. Is Woody showing."

"Woody?"

"Filmic American genius, Woody Allen. Napper movie."

"Napper? Oh, you mean *Sleeper*."

"Yes. Slipper. Part of curriculum is Slipper."

Xanthos had already informed Louise that he and his friend were both studying film production in graduate

100

school at the university on Iraklion. Clint Davenport, according to Xanthos, was an exchange student from the NYU Film School in "Apple—you know?" while he himself had matriculated from Athens, where the college education he had begun during the time of the colonels had been interrupted by the student uprising in which he had participated. This explained why he was so late in finishing his studies, for he was, as Louise had discovered, older than she had at first thought. Indeed, Xanthos was in his late twenties, only three or four years younger than she was herself.

At first, Louise had been hesitant to come to his cave in Matala. She was, after all, a married woman, and her husband was a famous as well as a wealthy man. Louise had only affectionate feelings toward Spiro, and she had no wish to embarrass him with any scandal. In the end, however, curiosity over her lover's life-style had won out. In her outdated black Greek peasant woman outfit with her distinctive red-gold hair covered by her Kriti headkerchief, Louise had scrambled behind Xanthos up the path climbing the sheer cliff wall of Matala to his cave. The climb itself had been an erotic experience.

Louise had seen the sunbathing and uninhibited denizens of the Matala caves from afar before, but this was the first time she had viewed them up close. During the climb, she had passed men washing their private parts with seawater they had hauled up the cliff. Following Xanthos, she had edged over narrow ledges where naked girls dozed wide-legged to keep their balance in pools of sunlight that would shift with afternoon. Louise had scrambled past couples joined in sex.

She was shocked and titillated to realize that not all of these were couples of opposing genders. Nor did it cool Louise's ardor toward Xanthos to find herself stepping over bodies merged in oral and anal couplings, as well as other, more bizarre pursuits. Indeed, by the time they reached their destination, Louise was as excited as if her lover had escorted her through a live pornographic orgy.

Xanthos was not unaware of the effect on her. As soon as they reached his cave, he stripped away her shapeless black garments. Seating her facing him across his lap, he

101

kissed her hungry lips and entered her in the same instant. Moving feverishly, Louise had realized that the sun warming them was spread over the face of the cliff, and she wondered if they, too, could be seen by others as they made love. Then, with a fierce surge of passion, she stopped wondering. Later, they had moved inside the cave, which was where they were now, coupling a second time, moving more slowly and intricately, harboring and savoring and prolonging their lust.

Awareness was the secret. Louise had never realized before Xanthos how alive to sensation she could be with every fiber of her being. There was not a nerve end that did not tingle to his touch, his kiss, his pressure, his movement. The rippling of his thigh muscles was alive and hot against her softer flesh. The sinews of his bottom moving under her clenching fingertips sent wild signals to her flesh around his stabbing, steel-hard penis. Her nipples burned hot in his mouth—first one, then the other—rising to his tongue, moving in tempo with the impalement between her upstretched, straining legs. Her hazel eyes looked up into his sun-leathered face, his dark eyes both limpid and loving and filled with mounting lust.

"To see is nice." Xanthos stopped moving and directed her gaze down between their perspiration-slicked bodies. He settled back on his haunches and withdrew so that only the tip of his phallus remained within her. "Is exciting." He flexed. He laughed.

"Don't tease me!" Staring, Louise slid into him, clutching.

"No, no! Resting." Still laughing, he moved inside her ticklingly and then partially withdrew again.

"Xanthos! Don't you dare make fun of me!" Louise flung her arms around his neck, impaled herself fully, and locked her long, supple legs around his writhing, muscular hips. "Do it!" she demanded.

"What is 'it'?" He pretended he didn't understand her.

"Damn you, Xanthos!" Twisting her hands in his long, curly hair she squirmed against his groin.

"Ahh, 'it.'" Laughing, he bent her double at the waist, and Louise felt the full weight of his body on her burning, hungry buttocks. "This 'it,' you mean!" He moved with deep, circular, intimate movements.

"Yes!" Louise panted, rising to him, holding to the moment, then slowly sliding down again. "Yes!" She repeated the movements. "Yes!" Yes!"

"Is now?" His stabbings were feral, demanding.

"Yes!" Louise dug her nails into Xanthos's rippling buttocks, clutching them, holding him deep inside her. "Now!"

His mouth on hers, Xanthos erupted deep inside her.

The long moment—an eternity—filled the sun-stippled walls of the vaulted cave of Matala.

Much later, Louise spoke. "I must go," she said.

"Is too soon."

"I know, darling, but I must. My husband is back from Malta. He'll be expecting me to greet him."

"Husband." Xanthos reached behind Louise for his shorts.

"Does that bother you very much?" Louise peered into the soft eyes anxiously. "My having a husband?"

"No." Xanthos's answer was flat, firm, and noncommittal.

Its echo stayed with Louise as she drove the Mercedes sports coupe through the gates leading to the Papatestus mountain villa. It troubled her because it told her nothing. Did Xanthos love her so much that he was willing to overlook her being married? Or was it his practice to seek out sexually frustrated married women simply because they easily fell prey to his lust? Nothing in Xanthos's tone had revealed either attitude. The question of which was true nagged at Louise's mind. She banished it, however, when she entered the villa and went to Spiro's study to greet him.

"Has Zelig returned?" Louise inquired after they embraced and exchanged perfunctory kisses.

"No. There was a message that he telephoned. He's been detained in Athens. He won't fly back until tomorrow."

"How was Malta?"

"Filled with intrigue." He smiled slightly. He did not specifically mention his meeting with the petroleum minister of Libya. Spiro never discussed business matters with his wife. In that respect he was quite old-fashioned.

In others he was not. "I think we must discuss this affair you are having," he told Louise now, bluntly but gently.

Taken aback, she stared at Spiro. His answering look told her that there was no point in denying it. This was no fishing expedition. Her husband knew.

Nevertheless, trying to gather her wits, Louise played for time. "Have you been having me followed?" she asked. managing to sound at least slightly indignant.

"Of course." Spiro shrugged. "But not to spy on you, my dear. Only for your own protection. Really. I am a man with many enemies. They would not hesitate to do harm to me and mine. It is a matter of course that I am kept under surveillance wherever I go and that you are as well. The revelation of your infidelity is merely a by-product of that surveillance."

Louise's mind was racing. She had known Spiro always as a loving and considerate man. Tact and courtesy, consideration and kindness, had always been the hallmarks of his attitude toward her. Nevertheless, Louise would have had to be blind and deaf not to have realized that there was another side to her husband. In the world of high finance, and that of the haute monde as well, Spiro Papatestus was viewed as a lion in its prime, dangerous—perhaps deadly—when crossed. His reach was long, his vengeance swift, his aim true. There were ruined men and dead men in the wake of his voyage to the pinnacle of worldly success. And there were also whispers of tawdry fates for those women he had discarded with displeasure. Yes, Louise knew, her husband could be utterly ruthless toward women as well as men.

Spiro knew about her affair. Was he toying with her? Was he really furious underneath his habitual calm? If he wanted to punish Louise for betraying him, it would be a simple matter for a man with his power to do so in a way that would annihilate her. Was he about to do that?

"I'm sorry," she said finally, cautiously, tense with trepidation.

"There is no need." His tone was as always soft, considerate, loving. "I'm not jealous."

She stared at him. Did he really mean it? "Then what—?"

"I do not want you to go to your lover's cave in Matala anymore," he told her. "It is not safe."

Louise took a deep breath. Long before Xanthos came along, Spiro had changed her life—and for the better. She cared for him; she really did. As a rule she had never had cause to fear him. What she usually felt for him was gratitude.

Regardless of the consequences, that gratitude was too great for her to lie to him now. "If I told you I would not see him anymore," she said simply, but still fearfully, "I would be lying."

"You misunderstand me, my dear. I am not forbidding you to see your lover. I am only insisting that you do not go to his cave."

"But where, then?"

"Why, here, of course. This is your home, too, Louise."

Louise shook her head against a swarm of bees. "Are you saying that you don't mind if Xanthos and I make love here?" she asked.

"Yes. That is what I am saying. I don't mind at all. As a matter of fact," Spiro added, taking his wife's hand in his, "I would very much like to watch."

The bees were dispelled; the confusion vanished; now Louise understood exactly what Spiro wanted.

18

W HAT JACK HOUSTON wanted from his wife, Buffy, and what she was capable of giving were two very different things, in Holly's opinion. Since the day of the fight, Holly had been watching their drama unfold at Riverview, and with it she had seen their confusion mounting. The attraction between them was electric, sometimes almost crackling, and yet it was overwhelmed by what Holly saw as a classic inability to communicate.

It was painful to observe. Jack loved Buffy fiercely for what she was, and yet he complained to Holly in confidence of his wife's inability to change, to adapt her life to their marriage. Buffy had been drawn to Jack by his comparative youth and virility, his masculine, virile qualities, and yet even to Holly, a quietly committed feminist, it was obvious that Buffy's conduct with other men must ultimately unman her husband.

Love! Holly sighed. Love was certainly taking a back seat these days to Jack and Buffy's other desires. But, despite everything, she knew that these two loved each other.

Holly listened now from the window seat in Nicholas's room as their voices rose in anger from the breakfast room downstairs. Buffy sounded sarcastic and shrill, Jack frustrated and angry. As he angrily stormed out of the front door, still shrugging into his overcoat, Holly wondered what they were fighting about now.

Oblivious to the foot-high snow, Jack cut across to the garage, ignoring the path that had been shoveled out. A moment later the garage door rolled up, and his BMW backed out too fast with tires screeching and wheels spinning over an ice slick. Then it shot forward, motor squealing a protest at too many revs too quickly, and shot down the estate road toward the Riverview gates.

Watching him go, Holly grimaced to herself with concern. The battle was escalating. She was afraid that Jack—

whom she knew was more impulsive than Buffy—might take some action from which there was no turning back. He had done it once before when he had used Holly's cousin, Patrice, to make Buffy jealous. It had worked, but the consequences for Patrice had been devastating.

Jack Houston was impulsive. He had been putting off making this visit for some time now, but his latest quarrel with Buffy had decided him. He would go today. His foot was heavy on the accelerator.

When Jack pulled his BMW into the parking lot of the nursing home in Riverdale, his energy seemed out of place, even to himself, as he stomped the snow from his feet on the rubber mat gracing a verandah where a few of the hardier and more ambulatory senior citizens of the home had gathered briefly to take the air. Self-conscious, he slowed his pace as he obtained a pass from the nurse at the front desk and strode down the hall past oldsters using wheelchairs and walkers to the elevator that would take him to room 316.

His knock at the door of the room went unanswered. Pausing a moment, he opened the door to see his grandfather sitting up in bed looking straight at the door. The old man had deliberately chosen not to respond to the knock.

"Hello, Grandpa." Jack laid the magazine he had brought on the night table beside the old man. There was a *Wall Street Journal*, copies of the latest *Forbes* and *Fortune*, and half a dozen stock market newsletters. "How are you feeling?"

"Love is bullshit," the old man replied in answer. Startled, Jack realized that he was picking up the conversation just where they had left off on Jack's last visit some months ago. "Love is the opiate of the people. Rockefeller senior said that."

"Religion, Grandpa. Not love. It's 'Religion is the opiate of the people.' And it was Karl Marx who said it, not John D. Rockefeller."

"Don't you quote Commie propaganda at me, boy."

"I'm sorry, Grandpa."

"Capitalism built this country. Capitalism made me what I am today."

Jack's grandfather was a pauper. Jack footed the bill to keep him in the nursing home. If he hadn't, the old man would be in a state institution. "Yes, Grandpa." There was no point in arguing with him.

"You can be rich, or you can make calf eyes, boy. Now which is it gonna be?"

"Rich, Grandpa." Jack grinned ruefully. "Could be I've O.D.'d on love."

"Stockwell widow clawing up the short hairs, boy?" The old man's watery blue eyes looked at Jack shrewdly.

Damn it! He really was amazing sometimes. The light could flicker out in those blue eyes, and he could turn into a vegetable in midsentence. Or, like just now, he could be sharp as a tack and stick his finger dead center to the crux of the matter.

"Drawing blood, Grandpa," Jack admitted, finally sitting down on a chair next to the hospital bed.

"There's some women do that. Best kind in bed, worst everyplace else."

"Careful, Grandpa. They'll string you up for the chauvinist you are."

"Chauvinist? What's that, boy? One of those things the young people do these days instead of the old in-out? New-left folderol? What, boy?"

"Never mind, Grandpa. It's not important."

"Chauvinist." His eyes bounced around like pinballs, his train of thought derailed.

"You were saying about money, Grandpa. About getting rich. About me marrying Governor Stockwell's widow." It was all related. It was why Jack had come today. Now he prodded the old man back into focus. "Governor Matthew Adams Stockwell," he said. "Government contracts. Insider trading."

"That son-of-a-bitch was my partner!" The old man snapped back with a vengeance. "He threw me to the wolves. I lost everything. I went to jail for eight years. And Matthew Adams Stockwell—he got rich. Richer, that is. The rich always get richer. He owes me, boy! He owes me!"

"He's dead, Grandpa," Jack reminded him.

"Left me with the mess and walked away with clean hands and all the marbles."

"The governor is dead," Jack repeated.

"The Stockwells, then, boy. All the Stockwells. They owe us. They owe all us Houstons."

"No argument, Grandpa." The old man had been saying it for years. "No argument."

"No argument, boy?" Jack's grandfather was jeering now. "What about that talk we had? What about 'I love Buffy, Grandpa. I really do'?" He mimicked Jack. "What about 'I love my wife'? What about all that bushwa, boy?"

"There have been some changes in our relationship." Jack closed his eyes briefly and then looked up at the ceiling.

"Do tell, Jackie. Do tell. Widow Stockwell twisting them 'stead of squeezing them, is she? Well, I always did notice that only limp thinks straight. But then again, Jackie, just how limp are you? And for how long?"

"I want what's due us from the Stockwells, Grandpa."

"Well, now. That limp, boy! Oh, my. Lady must have twisted really painful." The old man's eyes glowed. He had not seemed so alert and enthusiastic to Jack in years. "Well, then, grandson mine, let's you and me go for it."

"How, Grandpa?" The thought flitted through Jack's mind that maybe he was himself as crazy as the old man. His grandfather was an old ex-con who had lost all his money. Why should he be able to show him how to muscle in on the Stockwell fortune? And yet, crazy as the old man was, he was shrewd as well. His grandfather knew the world of high finance, where the weak spots were, where it was possible to infiltrate, how to parlay that infiltration into control. Yes, crazy as he was, he knew all the things Jack would have to know if he was to cut himself a piece of the Stockwell pie. "How?" Jack repeated. "How, Grandpa?"

"Start where the money moves fast and loose," the old man told him. "That's how."

"Where is that, Grandpa?"

"Insurance, Jackie. That's where the fast and loose money flows. Insurance." He went on talking, brisk and sure of himself. There was nothing senile about him now. His mind was focused. His knowledge was cogent, and his plan was sound.

Even as he listened, though, Jack was beset with doubts. Suppose he did get enough of the Stockwell pie to make Buffy take notice? Would that really change anything? Would she treat him as an equal then? Would it give him some control in their marriage? Would he then have the power to keep her from straying to other wealthy and powerful men? Or was he just kidding himself?

Insurance? Jack laughed ruefully. There was no insurance!

19

"INSURANCE." THE THREE syllables tripped off Beth Tyler's tongue as harshly as stalactites of ice falling from the roof of a polar cave. "Max is concerned. He thinks that we should be aware and wary."

"Insurance?" Carrie's tone said she didn't get it. "But why should we be concerned? Haven't Stockwell Industries always been into insurance?"

"Max doesn't say. Here's his letter. Read it for yourself." Beth handed it to her twin and turned away abruptly. She could have enlightened Carrie, but she wouldn't.

Indeed, it was all Beth could do to speak to her twin—or to Deke, either, for that matter. It was even harder with Deke. She had long ago accepted that her sister was what she was and had always been. Carrie had few morals—and sex certainly wasn't one of them. But Deke, with his insistence that he had thought it was she he was making love to, not Carrie, truly filled Beth with fury.

How stupid did he think she was to believe a cock-and-bull story like that? Didn't he realize how insulting it was? They'd been making love for months. How could he not tell the difference? If it was true, which Beth didn't believe for a minute, that would be the greatest insult of all!

Now Deke came up from below and saw Beth. That pleading, puppydog look Beth was coming to know and despise spread over his face. "Hi, Bethie," he said. "What's new with Mother?"

Beth had just returned from the Greenpeace mother ship with the letter from Max she'd passed along to Carrie. She didn't mention it to Deke. If Carrie wanted to show it to him, let her. Anyway, the letter hadn't really been the purpose of Beth's visit. The purpose had been for her to be brought up-to-date on what role their small sailing vessel would play if and when Papatestus tankers attempted to transport Stockwell oil down the coast of Crete and across the Libyan Sea. That had been the purpose, but it had not been related to the even more important information that Beth had brought back.

"When we're all assembled, I'll update you," she snapped at Deke. "I'm not going to repeat myself." In the past, of course, she would have told Deke immediately. But that was in the past. Now Beth turned her back on him and strode alone to the foredeck.

Carrie's laugh followed her. "You're in the doghouse, stud." She slapped Deke familiarly on the rump. "Now how about I give you some advice?"

"Such as?"

"When I'm not with the twin I lo-ove," Carrie sang out, "I lo-ove the twin I'm with."

"Very funny." Deke started to move away.

Carrie blocked his path. "Seriously, Deke. It was damn good. You know it was. If Beth hadn't come in when she did and carried on so—"

"She had every right to be furious."

"Oh, sure. But that's not the point. The point is we had a good thing going. I really turned you on. You know I did. It wasn't like with Bethie. Admit it."

"It was different. Not better, just different. And I guess that did excite me."

"Not better?" Carrie took a step forward so that the

111

visibly outlined tips of her breasts grazed Deke's bare chest through the thin T-shirt she was wearing. "Really not?" She rubbed against him.

Deke took a quick step backward. "It was really a lousy trick for one sister to play on another."

"My God, you're a prig!" Carrie laughed in his face. Then she turned her back on him and walked away. Deliberately, provocatively, she rotated her bottom as she went.

Carrie repeated the movement for Deke's benefit later on, when Beth called all the crew together to hear what she had been told at the mother ship. He scowled and looked away. Beth, however, noticed not Deke's reaction but her sister's actions and felt the rage welling up inside her again.

Suppressing her anger, she forced herself to sound reasonably calm as she started to speak. "Greenpeace has come into possession of certain information," she told them, "involving Zelig Meyerling."

The name got everyone's full attention. No one aboard the vessel had to be told that Zelig Meyerling exercised a major influence on the European policy of the United States regardless of which party was in power.

"He's on Crete," Beth told them. "Staying at the Papatestus villa."

"Papatestus!" The man who spoke—little more than a boy, really, for his age was the same as Beth and Carrie's—was a Berber from Morocco new to Greenpeace. His name was Yusuf al-Bekka. "Papatestus, the armaments wholesaler for the Zionists!"

Ignoring the interruption, Beth continued. "The cover story being leaked is that Meyerling is on an unofficial mission for the Reagan administration aimed at putting pressure on Prime Minister Papandreou to keep Greece in NATO. That much is true. Now Mother has learned that in line with this goal, Meyerling will make an offer that Papandreou will find hard to refuse. It is an offer which Greenpeace regards as a major threat to the peace and ecology of the area."

"Explain, please." Yusuf al-Bekka was visibly agitated.

112

"Papandreou is a Socialist, but he recognizes that Greece either has to catch up or resign itself to being a third-class country in a nuclear world and a computer age. Many of the most politically powerful people in Greece—and not all of them on the right, by any means—think the future of the country hinges on access to American computer technology—and nuclear power. According to Mother, Meyerling will offer a deal whereby Stockwell Industries, with administration blessing, will provide computer chips and nuclear reactors to Greece in exchange for guarantees of maintaining the NATO bases and beefing up the forces they service on Greece."

"He'll sell Greece on going nuke," Deke exclaimed. "That's his mission."

"He must be stopped!" Yusuf al-Bekka pounded a fist into the open palm of his other hand.

"Nuclear reactors." Another crew member voiced what that meant. "Then Stockwell will also be shipping uranium into Greece."

"And that's where cousin Spiro comes in," Carrie realized. "He'll supply the transport. That really makes it a family affair."

"What do you mean?" Yusuf al-Bekka was not following Carrie.

"Spiro Papatestus's wife is our cousin, mine and Beth's. Zelig married Holly Stockwell, which also makes him a cousin by marriage, although a more distant one. Our family—the Tylers—owns a considerable chunk of Stockwell Industries. Deke's grandfather was Governor Stockwell. So it really is a family affair. And," Carrie added impishly, "not the first in our family."

"What are you two doing in Greenpeace?" the Berber wondered aloud.

"We are standing up to our family and to Stockwell Industries the same way we stand up against all the polluters and arms dealers of the world." Beth's response was didactic, but firm.

"Standing up?" Yusuf al-Bekka snorted. "And will you stand up to eliminate this Zelig Meyerling before his purpose is realized and the nuclear plague spreads?"

" 'Eliminate'?" Beth stared at him.

"Yes." He bared his teeth in a humorless smile. "Off the pig." It was an Americanism picked up from the movies and uttered with conscious contempt. "Kill him."

"I don't think you understand." Beth spoke very carefully and even more firmly than before. "We don't kill people. Greenpeace is nonviolent. It's against our most basic policy to even contemplate an action like that."

"A thousand pardons." The apology was ironic, the bow that accompanied it downright insulting. "Then by all means let this Meyerling die of natural causes. But before—not after—he has nuked southern Europe and North Africa." Yusuf al-Bekka turned and strode aft, away from the group.

"Please don't leave." Beth was conciliatory. "We're not through."

"I must meditate," Yusuf called back, deadpan, "on the natural causes to which man may fall prey."

Carrie was the only one who laughed.

Later that evening, after the meeting had ended, Carrie strode aft to find Yusuf al-Bekka still sitting on the deck and looking out to sea. "Hi," she greeted him.

"Hello."

"Sulking?"

"No. Considering."

"Oh?" Carrie cocked her head quizzically, her apricot curls tumbling loosely over one shoulder.

"I am thinking of leaving Greenpeace. All this commitment to peace and conservation, but then they immobilize themselves with interminable discussions about ethics. Even when there is action, the organization is so damnably pure that the effect gets lost in concern for the ones being acted against. I've had enough." Yusuf's scowl was menacing.

"I'd be sorry to see you go." Carrie smiled and moved closer.

"Why?" Yusuf asked. "You don't even know me."

"Maybe. But I've noticed you. You're very attractive. You have a high energy level." Carrie laughed intimately. "Of course we're from different cultures, and so maybe I'm not getting through to you."

114

"Perhaps you are not." Yusuf was noncommittal.

There was a long silence.

"They say Arabs know where to get the best kayf." Carrie tried another tack.

"I am Muslim. I use neither drugs nor intoxicating beverages."

"Next thing you'll be telling me you believe in chastity."

"I follow the Koran in such matters," Yusuf assured her.

"No hash. No booze. No sex." Carrie sighed. "This is not going to be a fun relationship."

Again there was silence.

"Do you really want to kill Zelig Meyerling?" she asked Yusuf finally.

"His life is not important." The Berber shrugged. "What is important is how it can be rendered useful rather than destructive. There are people who understand that. Various groups in Libya, for instance."

"Terrorists?"

"To some. Freedom fighters to others. Either way, they would know how to deal with Zelig Meyerling to prevent the nuclearization of Greece."

"Greenpeace would never have anything to do with people like that."

"Of course not." Yusuf was sarcastic. "These people deal with realities."

"Oh, sure." Carrie was flip. "Setting off bombs. Hijacking airplanes. Holding people hostage. Realities."

"Such actions are sometimes justifiable. If, for instance, by taking a very important man such as Zelig Meyerling hostage, nukes could be kept out of Greece—"

With a thrill that was both delicious and ominous, Carrie realized that Yusuf was serious. He really would not hesitate at kidnapping, or murder. If Carrie had been drawn to him before, she was even more strongly attracted now. She had never met a man of such strong convictions before; and if those convictions were deadly, it didn't bother her. In fact, its effect was like an aphrodisiac.

115

"You're a very dangerous man." Impulsively, she leaned over and kissed him on the lips. "Very dangerous."

Her face lingered close to his, but he did not return the kiss. He seemed almost not to have noticed. He simply kept on staring out over the stern toward where the starlight revealed the outline of the southern shore of Crete.

20

ON CRETE, BEHIND the mountain villa that was the centerpiece of the Papatestus estate, there was a small cottage until recently occupied by a peasant family that had labored in the olive groves. In February, with all save the most bitter of the olives harvested and the silver-tipped leaves of the trees curled in waiting for springtime, the cottage stood empty. Here, Xanthos Konstantin, and his American friend, Clint Davenport, took up residence at the invitation of Spiro Papatestus.

There had been no difficulty in bringing this about. Spiro had himself arranged a meeting with Xanthos to discuss the arrangement. He had explained to his young countryman that it was neither seemly nor safe that Louise should visit him in the cave. Would it not be better for all of them, he suggested, if Xanthos accepted his hospitality and made use of a cottage on his estate that was at the moment standing empty?

"I love my wife." Spiro had been most persuasive. "But I don't own her. We are adult, the three of us. You two are young. I, alas, am not." He made a moue that laced his face with a spiderweb of wrinkles and aged him ten more years on the instant. "You can provide her with those youthful contentments which are beyond my years. And I will be happy to see her so satisfied."

Xanthos's nod dismissed any need of a glossary. There would be no need to resort to the French definition, "ménage à trois." It was understood.

Still, Xanthos expressed a concern. "My friend," he said to Spiro. "We have planned to take our sabbatical together. I cannot just desert him."

"Of course not. You must bring your friend here to stay with you." Spiro's hospitality was unhesitating. "He is an American, is he not? So is my wife. But of course you know that. They will have much to talk about regarding their native land, I am sure."

And so it was settled. Xanthos Konstantin and Clint Davenport moved into the cottage. Louise visited frequently.

Sometimes the two men took tea with Spiro and Louise. On one such occasion, Clint remarked that there was a Buñuel flick showing in Iraklion that he would love to see. Spiro immediately said that he must choose a car from among those in the garage and drive himself to see the film. Clint accepted happily. When Xanthos begged off accompanying him, he quipped that love really shouldn't be allowed to interfere with classic cinema and went off by himself.

That afternoon, when Louise started for the cottage. Spiro intercepted her on the path. Firmly taking her arm, courtly as always, he escorted her to her waiting lover. When Xanthos opened the door to their knock, he was not surprised.

"Please," Spiro said, "take no notice of me. I just thought you wouldn't mind if I warmed my aging bones by the fire while you amuse yourselves."

He went straight to the fireplace. The ashes were cold. Nevertheless, he sat down in front of it with his back to Louise and Xanthos.

Louise started to say something, but Xanthos put his fingers to her lips, hushing her. He led her into his bedroom, leaving the door open behind them.

Xanthos sat on the edge of the bed and drew Louise to him. Again Louise attempted to explain. This time Xanthos cut off her words with a kiss.

His hands slid up under the blouse she was wearing

117

and cupped her naked breasts. He thumbed the nipples, and her breathing quickened. His tongue in her mouth was demanding.

"Xanthos," she panted when the kiss was over.

"My love is big for you." He guided her hand to his jeans.

"My husband—"

"Is ready." Xanthos reached under her cotton skirt and removed the panties Louise was wearing.

"I wanted to tell you," Louise moaned. "But I didn't know how." Her thighs parted to his fingers. The lips of her vagina nipped damply at his knuckles.

"You want," Xanthos judged. He pulled off his shirt and jeans. He stood before Louise, naked and erect. They both ignored Spiro, watching them now from his place in front of the fireplace in the next room.

"He's watching," Louise murmured as she swayed voluptuously under her lover's hands while he quickly undressed her.

Xanthos bent, kissed her breasts, tongued the deep valley between them, licked her quivering, blood-red nipples. He sank to his knees, and his mouth moved down her body. His lips sent shivers over her flat belly and then her lissome, trembling thighs.

Her hands tangled in his hair, Louise stood quaking. She felt herself opening to him. Xanthos's mouth caressed her intimately. Louise whimpered aloud, bearing down to the spearing of his tongue. Her hands tangled in his mop of too long curly hair. Her pelvis pushed forward, grinding with the quest for release, and then—just as she cried aloud—her eyes met those of Spiro standing in the doorway.

Her young lover ignored Spiro. Even as Louise was falling back to the bed with the last of her climax, he was mounting her. His strong hands reached under her bottom and lifted it off the mattress in a quick jerk as he entered her to the hilt with one strong thrust and then moved in and out more slowly with long strokes. "Is good?"

"Yes. Yes," Louise panted, arching up to reach him.

"Is even better with watching."

"Yes. No. Yes." At first Louise had moved deliciously in concert with Xanthos. Then she had seen her husband standing over them with his own lust revealed. He was smiling at her, stroking himself. At that point Louise, with Xanthos's hands firmly cupping her bottom, began thrashing wildly, control slipping from her grasp.

Even with the powerful push of her mounting orgasm, Louise was struggling with the conflicting emotions twisting her in their grip. She was suffused with embarrassment, and ashamed as well, yet there was a voluptuous joy in bringing pleasure to both her lover and her husband at the same time she herself was coming. Then, explosively, sensation banished thought.

Colors danced over her head, and when they subsided, Xanthos was lying naked beside her and Spiro had gone back into the other room. Louise tried once again to apologize to Xanthos for not having warned him in advance that her husband intended to watch. Again Xanthos shrugged it off. Obviously he had no objections to being observed by Louise's husband as he made love to her.

Is Xanthos only a stud, then, with no real feeling for me? Perversely, Louise was disturbed at her lover's equanimity. If he cares for me, then how can he stand making love under the gaze of my masturbating husband? Still, if he didn't care, didn't feel some love for me, would Xanthos pay such a demeaning price to take me into his bed? Does he ravish me for my husband's pleasure out of indifference or out of desire? What was the answer? What was the truth? Only Xanthos could know, and he wasn't telling.

"Excuse me." Louise's disturbed thoughts were interrupted by her husband, fully clothed now, standing in the doorway. "I wonder if I might have a word with Xanthos."

Pulling one of the sheets around himself, Xanthos started to get out of the bed.

"No, no. Do not disturb yourself." Spiro held up a trembling hand. "I only wanted to ask if you and your friend would oblige us by joining us for a small dinner party on Thursday night. There will be two extra women guests, and I would be most grateful if you would help us balance the table."

"What about Zelig?" Louise interjected. "Won't he be back by then?"

"He's scheduled to return that afternoon," Spiro granted. "But you know Zelig. He's detained by weighty affairs of state as often as not. And besides, he's married. These are two single ladies. And you know how happy it makes single ladies to find that their host and hostess have arranged to have single gentlemen for their dinner partners."

"We will be happy to come," Xanthos answered Spiro in Greek.

"Good, then. It's settled." Spiro glanced at his watch. "Ahh. I must hurry off. There is some business which I must see to before dinner. I will see you back at the house, my dear." He blew a kiss to Louise. "Good afternoon, Xanthos," he said in Greek. "Thank you for you hospitality."

"Is my pleasure."

When her husband was gone, Louise snuggled up to her lover. "I'm glad you'll be joining us for dinner," she told him.

"Joining two unweddinged lady dining partners?" he teased her.

"Not for me to worry, Xanthos. These two ladies aren't interested in men. They are only interested in each other."

Xanthos smiled.

"One is American, the other English. The American is a cousin of sorts. She's Lisa Stockwell, and the English woman is her traveling companion. Lisa is Michael's little sister."

"Michael? The one who plays with tennis and Congress? Is coming, too?"

"Yes, the congressman. And no, he won't be here. He's in Athens."

All thoughts of her cousin were banished as Xanthos's hands reached for the moist cleft between Louise's legs and his mouth closed upon her nipple.

21

THE WOMAN BETWEEN the silk sheets of Congressional Representative Michael Stockwell's bed had skin soft as silk and a bosom designed for pillowing. Add to that raven hair, dark eyes, and limbs accomplished as any contortionist's, and the most stone-hearted whistle blower from the Government Accounting office would have had to judge the congressman's hospitality justified.

She was Greek. Her father was with the government and had something to do with organizing tours of the Acropolis, which was where they had met. She had snagged her skirt on a fragment of pillar alongside a sign that cautioned tourists in three languages not to touch it. Trying to obey the injunction and free herself at the same time, the young woman had displayed a great deal of shapely thigh. Michael, who had come to the Acropolis determined not to miss any of the sights he might have passed up on previous visits when he was young and foolish, had immediately responded to this one.

After he helped the lovely Greek lady free herself, he had taken her for coffee and baklava and then insisted on showing her the fabled artifacts of the newly decorated lounge of the King George V Hotel, where he happened to be staying. From there it was only a short elevator ride to his room, where he learned that her name was Leila.

Michael was murmuring the liquid name into the pronounced cleft between her remarkable breasts when the telephone rang. Leila's affectionate eyes, deep and dark, met his. The corner of her generous mouth curved fatalistically. Reaching over to the night table, she picked up the telephone and handed it to Michael. The wire coiled teasingly over her naked belly.

"Hello? Yes, this is Representative Stockwell. Oh. How are you, Mr. Ambassador?" Michael's body straightened with respect. Leila sighed. Michael listened for a very long time without saying anything.

When he finally did speak, his words were respectful and brief, indicating a great deal of concern. "Yes, Mr. Ambassador," he concluded. "Of course. I'll see to it immediately." He hung up the phone and gazed down at Leila sadly.

"Your enthusiasm"—her eyes strayed down and up his lean tanned body—"seems to have abated."

"I'm sorry. I'm really sorry, but something has come up. I really must ask you to leave immediately. But not permanently," he added quickly. "If you could just go down to the bar and have a drink, I could join you in about an hour, and then—"

"Then?"

"My enthusiasm will astonish you, I promise."

"Spoken as a true American." Leila stood, naked, and began retrieving her clothes from the various parts of the room where they had been discarded. "I do not take kindly to rejection," she told him. And yet she did not appear to feel rejected or to be angry, either. Even stooping to retrieve a pair of bikini panties under the bed, Leila was dignified.

Michael, on the other hand, scurrying around naked to help her, was clearly distracted. Even in his hurry and awkwardness, however, his charm manifested itself. "I promise you that I'm not rejecting you," he told Leila. "This is government business. An emergency. Confidential. I have to make a call which is also very confidential. Please, please wait for me in the bar."

"A congressman?" Leila laughed and finished dressing quickly. "Surely you are in the wrong branch of government. Diplomacy is your strength."

"I'll be down as fast as circumstances allow." He escorted Leila to the door of the room and closed it gently behind her.

Once she was gone, Michael's features automatically arranged themselves into an expression of grave concern. He found a robe in the closet and, perching himself on the edge of the bed, he picked up the telephone and asked the switchboard at the King George V desk to get him the transatlantic operator.

It took a few moments. During that short time, Michael

put Leila completely out of his mind. His thoughts were completely occupied by what the ambassador had told him and the message he would have to deliver once his call was put through. No matter how tactful he was, it would be painful. Michael sighed, and for the moment, at least, his distress was genuine.

"Did you wish to place a transatlantic call, sir?" The operator's voice crackled in his ear.

"Yes, please. Person to person to the United States. New York State. Town of Riverview Heights. Riverview Manor."

"And the name of the party, sir?"

"Holly Meyerling." Michael repeated it slowly and distinctly. "Mrs. Holly Meyerling."

22

HOLLY FOLDED HER arms and peered into the mirror over the marble sink in the bathroom adjoining her studio over the Riverview library. Her aquiline features, crowned by carefully cut pale golden hair, reflected back an image that was delicate, graceful, and aristocratic. Nevertheless, it did not pass muster under her scrutiny. Peering closer, she judged it pinched, lacking in color, even lifeless. Oh, yes. It was a face trapped in ennui and weary of marking time.

Damn you, Zelig! Holly and her image agreed. I'm turning into a sex-starved hag, and it's all your fault.

Before meeting Zelig, after the breakup of her first marriage, Holly had resigned herself to a scholarly and rather placid and unerotic existence. Then Zelig had come along with his charm and his humor, his sophistication and his love. He had swept Holly—who was really old enough to have kept a better balance—off her feet. He had aroused her, unleashing her passions, turning her placidity to wildness in bed, and he had married her. And then—damn him!—he had left her alone.

Circumstance, yes, of course. Not really Zelig's fault. Yet . . . I'm turning into a Buffy. No Riverview footman will be safe from me. My lustful seizures will become the scandal of the Hudson River Valley. Holly grimaced.

Oh, no! She wagged a finger at her image. Control, old girl. She turned away from the mirror. Soon—only another week or so, and Nicholas would be well enough to travel, the doctor had said—soon she would be joining her husband on the glorious island of Crete. And, Holly promised herself, our reunion will be so depraved as to make those randy old Greek gods blush.

Meanwhile, she counseled herself, sublimate. Determined, she left the bathroom and marched over to the work table set at a right angle to her desk.

Holly sat down in her swivel chair and contemplated the carefully arranged stacks of paper there. During the last occasion she had spent working on the Riverview history, she had been keying documents and notes she had compiled to the events related in the satiric novel based on George Cortlandt Stockwell's family. There was no concrete proof that the boy, Horace Stockwell, had come upon his mother and his uncle in an act of adultery, but there were letters and diaries and even records from the period that attested to the strained relationship between Horace and his mother. These documents supported the account of the dramatic, even dreadful, events that followed Horace's discovery of the lovers in the novel.

To make sure that she was not exaggerating the evidence, Holly now reread that portion of George Lincoln Stockwell's work dealing with the events following Horace's discovery. . . .

''How can I make you understand?'' Margaret Adams Stockwell stared into the impassive face of her eleven-year-old son with a look that combined anguish with pleading.

''Oh, I understand, Mother.'' Horace revealed no sign

of his own inner turmoil. His voice was tightly controlled, cold, and loveless. "I understand quite well."

She had followed Horace downstairs after he had stumbled upon her lying naked in the arms of her brother-in-law. Tearing herself from her lover's arms, Margaret had flung on her clothes. "Lord forgive me!" she had kept repeating. "Sweet Jesus forgive me. I must go to him."

"Margaret, wait— We must talk—we must make plans—" But she was gone, lost to Roger, the claim of motherhood stronger than their passion and his need.

In the void of her leaving, the despair that had held Roger in its grip on the night their affair had begun once again closed in on him. He would lose her as surely as once he had lost Ursula! He knew Margaret. Her love for him could survive anything, but it was no match for her maternal instinct. No, not instinct; say rather duty. That deeply ingrained maternal duty would take her from him. And without Margaret his life again would be devoid of meaning.

Now, facing her son, Margaret somehow tried to get through to Horace. "You say you understand, but you can't," she pleaded. "You're only a child. It's not just what you think. It's not just—" Margaret had no words to explain that which she so deeply felt but perhaps did not really understand herself.

"Barnyard breeding." Horace finished her sentence in a flat, uninflected voice. Once he had heard his father use the phrase with sneering contempt to describe the behavior of the adulterous wife of a Hudson River Valley neighbor. Horace knew that it was the sort of judgment a gentleman was expected to pronounce in such circumstances. "Is that what you mean, Mother?" Mother! With all that the word implied, Horace almost lost his composure. The effort to maintain it caused his next words to come out even more savagely. "Is that what it's not? Barnyard breeding?"

"Horace, please!" Her voice broke. "We are not animals." She was sobbing then. "I am not an animal."

Horace would not let himself show sympathy. His

father would not have been moved by her tears. Everett Stockwell would not have been so unmanly, and neither would his son. The face Horace turned to his mother was deliberately stony. "That, Mother," he told her, "is precisely the point. We are not animals."

The judgmental expression in her son's pale eyes was more than Margaret could bear. "I don't know what to say," she wept. "I don't know what to do."

"Why, Mother, there is nothing to say. There is nothing to do." Although Horace's voice broke with concealed emotion, before leaving, he made her the sort of small, polite, ironic bow his father reserved for those of whom he was contemptuous.

"Horace—?"

"Yes, Mother." His back was still to her; he did not turn around.

"Your father . . ."

"Father. Yes, Mother?"

"Will you— Will you tell him?"

There was an instant of silence, then Horace spoke. He did not answer the question. "I will see you at dinner, Mother," he said. And then he was gone.

Horace went straight to his room. Closing the door behind him, he moved a small bureau against it so that no one could enter and catch him unaware. Then he threw himself onto the bed with his face pressed into the eiderdown pillows to muffle the sounds and sobbed uncontrollably.

Confused both in thought and emotion, Horace recognized that crying was the one result of his mother's infidelity he understood. His father would not approve. He believed that crying was unmanly. And through his tears Horace believed that his mother's betrayal had robbed him of his manhood, just as it had robbed his father.

He knew that this robbery of Father by Mother, this cheating—Horace realized the enormity of her act while only dimly comprehending its sensual and emotional components—was wrong. The picture of his mother, naked and making those sounds in the arms of his uncle

Roger—this image overwhelmed his efforts to make sense of what he had seen. It made his skin crawl, made him feel dirty, knotted his belly with a squeamishness toward all that was motherly, all that was womanish.

If he told his father, Everett would take his pistol and kill Uncle Roger. Horace was sure of that. Then Father would beat Mother. Horace shivered. The first picture was exciting, but the second made him uncomfortable. Mother deserved to be beaten, of course. That was what husbands were supposed to do to unfaithful wives; everybody knew that, and Father certainly believed it and would act accordingly. Yes, Mother deserved to be beaten, and yet—

She was his mother.

When Margaret did not appear at dinner that night, Everett Stockwell announced to his three children that their mother was not feeling well.

"Female trouble." Father grimaced. This intimation to Horace of their mutual maleness was his father's way of declaring filial intimacy. The remark brought an uncomfortable flush to the cheek of Horace's older sister, Mercy. His younger sister, Deborah, merely looked puzzled.

Deborah was also puzzled by the absence of her uncle Roger from the dinner table. "Does Uncle Roger have female trouble, too?" she inquired. Deborah knew better, of course, but sometimes such deliberately "cute" remarks directed people's attention to her and made them cluck over how clever she was.

This time the effort did not succeed. "Don't be silly," Father told her coldly. "Now be quiet, Deborah, and eat your dinner."

Female trouble . . . The phrase stayed with Horace later when he went to bed. It was related, he was sure, to his mother's unfaithfulness. He lay awake trying to fathom the connection. He thought hard about it and about what action he, Horace, should take. Should he tell Father so that he might punish Mother? He still couldn't decide. Then, overtired but not sleepy, some advice he had once inadvertently overheard his father giving to his uncle Roger popped into his mind.

The subject had been control and discipline in the home. "You are a bachelor, Roger, so you cannot understand the necessary subtleties," Everett had told his brother. "With children and wife, as with servants, a threat is more powerful than a punishment. A threat may be exercised over and over again, but once a punishment is executed, it is over and done with. In the act of execution, it has lost its force. But a threat—ahh, that can become more dire with each utterance."

More dire with each utterance . . . Horace thought about that overheard remark long and hard through the sleepless night. The phrase became the cornerstone of the course of action he decided to follow.

Horace embarked on his plan the next morning. After his father had left the house to see to some business or other, and his sisters were busy at lessons, each with her own governess, Horace had marched to his mother's room. "I would speak with you, Mother," he said with a new attitude that was polite but devoid of respect.

Margaret, fearing the condemnation she could read in her son's eyes, steeled herself. "Yes, Horace?" But when her gaze met his, it found neither hurt nor anger, but only a pale, bland, appraising look that was the more chilling for its studied lack of emotion.

An eleven-year-old boy shouldn't look like that, she thought automatically. His expression reminded her of something. It nagged at her later, but she could not recall. Then it came to her. It was similar to the loveless look her husband bestowed upon her when he was weighing the decision to make love to her. Yes, the boy's look was the look of a man deciding how best to use a woman for his own satisfaction.

"I have a duty to Father," Horace began. "I am his son."

"You are my son, too," Margaret said softly.

Horace ignored the interruption. "I owe him devotion and loyalty. As," he added carefully, "do you, Mother."

"Horace—"

"As do you," he repeated, cutting her off. "I could

128

never betray Father. He trusts me. As he trusts you, Mother."

"You have decided to tell him." Margaret was filled with dread.

"Surely that is my duty, Mother." Horace paused significantly and then continued, "But—"

"Do not toy with me, Horace!" Margaret erupted. "I am your mother."

"And therefore deserving of my respect." The irony was the more cutting for the absolute lack of sarcasm in Horace's little-boy voice. "Very well, then, I have decided not to tell Father, if—"

"If?"

"If certain conditions are understood, accepted, and put into effect."

"Please, Horace. I can't stand much more of this, I promise you. Say what you have come to say."

"You must put an end to it, Mother. You must cease your betrayal of my father. Nothing like it must ever happen again."

"Yes, Horace." Consumed with shame before the son she had borne, Margaret surrendered quickly and completely. "It will never happen again. I promise you that."

"You are not to see him, Mother."

"Alone, you mean. I will not. I swear it. But it will not be possible to avoid encountering Roger here at Riverview. He lives here, after all."

"He must leave." Horace's tone was final.

"Leave? But Riverview is his home."

Horace frowned, and his voice raised an octave. "He must leave my father's house."

"You don't understand, Horace. Riverview is not your father's house. It belongs to your uncle Roger. We live here—your father and I, you and your sisters—at *his* invitation."

His mother's words gave Horace pause. It was true. Not long ago, his father had mentioned the status of Riverview to Horace. "Providence is not always practical, nor fair, my boy," Everett had remarked. "Your uncle Roger is both wifeless and childless, while we constitute ourselves a family. Riverview is far too large for him, albeit well suited to our situation. Nevertheless, we are dependent on your uncle's hospitality.'' Small boy though he was, Horace had been aware of the resentment in his father's tone despite his next words. ''Of course we must be very grateful to him.''

Horace had not felt grateful. This news had made him feel insecure. Now he faced that insecurity once again. The ownership of Riverview had to be considered. They could leave, of course, he and his mother and father and sisters, but truly Horace did not wish to give up living at Riverview. It was much nicer for him here than it had ever been in the crowded, dirty city.

Horace's mind raced. He thought hard. Finally he spoke. ''It is Uncle Roger who must leave,'' he decided. ''You will convince him to go, Mother.''

''But Horace, I can't—''

''Oh, but you can, Mother. You will tell him that if he is not gone by Friday hence, I will tell Father that his brother and his wife are lovers. Father will kill him.''

Even as he spoke the words, Horace felt the first thrill that comes with exercising power. His mother's face drained of all color as her eyes widened with alarm. She opened her mouth as if to speak, then closed it again. Her eyes searched frantically for some sign of sympathy, compassion in her son's frowning visage. She saw none.

Finally she said, ''Your uncle Roger is no poltroon. He served with great valor and distinction in the war, and—''

''You will tell Uncle Roger that Father's anger will most likely be directed at the wife who betrayed him. If he truly cares for you''—Horace was heady with the exercise of control now—''Uncle Roger will not want you to risk Father's wrath.''

''Your father would not—''

''Wouldn't he, Mother? Are you quite sure?''

Margaret stared at her son. In truth, she was not sure. Everett might indeed be capable of doing her harm, even of killing her, under such circumstances as these. It was not the realization of that which came as such a shock to Margaret at the moment, though. It was, rather, the knowledge that her son would not hesitate to put her in such danger.

130

"Do it, Mother," Horace said now into the silence. "Make sure that Uncle Roger leaves Riverview."

"All right, Horace." Horace's newborn ruthlessness defeated Margaret. "I will tell Roger that he must go." Sick at heart, she hugged her full bosom—the unconscious clutching of a child—and watched as Horace made her a small, polite bow and started to leave. "Horace!" The cry, a plea, wrenched itself from her lips.

"Mother?" He turned back inquiringly. "Is there something you want from me?"

Margaret bit her lip and looked at her eleven-year-old son behind the invisible shield that would in future always stand between them. "Try not to hate me, Horace," was the best she could manage in answer to his thin, raised eyebrows.

"Of course, Mother. I will try. I promise you that I will try." And then he was gone.

Actually, Horace didn't hate her. He was bitter about the betrayal of the father who was his ideal, but hatred of Margaret would have required a depth of emotion that pain dictated should be closed off from him. At first he had been confused, and now the confusion was hardening into a contempt for her weakness. Yes, his attitude had changed, but not to one of hatred. From this day forward, he would simply regard his mother as someone to manipulate and control toward objectives and ends that he would define and redefine as he went along. He could deal with that; he could not deal with the wreckage of his love for her.

From the first, Margaret was helpless. Now, after Horace left, her blue eyes filled with tears. It was terrible that her own son should control her in this fashion, but it was worse for him. What sort of manhood would be shaped by the power he brought to bear on her?

Wiping her eyes, she left her room to seek out Roger. She found him in his study where it had all begun between them. When she entered, he looked up with a gaze that regarded her without hope. Before she even spoke, he acknowledged her decision. "It was a chimera," he said. "It was never real."

"It was hopeless." The admission was wrenched from

131

Margaret's throat. "I am a wife. A mother. I was weak. I could not withstand the temptations of the flesh. But now it is over."

"Over." Roger echoed her dully.

"We must not meet. We must not even see each other."

"But how—?"

Margaret told him then of Horace's ultimatum. "You must leave Riverview," she concluded. "You must!"

Here, he had met and wooed Ursula. Here, she had died. And then at his most despairing moment, he had rediscovered love.

"Leave Riverview!" Roger's look was stricken. "Margaret, to cease being lovers is harsh punishment, but to leave Riverview, never to see you again—"

"There is no choice."

And indeed there wasn't. In the end, Roger was forced to accept that. He could not stay and put Margaret's life at risk. And yet he could not live without her. . . .

It was Horace who found his body. Later that day, walking past the barn, he had noticed that the door was open. When he went to close it, he heard the sound of creaking. The draft from the open door was causing a weight suspended from the rafters to sway and make them groan. Going inside the barn to investigate, Horace peered upward through the dimness. It took him a moment to discern what the weight was. Then, with a start, he made it out.

Colonel Roger Stockwell's body was hanging from the rafters, from a rope pulled taut around his neck. His gray eyes were open and bulging. His tongue was visible between parted lips; it was quite blue. His body dangled, swaying, making the rafter creak with its weight.

Horace sucked his breath in sharply. He stared at the dangling corpse. He had never seen a dead person before, but he was not afraid. Cutting himself off from one emotion, Horace was not growing beyond reach of others. Denying love, he could not feel fear—or grief.

Calm in the presence of death, Horace reflected. With Uncle Roger gone, Riverview would now belong to his father. And someday, when he was older, after his father died, it would be his. It would not go to his mother; he would have to be firm about that. It would not go to his sisters; they were girls and would marry and leave. And so it would be his, all his.

Yes, one day Riverview would belong to Horace.

23

THE SOUND OF footsteps on the spiral staircase leading up from the Riverview library to her studio distracted Holly from her reading. She put the papers aside to answer the knock at her door. She found Jack Houston standing there.

"I saw your light," he explained. "I thought maybe you'd offer me a nightcap."

"Of course, Jack. Come in." She could smell liquor on his breath, but he wasn't drunk. "It's good to see you."

Holly had seen very little of him lately. He and Buffy had obviously been avoiding each other, and in avoiding his wife, Jack had been avoiding Riverview and Holly as well.

"Scotch?" she asked him as he settled onto a small couch.

"Yes, please. Rocks if you have them."

"I do." Holly fixed two Scotches over ice, handed him one, and sipped at the other herself. Sitting down next to him, she noticed with concern the deep circles under his eyes.

"How's Nicholas?" Jack inquired.

"Coming along nicely. A week or so, the doctor says, and he'll be ready to travel."

"I have this little zap robot for him," Jack told her. "I saw it passing a toy store one day and thought of Nicholas. I keep forgetting to give it to him. So many damn things on my mind."

"That's so nice of you, Jack." Holly was touched. She reached over and squeezed his hand. "Thinking of Nicholas with everything that's going on in your life."

"Nicer if I'd remembered to give it to him." Jack grinned ruefully.

"Well, you will." Holly took another sip of her drink and looked at him over the rim of the glass. "How's your life going, Jack?" she asked gently.

"All right." He shrugged, then frowned. "Lousy."

"Buffy?"

"A bitch." Jack took another long sip of his drink as he met Holly's level gaze. "The situation, I mean. Her, too, I guess." He laughed without humor. "We don't exactly communicate."

"Poor Jack. You love her so much." She squeezed his hand again.

"Yeah, and I *hate* her so much, too." He drained his drink, his eyes asking for another.

As Holly went to pour it for him, Jack's gaze followed her across the room. She walked with an easy grace that was sensual without resorting to the hip-swaying gait that Buffy, even in the highest of heels, had learned to perfection. Her face free of makeup, garbed in faded jeans and a bulky fisherman's sweater, she looked no older than nineteen. Certainly not like a Hudson River heiress married to one of the most important men in the nation. With the gentle curves of her tall, lean body, her silky gold hair, and ice princess features, she was the antithesis of his wife. Jack drew in his breath with admiration, recognizing that the quiet, more formal beauty of Holly could be just as arousing as his stunningly sexy wife.

"Have you heard from Zelig?" he asked, changing the subject from his own painful marriage and forcefully reminding himself of her married status.

"Last Tuesday. He's very busy. Really on the run."

"You must really miss him."

"Oh, yes." Holly handed him a fresh drink. "I'm damn lonely." Her eyes met Jack's, then, blushing, she looked down. All day long she had been thinking of the

134

pleasure she should have been looking forward to—of honeymoon nights in Zelig's arms. Now all her nerves were alive with expectation and passion.

"I wish I'd known, I would have kept you company. We could have had dinner, taken in a show or something."

"That would have been nice. You know what," Holly realized, "I haven't been off the grounds since Nicholas had the accident."

"You poor kid." Jack was genuinely concerned. "What a lousy friend I am," he apologized. "I should have seen to it that you got out."

"Well, you've had your own troubles on your mind."

"Oh, yes." Jack was bitter. "My marriage. Your husband's away and my wife's at home, but you know, Holly, I'm probably lonelier than you are. Not to mention frustrated."

"Frustrated. Yes." Holly bit her lip. Suddenly she was very uncomfortable. Jack had touched on feelings that in Zelig's absence she had been pushing away from herself.

"You feel that way, too." Jack answered his own question. "Well, of course you do, with Zelig gone all this time."

Their eyes met with unanticipated candor. Holly lowered hers immediately. She and Jack were friends. Good friends. That was all. Wasn't it?

"Holly—"

Jack's tone caused her to look at him again. His commanding blue eyes were hypnotic. Recognition hung silently between them. They were friends, but there was a strong attraction between them. They had never pursued it, but it had always been there.

"No, Jack—" Holly's voice was weak, barely a whisper.

The words seemed not to register on Jack. He set his second drink down on the end table, half-finished. He moved toward Holly.

Holly felt confused, attracted, tempted, and guilty even before Jack put his arms around her and kissed her. Yet she could not stop herself from returning the kiss. Outwardly cool and composed and even elegantly passionless, beneath the surface Holly had always been easily aroused to passion. Now, Jack's lips were claiming hers with an insistency, an urgency that she met with her own. His kiss was not harsh, not gentle. As the kiss continued, Jack's hand moved under her sweater to caress her breast. A thrill coursed through Holly as she pressed into his palm, feeling her nipple harden. His other hand slid down the small of her back, sending shivers of pain and heat down her body as her thighs separated slightly. It had been a long time, such a long time!

Jack's hand slid down between her legs, rubbing firmly against her jeans, then reaching higher. Holly heard herself moan as he touched her. She felt herself start to respond. However, with a strong effort of will, she made her lips stop clinging to his and pulled away.

"We can't!" Holly drew back from him, startled by her own strength. Her body throbbed with desire, and her face was flushed. Pushing her tousled hair back, she looked Jack squarely in the eyes. "I'm sorry, Jack. You're my dear and good friend, and I'll always be grateful to you for saving Nicholas's life. But I can't do this. I am attracted to you, but my marriage to Zelig means too much to me."

Jack looked at her with a half smile that managed to be disappointed, bitter, and understanding all at the same time. He shrugged. "Okay." He picked up his glass and drained it. "Then I guess you should fix me another drink."

"Of course." As Holly started over to the counter where the bottle of Scotch stood, the telephone rang.

She veered over to the side of the room to answer it. "Hello."

"Person-to-person call from Athens, Greece, for Mrs. Holly Meyerling," the operator's voice said in her ear.

"This is Mrs. Meyerling." She waited. "It's from Athens," she told Jack as the receiver made clicking noises in her ear. "It must be Zelig."

"Husbandly instinct." Jack shrugged. "Possessive timing."

"Holly, this is Michael." The voice on the phone surprised her.

136

"Michael." Feeling Jack's inquiring eyes on her, she covered the receiver. "It's my cousin Michael," she said, her tone puzzled.

"Listen, Holly, something has happened."

"Happened? What do you mean, Michael. Is it Zelig?" Holly felt her stomach lurch. "Has there been an accident? What?"

Alerted by her tone of voice, Jack was observing her very closely now.

"No accident, Holly. Zelig is missing."

"Missing?" She sank onto a straight chair. "What do you mean, missing?"

"He was supposed to be at the embassy early this morning, and he never turned up. They think he's been kidnapped."

"Kidnapped?" Holly was dazed. "But why—?"

"The embassy thinks it's political. They think he's being held hostage."

"Hostage? But who would—"

Jack strode across the room to her. He held her outstretched hand. She pulled him toward her.

"They don't know who, Holly. There are a lot of different groups who might find it advantageous to hold Zelig Meyerling hostage."

Holly was sobbing now, and her words were becoming garbled. "Terrorists? My God, Michael, do you mean that Zelig is being held by terrorists?"

BOOK THREE

24

HOLLY MOVED THROUGH the forty-eight hours following the call from her cousin Michael like a sleepwalker. For several hours she had cried, but once the family had rallied around her she had tried to regain her composure. Her anxiety was still so great that she functioned as she had to, but she didn't allow herself to feel. If she had, she would have crumpled.

Riverview was in turmoil. Reporters camped outside the gates as family and government officials came and went. Inside, decisions had to be made, plans put in motion. Holly would go to Greece, of course. Her presence— the presence of a granddaughter of a New York State governor who had almost been president of the United States, of the wife of a former secretary of state—would be a lever on the Greek government and on the U.S. State Department as well. Her beauty would guarantee considerable media coverage, and her ongoing vocal presence would ensure that Zelig Meyerling would not become just one more forgotten American hostage.

The official line was never to negotiate with terrorists. But the official line, Holly knew, was all image and little substance. No hostage had ever been *recovered* without negotiations, and none ever would be. The three possibilities were death, ongoing captivity, or an exchange deal.

Holly was determined not to allow martyrdom for Zelig. She wanted her husband back, and she wanted him back alive. Toward that end she vowed to use every weapon at her disposal: her beauty, her social position, the wealth of her family, her political influence. Fired by her determination, her only other consideration was Nicholas. Although he had been out of bed for almost a week now, he was still convalescing. Even though the Hudson Valley was going through an unseasonable mildness—a pre-March thaw of pale green buds poking through the slush on their way to crib death in a resurgence of winter—the doctors had thought it best that Nicholas remain indoors.

Now, with this latest crisis, they left the decision up to Holly. Yes, Nicholas was well enough to travel to Greece as long as efforts were made to take care that he didn't overexert himself either during the journey or after he got there. Still, it would be better if he stayed indoors at Riverview for another few days and then proceeded step by step to resume the normal activities of a five-year-old.

But Holly knew that she would be very busy in Greece, and she would not have time to devote to Nicholas. In Greece, he would be among strangers, and there would be no boys his own age who spoke his language with whom he might play.

Nicholas would undoubtedly be bored and lonely. And—Holly had been a mother long enough to admit this to herself without feeling guilty—he would be an irritating distraction to her at a time when she wanted to focus all her energies single-mindedly on dealing with the plight of her husband. Still, she didn't like to leave Nicholas rattling around all by himself in the eighty-eight-room mansion with nobody but servants to take an interest in him and to supervise him.

"I'll be here," Jack had offered quickly. "I'll look out for Nicholas."

Holly had been touched by Jack's offer. She knew that he meant it sincerely, but she also knew that Jack had business concerns that often took him away from Riverview and a social life, particularly since his estrangement with Buffy. Jack meant well, but if he did indeed have the willpower to stay home for who knows how long with a five-year-old boy, it would be torture for him.

"Maternal instincts aren't exactly my strong suit, darling"—even Buffy had tried to be helpful in the midst of the crisis—"but I will keep an eye on the little monster while you're in Greece if you like, Holly."

Nicholas, in whose presence Buffy had made the offer, stuck his tongue out at her behind her back. Holly scowled at him until the tongue went back in his mouth. Then she politely thanked Buffy but said she was making other arrangements.

James had moved quickly to relieve his niece's mind of all concerns about Nicholas. "I'm going to Greece with you," he informed Holly. "We have reservations on the first Olympia plane nonstop to Athens Wednesday morning. In our absence, Patrice will stay at Riverview and see to Nicholas."

Fortunately, Holly's cousin Patrice O'Keefe, who had been married briefly but was childless, was genuinely fond of Nicholas and enjoyed spending time with him. "Keeping him amused keeps me amused," she had told Holly once in the past.

"You should have been a mother," Holly had replied with a laugh. "You'd get over that quickly enough."

Her cynicism, however, was all on the surface. Underneath, Holly's concern for her son was abiding. After his accident she had spent hours every day talking to him, playing with him, amusing him. Even now, her mind on Zelig and her faith in Patrice quite firm, she worried about how her little boy would fare in her absence.

In the blunt manner of children, Nicholas alleviated her concern. "I won't miss you at all," he told Holly. "I'll have cousin Patrice to play with." He was truly delighted at the prospect; he adored Patrice. "Cousin Patrice never hollers that I hit too hard when we play slapjack the way you do," he added.

"Well, I'll miss you," Holly responded wistfully.

"You can come right back after you find Zelig, Mommy." Sometimes insensitive like all children, Nicholas was nevertheless by nature soft-hearted. Now he was trying to be reassuring. "Then we can play four-handed. Me and Cousin Patrice against you and Zelig."

"Oh, baby!" For a moment, Holly's composure cracked. Then she regained it. "It may be a while," she told Nicholas seriously. "You may have to be patient."

"How long, Mommy? How long do you think it will take to find Zelig?"

"I don't know." Holly turned away from Nicholas abruptly to hide the tears brimming in her blue eyes. She made believe that she was studying her reflection in the window fogged over by the unseasonable defrosting. Peering at her blurred image, she patted down a few tendrils of sleek golden hair. "I don't know."

Through the running beads of mist covering the window, she could see the melting snows turning the vista of Riverview from snow white to mud brown. Her eyes followed the sloping terrain down to the Hudson River, high now with the thaw's slush, running strong but not turbulent, flowing into the ocean she must cross to find her missing husband. "I don't know how long it will take to get Zelig back," she whispered.

Still gazing out the window toward the river, distraught, Holly's mind barely registered the two tiny figures in the distance where the path from the boathouse started up the hill to the main house of Riverview.

25

JAMES LINSTONE STOCKWELL and his daughter Patrice paused to take a deep breath before starting up the hillside. They smiled acknowledging the prospect of doing battle with slush, muck, occasional ice-slick rocks, and gravity. Still, the temperature was in the high forties, and the wind off the Hudson was at their backs and not strong.

The Riverview estate was not at its best this time of year. Clearly defined seasons were the couturiers demanded by the Hudson River Valley. The riotous wildflower hues of springtime, the red-gold hazes and pewter storm skies of summer, the earth colors of autumn, and the startling pine-green black-and-white contrasts of winter—such was the finery demanded by breastlike mountain rises, smooth, flat meadows, and the clefts of river valleys. On a day such as this, Riverview, one of the valley's greatest estates, one of the wealthiest in the Northeast, had the scraggly, barren look of ancestral English lands gone to pot and on the block for taxes.

By contrast, and despite their lumbering all-weather boots, James and Patrice looked quite smart, due partly to their Abercrombie & Fitch garb, but partly also to the refined integration of those born to the world of country gentry. Father and daughter enhanced the lackluster scenery. James, tall and slender, gray-haired and distinguished, slogged through the mire with the ease and surefootedness of the natural athlete he was. The legs are the first thing to go, they say, but James's long legs, at age fifty-three, were as springy as they were on the tennis courts during his daily two sets. And, as always, the outdoors liberated his spirit from the conservative side of his nature that prevailed in the boardrooms of Wall Street.

Beside him and more than a head shorter, Patrice was petite, but equally nimble and in tune with her woodland surroundings. Her cheeks were flushed under her wavy chestnut hair, and her deep brown eyes sparkled. For once she had forgone her eyeglasses, and, like her father, she looked very *Town & Country*-ish in lined tan corduroy slacks and a short, chocolate-brown down jacket.

"Wait a minute." Her father's hand on her arm stayed Patrice as she started the final ascent back to the house. "We came out to talk," he reminded her. "It would probably be better if we get it over with before we rejoin Holly."

"You're right, Dad. I got so carried away being in the

out-of-doors—it's what I miss most living in the city—that I forgot the reason for our little hike.'' She sighed. ''It's been almost two days,'' she said.

''Yes.''

''And?''

''And nothing,'' her father told her. ''No word from Zelig's captors, whoever they are. No demands. No ransom note. We don't know any more than we did the day he was abducted. He went to Athens from the Papatestus villa in Crete. Drove his car to the Iraklion airport and took the shuttle flight. Saw your brother Michael at the King George V Hotel. They had a drink together. Several hours later he was due at the American embassy, but he never arrived at his destination.'' James brushed off an outcropping of rock and then took off his glove and slapped it against the boulder to shake off the dirt. ''Sit down,'' he suggested.

Patrice sat. ''There's also the question of why,'' she reflected. ''Why kidnap Zelig?''

''Why not?'' James answered his daughter's question with another. ''What more likely candidate for abduction than Zelig Meyerling, former secretary of state, secret emissary of the Reagan administration, Cold War hawk and modern-day NATO architect, pro-Zionist truce maker, outspoken proponent of both nuclear energy and nuclear arms parity, a rad-lib threat to the conservatives, a neo right-winger to the liberals, and husband to a member of one of the world's wealthiest families that also, incidentally, controls one of the world's most diverse and influential multinational corporations? That's perhaps the biggest problem. There are just too damn many people with too many damn good reasons to abduct Zelig.''

''That's true, Dad. But the flip side is that to every one of them Zelig would be worth more alive as a hostage than he would dead.'' Patrice stood up and grinned. ''My fundament is turning to popsicles,'' she announced, rubbing her bottom ruefully.

''That's the trouble with youth today. Too soft.'' James took her place on the rock.

''Not your progeny.'' Patrice grinned at him. ''We're all hard as nails.''

"Except Lisa." James sighed, serious. "I worry about your sister. She seems to have no focus, no direction. Worse, her energy level always seems so damn low."

"You haven't seen her in a while," Patrice reminded him. "Maybe things have changed." Absentmindedly patting her father's hand, she tried to sound reassuring. "Lisa isn't like me," she told him. "But she is a Stockwell. She'll come out all right." Patrice paused. "Is Lisa meeting you in Athens?" she asked finally.

"No. I'll see her in Crete. She was at Spiro's villa when they got news of the kidnapping. She's been there ever since." James frowned. "That Fitzsimmons girl is with her."

"Don't jump to conclusions, Dad," his daughter advised him. "You've never even met Winifred Fitzsimmons." Her father, Patrice knew, did not accept the relationship between Lisa and Winifred. A product of his generation, James undoubtedly knew that Lisa was a lesbian but did not discuss it. He regarded her homosexuality as an aberration, an illness. Blaming her companion, he believed that if Lisa could only be separated from Winifred Fitzsimmons, she would be cured.

"Michael will be waiting to meet us in Athens." James changed the subject. He stood up and slapped at his own bottom to restore the circulation robbed by the coldness of the rock on which he'd been sitting. "He's been holding down the fort, keeping on top of the embassy, handling the media, leaning on the Company—all that sort of thing."

"The Company? You mean the CIA?"

"The U.S. intelligence community. Whoever's involved. Michael's not been letting it rest. He's been flexing his congressional muscle for me until I get there and exercise some Stockwell muscle of my own."

"Michael behaving congressionally." Patrice smiled. "I wonder if it's interfering with his bed hopping."

"Underneath that playboy image"—James defended his son—"there is the same kind of genuine political ability that the governor had."

"And blew between the sheets, Dad. Don't forget that."

"Don't be envious of your brother." James had always been close to his children. And, unlike many of the fathers of his class, he knew his children. Even so, he was always mildly surprised to realize that the same jealousies that had prevailed through childhood and adolescence continued into adulthood. "Michael is not the lightweight he appears to be. I have faith that he will rise in government well beyond your expectations, Patrice. He is smart, and he is ambitious."

"Sure, Dad. It's just that all Michael's hormones are steroid." Ignoring her father's frown, Patrice started up the path. "It gets cold standing in one place." She explained the move. She fell silent then, as they began the climb, as did James. Finally, though, Patrice spoke the thought that had been on her mind since they began their hike together. "Will you look up Vanessa Brewster while you're in Greece?" she asked carefully.

"Of course." James's voice was firm.

"I used to think those steroid hormones skipped a generation between the governor and Michael. I guess I was wrong."

James stopped and put his hand on her arm, restraining her from walking farther. "I know how clever you are, Patrice. You don't have to be vicious to prove it."

Patrice knew by James's tone that her father didn't appreciate her sarcasm. Nevertheless, she felt defensive. "She's an adventurer, Dad. I can't just stand by keeping my mouth shut and watch you make a fool of yourself over her the way you did before."

"This is not your concern, Patrice. I'm a grown man. I don't need you to supervise my love life, or to pass judgment on it."

"You're my father. I feel an obligation to—"

"There is no obligation, Patrice." James cut her off. "Furthermore, you have no right. None whatsoever. But I will tell you this: even if you did, Vanessa Brewster is not the kind of woman that need cause you a moment's concern. She is neither a gold digger nor an opportunist." James continued his hike up the hill.

"Then what is she?" Patrice demanded, trailing after him. "My God, Father." Only at her most disillusioned

146

with James did she substitute "Father" for "Dad." "This is the woman who was in bed with the Governor when he died. The governor! Your father! And for all we know, she may have killed him with her lovemaking. Not an opportunist? Then what was she doing with a man almost forty years older than she is? And what is she doing with you, Father, who, I might point out, is also considerably older? Do you seriously believe she isn't interested in the Stockwell fortune, the Stockwell prestige, the Stockwell power?"

"Power attracts Vanessa," James granted. "But not because she herself wants to manipulate it. And as for money and prestige, I can assure you they really do not matter to her."

"How can you be so naive?"

"Listen to me, Patrice. I have known happiness with Vanessa that I did not know was still possible for me. If I can recapture that happiness in Greece, I shall. If she is willing to pick up where we left off when she left, then I will be grateful."

Patrice sputtered, then burst out, "Are you in love with this woman?"

"Why, yes," James answered, sounding a little surprised at the admission himself. "I suppose I am."

"Then, Father"—Patrice's full lips were pressed together into an uncharacteristically thin, tight line—"there is nothing more to say."

"Not on that subject," James agreed. They were almost to the ridge now, and James put his hand on Patrice's arm to slow her down. "We do have to have a few words regarding the board before we go inside," he reminded her.

"All right, Dad." Patrice's tone softened. She did not want them to remain angry with each other on the eve of his departure. Who knew how long he would be gone?

"I've spoken to your uncle David about your taking my place on the board. He's agreeable."

"That's a surprise."

"David and I ran things together without a board for many years before the deaths of the governor and Mother," James reminded her. "We always got along.

147

We respect each other's professionalism. Whatever doubts he may have, David honors my judgment. And my judgment is that you are qualified to take my place on the board. I have absolute confidence in your ability."

"I'll do my damnedest not to disappoint you, Dad." Patrice was touched by his faith in her.

"I think, and David agrees, that Max will back up this move."

"Yes. Max and I have always gotten along," Patrice mused as she considered the reactions of the other board members. They would not welcome her with open arms.

"Anyway, as David and I see it, Peter will probably oppose you. He might even insist on a vote to bring the matter back to the probate judge for an opinion. If that vote should pass, the judge's decision would be anybody's guess."

"Peter and I have never liked each other. He was a nasty little boy, and now he's a nasty young man."

"He does tend to see any sort of brouhaha on the board as an opportunity to be turned to his advantage," James conceded.

"That leaves Buffy and Halsey De Vilbiss," James continued. "Halsey will act strictly out of what he perceives to be self-interest, of course. Still, I may have ways of putting pressure on him from a direction he might least expect. As for Buffy—"

"She'll come down against me." Of that Patrice was certain. "Buffy doesn't like me." She didn't tell her father why. He did not know that Buffy's anger was directed at her because Patrice had had a brief affair with Jack Houston. Of course, Buffy and Jack had not been married then, and in truth, it probably bothered her, Patrice, more than it did Buffy. She had imagined herself more than a little in love with Jack. But Jack had made it so obvious that he didn't return the feeling that Buffy never really had any reason for concern. Still, Buffy would not want another woman on the board—not one, anyway, who was both attractive and younger than she was.

They were at the top of the embankment now. James, taking Patrice's arm, helped her over the final crest. Half-

148

way to the manor house, they encountered Jack on his way to the garage.

"Hi, James," Jack greeted her father casually, and then turned to Patrice. "It's good to see you, Patrice." Jack always felt a twinge of guilt when he saw Patrice, but it had been a while and she apparently had taken the affair more casually than it had first seemed. In his eyes, she was too sensible to suffer from a broken heart. He'd never meant to hurt her—he had meant to hurt Buffy, who had been treating him too casually, not taking his proposals of marriage seriously. "How have you been?"

"Hanging in there, Jack. And you?" Outwardly, Patrice was casual. But her heart, as always, was doing a number on her, beating out a quick rhythm to remind her of how deeply she'd once thought she was in love with Jack.

"The same. Hanging in there." His outdoorsy blue eyes regarded Patrice approvingly. "You're looking real good," he told her.

"Thank you." Surely he and her father both must hear that pulsing tattoo!

"I hear you're going to be staying here with us at Riverview for a while."

"Yes. I'm going to keep an eye on Nicholas for Holly."

"Well, it will be really nice to have you here." Jack raised a hand casually before continuing on his way to the garage.

Really nice? Could he actually have come down as hard on those two words as the echo now in Patrice's mind? Stop it! Patrice told herself. He's married now. Still, according to Holly, things weren't exactly going smoothly between Jack and Buffy.

As she walked beside her father, Patrice's eyes followed Jack to the garage. Where was he going? she wondered. And where was her fancy leading her?

26

THE TRIP FROM Riverview to his grandfather's nursing
home took Jack forty minutes. When he arrived at the
home, the scene was SRO on the verandah, rockers and
walkers all bundled up to watch the snow melting into
Yonkers. Grandpa, of course, wasn't there. He preferred
his room, where there was privacy, TV, and a candy stri-
per whose skirt rode up in back every time she bent to
retrieve the bedpan he'd been sure to shove well under
the bed.

"En-*tah!*" Usually he didn't respond when anyone
knocked on his door, but this time his reaction was immediate and hearty. Beaming a welcome at his grandson,
he turned off the soap opera on the TV. "Only one way
out," he greeted Jack. "Thought about it. Kill the
widow."

"Kill Buffy!" Jack had come to expect just about anything from his grandfather, but nevertheless he was
shocked.

"Not Buffy. Heather. Kill Heather!"

"Heather?" Jack stared at him. "Who is Heather,
Grandpa?"

"The widow. Got to kill her, boy. Got to. It's the only
way. Write her out."

"TV," Jack realized. "Heather is a character on TV."

"*Spend the Heart Freely*, boy. Never miss it. More action
than the Superbowl. That widow, though! A man-eater.
After all the men and the oil field, too. Her contract has
got to be canceled."

Jack flinched at the comparison to his own wife. "Could
we put the soaps aside, Grandpa? I came to see you about
business."

"Business." The old man's eyes clouded over. "I'm
retired, boy. Retired courtesy of Governor Matthew Adams Stockwell and his New York State penal system. I
don't do business."

"My business, Grandpa. The insurance business. You said you were going to call somebody and . . ."

The old man stared blankly at him. Then, slowly, his eyes refocused. A slick smile encircled his prune-wrinkled mouth. "Think I'd forget that, Jackie? Think your old grandpa's marbles are on a downhill roll? Well, think again, boy. I made your call. I set up an appointment for you. The back door is open, Jackie. The matches are waiting. Insurance. Reinsurance. That's one business, boy, where the shots can be called at the grass roots. And your old grandpa, why, he has opened the gate to pasture for you, Jackie boy. 'Course, you got to contribute some effort, too. You got to meet your partners halfway."

"You lost me three turns back, Grandpa. What do you mean?"

"Entry, Jackie. It's going to be possible for you to influence paper. And that's the only influence that counts, Jackie, not people, believe me. Yessir! You will be able to lean on paper and make it multiply, or disappear, whichever is most profitable. You do that enough, boy, and what you have done is, you have dropped an army of termites right down into the foundation of Stockwell, Inc. The termites gobble, and the structure starts shuddering, and then one day . . . And the itty-baby grandson that is positioned right, why, he gets to pick up all the pieces. Only like I say, first you have to do your part."

"Which is?"

"Infiltration, boy. We have to know just what high-risk paper the Stockwell board is shuffling. And, since you are married to a member of said board, Jackie—"

"Not a chance, Grandpa." Jack interrupted. "Buffy won't even let me into her bed, let alone her boardroom."

"Powers failing, are they, stud? Well, many's the ambitious man's come a cropper with uncut mustard."

"The problem isn't cutting it, Grandpa. The problem is access to the jar. My wife and I are not sleeping together. We don't even talk these days except for an occasional shouting match."

"You have to have access to the Stockwell board, boy. Without it, my connections won't give you the time of day. I'm saying they specified, Jackie. I'm saying they spelled out that unless such conditions are met, there is no deal.''

"And the conditions are access to the board," Jack mused. "But that doesn't mean it has to be my wife, does it?"

"You can sleep with Governor Matthew Adams Stockwell himself, boy. Just as long as you make yourself privy to just exactly who the policy paper's being bought from.''

"The governor's dead, Grandpa. Almost two years." Jack's voice was weary. "But there is someone . . ." And the way she looked at me today, Jack thought, not proud of himself, that someone is not going to object to my pulling her bows. "I think I can arrange it." He sighed.

"You do that, Jackie. And you get yourself to the library tomorrow at two sharp.''

"The library?" Jack's eyes narrowed on the old man. Was he fading out again? Was he back with *As The World Turns* or some other soap? "What library?"

"Lincoln Center branch, boy. Music reference section. Orchestra collection room. Two sharp. Old friend of mine will meet you there.'' Grandpa cackled, sudden and sharp. "Old jailhouse buddy from back when."

"How old?" Jack was suspicious.

"Halfway twixt you and me, Jackie. Don't you worry. This is a man with both kidneys and never heard of prostate. Sharp ears, his own teeth, and remembers the Dow six days back in a row. Not senile like me, Jackie.'' The old man's lips curled in a grimace that might have been either a smile or a snarl. "Not doddering like me."

"Now, Grandpa—"

"Bucket shops. Messenger scams. Platform man in three top banks. Phony copper mine certificates. Oh, and up-to-date, too. Computer theft. Figures and chips. Goodbye, Mister IBM Chips!'' The cackle went up the register and off; the old man's eyeballs bounced the bumpers.

Was the old man back in never-never land again? Was any of what he was raving about for real? Was anything he'd said today rooted in reality? Was it all just a hodgepodge of old gangster movies on TV, soap operas, and cartoon shows? Was there a jailhouse buddy? Was there really a scheme in the making? Was it wishful thinking—

revenge on the Stockwells—with daytime TV icing? And how crazy was he himself, Jack wondered, to build his hopes on this off-balance old coot's fantasies? Even so . . .

"What's his name, Grandpa?" Jack inquired.

"Hey, boy? Name?" The old man yawned, wide, showing off the back of his throat, not a pretty sight.

"The man I'm going to meet, Grandpa. The man in the library. Who is he?"

"Oh, that name. Well, that doesn't really matter, boy. He's the Don. That's the only name you need, boy. The Don."

I am crazy, Jack decided. Why do I listen to him? The Don? This is insane. It really is insane!

27

"MADNESS! IT REALLY will be madness." Michael was telling Holly and James what to expect as they prepared to ascend to the royal suite of the King George V Hotel, where the press was waiting. The royal suite had been reserved for them by Spiro Papatestus, whose custom it was to take up residence there himself whenever business took him to Athens. Now it was the setting for a media event that would be, as Michael was explaining, the journalistic equivalent of a three-ring circus. Zelig's abduction was the hottest story of the year, and his beautiful socialite wife—a Stockwell by birth, no less—was as much its focal point as Jackie Kennedy had been the center of attention in the wake of the president's assassination.

An hour earlier, Michael Stockwell and Louise Papatestus had met Holly and Michael's father when their plane landed at Athens Airport. Thanks to Spiro's influence, Greek army soldiers had run interference to get the group out of the airport without being waylaid by the international press contingent massed to interview them there. In the Rolls-Royce limousine transporting them to the hotel, Louise had informed Holly that Spiro himself was in Malta, making inquiries of his Libyan and Syrian contacts regarding the possibility of Arab terrorist involvement in the kidnapping. Concerned and sympathetic, Louise held Holly's hand as Michael explained that the American embassy had arranged for an immediate news conference at the King George V.

"Better to get it over with quickly," Michael told Holly and James. "There will be a Mr. Hartwell from the embassy there to speak for the administration. He'll do his best, I'm sure, to keep some order. Still," he had added, "it really will be madness."

It was. A picture being worth a thousand words, and Holly a newly wed wife who was both beautiful and fabulously wealthy, the initial turmoil involving the highly competitive newspaper, wire service, and magazine photographers, as well as the television cameramen, was uncontrollable. Nor was the situation calmed by Holly being accompanied by Mrs. Spiro Papatestus, former model Louise Tyler, whose face and figure had adorned countless covers of international publications. As soon as they arrived, the flash bulbs started popping, and the cameras dollied up to graze the two women's noses with their lenses.

At the very beginning of the picture taking, Michael drew his father on one side. "I'm going down to my own suite now, Dad," he told him. "Five oh two."

James was surprised. "You're not going to stay for the press conference?"

"Best if I don't, Dad. Things are happening very quickly. I want to see what messages have been piling up while I was at the airport. And it's best if someone responsible stays by the telephone. There could be a contact made. Demands from the kidnappers. Any number of related matters. You can handle things here without me. Hartwell from the embassy is a good man."

"He's an administration man." James sounded doubtful. He did not have a great deal of faith in either Hartwell

154

or the Reagan administration. His republicanism, as he was the first to admit, was most comfortable when represented by a power structure based east of the Mississippi and tempered with moderation. "But it's all right, Congressman," he told his son. "We'll manage."

"Five oh two," Michael repeated. "Come down when this circus is over, Dad."

"Will do. And Michael—" James called after him.

"Yes?" Already pushing his way through the crowd of reporters, Michael turned around.

"I'm very impressed with you, son. Very impressed."

Michael nodded. As he turned away and continued toward the door, there was an expression on his face that had not been there in many years. The last time it had appeared was when he heard his father's reaction to Michael's being named valedictorian of his graduating class at St. Andrew's Academy.

After Michael left, James elbowed his way to Holly's side. After several minutes Hartwell, the embassy man, was finally able to declare a moratorium on photographs. James then took his niece's arm and lent his support to her as they mounted the makeshift podium.

Behind them, Louise slipped toward the back of the room. She took a folding chair not far from the door and tried to make herself as inconspicuous as possible. Louise was used to the attention she had received, but the focus now must be on rescuing Zelig Meyerling, and she did not want her presence there to distract from that.

Louise watched as Mr. Hartwell, forceful as his chalk-striped diplomat suit was proper, called the press conference to order. "Mrs. Meyerling and Mr. Stockwell and I will take your questions one at a time," he announced. "One follow-up question, no more. This is a very trying situation for Mrs. Meyerling. If the strain is too much for her, I will terminate these proceedings. Those are the ground rules. Let us begin. The lady from Reuters first, please."

"Mrs. Meyerling, it has been less than three months since your wedding. During most of that time your husband has been in Greece while you have remained in America." The Reuters reporter was a middle-aged woman, square built and businesslike, who spoke English with just the trace of a Belgian Flemish accent. "Was Dr. Meyerling in Greece on a mission for the United States government? If so, please comment on any connection between it and his abduction."

"When my husband went to Greece, I remained behind in order to be with my five-year-old son, who was convalescing from an accident. Yes, Zelig was on a mission for the administration." There had been far too many leaks for Holly to deny it. Besides, as she saw it, acknowledging the mission was a way of holding the administration responsible for Zelig's fate. Beside her, Mr. Hartwell frowned, indicating that he disapproved of the tactic. James suppressed a grim smile. "But I don't know the details of his mission," Holly added.

The reporter followed up. "And at his news conference last night, the president expressed 'the gravest concern' over 'the possible abduction of Zelig Meyerling.' In the past, the administration has insisted that its policy is never to deal with terrorist hostage takers. Have you received any indication that the administration might soften its position on this in the interests of rescuing a man of the stature of Zelig Meyerling, whose predicament may well be the result of his having acted in their behalf?"

"There have been no discussions about this as yet between the administration and myself."

Hartwell's sigh of relief was premature.

"When such discussions take place, will you ask the administration to make such a deal to save your husband's life?" The Reuters reporter tried to sneak in another question.

"Please play by the rules." Hartwell stepped in and came down hard. "We'll take the next question from—"

"No, wait." Holly interrupted him. "I would like to answer that. The answer is yes. I think that the administration has an *obligation*"—Holly spoke the word defiantly—"to my husband. If that means softening their position in regard to hostage situations, then so be it."

As James nodded his support, several questions were shouted into the resulting hubbub. Holly made no effort to answer them as Hartwell pounded with his fist against the microphone until some semblance of order was restored. He did not look happy.

"You, sir." Hartwell pointed to a reporter from the London *Times*.

"Are you saying, Mrs. Meyerling, that you expect the government of the United States to alter a policy it has held to through several hostage situations in the interests of your husband? And Mr. Stockwell, sir, does this also accurately reflect the position of the Stockwell family?"

"I stand by what I have said," Holly refused to back down.

"Dr. Meyerling's safe return is the primary concern of the Stockwells." James stood equally firm.

"Is it the position of the Stockwell family, then, sir, that their protégé Zelig Meyerling, now an in-law, deserves preferential treatment over other hostages such as wire service chiefs and university executives?"

James responded strongly. "That is a 'Do you still beat your wife?' question if ever I have heard one. We are concerned here with a specific situation, and I see absolutely no point in speculating about such hypothetical choices."

Upset by the loaded phrasing of the question, Holly once more spelled out bluntly her own position. "I don't speak for the Stockwell family. I speak for myself. I am a woman whose husband may be in very grave danger. Rightly or wrongly, his safety comes first with me."

"Before the safety of other hostages who—"

"*You have had your two questions!*" Hartwell roared. "*Athens News* now." He gestured to a thin Greek man whose hand had been waving in the air.

"Zelig Meyerling has long been known for his strong pro-Zionist stands," the Athenian said softly. "Does the administration believe that the Arabs are responsible for his abduction?"

"We make no assumptions and investigate all possibilities." Hartwell chose his words carefully. "As you say, Dr. Meyerling has been pro-Israel for years. During that time, nothing ever happened to him. So the question is, Why should the Arabs act against him now?"

"Was his mission to Greece involved with Mideast problems?"

"I am not authorized to comment on whether or not there was any such mission, and what its nature may have been." Hartwell quickly called on the *Time* magazine reporter.

"I'd like to follow up on that with a question for Mr. Stockwell," he said. "Many hostage incidents from 1973 right up through the present have been traced to the Abu Nidal group with rumors of both Libyan and Syrian sponsorship. Zelig Meyerling has been outspoken in recommending that the United States respond militarily. Has there been any indication that he may have fallen into the hands of Abu Nidal?"

"Not to my knowledge at this time," James replied.

"Perhaps, Mr. Stockwell, you would comment on this, then: Dr. Meyerling was staying at the Papatestus villa on Crete. Our stringer in Malta reports that Spiro Papatestus has been seen at a Valetta cafe in the company of the Libyan minister of petroleum, Ezzadine al Mabrouk. In the past, Ezzadine al Mabrouk has been a conduit to terrorist groups rumored to be sponsored by Libya—groups such as Abu Nidal. Mr. Stockwell, is Spiro Papatestus negotiating for Dr. Meyerling's release?"

My God! In the back of the room, Louise was shaken not so much by the question but by a new awareness that her husband was right: they were under constant surveillance. He was followed. For people like us, there is no privacy.

"Spiro Papatestus is a good friend and related to Mrs. Meyerling and myself by marriage." James chose his words carefully. "Other than that, I'm in the dark."

"Mrs. Meyerling." At a signal from Hartwell, the *Newsweek* reporter followed up on her *Time* magazine colleague's question. "If Mr. Papatestus could influence the Arabs on behalf of your husband, he would, would he not?"

"I'm sure that he would. As my uncle said, Spiro Papatestus is a friend."

"Is he 'a friend' authorized . . ."

Louise did not hear the rest of the question. At that

moment there was a garbled murmur in her ear, a breath, warm and intimate. "A distraction," were the words she heard. "We must have a distraction." The hands on her shoulders were strong, preventing her from turning around, but at the same time there was something intimate and sexual about the touch that signaled to Louise that the whisperer kneeling behind her was Michael Stockwell.

"What?" she said, losing track of the give and take between the reporters and those on the podium. "What did you say?"

"Something's come up. We have to get Dad and Holly out of here and down to my room without making it obvious that they've been summoned."

"But what can we—"

"I don't know. I only know we have to do something quickly." The urgency in Michael's voice was unmistakable.

"All right." Louise reacted automatically. She got to her feet.

As she rose, Hartwell was calling upon the representative from *Atlas*, the most widely read journal of opinion in the Mideast. Gray-haired and distinguished, the Jordan-based correspondent was smoldering. The questions and answers regarding the probability of Arab involvement in the Meyerling kidnapping had deeply upset him.

"The Arabs." He spoke slowly and ironically. "Everybody's favorite villain. When will the Western media learn that there is no such thing as 'the Arabs'? Anti-Israel as it is, the Arab viewpoint runs a gamut. We are no more monolithic than the Communists or the democracies. There are differences as great among the Arabs as between China and Russia and Yugoslavia, or Sweden and the United States and South Africa."

"That is a provocative statement, not a question," Hartwell pointed out. "Your question please, sir?" He did not notice Louise in the back of the room as she started down the aisle bisecting the row of folding chairs.

"Very well." Neither did the *Atlas* correspondent pay attention to the progression of the tall international beauty with the crown of red-gold hair as she strode toward the podium. "Aside from my nefarious fellow Arabs, Mr. Hartwell, does the American government have any leads which might point to other groups having abducted Dr. Meyerling? And if so, will you please name the groups under suspicion."

"Other possibilities are of course being considered. It would be premature to name those under investigation. It wouldn't be fair to—"

Almost to the podium, Louise paused and looked around her as if disoriented. A low sound came from her throat. Her hand fluttered to her forehead, claiming attention.

"Of course not. Only the Arabs may be named. All right!" The Arab reporter cut off Hartwell's protest and started to phrase his second question. "Recently, various radical European peace groups—" He broke off as Louise moaned a second time, louder, and swayed. Like everyone else in the room, he stared as Louise's tall, graceful body crumpled to the floor in a faint.

"You can put me down now." The closing of the door to Michael's suite shut out the sounds of the reporters trailing in their wake, and Louise opened her eyes to find herself staring up Michael's square chin to his Robert Redford cheekbones. Handsome, but decidedly not her type. "Please," she added.

Michael grinned. "First time I've ever had you in my arms. Why not let me enjoy it?"

"Because I'm not enjoying it," Louise said sharply. Something about Michael reminded her of the boys she had dated in high school and college.

"That's gratitude!" He dumped her unceremoniously on the couch. "The next time you faint, I'm just going to let you lie there."

"I didn't really faint, and you know it." Louise stood up and smoothed down her jacket and skirt. "Where are Holly and James?" she asked.

"They're right behind us, hacking their way through the media forest."

As if on cue, Holly and James entered the suite. James pushed the door shut firmly behind them. Concerned,

Holly strode straight over to Louise. "Are you all right?" she wanted to know.

"I'm fine."

"You should be lying down."

"I'm okay, Holly. Nothing really happened."

"You fainted." James was already heading for the telephone. "That's not nothing. I'm going to call—"

"Don't do that." Louise's tone was exasperated, but to Holly and James it seemed only further evidence that she wasn't well.

"Put down the phone, Dad." Michael stepped in. "There's nothing wrong with Louise. It was a trick. I had to get you and Holly out of there, away from the reporters."

"Something's happened," Holly realized. "Tell me."

"There was a call from the British embassy." Michael filled them in tersely. "They wanted to talk to Spiro."

"Spiro?" Louise echoed. "What about?"

"They wouldn't tell me. When I told them he wasn't here, they asked if I could put either my father or Holly in touch with them. They said it was urgent. I said you'd get right back to them."

"They've heard something about Zelig!" Holly had gone quite pale.

"Don't jump to conclusions." James took her by the arm. "Come in the bedroom, and we'll call them back right away."

"I left the number for you on the nightstand," Michael called after his father as James and Holly went in the bedroom and closed the door behind them. There was an instant of strained silence. Then he turned to Louise. "How about a drink?" he suggested.

"Sherry would be nice."

He fetched it. "You're looking very well, Louise." His eyes followed the classically voluptuous curve of her body up and then down. What a waste, he thought. Married to that Ancient Mariner.

"Thank you." She didn't miss his appraisal or his interest. She understood its nature very well. She had known many men like Michael, and she had known Michael himself since he was a little boy. His lust was transparent. "How does the British embassy come into it?" she asked.

"It's very complicated," Michael told her. "But fortunately you've come to just the right person to explain it. As a United States congressman, I am privy to all sorts of information regarding the operations of foreign embassies abroad. I'll tell you what—after the press conference, have lunch with me, and I'll explain it all to you."

"Sorry. I have shopping to do." Louise gave him one of her stoniest stares.

"I know all the best stores," Michael quipped gamely.

"I never go to the best stores." The firmness of Louise's tone stressed the rejection in her reply. She was not interested in the handsome congressman. "And I prefer shopping alone."

Michael, not used to being rejected, frowned. To Louise, his expression was that of a sulky little boy. He was not accustomed to being so summarily dismissed by attractive women. His ego did not take kindly to it.

I do believe he'll stamp his foot next, Louise thought to herself, not amused. She thought of Xanthos then, of making love with him. Michael with his clean-cut, All-American good looks seemed far too tame by comparison.

The strain between them was relieved as James and Holly emerged from the bedroom. Quickly and tersely, James summed up their return call to the British embassy. "They've received a request—an anonymous request. The caller claimed to be a Palestinian freedom fighter and said that if the underground was contacted through the usual channels by the Church of England, the contact would then be routed on to his people, who are prepared to discuss a matter of international concern."

"The Church of England?" Louise was perplexed.

"The British embassy believes the caller's people want to talk to Terry Waite."

"Who is Terry Waite?" Louise asked.

"He is the special representative of the archbishop of Canterbury and the Anglican church's chief hostage negotiator. He's had remarkable success with both the IRA and the Provos in northern Ireland. More recently he's been active in the Mideast." Michael turned to his father

162

and Holly. "Did the caller say he was willing to negotiate Zelig's release with Terry Waite?"

"Zelig was never mentioned." Holly's tone was grim.

"Then what makes the British think—?"

"The timing," James told him. "Although no specific names were mentioned, the fact that this dissident group—whichever group it is—has called and asked to contact Waite just after Zelig was kidnapped would indicate that a connection is likely. Certainly we have to act on that assumption."

"Why did the embassy ask for Spiro first?" Louise asked.

"They know about his Libyan contacts. They want his opinion on the bona fides of whoever it is who's trying to contact Waite."

"I'll see that Spiro contacts them," Louise promised.

"Good." James glanced at his wristwatch. "We'd best get back to that press conference," he told Holly. "We don't want those media vultures speculating any more than necessary."

"Tell them you waited with me until I was feeling better, and now I've gone to see my doctor," Louise advised.

"You're not coming back in with us?"

"It will look better if I don't. And besides, I have some shopping to do."

"Solitary shopping." Michael's tone was heavily sarcastic.

Louise ignored it. She offered each of them in turn her white-gloved hand—Michael for but an instant—and then she was gone.

28

BACK IN THE royal suite, Holly and James were impatiently awaited, particularly by the *Atlas* correspondent whose question had been interrupted by Louise's swoon.

"I was about to ask," he reminded them, "about radical European groups who might be involved in the abduction. Recently, *The Spectator* of London speculated that Zelig Meyerling, in his role as U.S. government emissary, would offer Greece a nuclear reactor and guarantee uranium to fuel it from Stockwell Industries. In return he would seek a guarantee by the Papandreou government of Greece's NATO commitment and a beefing up of American bases and forces in Greece. Specifically, is Greenpeace, which opposes a nuclear capability for Greece on both environmental and world peace grounds, under suspicion? And if so, does that suspicion extend to those Stockwell relatives associated with Greenpeace?"

"To my knowledge, Greenpeace is committed firmly to a policy of nonviolence." Hartwell fielded the question. "They have never been known to abduct anybody, or to hold any hostages. And I have no reason to believe that any members of the Stockwell family involved in Greenpeace would do Dr. Meyerling any harm."

The Australian newsman now called on by Hartwell directed his remarks to James. "On the heels of Zelig Meyerling coming to Greece, one Halsey De Vilbiss, a member of the board of Stockwell Industries, met with Spiro Papatestus here in Athens. As has been noted, Mr. Papatestus is in contact with the Libyan minister of petroleum. It is no secret that Stockwell Industries is having a problem getting its crude refined. It is also no secret that Libyan refineries are standing idle. Before coming to Greece, Zelig Meyerling headed the Stockwell Institute, a think tank that in the past has advised the U.S. government. It is rumored that there is a connection between his mission for the Reagan administration and a deal between

Stockwell Industries and Libya. Your comments, Mr. Stockwell, please."

"The Stockwell Institute has always been center of the road in terms of Republican politics, and the Reagan administration does not look to it for policy." James's answer was short and to the point.

Hartwell gestured for another questioner. "You, sir." He had not identified the reporter he selected, and the choice was unfortunate.

"Anatole Koronski, TASS." He identified himself as the representative of the official Soviet Union press agency. "So far there has been no consideration of right-wing involvement in the abduction. The followers of the Greek colonels, for instance. Meyerling opposed the colonels. Other powerful American interests did not. Indeed, they supported them with both money and intelligence information. I refer, of course, to the CIA. Now, Mrs. Meyerling, do you grant the possibility that either Greek or American right-wing interests committed to the toppling of the Papandreou government might have the strongest reasons for wanting your husband out of the way?"

"I have faith that the American government will look into all the possibilities," Holly told him.

"Right-wing fanatics exert great influence in the Reagan administration, Mrs. Meyerling. Will they then investigate themselves?"

"No comment."

Hartwell and James both nodded approval—as much at the coldness of Holly's tone as at her words.

"Mrs. Meyerling—" The next question came from a pool reporter for the far-flung Rupert Murdoch newspapers. "Have you and your family considered that your husband may have been kidnapped by some faction of organized crime? The Stockwells are, after all, involved heavily in both real estate and insurance. The mob has been making inroads in both areas. Could not the seizing of Dr. Meyerling be a ploy to exert pressure on the Stockwell family?"

"I hadn't heard that possibility mentioned before,"

Holly's response was thoughtful and cautious. "Certainly it bears looking into."

"It might even be a simple mob kidnapping for ransom," the Murdoch man pointed out. "Would you comment on that, please."

"It could indeed be just that," Holly granted.

Unwittingly, she had supplied the *New York Post* with its next day's headline: ZELIG'S BRIDE FINGERS MAFIA IN DIPLO-NAP CASE!

Hartwell called on a reporter from Crete.

"Mrs. Meyerling," he asked, "there is a strong Greek movement to have NATO bases removed from Greece. Your husband stood in opposition to this. It has been mentioned here before that persuading Greece to remain in NATO was the reason for his trip. Will you either confirm or deny this?"

"I can do neither."

"If contact is made by the abductors and it turns out that their price for releasing Dr. Meyerling is the severance of Greece from NATO, what will you do?"

"Don't answer that!" Hartwell broke in quickly. "Neither Mrs. Meyerling nor Mr. Stockwell can have any opinion regarding such an unlikely hypothesis. It is a matter of United States foreign policy."

"Will you respond to the question for your government, then, Mr. Hartwell?"

"No. I will not." Hartwell was showing strain. "This press conference is over."

Flanked by James and Hartwell, Holly made her way through the crowd of reporters and past the television cameras from the royal suite to Michael's more modest quarters. Here Hartwell left them to return to the embassy. After he'd gone, Holly, pleading exhaustion, excused herself to go into the bedroom and lie down.

The door had just closed behind her and Michael was mixing his father a drink when the telephone rang. He answered it. A woman's voice, American from the sound of it, asked to speak to Holly. Michael knocked at the bedroom door and told Holly there was a call for her.

166

She picked up the phone from the nightstand phone beside the bed. "Holly Meyerling here," she said.

"Mrs. Meyerling." The voice on the other end did not identify itself. "I have to talk to you."

"To whom am I speaking?"

"That's not important. What is important is that we meet. Can you come at five-thirty this evening to the out-door cafe in the Syntagma Square park directly opposite your hotel? Just take a table. I'll recognize you."

"Who is this?" Holly asked. "Why should I agree to meet you?"

"I have information, Mrs. Meyerling." The woman took an audible breath. "Information regarding the kid-napping of your husband."

29

LATER THAT AFTERNOON, four P.M., Athens time, Michael and James sat across from each other at a table in the Syntagma Square outdoor cafe and sipped their drinks. The reporters had cleared out, and Holly was taking a nap. James, adding soda to his Scotch, regarded Michael's ouzo with distaste.

"How can you drink that?" he asked. "It tastes like licorice, and it's twice as sticky."

Michael shrugged. "When in Rome . . ."

"This is Athens."

"Same principle."

"No wonder the country's in the shape it's in, when our congressmen can't tell Greece from Rome," James joked.

"It's not congressmen you should be worrying about," Michael told his father. "It's the White House."

"Oh?"

"Zelig was the last man the administration should have sent over here."

"Criticism of the administration from you, Michael?" James raised an eyebrow. "I am surprised. I thought you were a dedicated Reaganite."

"Loyal. Not necessarily dedicated. I'm a politician, Dad. I always check which side the pita's buttered on and make damn sure that's the side that's face up when it drops."

"And Zelig was dropped facedown?"

"His views on Greece are well known. There's a strong voice with policy input that's diametrically opposed to them. Zelig's disappearance at this particular point in time is—well, fortuitous—from their point of view."

"Are you saying he might have been snatched by American right-wingers?" James narrowed his eyes at his son.

"Well, not exactly *by* them. For them, maybe."

"The CIA—?"

"Whoever." Michael shrugged and licked the ouzo crystals from his upper lip. "Probably not the CIA itself. But . . ."

"You sound like that Moscow mouthpiece from TASS."

"I'm not saying that's what happened. I'm only saying it is one outside possibility."

"Jesus." James was disgusted. "What the hell is the country coming to, anyway?" He scowled at his son. "And you, Michael? Were you against Zelig trying to patch things up with the Papandreou government?"

"They're Socialist and maybe leaning toward Moscow. The colonels may have been gangsters, but they were pro-American gangsters. We should be withholding support from the Papandreou government, not making deals with it. Still, I would never go along with anything like kidnapping Zelig."

"But you do play ball with the cowboys, Michael."

"I'm a team player, Dad. To get elected, I have to get nominated. A politician has to compromise just to get a chance at bat."

168

"At bat for what, Michael? You were only just elected to Congress."

"Maybe so, Dad. But I still have to look to the future. The Gipper's people are in control of the Republican party these days. If you're a Republican, you either play ball with the right, or you don't play."

"And you play," James sighed. "Well, Michael, you're a chip off the governor's block all right. After senator, then what?"

"I'll be older then, and presidential fever is genetic."

"Thank God it skipped me," James said fervently, draining the last of his Scotch. "One word of advice, though, Michael. Americans are a very moralistic people. You'd better clean up your bachelor act if you've got your eye on the White House."

"Are you kidding, Dad? Warren Harding's backstairs mistress. FDR and Lucy Mercer. JFK and everything from Marilyn Monroe to Mafia molls. Even the Gipper getting a divorce and marrying Nancy with a bun in the oven." Michael ticked them off. "Americans moralistic? On the contrary, Dad. The country loves a lover."

"You're right, Michael. I'm behind the times. Ignore all fatherly advice, and your head will end up on Mount Rushmore." James stood up. "I'm going to stroll over to the British embassy," he announced, "and see if they've heard anything further regarding the possibility of a negotiation through Terry Waite."

"Good luck, Dad. Catch you later."

After his father left, Michael ordered another ouzo. Sipping it slowly, he stared into the late-afternoon sun-rainbowed fountains that were the centerpiece of Syntagma Square. Thinking about Louise Papatestus, he scowled to himself. He couldn't get her disinterested hazel eyes and long, tousled red-gold tresses out of his mind. By rejecting him, she had made herself all the more desirable.

That was probably why, for an instant, he thought he glimpsed her cutting across Syntagma Square. The vision was quick, and peripheral, and Michael had to pivot quickly in his chair to check it out. Yes! There was that crown of loose, long apricot hair gleaming in the late-afternoon sunlight. On impulse, he got to his feet and strode diagonally across the square to intercept her.

But it wasn't Louise. Drawing closer, Michael saw that this woman was much shorter—and younger. Also, she was wearing a denim jacket, jeans, and an oversized turtleneck, whereas when Louise had left the King George before, she had been smartly dressed in a tailored designer suit and a contrasting jacquard blouse. Still, there was something familiar about this young woman. Michael sped up and walked past her for a clearer look.

"Carrie!" he exclaimed. "Carrie Tyler." Of course. All the Tylers—Louise, Carrie, all their cousins and siblings—had those same almond-shaped hazel eyes and that apricot-colored hair.

"No." Michael was corrected with a certain amount of irritation. "I'm Beth. Sorry to disappoint you, Michael."

"I'm definitely not disappointed." By habit, Michael was gallant. "Not only have I run into beauty, but brains, too. Let me buy you a drink."

Beth allowed him to lead her back to his table. "If only you were as ethical as you are eloquent."

"What's wrong with my ethics?" Michael masked his irritation and signaled the waiter for two more ouzos.

"The mealy in your mouth when you make speeches and the company you keep."

"Can't argue with that." Michael didn't take offense. He couldn't take Beth seriously. Besides, there was a certain warmth in her tone. "You've convinced me. I'll throw it all up and join Greenpeace."

"They'd never take you. Handsome as you are, you'd tarnish their image."

"Why, Bethie, I didn't know you thought I was handsome." Michael reached over and took her hand, casually flirting with her.

"Just a statement of fact." She blushed but did not try to remove her hand from his.

"What brings you to Athens?"

"Greenpeace business. I had to arrange for some supplies to be dropped off for us in Crete." Beth picked up

170

the small tulip glass of ouzo the waiter set down in front of her and sipped the thick, sweet, clear liqueur.

"You're sure you aren't dropping off the ransom note in the Meyerling kidnapping?"

"That's not funny." Beth's voice rose in defense. "Greenpeace doesn't take hostages, or do anything else to hurt people."

"I know. I know." Michael held up his hand palm out in a gesture of peace. "But you'd be surprised what some others think. Particularly after that caper you pulled with the Papatestus shipment of Stockwell uranium. That was obviously aimed at embarrassing the family. Well, we're a lot more than embarrassed with this thing with Zelig."

"It really is awful. But it's absurd to think Greenpeace would have anything to do with it."

"Sure." Michael's tone was placating. He changed the subject. "How have you been, anyway, Beth? Are you and Carrie and Deke still all together on that sloop lying in wait for polluters and arms shippers?"

"Yes. For the time being."

"And are you and Deke still an item?" Michael remembered having heard via the family grapevine that his cousin Deke and Beth were lovers.

"No." Beth's answer was short and unhappy. "That's over." She took another swallow of ouzo.

"Carrie?" It wasn't hard to guess, knowing the people involved.

Beth nodded.

"Want to talk about it?" Michael's tone was sympathetic.

"Definitely not." The pink tip of her tongue slipped out briefly to lick the licorice sugar from the rim of her goblet. "Change the subject. Have you heard how Holly is coping? This business with Zelig, I mean?"

"She's in Athens. She got in this morning. She's right across the street at the King George, as a matter of fact. Why don't you come on up and say hello to her? She can use all the support she can get."

"You mean now?"

"Why not?" Michael signaled the waiter and paid the check. He took Beth's arm and guided her across the busy street and into the King George V. The concierge regarded her jeans and denim jacket askance from his little booth just inside the lobby, but then he recognized Michael and tipped his gold-braided cap politely.

Beth stuck out her tongue at the concierge.

It happened so unexpectedly that Michael's jaw dropped. When Beth giggled at the expression on his face, he reacted. "Why on earth did you do that?" he demanded.

"I was here just half an hour ago," Beth explained. "I asked to use the loo. He wouldn't let me. He threw me out. Snobby twit."

"The bathroom is reserved for guests of the hotel," Michael explained as he guided her past the operator into the express elevator to the royal suite.

"Not the one in the cocktail lounge."

"For patrons of the lounge, then."

"Michael, there's something you should know. You can cut farm subsidies and food stamps and even Social Security, but when you lock the downtrodden out of the johns . . . then comes the revolution!" The elevator stopped, and Beth exited ahead of Michael.

She followed him through the ornately gilded doors into the huge sitting room and flopped down on a Louis XIV divan. "Comes the revolution!" she murmured as Michael went to fetch Holly.

He knocked at the door of the bedroom Holly was using. When there was no answer, he opened the door and peeked inside inquiringly. The bed was rumpled but empty. "Holly?" he called, thinking she might be in the bathroom washing up.

"She isn't here," Beth called from behind him. "There's a note here for James. It said she's gone out and will be back in time for dinner."

"Oh." Michael rejoined her.

"If I hadn't found this note," Beth told him. "I might think you planned this to get me up here alone with you."

"My God, Beth. We've known each other since we were kids. I wouldn't try to seduce you like that."

"Why not? You seduced Carrie. She told me you did."

"Like hell. It was the other way around."

"Oh? Well, we are twins." Beth's hazel eyes gleamed.

"Are you sure you're not Carrie?" Michael was confused. "You sure do sound more like Carrie than the Beth I've known all my life."

"Well, maybe I've decided it's about time I stopped fading into the woodwork while Carrie has all the fun," Beth told him. "If I was Carrie, though," she added, "I'll bet you'd have made a pass at me by now."

"If you were Carrie, I wouldn't have to make a pass at you."

"Oh? Is that so?" Beth got up and walked to where Michael was sitting on a straight-backed French empire chair with thin, curved legs. The chair was not as fragile as it appeared. It held her weight easily as she settled onto Michael's lap. She clasped her hands around the back of his neck and kissed him.

I'll be damned, Michael thought as his hand moved automatically to the softness of her breast rising against the cotton turtleneck. Is it possible, he wondered dizzily, that this is Carrie pretending to be Beth coming on like Carrie?

"A politician should know better than to pigeonhole people." The kiss over, the tip of Beth's tongue tickled Michael's ear as she murmured into it. "And that goes double—pun intended—for pigeonholing twins."

"Why do I have the feeling that you're trying to prove something?" The small, firm breast nuzzling Michael's palm through the material was rising and falling rapidly.

"Why do you feel that you have to go on talking?" Beth countered. She pushed back from him a moment and slipped off her short denim jacket. Then she pulled the turtleneck free from the waistband of her jeans and raised it. Her firmly molded, uptilted breasts appeared, the berry tips aroused and quivering.

Michael responded. He leaned in and kissed the deep cleft between her bare breasts. Beth laughed with pleasure as she felt his tongue. When his lips closed around one of her nipples, her laugh turned to an audible moan of excitement.

He sucked at her breast, licking the nipple at the same time with his tongue. Beth writhed over his lap, eliciting

173

a hardening response. Again Michael was reminded of Carrie and that time they'd made love a year or so ago. He guided Beth's hand to the zipper of his pants.

"What do you want me to do?" Beth's voice was tremulous in his ear.

So this was Beth. Carrie, of course, would not have had to ask. "Unzip it," he told her.

Beth stood up and leaned over him. "Now take mine off," she said, squeezing him intimately.

Michael opened her belt, unbuttoned her jeans, and pulled them and her panties down. The red-gold triangle of her pubic hair was moist with her desire.

"Jesus!" Michael cupped Beth's bare bottom and pulled her to him. Half-stumbling, she settled to his lap again, straddling him. Panting, her short fingernails digging through the material of his shirt into his shoulder, she impaled herself. Michael rose, hard and eager, to meet her.

"That's it!" Beth was beside herself. "Fuck me!" The unaccustomed word fell harshly from her lips.

As Michael complied, she started to sob and to move more and more violently. "Beth!" she babbled. "I'm Beth! There's a difference! Not Carrie. Beth! Tell me you can tell! Tell me you can tell the difference!"

"I can tell the difference," Michael muttered. A tiger by the tail! he thought, straining, feeling the pressure building in his scrotum, ridging the shaft buried deep inside Beth. A tigress! he amended as she bore down hard, her lower body shaking with spasms.

"I'm Beth!" Her explosion triggered his.

"Beth!" he echoed, clutching her close, prolonging her climax and his own as well. "Beth . . ."

A while later Michael waited while Beth finished up in the bathroom. She came out smiling. "My only problem is making sure he knows," she announced.

"Who knows what?" Michael was bewildered. Surely she wouldn't tell Deke about this.

"The concierge in the lobby. I want him to know that I have used one of the King George V Hotel's lousy bathrooms. And in the royal suite, no less."

174

Michael was relieved. He laughed out loud. "I'll swear out a statement, and you can have it notarized and hand it to him yourself."

"On official U.S. congressional stationery," Beth suggested, starting to smile.

"Absolutely." Michael returned her smile. "Listen," he said. "I'm curious. Why have you become so competitive with Carrie sexually?"

Beth reddened. "That's not true."

"I'm not deaf. And I'm not dense, either. Plus I have this uncomfortable feeling that if you hadn't known that Carrie and I made it, this afternoon would never have happened. You don't have to tell me what it's all about if you don't want to. But I wouldn't be human if I wasn't curious."

Beth thought a moment and then shrugged. "All right." She told him about finding Carrie in bed with Deke. "And," she finished, "he said he thought it was me. He still claims that's true. Like I should be happy to hear he couldn't tell the difference between me and Carrie."

"Your twin stole your lover," Michael summed up.

"She didn't steal him, she just used him. Then she moved on to someone else. A fundamentalist Moslem fanatic, no less."

"Carrie won't get much action there," Michael pointed out. He thought a moment. "So Carrie used Deke, and you used me," he realized.

"Not really." Beth blushed. "I am attracted to you."

"Well, I don't have a hump on my back and run around ringing cathedral bells," Michael said dryly. "I suppose that made me acceptable."

"Why are you talking like that? Wasn't I any good?" Beth asked in a small, woeful voice.

"Don't be silly." Michael relented. "You were great. It was marvelous."

"As good as Carrie?"

"Much better. Much more passionate." Truly, Michael couldn't remember too well what making love to Carrie had been like. However, he was not by nature an unkind man, so he had cultivated a postcoital technique of always

175

telling women what he assumed they wanted to hear. "Carrie isn't in your league. If Deke really couldn't tell the difference, he must have been zonked."

"You're really sweet to say that, Michael."

"I mean it." Michael glanced at his watch. "And to prove it," he said, "why don't we go down to my room for an encore. If we hang around here, James or Holly will come back, and we'll have blown the chance."

"Okay." Beth grinned, reassured that she really had pleased him, that she really wasn't an erotic wimp compared with Carrie. "I can catch up with Holly later tonight." She linked arms with Michael. "To tell the truth, I'd forgotten all about her. Poor Holly. I wonder where she went."

30

HOLLY WAS RIGHT across the street from the King George IV Hotel at the very same outdoor cafe where Beth had encountered Michael. She was dawdling over a dry martini when the woman she had come to meet finally arrived.

"Sorry to keep you waiting," the woman apologized, trying and failing to smooth the wrinkles from her rather baggy skirt as she sat down across from Holly. "My taxi got caught in the rush-hour traffic. Sometimes I think the most ancient ruins in Greece are its potholed roads." She patted some loose tendrils back into the bun of her brown hair, but they immediately sprang free again.

"Madam?" The waiter was at her elbow.

"I'll have one of those." She nodded toward Holly's drink. "I suspect I'll need it," she observed to no one in particular as the waiter moved away. She smiled nervously at Holly from a face free of makeup.

Holly waited in silence.

"I don't think I'll introduce myself," the woman said with a small, abrupt laugh. "I mean, I could make up a name, but what's the point?"

"None at all," Holly told her. "I recognize you. You're Vanessa Brewster."

"Damn. I was hoping you wouldn't remember me. I mean, we've never met, have we?"

"Not really. But there were pictures of you in the paper when my grandfather died. You were at the funeral, and I was in probate court the day you testified over his estate."

"I see." Vanessa waylaid her drink on its way from the waiter's hand to the table and took a large swallow.

"Why should you care if I know who you are?" Holly asked. "Why are you so nervous? And why did you want us to meet like this?"

"It would have been easier if you hadn't identified me, if you didn't know I was involved with your grandfather. I suppose you know about James and me, too."

"Yes, I do. Uncle James is here with me, you know. I'm sure he's going to want to see you."

"He may change his mind about that."

"Why should he? What is this all about, anyway?" Holly's tone turned insistent. "You said on the phone you had some information about Zelig."

Vanessa gulped down the rest of her martini. She took a deep breath. "He was with me before he was kidnapped," she said.

"With you?" Holly looked at her blankly.

"I'd taken a room in the Plaka. That's where he was."

"In your room?" Holly blinked.

"Yes." Vanessa looked down at the cocktail napkin in front of her. "We made love. I'm sorry."

"You made love?" Holly shrank into herself. Her next words were cold: "I see."

"Look," Vanessa said, "I don't know how to say this, or even if you'll hear it, but I have to try. It didn't mean anything. It really didn't. Zelig was here alone away from you. I was here alone away from James, and—"

"James." Holly's voice was flat. "You do like the men

in my family, don't you Miss Brewster." She eyed her coldly, seeing a drab, thirtyish woman, her unmade-up face lined with strain. I am much more attractive. Much more. How could Zelig? How could he? "Yes, you certainly do. First my grandfather. Then my uncle. Now my husband."

"Please, Mrs. Meyerling—"

"Do me a favor, will you, Miss Brewster? Stay the hell away from my son. I mean, he's only five years old, but—"

"I don't blame you for being angry," Vanessa said quietly. "If it makes you feel better, go right ahead. From where you're sitting, I've got it coming."

"From where I'm sitting—" Holly's voice started to rise. She closed her lips firmly and looked down at the table in front of her, making an effort to stay in control. She saw her fists were clenched and put them in her lap where they would be concealed by the tablecloth. "From where I'm sitting," she repeated in a low, calm voice. "And just where is that, Miss Brewster?"

"I'd really like to answer that. Your husband and I had a brief, meaningless affair—a physical release, for Zelig a way of easing the tension he was under. Nor did we kid each other that it was any more than that. He was not—is not—in love with me, not even infatuated, nor I with him. I love James. Zelig loves you."

"How neat. How very neat. Such a tidy package. Such a reasonable arrangement. Tell me, Miss Brewster, do you rationalize all your affairs with married men so ingeniously?"

"I guess it's no use." Vanessa nodded more to herself than to Holly. "I should have known better than to try to make you understand."

"Oh, but I do understand. And I'm grateful, too. After all, Zelig and you must have waited a full eight weeks from our wedding day before jumping into bed together."

"It's useless. I just wish you weren't so—so—" Vanessa groped for the right word. "Sensitive," she decided finally.

"Sensitive?" Holly's voice rose to a shriek. "What

would you know about that, Miss Brewster? I wouldn't expect that sensitivity is exactly your strong point."

"The hell it isn't. If I wasn't sensitive to your hurt, I wouldn't have bothered trying to ease it. If I was a callous woman, I wouldn't even be here."

"I wonder about that. Just why are you here, Miss Brewster? Why did you arrange this meeting? Why confess at all?"

"I thought the information might be of use in getting Zelig back. I thought it might be helpful to fill the gap in his movements that day. I really did hope you would see that the important thing is Zelig's return, not an interlude that was really the most casual of infidelities. Really, Mrs. Meyerling." Vanessa leaned her face close to Holly's and earnestly tried to get past her hostility. "Isn't that what's important? Getting Zelig back?"

"Yes. But coming from you, it's just more rationalizing."

"Can't you stop yourself from being so judgmental, Mrs. Meyerling? Zelig was gone two months. Two months without sex is a long time for a man like Zelig. Surely you must see that."

"I lived through the same two months," Holly erupted hotly. "And I did not—"

"But were you never tempted, Mrs. Meyerling? Truly now. Were you never once even tempted?"

Righteously, Holly started to deny that she had been. Then her deep blue eyes met Vanessa's clear gaze. She cut off the words before she spoke them. She said nothing.

Holly was thinking of Jack.

31

Jack Houston surrendered his queen to the ace and spread his hands to indicate he had no more cards. "You win the war," he told Nicholas.

"Then you have to come belly whopping with me," the little boy declared. It had snowed the night before, and all through the card game his eyes had strayed hungrily out the window and over the steep, smooth white slope running from the edge of Riverview's formal gardens to the start of the natural woodlands.

"Sorry, champ. No can do. I have to go into the city on business."

"But I won the war. That means I get to do what I want."

"Tomorrow, Nicky. Believe me, I'd rather go sledding with you here then hack those roads into Manhattan, but I have an appointment I just can't break."

"Can I go belly whopping by myself, then?"

"Don't see why not. But you'd better check it out with Patrice first. She's the boss."

"It's not as much fun all by myself," Nicholas grumbled, as he went off to look for Patrice. He was sure she'd give her permission without any trouble. The doctor even said it was good for him now to get out in the fresh air because he was almost all better. He just hoped Patrice wasn't busy and that she'd go belly whopping with him. It really wasn't as much fun alone.

With Nicholas gone, Jack changed quickly into a suit and tie and pulled on a car coat. Ordinarily he would have had plenty of time to get into the city and keep his appointment, but in the wake of last night's snowstorm there was no telling what shape the roads might be in.

Hurrying down the broad staircase, he encountered Buffy on her way up. She was wearing a chalk-stripe dark gray suit with a white silk blouse unbuttoned at the collar.

The rise of her opulent bosom was bisected by an Annie Hall necktie with a rep stripe. The cravat, Jack knew, was from Tripplers. There had been times in his life when the price of the tie would have kept him in hamburgers for a week.

The outfit was very becoming to his wife. Buffy looked not just stylish, but quite beautiful as well. Must have a heavy date, Jack thought to himself cynically. But the cynicism didn't quite work. Estranged as they were, the thought of Buffy with another man still hurt.

"Good morning, darling." Buffy's greeting was high-spirited. Her violet eyes danced, and she tossed her blue-black curls in a manner so like a southern belle it amounted to self-parody. "And where is my handsome young husband going this morning?"

"Business." Jack's tone was truculent. "An appointment in the city. And from the way you're got up," he added sarcastically, "you can't be bound for a quilting bee with the ladies from church."

"Stockwell board meeting, angel. And I'm not 'bound' anywhere. We're having it right here at dear old Riverview."

"I see. And will there be a vote today on whom my wife is to seduce next?" Jack brushed by Buffy and continued down the stairs. "Don't bother letting me know how it comes out," he called out without turning around.

"Celibacy doesn't agree with you, angel." She raised her voice after his retreating back. "It's making you bitter and testy."

"What the hell would you know about celibacy?" The front door slammed so hard behind Jack that the shutters on the windows rattled.

A little more than an hour later, Jack seated himself in the music reference section of the general Library and Museum of the Performing Arts. The orchestra collection room, with its world-famous resource of scores and parts for every conceivable instrument and voice ranging from baroque and German lieder and the ancient atonalities of the Indian subcontinent to punk, reggae, and hard rock, was the place his grandfather had set up the appointment for Jack to meet the Don.

181

Jack, looking around, noted that there weren't many people in the room, and the dozen or so who came and went were just about all students, pale and dedicated, their ears tuned to the musical scores they were poring over. Toward the back, a middle-aged Oriental man was sitting with his cashmere overcoat on and carefully copying out a part from a score onto lined music paper. Beside him on the table there was a violin case. As he copied the notes neatly with his right hand, his left hand rested on the violin case firmly and possessively.

Where the hell was the Don? Jack drummed his fingers on the table impatiently. The room seemed overheated to him. He took off his car coat. He waited. It was twenty minutes past the appointed time, then a half hour, and still no Don.

Jack scowled. He looked at the clock on the wall, checking it against his watch. As he lowered his eyes, his gaze met that of the Oriental man.

The man nodded curtly. Jack blinked. There was a second nod, just a trifle impatient, and then the Oriental man turned his attention back to the score he'd been copying. He inscribed some additional notes on the copy paper.

Hesitantly, Jack got to his feet and walked over to the man. "Excuse me," he said. "I had an appointment to meet someone here, and I was wondering if—"

"Sit down, Mr. Houston. Take a load off." The Oriental man spoke with a faint southwestern drawl.

Jack sat. "Then you're the one I'm to meet?" Surprise crept into his voice.

"Seems so."

"You're the Don?"

"The Don." He chuckled. "Haven't heard that since my days in the slammer. How's your granddad?" he asked.

"Getting older," Jack told him. "But good for his age, I guess."

"He's one tough old bird. Hangin' in there; that's his life-style. Don't expect he'll ever change that."

"He hasn't." Jack felt as if he'd somehow fallen into a tea party with the Dormouse. The Don? He hadn't exactly expected a Mafioso with a scar on his cheek and a pinkie ring, but still, a Sicilian, or at least an Italian-American, would not have been out of line with the expectations raised by the name and his grandfather's description of the man's activities. Instead, here he was sitting across from a conservatively dressed Oriental whose accent made him sound like John Wayne.

Still, there was that violin case. The Don's hand never left it. Just the right size, Jack knew from his days as a mercenary in Africa, for a Bugatti submachine gun.

"Don't fret, Mr. Houston." The Oriental man's smile was understanding. "Your granddad may have laid on that Don business a mite heavy, but he steered you to the right place. And I can lay some claim to being the Don. As it happens, Don is my rightful name. Sun Kai Don."

"Sun Kai Don."

"Not rightly Corleone." Sun Kai Don smiled laconically. "Fact is I'm Chinese-American. Born and raised in Cottonwood, Arizona. Call Chinatown here in New York home now, though."

"You moved from Arizona to New York?" Jack was still trying to get a handle on the situation.

"Not exactly. I moved from Arizona to Texas. From there I went to Atlanta—the federal pen, which is where I met your granddad. Then I came to New York. Upwardly mobile all the way, though, you might say. Just kept moving on up, and here I am in the grand old Apple."

"Here you are," Jack echoed.

"Rightly a self-made Don." His eyes crinkled as if from too much time in the saddle squinting against the sun. "While you, according to your granddad, are still in the making. That right?"

"I guess so."

"How old are you? Thirty something? That's a mite old to still be stretching for the brass ring."

"I'm a late bloomer."

"That so?" Sun Kai Don stroked his cheek with one finger as if testing for stubble and found it smooth. "Sprouting in a lot of directions, too, from what your granddad says. Bellhop. Soldier of fortune. Safari guide. Travel writer. Now, husband to a wealthy widow."

183

"That last is *not* one of my professions," Jack protested.

"That a fact? Too bad. It's the only one will put you in reaching distance of the brass ring."

"Let's get down to cases." Jack was tired of the verbal fencing. "Grandpa said you can help me out in the high-risk insurance field. Can you?"

"Quiet down, boy! This here is a library, not the back-room of a saloon." Sun Kai Don was disapproving.

"Can't we just get on with it?" Jack's voice stayed loud.

"Shh, boy. Shh." Suddenly Sun Kai Don's mouth curved upward on one side, a cowboy smile. "Don't hear that much any more. 'Shh,' I mean. When I was a boy they didn't let 'em out of library school without they could pass 'Shh-ing one oh one.' Not anymore. Libraries these days aren't s'posed to be quiet anymore. The kids don't respect the librarians, either, and it's no wonder. Everything's changed. Everything's different. Not much respect for anything anymore."

"Yes, well . . ."

"No respect. The young don't respect their elders anymore. Yessir. No respect anywhere."

"Listen, could we just—?"

"No respect. Take my daughter. She just runs wild. Running around with a Korean. A Korean. Tarnation! Raised to be a decent Chinese girl, and she thumbs her nose and takes up with this Korean."

"How old is she?" Jack gave up and went with the flow.

"Twenty-eight. Twenty-eight years old and no respect for her father, or her family, or anything else. A Korean! I gave that girl everything, and now she'll end up peddling Bibb lettuce on First Avenue."

"I'm sorry. But listen, could we talk about this high-risk insurance business?"

"Not here, boy." Sun Kai Don shook his head disapprovingly. "This place here is a library. A music library."

"If you don't want to talk here, why did you arrange to meet me here?"

184

"Had to transpose some Joplin arrangements to violin."

"Joplin? You mean ragtime?"

"Well, good for you, partner. Yes, ragtime. Although strictly speaking, my special thing is jazz violin."

"Jazz violin." Jack took a deep breath. "Well, listen, if you don't want to talk here, is there someplace else we can go?"

"Not just now, boy. I have another appointment." Sun Kai Don looked at his watch. "Fact is, I should be making tracks to it," he said.

"I don't get it. If you don't want to talk business here, or now, then what is this meeting all about?"

"Just checking you out, boy. Never get involved with a man before I check him out."

"And?" Jack was exasperated. "Do I pass muster?"

"You'll do, old buddy. In my expert opinion, you'll do. Now the way it works is, I'll be in contact with your granddad. We'll set up another appointment. Real soon. And then we'll have us a real serious talk about business and such. Meantime, you just be sure we have the access we need to those Stockwell board records. Have to know the paper flow before we light any matches, bucko. Without we know that, the only thing going into the cashbox is ashes."

"I'll have access when the time comes." I'd better not waste any more time rekindling that romance, Jack thought to himself unhappily. He really didn't like using Patrice in this manner, but he was even less willing to patch things up with Buffy. No, he had to earn Buffy's respect, to make her see that he was more than a stud she could ignore when a man with more power came around.

Sun Kai Don stood. "Got to be moseying along now," he drawled.

Jack watched him go. Then, with a start, he realized there was absolutely no reason for him to go on sitting in the orchestra collection room himself. He put on his car coat and started out.

When he reached the exit, there were three or four people backed up. There was evidently some sort of altercation going on at the turnstile where the guard stood. Jack peered around them and saw the guard arguing with Sun Kai Don.

"Look, mister, you have to open it up so I can check there are no books, or symphony scores, or anything like that in there. Those are the rules."

"I am telling you, friend, that the only blamed thing in there is my violin."

"Open it up, mister. 'Til you do, you can't come through here."

"But it's an Amati. There's a draft here would turn a Laramie stud bull into a mule. It's plumb old, this instrument. Sudden change in temperature like that could make the catgut pop."

"Hey, mister, you're holding up the line," complained someone behind Sun Kai Don.

"Don't meddle in this, friend. It's not your business."

"If you don't open the goddamn violin case, shrimp, I'm going to make it my business."

Jack thought to himself that threatening Sun Kai Don was not a very wise thing to do. The middle-aged Chinese turned a look on the man who had insulted him that would not have been out of place at the O.K. Corral. Slowly, he undid the straps, and then the zipper sealing the violin case. All the time he kept looking at the man who had interfered. Jack tensed as Sun Kai Don turned back the cover.

"Oh, God!" A young woman on the line reacted, horrified. "It really is an Amati. For God's sake, cover it up. Quickly." Jack, expecting a Bugatti submachine gun, smiled.

32

"UNCLE JAMES TAKES off for Greece without giving us any notice whatsoever, and now he expects us to make Patrice a member of this board just as if it were some kind of royal prerogative to be passed on from father to daughter by divine right." Peter Stockwell snorted derisively, addressing the governing board of Stockwell Industries, which had gathered once again in the third-floor conference room of the west wing of Riverview.

Patrice O'Keefe was unintimidated. She had expected Peter to be difficult, and he had not disappointed her.

"You wouldn't be here if your father wasn't Jonathan Stockwell. *You* replaced him, remember." Patrice's calmness was itself a rebuke. "Uncle David wouldn't be here if he hadn't married Alice Stockwell. Buffy is here"—Patrice shot her a conciliatory smile to soften the words—"because she married the governor. Even Mr. De Vilbiss is here as a representative of a member of the family."

"But not every member of the family serves on this board or is represented on this board." Peter's tone was scathing. "We who do serve bring certain skills with us, and experience, too."

"Well, since I'm chairman today," Max Tylor interjected, "it's my ruling that Patrice may stand in for her father until his return."

"The hell you say!" Peter exploded. "This isn't some goddamn gay meeting to elect a drag queen, Max. This is business!"

"Nice try, Max." Buffy chuckled.

"We have to decide unanimously to accept her or reject her," Peter insisted. "And since I vote nay, that's the end of it. Go away, Patrice. Don't go away mad. Just go away."

"You know what you can do, Peter," Patrice replied with exaggerated sweetness. "Only it's a biological impossibility," she added. She may have looked small and

187

vulnerable sitting there with her tortoiseshell glasses sliding down the bridge of her nose, but the movement of her index finger on the bow of her blouse was remarkably like the stroking of a trigger about to be pulled. There was steel beneath her softness.

"Whoa!" David Lewis protested. "There's nothing in our bylaws about it having to be unanimous. A simple majority one way or the other is enough."

"If you want to get technical, Uncle David," Peter snapped back, "it really is a matter for the probate judge to decide."

"Nobody here wants to start with the probate judge again, Peter." It was Halsey De Vilbiss who voiced the objection. "I don't see why we can't decide the matter among ourselves by a majority vote."

"Then call the vote," Peter was disgusted, but he was also sure of himself. He had spoken to De Vilbiss before the meeting, and Buffy, he knew, disliked Patrice.

"Very well." As presiding officer, Max had no choice but to accede to the request. "All those in favor of Patrice serving on this board in place of her father during his absence?" He raised his own hand.

David Lewis's hand also went up.

Patrice smiled blithely and raised the hand that had been toying with her bow. "Counting Daddy's vote, that makes three in favor," she announced.

"The hell it does!" Peter exploded. "Uncle James isn't here."

"I have his proxy," Patrice insisted.

"No proxies allowed." Peter glared.

"He's right, Patrice. I'm sorry." Reluctantly, Max Tyler had to agree with Peter. "Two in favor." He sighed. "Opposed?"

Peter's arm shot up. Halsey De Vilbiss raised his hand. Buffy did not.

"Two against," Max Tyler announced. "The vote is a tie."

"Buffy?" Peter had noticed her staring out the window at the newly frozen icicles wielded by the gargoyles scampering over the facade of Riverview's main house.

188

Annoyed, he assumed she had simply been daydreaming and so had missed responding. "How do you vote?"

"I abstain."

Surprised, Patrice stared at Buffy.

"What do you mean, you abstain?" David Lewis was disapproving. "You can't abstain. If there's a tie vote, this board will be immobilized, and we'll have to go back to the probate judge."

"I can't help that. I still abstain."

"She has a right to abstain," Max Tyler granted unhappily.

"Absolutely." Peter was not displeased. His mind was already racing ahead to the advantages that might accrue to him as the most junior member of the board during the time the probate judge heard arguments regarding Patrice's eligibility.

For reasons of his own, however, that was the last thing Halsey De Vilbiss wanted. Anything that would interfere with the board's decision-making process would cause a delay that threatened the project he was pushing behind the backs of the others. Toying with one of the gold buttons of the navy-blue blazer the southern California clothing salesman had assured him was all the rage among New York corporate executives, De Vilbiss was reminded that the salesman had lied. The other men present were all garbed in subdued versions of gray flannels and blue worsteds. De Vilbiss felt keenly the disapproval implicit in the narrowness of their lapels. Nevertheless, sartorially gauche as he was, Halsey De Vilbiss was neither a fool nor lacking in tact. "Perhaps Mrs. Houston would care to explain her abstention to us," he suggested a little too smoothly.

"And perhaps she wouldn't." Buffy's tone reminded the others present that a parvenu is, after all, a parvenu.

"I'd like to hear why you're abstaining," Patrice told Buffy honestly.

The older woman looked at her from violet eyes. The carefully applied deep violet eyeliner did not in this instance hide their shrewdness. "Careful, Patrice," she said. "I might change my mind."

"Why, Buffy?" Patrice decided to take the chance. "How come you're not voting against me?"

"Sisterly solidarity." Buffy's tone was light, flippant. "I'm tired of wearing old-school neckties over my Schiaparelli blouses just to prove I'm one of the boys. Another soprano voice might be a healthy addition to this board."

Playing with her bow, which she would never trade in for a necktie, Patrice studied Buffy over the top of her glasses. Despite Buffy's flippancy, she realized, there was an underlying truth to the reason she had given. "Then why," Patrice asked slowly, "why don't you vote *for* me instead of just abstaining?"

"Ah, well, Patrice, my dear. I don't think that would be very wise. You are, after all, so much smarter than— umm—the boys on the board. You're young, and you are, in your petite and calculatedly understated way, not unattractive. Men—boys—are all too susceptible to that. In short, I won't vote for you for the same reason I won't vote against you. You're a woman."

"You're a bitch," Patrice answered. Strangely, the way she said it, and the way that Buffy took it, the epithet expressed more admiration than insult.

David Lewis, however, was insulted by Buffy's rationale. "I do not take kindly to being categorized as susceptible to feminine wiles," he told them stiffly.

"Still," Max reminded the others, "this doesn't solve our problem as to seating Patrice. We're at an impasse."

The impasse was interrupted by a discreet knock on the door, followed by the entrance of Berkley, the Riverview butler. David Lewis was both surprised and annoyed by the intrusion. Berkley knew better than to disturb a board meeting.

"I beg pardon," Berkley said in his usual diffident tone. "There's a long-distance telephone call for Mr. De Vilbiss."

"Mr. De Vilbiss is in conference," David Lewis reproved Berkley.

"That is what I said, sir, but the lady insisted. And—"

"And?"

"The caller is Mrs. Sarah Stockwell Tyler, sir."

Halsey De Vilbiss scrambled to his feet. "I'll take the

call," he said firmly. "Is there another phone where I can talk without disturbing the board?"

"If you'll follow me, sir."

Berkley led De Vilbiss to an anteroom, indicated a phone on a carved teakwood coffee table, glided out, and closed the door behind him. "Hello there, Mrs. Tyler." De Vilbiss picked up the phone. "How are you feeling?"

"I am eighty-seven years old, Mr. De Vilbiss. Don't ask foolish questions."

"Sorry. What can I do for you, then?"

"I've had a phone call from my nephew, James. Seems he wants his daughter to replace him on the board."

"Curiously enough, the board has just been discussing that," Halsey told his client. "Voting on it, as a matter of fact."

"And how did you vote, Mr. De Vilbiss?"

"In my judgment, Patrice O'Keefe lacks the maturity and experience to serve on the board."

"You voted against her?"

"Yes, ma'am, I did."

"Then go back in there and vote the other way, Mr. De Vilbiss."

"Don't you trust my judgment, Mrs. Tyler?"

The laugh in his ear was suspiciously close to a cackle. "Change your vote, Mr. De Vilbiss."

"You pay me for my advice, Mrs. Tyler." Halsey's tone was more unctuous than his words. "Why disregard it?"

"James is my nephew. Patrice is his daughter. They're family. I've spent most of my life turning my back on my family. Now the creak in my bones says they're all I've got. Family. That's one reason."

"Is there another, Mrs. Tyler?"

"They're family, and you're a southern California lawyer. Change your vote, Mr. De Vilbiss. Good-bye." The phone clicked in his ear.

Halsey returned to the conference room and informed the others that he was changing his vote. Peter protested. There was some argument back and forth, but finally Max Tyler pounded on the oak conference table for quiet. When he had it, he announced the new vote tally in a firm voice. "Three for, two against, one abstention. The yeas have it. Patrice Stockwell O'Keefe is accepted as a member in good standing of this board, replacing her father, James Linstone Stockwell. Let us move on to the business of the day. Insurance is first on the agenda."

"I have here a list of reinsurance offerings in blocks of half a million each." Peter resigned himself to Patrice's presence on the board and plunged into his pet project. "The list totals three million five. I'd like board approval to purchase."

"I'd like to hear who the sellers are first, please," Max requested.

"All right." Peter scowled. He read from the list. "Casualty Insurance Company of Taiwan. Brooklyn Mutual. Caracas Fidelity and Loan. Liverpool Fire and Theft. SoHo Independent of New York. Jakarta Limited. And Pan-African of Nairobi."

"SoHo Independent of New Y ..." The name drew Patrice's attention. "Isn't that an Imalda investment front?"

"Could be," Peter said. "So what?"

"So plenty!" Max Tyler reacted. "I for one don't think—"

"Put a lid on it, Max." David Lewis stepped in. "We've already wasted too much time today. You can't have purity and expect to buy and sell in the high-risk insurance market. And we've already settled that that's what we're doing."

"All right. But even so, I'd like a breakdown of the offering from Jakarta Limited. Insurance, you'll remember, is my business, and they're new to me."

"Listen, Max," Peter reacted hotly. "If we don't snap up these offerings, there are plenty of others who will. You can be sure that Lloyd's of London, the Brazilian government's Instituto de Resseguros, or Den-Har down in Florida will all be all too happy to pick up these policies."

"Is there some reason you don't want to tell me the components of the Jakarta Limited offering?"

"Oh, for Christ's sake." Peter shuffled through the papers in front of him.

Patrice observed the interplay between Peter and Max

carefully. Her father had voted along with the others to move Stockwell investment funds into the reinsurance area, but privately he had confided to Patrice that he had some reservations. "The paper moves too fast, and it's in the air too long," he told her. "The profits are big all right, but so are the chances of really dirtying our hands. Insurance is service—not steel, not oil, not manufacturing. It's nebulous, ephemeral. And fire insurance is—well, highly inflammable. It's too damn easy for that kind of operation to go up in smoke itself."

"Why get involved at all then, Dad?" Patrice had asked him.

"Greed." He had answered her honestly. "That's how the Stockwell fortune was built, Patrice. Greed."

Greed was clearly behind Peter's impatience now as he read off the list of insurance companies underwriting the policies being offered to Stockwell, Inc. by Jakarta Limited.

Max Tyler stopped him at the fifth name. "Hewlett Fire and Theft," he repeated. "How much of a share?"

"One twenty-five. Peanuts."

"Then turn it down."

"Why the hell should we?"

"What is it, Max?" Patrice realized that he wasn't just trying to make waves.

"There have been six fires of suspicious origin in the South Bronx in the last month," Max replied. "Four of the owners of the possibly torched properties cashed in on polices written by Hewlett Fire and Theft."

"That doesn't matter, Max." David Lewis spoke to him as if explaining simple arithmetic to a child. "The lag time will take care of anything like that. The total package will more than even it all out."

"Goddamn it, we are encouraging arson."

"Even if that were true," Halsey De Vilbiss interceded, "I don't see that it matters. The South Bronx is an eyesore. It should be burned to the ground."

"How the hell would you know? Since they don't have any surfing there, you've probably never even been to the South Bronx. People live in those buildings. The apartments in them are homes to thousands of families. And when we underwrite the underwriters who are insuring the landlords who are hiring the torchers to burn them out so they can collect insurance and then rebuild—high-priced condos probably—with the help of government funding, we become parties to the crime of arson.''

"Don't get so emotional, Max," Peter told him nastily. "Your mascara will start to run."

"That was uncalled for, Peter." For the first time Patrice entered the discussion. "I think Max has a point. We don't have to do business with sleazebags. The hundred and a quarter is a drop in the bucket. I suggest we simply don't buy the Hewlett Fire and Theft paper."

"It doesn't work that way. It's part of the package. We'd have to turn down the whole half-million offer from Jakarta Limited."

"Do it, then." Max was adamant. "If they're underwriting Hewlett Fire and Theft, their other paper's probably inflammable as hell."

"There's a principle here," David Lewis reminded them. "We aren't moralists, and we aren't police. We're businessmen. Business people," he amended quickly before Patrice or Buffy could react. "Our only concern should be the investment. Will it pay us a reasonable return? As we've discussed previously, it will. I move we authorize purchase of the whole three-million-five package."

With Max Tyler voting nay and Patrice abstaining, the authorization was granted.

Patrice had abstained rather than siding the Max because she felt she really wasn't well-enough acquainted with the reinsurance investment program to jump to any conclusions about it. Obviously its importance within the structure of Stockwell Industries was growing, and she decided that she would make it her business to study it thoroughly. She would ask Peter for copies of all the relevant documents. More, she would insist on having them. Patrice knew she had to earn the respect of the board members, and since she had confidence in her own abilities, she was certain that with the help of a little homework, she'd have the entire matter in hand in time for the next board meeting.

Decided, Patrice focused on the next item of business.

It was the sore tooth of Stockwell Industries—the problem of getting their crude oil refined. Heads had turned toward Buffy, only to meet with disappointment. "Grebbs Refining is out, at least for the present," she told them. "Texas is unlikely."

Buffy ignored the questioning looks directed her way. Patrice, however, knew from Holly about the fight between Jack and Jimbo Grebbs, so she wasn't surprised. For once Buffy's allure hadn't turned the trick.

"Perhaps now," Halsey De Vilbiss suggested, "the board might reconsider the Libyan option."

"Maybe we should," Peter said thoughtfully.

David Lewis and Buffy both nodded reluctantly.

"I guess it makes no difference," Max Tyler said sarcastically, "that Qaddafi may well be implicated in the kidnapping of Zelig Meyerling."

"It makes a difference to me," Patrice said quietly.

"I don't see what one thing has to do with the other." Halsey De Vilbiss clasped his hands in a way that displayed the ostentatious gold cuff links he was wearing.

"You wouldn't." Max turned his wrath on him. "You don't care who gets hurt. You've been pushing for this deal to have our oil refined in Libya from the first. Even after the board turned thumbs down on it, you went right on wheeling and dealing to bring it about."

"Are you accusing me of something?" Halsey puffed up with indignation.

"Damn right I am! You even flew into Athens to meet with Spiro Papatestus to discuss transporting our oil in his tankers."

"How do you know that, Max?" Patrice asked him. She considered it a very serious breach if Halsey had indeed defied the board that way.

"Beth wrote me about it. It seems that Mr. De Vilbiss was seen going up to the royal suite of the King George V Hotel to meet with Mr. Papatestus."

"Sure I was in Athens," De Vilbiss conceded. "I do have other business besides Stockwell, you know. I'm an attorney. I went to Athens to meet with a client."

"He flew in, saw Papatestus, and flew out," Max Tyler told the others. "Altogether, he wasn't in Greece more than three hours. And two days later Papatestus was seen meeting with the Libyan minister of petroleum in Malta. You'll remember that's Ezzadine al Mabrouk, the very fellow that Mr. De Vilbiss here bragged about being able to use as a go-between."

"I was in Athens on business for another client," Halsey insisted.

Nobody believed him. The board voted to shelve reconsideration of any deal to refine Stockwell crude in Libya until such time as the circumstances surrounding the abduction of Zelig Meyerling came into clearer focus. Shortly after reaching this decision, by common agreement, they adjourned.

Patrice escaped from the others and went down to the center parlor in the main house. She needed a drink, and she didn't want to have to rehash business with anyone while she had it. Berkley had laid a fire, and she was curled up in front of it on the sofa with her shoes off and a vodka gimlet in her hand when a voice from behind her made her raise her head.

"Some people really know how to live." A warm, fond laugh followed the greeting.

"Hello, Jack. Did you just get back from the city?"

"I did. And I'm frozen. I'm badly in need of one of whatever you've got in your hand—that is, if it's alcoholic."

"Only six parts. The seventh is lime juice. I'll make you one."

"You're an angel. Easy on the lime juice, though. It makes me lose control."

Jack laughed. "On second thought, give me six parts lime juice and one part vodka. Then we can discuss my libido problem."

Patrice flushed. "That's the last problem I'd have thought you'd have, Jack." She handed him the drink and sat down on the couch.

"You misjudge me." He sat on the couch beside her.

"Poor boy. Let me guess. Your wife doesn't understand you." Patrice could feel that her face was growing redder. Her nervousness made her joke, but she also felt a thrill of pleasure sitting next to him. God, how she wanted him! Remember, she cautioned herself. Remember what happened last time.

"My wife has other interests. 'Extramarital,' I think is the proper description."

"And so you figure that sauce for the goose is—" It was a one-night stand, that's all it was. He said it wasn't, but it was. And then he ditched me for Buffy. Remember, Patrice! Remember how that hurt! Don't do this to yourself. Get up and walk before it's too late. Instead, she caught her breath sharply as Jack moved closer and took her hand.

"Isn't it?" he asked, looking into her eyes in a way calculated to melt any resistance Patrice might have had. "Isn't it sauce for the gander?"

You're going to get hurt! "Yes. I suppose it is." Hurt bad? But she couldn't help herself. She was too attracted to him to resist him. And since their affair, she had not seen any other man. She had immersed herself in business. "I just don't know if I want to be gander sauce," she added feebly, unable to meet his intense blue eyes.

"Don't you?"

Jack leaned in then and kissed her just as Patrice had known all along that he would. She responded first tentatively, then fiercely. Had there ever been any doubt that she would? Her common sense and her memory had always taken second place to her desire for Jack.

33

"THE SEX DRIVE?" Lisa Stockwell's gaze moved around the dinner table from one face to another. "It can be as powerful as you like, but that power is independent of direction. There is no morality any more than there is any logic. There is only lust and the sex object. And in many cases the lust is free floating—like anxiety in Freudian psychology—just a tired old bumblebee looking for the nectar of warm flesh.''

''You make it sound like Count Dracula, my dear.'' Spiro Papatestus, Lisa's host, was the only one at the candlelit dinner table who was amused by the young woman's ramblings. It was not that he was insensitive to the tension among those dining outdoors on the patio of his villa. Rather, it was that he alone held fast to the classical Greek viewpoint, which regarded life as drama and conversation as the dialogue necessary to move the plot along. To monologues such as Lisa's in particular, Spiro lent an ear attuned to Greek choruses.

Lisa's father's reaction to his youngest child's high-pitched and deliberately outrageous tirade was quite different. James was more than offended by it; he was deeply disturbed. The anger behind Lisa's words was so clearly directed toward Lisa's lover, Winifred Fitzsimmons. The outburst pointed up just how unnatural their relationship was. James had tried, but he could not accept it.

Winifred was looking down at her brandy snifter steadfastly, avoiding Lisa's gaze. All through her diatribe Lisa had stared straight at her. Winifred's fair English complexion had mottled red with embarrassment, but she had refused to raise her head and meet Lisa's eyes. Even now, as Lisa spoke to her directly, Winifred would not look at her.

''Doesn't that apply to you, Winifred?'' Lisa inquired, her voice edging toward shrillness. ''Weren't you just a bumblebee on the rebound when we met?''

Winifred bit her lip. She said nothing. Her head remained bowed.

''Surely if Winifred had an unhappy experience and doesn't wish to discuss it . . .'' Gently, Louise tried to deflect Lisa, to break the tension she was creating.

''Surely.'' Lisa's laugh rang false. ''What do you think, Holly?'' She turned to her cousin, who had been quiet and reflective, wrapped in her own concerns, all through the meal. ''Do you think we should let Winifred off the hook?''

"What?" Addressed directly, Holly was prodded into paying attention. "Oh, yes. It should be Winifred's choice."

"Winifred's choice." There was an eeriness to Lisa's thin, hollow-cheeked face as she stared now at Holly. The candlelight stressed the translucence of her skin and the prominence of her cheekbones. "Her first choice, Holly? Or her second choice?"

The sharpness of the innuendo got through to Holly. Holly, who had known Winifred when she had lived in England, was well aware that Holly, herself, had been Winifred's first choice. That experience had been painful not only for Holly who had to reject her friend's feelings, but also for Winifred who had been unable to accept Holly's rejection. But how did Lisa know about it? Taken aback by the way Lisa's eyes burned deep in their sockets, Holly reflected that her cousin looked more than thin; she looked ill, like a flame's last bright burning before it extinguishes itself. Seeking an explanation, Holly automatically turned toward Winifred.

Winifred's head stayed down, but her eyes looked up from under long lashes, and the look in them as they returned Holly's glance was pleading. Holly caught her breath sharply. I can't get involved in this, she thought to herself. I have to deal with my own real problems. Whatever Winifred felt about me, she was mistaken. I don't have the time or the energy in the middle of all that is happening to worry about them. And the topic—lust—was not one she cared to dwell on. Already, she could feel anger rising up within her. Damn Zelig! How could he have done that to her?

"Sometimes our view is warped, and what we think was the past never really was," she told both Lisa and Winifred. "And in any case, real or *imagined*," Holly emphasized the word, "the past is done, over, finished." She stood up. "I'm rather tired," she said. "If you'll all excuse me—" Tall, slender, golden-haired, beautiful despite the strain she was under, Holly exited with a bearing that could only be described as aloof.

"Class," Lisa said. "Is that what it is, Winifred? Class?"

199

"It is in the blood." Spiro stepped in smoothly to deflect any escalation of Lisa's hostility. "All of you Stockwells have it. Even so distant a relative as my Louise. It is one of the reasons I married her. That, and her beauty, and her intelligence."

Louise was touched by his absolute sincerity. "Thank you, my husband." She stood and curtsied. "I think that I'll walk in the gardens before turning in," she said. "Would you care to join me, Spiro?"

"I will catch up with you later." His eyes watched Louise fondly until she turned the corner of the path. The expression on his strong-featured, weathered face was that of a mature man who would always be quite smitten with his somewhat younger wife.

There was the slightest chill in the night air of Crete as Louise started from the edge of the garden through the grove of olive trees. The tips of their leaves gleamed silver in the moonlight. Their gnarled and twisted branches formed shapes that lent the grove a feeling of enchantment under the clear, star-sprayed, mountain-shore sky. Her step quickened in anticipation of the true enchantment she would find with Xanthos Konstantin.

He was expecting her. His welcoming kiss was passionate. "The husband?" he inquired.

"Spiro will be along." Louise stroked his cheek with fingertips that tingled. "Clint?" she asked.

"Out." His hands were impressed by the satiny feel of the evening gown Louise was wearing. "Is returning later."

"Much later, I hope." Louise nibbled the muscle where his strong shoulder met his neck.

"Heated tonight?" Xanthos teased.

"You Greek devil!" She laughed. "You know me too well."

"Is well. Not too well." He carefully left the door off the latch and led Louise into the bedroom he and Clint shared. He turned to her, and they embraced again.

His kiss was hot, urgent. His tongue filled her mouth, hard, thrusting, an anticipation of the coupling to come. Louise's hands slid over his back, savoring the way his

200

muscles rippled under the rough cotton work shirt he was wearing. Her hands slid down, clutching his rudely grinding buttocks. She clenched them shamelessly, pressed in to him, felt the long, swelling heat of his readiness.

Xanthos undid the buttons at the back of her satin gown, his fingers rough as they worked their way down. They played thrillingly down her spine, then down still farther, discovering the cleft, impudent, teasing through the silk of her panties. The gown dropped to Louise's ankles.

Louise laughed breathlessly. "Devil!" She pushed her hand under the waistband of his denim pants. Her nails dug into the rippling, molded muscles of his haunches. "Devil!" Her tongue was in his ear. Sometime, somewhere, during these last few weeks, the dam had burst. Louise was as brazenly voluptuous now with Xanthos as once she had been shy and withdrawn from all men. She reveled in her wantonness. "Brazen devil!" Her fist encircled him.

Xanthos growled deep in his throat. He pushed her back on the bed. He unbuttoned his pants and kicked them free. He fell on her, drawing the large, swollen, agitated nipple of one of her breasts into his mouth. He sucked it while he pulled the silk panties free of Louise's writhing hips.

Clutching his head to her breast, Louise stretched her long, lightly muscled legs toward the wood-beamed ceiling of the peasant cottage. "Do it, devil!" she urged.

Dark eyes narrowed, a small smile twitching at the corners of his hawklike mouth, Xanthos stood, and with neither modesty nor self-consciousness, he posed for Louise, displaying his erection. And then, when her eyes told him she could not stand to wait one instant longer, he fell on her, bent her long, lissome body in two, and penetrated her fully.

Legs on his shoulders, ankles locked around his neck, she stared down the length of her body with smoky hazel eyes, gazed between the heaving mountains of her breasts, followed the rivulet of perspiration to her navel, watching her silky golden mound rise and fall to his

201

thrustings, his pounding, felt her heart beat wildly as she saw the engorged length of his dark penis enter her to the hilt, and then withdraw and then reenter, its crest and then its length stroking her aroused clitoris.

Xanthos twisted—an unexpected movement, a sudden, indescribable thrill. Both half-moons of Louise's round, firm bottom pushed up toward the ceiling in response. She gasped. Her long golden lashes fluttered in surprise. It was a moment before her eyes could focus again. When they did, they saw the seamed Olympian face of her husband gazing down on their coupling with benign approval.

"Magnificent." His off-white dress trousers were buttoned, their modified pleats undisturbed by lust. And yet his ageless, fathomless eyes bespoke a passion so intense as to demand the ultimate response from Louise.

Whimpering and then almost crying, her nails drawing blood, her limbs enveloped Xanthos, and she came with a series of tearing, wrenching movements that commanded the fullness of his lust in response.

"Don't stop," Spiro said when they lay parted, panting, catching their breath. It was not a command. He did not order; he made no demands. It was rather a suggestion, an urging, a hope that there would be more pleasure for the three of them.

Louise fetched a basin of water. She sponged herself off. She washed Xanthos. As she patted him dry, his penis stirred. On impulse, she pressed it to her cheek.

Eyes glittering, Spiro suggested she take it in her mouth.

"I've never—" Louise responded.

"You might enjoy it. If not, you could always stop."

Pink and trembling, Louise's tongue appeared between her bee-stung lips. The cloud of her red-gold hair fanned out over Xanthos's groin. As he stretched to stroke between her thighs, her mouth enveloped him. Looking up, she saw Spiro smiling approval as he unzipped the white dress trousers.

Her head was spinning. She felt faint. Crouching, she was reduced to the sensation of the lust coming alive deep in her mouth. She looked up at Spiro.

"Yes," he said. "Oh, yes, my darling." He fondled his own naked lust voluptuously, patiently.

Deep inside Louise something gave way, snapped, surrendered. She lowered her head to Xanthos, parted her lips, and took Xanthos deep in her mouth.

34

VANESSA BREWSTER'S ANXIOUS smile of conciliation did not melt James Stockwell's haughty demeanor as he confronted her. He stood over her tall and slim and elegant, hair flat and cobalt gray at the temples, eyes pale, chilled, unforgiving. His poise was a jarring contrast to the setting.

James had sought her out at Kommos, the archaeological dig where Vanessa had been camping out in order to be close at hand as shards were reconstructed into artifacts to be deciphered by the expert in linear one. To his cryptic readings Vanessa applied her expertise as an anthropologist and rendered ancient thought—legend, history, lives—into the vernacular. The ever-present swirls of dust enclouded her surroundings.

Archaeological digs are rarely sightly during the process of discovery. Kommos was less so than most. Whatever its glory in antiquity, its uneven excavations looked particularly shabby and drab—gray-brown mounds and motes and dull umbra jagged edges overwhelmed by the cerulean Cretan sky and the white-edged, blue-green curls of surf nibbling the golden shore beyond the dig. Brown hair snooded, rumpled and uncaring, Vanessa fit right in with these surroundings. Only her green eyes on James—their gaze piercing and yet pleading—disturbed the tranquillity.

"So she told you," Vanessa said.

"Yes." One word, one syllable, and yet its coldness testified that James doubted the pleading in her eyes, the regret in her voice, the past that they had known together, any chance of future reconciliation.

"I hoped she wouldn't. But of course that was foolish. Naturally she would."

"She had to, and the authorities. They will want to talk to you. And Holly is my niece. We are very fond of each other. We care about each other's welfare. She would not stand by idly knowing that I had been betrayed and fail to inform me."

"Betrayal?" Vanessa's eyes were questioning. "Is that what it was?"

"Of course. What else?"

"But we never promised each other fidelity. I've been in Europe for some time without you. You've been alone in America. We *are* adults."

"And we should have the adult ability to exercise self-control."

"Why?" Vanessa folded her arms akimbo, a most unbecoming pose that mashed her abundant bosom to shapelessness. "Why exercise self-control? Life is finite. Moments without enjoyment can never be relived."

"Spare me your sophomoric hedonism. Loving concern imposes its own restraints. One imposes them on oneself. If one truly cares, truly loves, one does so gladly."

" 'One'? For God's sake, James, this isn't a Stockwell board meeting. There is no 'one.' There is you and me. Whatever I did to hurt you, 'one' didn't do it, I did. Me. Vanessa."

"I beg your pardon." He was sarcastic. "Being cuckolded always renders my speech more formal."

"I didn't cuckold you, James. We're not married. I was free, as were you."

"Of course. Free as birds in flight. And no more intimate." James turned away.

"What nonsense. Of course there's intimacy between us. Listen, darling." Vanessa was very earnest. "I care for you. You know that. You care for me. I know that. You're hurt because I went to bed with another man. And just maybe, James, you're most hurt of all because I was unfaithful, and you weren't. But it wasn't important. It was an itch that I scratched, no more. We can't let something so unimportant wreck the very real and loving relationship between us. Please, James. Don't let that happen."

James was shaken. It was true. A large part of his resentment was due to the fact that he felt so very foolish to have refrained from sex with other women while Vanessa had indulged herself. True, they had never made any verbal agreement to be faithful, but still . . . "And what guarantee have I"—he chose his words very carefully—"that if circumstance puts an ocean between us, you won't indulge yourself again?"

Vanessa stared at him. Although her emerald gaze turned cold, inwardly she sighed. How could she care so much for a man twenty years her senior who was so immature, so downright naive? "None," she told him. "You have no guarantee. I'm a woman of large sexual appetites. I cannot imagine that I would go for months on end without sex."

"I see." There seemed nothing further for James to say.

"You have the same option, James. I'd understand."

"But I wouldn't. I *believe* in fidelity."

It was no use. The gap between them was unbridgeable. In Vanessa's eyes this man she had somehow allowed herself to fall wholeheartedly in love with, this man who was a joy beyond all others in her bed, this man was not a man at all, but a child who would always have polite tantrums at the prospect of any other children playing with his toys. But, Vanessa reminded herself, I'm not a toy. No, I am no man's toy, not even his. And so, yes, the gap was unbridgeable.

"I have to go." A whisper of misery escaped James's control with the words. Why couldn't she at least agree that fidelity was preferable; that loving one, you shouldn't need another. "My daughter is expecting me for lunch."

"Has Patrice come to Greece with you, then?" Hurting, Vanessa retreated to small talk.

"No. I meant my younger daughter, Lisa. She's here in Crete with a friend. Like Holly and myself, they're guests at the Papatestus villa."

"I see." Vanessa remembered the concern James had expressed to her about Lisa during their affair. "How is Lisa?"

"Thin. Painfully thin." James sighed. "And unhappy. Very unhappy."

"I'm sorry." Vanessa reached out and touched his hand.

For an instant, despite everything, James believed her concern. Still he would not relent.

"I'm sorry. I really do have to go." This time he was firm. He nodded curtly and turned on his heel. He walked ramrod stiff up the sharp angle of the dust-sliding hillock.

"Will you come to see me again, James?" Vanessa called after him. Her heart, had he not been turned away, was in her emerald-green eyes. Her pride was of no matter to her, and she would have been very quick to offer it up had she not known that his pride would not let him accept even that sacrifice. "Will you?"

"I don't know," he replied without turning around. "I don't really know." And then he was gone.

35

HOLLY CONSIDERED THE contents of the trunk and smiled wanly to herself. The domestics of Riverview, schooled in anticipating any possible needs of the family they served, and charged with packing the necessaries from Holly's study above the library for her emergency flight to Greece, had included all the papers on the project on which the young mistress was working. Holly, distraught over the abduction of her husband, had not intended to pursue her history of Riverview from the far-off shores of Crete. She had anticipated constant and frenzied activity upon her arrival in Greece. Instead, however, the time had been marked by the tedium of waiting, of doing nothing at all because there was nothing to do.

The first move was up to the kidnappers. Knowing this did not ease Holly's anxiety. Indeed, the enforced idleness of waiting had become intolerable. Yet there was nothing to do but wait. Until contact was made, their demands revealed, it was impossible to even discuss what might be the best course to secure Zelig's freedom.

So Holly waited. She fretted, brooding over his infidelity. She felt hurt, confused. One minute she would be angry, unforgiving, and the next she would be nearly sobbing at the thought of not seeing Zelig again. She measured out in eternal minutes the tedium of her own impotency. There was nothing she could do to help him. She was immobilized, upset, and very bored.

And finally, feeling guilty, but having somehow to get through the days, Holly had picked up where she left off with her researches into the early history of Riverview. . . .

To the boy Horace, the suicide of his uncle, Colonel Roger Stockwell, was a confirmation of his own ability to control situations and effect events. At an early age he was mastering the techniques of his father's power. His mother, broken in heart and spirit, her sin his lever, was at his mercy.

At first his demands were no more than might be expected from one of Horace's tender years. He was flexing his power, as it were. The flexings were hateful, perhaps, but they were also quintessentially adolescent. That was certainly the case when Horace conducted his first major test of the new balance of power. "The stallion, Mother," he had said in a voice as devoid of emotion as ever his father's had been. "The chestnut. I want it to ride for myself alone."

"Your father doesn't think you're old enough yet for your own full-grown riding horse," Margaret reminded her son. "You have your pony. And the chestnut has to be properly broken. After that it is to be given to Mercy."

"If Father thinks I am not old enough, it is because you have said so. Now, Mother, please be so good as to say otherwise. I want the stallion broken to me. It is not a proper mount for Mercy. A mare will suit her better."

"Your father—"

"Shall I talk to him myself, Mother?" Horace looked at her for a long moment from his flat gray eyes.

The detachment of his gaze almost made Margaret miss the threat lurking in the pupils. When she did recognize it, she shivered. "That won't be necessary, Horace," she said. "I will speak to Father."

If a look, or an inflection, was all that was needed to bring his mother to heel, Horace nevertheless did not balk at using stronger measures to exert his power over others. His attitude toward menials was imperious. Nor did he hesitate to establish his authority by physical means. Such was the case on the afternoon that Margaret came upon Horace bullying the coachman's son, Willie, in the barn.

Willie was two years younger than Horace, twenty pounds lighter, and several inches shorter. Horace was holding him down with his foot and striking his buttocks with a riding crop. More than his brutality, it was the look of unmitigated pleasure on Horace's young face that struck Margaret when she stumbled on the scene.

"Stop!" The word exploded from her lips with such forceful loathing that it did indeed stay Horace's hand.

The victim pulled away from his tormentor. He stood up, sniveling. "It's my birthday, mistress," Willie sobbed. "Ma gave me treacle of molasses for a treat." He wiped his nose with his sleeve. "And now Master Horace says I must give it to him 'cause my pa was 'dentured. When I said it's not true, mistress, that Pa ain't 'dentured since the Tories lost the war, Master Horace pushed me down and beat on me and all the time hollering he'd show me whose property me and my pa and my ma, too, was."

"Well, you're not indentured. Willie, none of you," Margaret assured him. "Now stop crying and take your sweet and run along. There's a good boy. I want to talk to Horace alone."

When Willie was gone, Margaret looked at her son sadly. "Your father would not approve such behavior," she told him softly. "He doesn't hold with mistreating servants. You know that."

Horace shrugged coolly. "That's probably so, Mother," he said. "Father would disapprove. He might even punish me. If he knew. But then there are so many things Father might disapprove of if he knew. So many punishments . . ."

Young as he was, the guiding principle of Horace's life was already established. There were two kinds of people in the world: the rulers and the ruled. Like his father, he was born to rule. His authority would always be absolute over those others, be they servant child or the mother who had borne him.

Nothing would stand in the way of Horace's desires, whether for treacle or grog or rich food, a steed to whip or a wager to lay, a mother to dominate, or a wife, wealth to wallow in, or women.

Horace was seventeen in 1795, the year his older sister, Mercy, was married. Her bridegroom would carry her away to far-off Pennsylvania, and Horace's mother and sisters were quite weepy at this prospect. Nevertheless, Margaret had rallied to organize the wedding. Horace observed the preparation with his usual cynical eye.

The nuptial arrangements were lavish. No less was expected of one of the Hudson River Valley's great estates. Already Everett Stockwell's land deals scooping up property at the lower tip of Manhattan Island were earning him the respect that comes with business success and the vast accumulation of wealth. It was taken for granted—by Everett and by their wealthy neighbors—that the wedding of Mercy Stockwell of Riverview would be *the* social event of the season.

Horace watched his mother oversee a horde of workmen constructing a temporary outdoor dance pavilion and long banquet tables, a kitchen staff on loan from adjoining estates and augmented by specialists in the mixing of bev-

209

erages from Fraunces Tavern, a gaggle of fluttery, fast-talking French couturiers charged with making gowns for all the principals on down to the bridesmaids and flower girls, and a household staff in mute rebellion at the brashness of all the interlopers. Margaret was also charged with preparing her daughter for the intimacies of her wedding night, as well as synchronizing a series of wedding rehearsals with the local minister—once a Church of England vicar, but now reduced by the constitutional separation of Church from State to a mere clergyman of the Episcopal church. Task piled upon task, and Margaret was kept so busy that she had no time left over for brooding on, or dealing with, her son Horace.

It was not until the day of the wedding itself that Horace returned to his customary place center stage in Margaret's concern. Margaret, finding it necessary to avoid her husband, Everett, had run out to the stables. Flight was necessary because the orchestra hired for the occasion had just launched into a waltz—Margaret's farewell gift to her daughter, Mercy. The waltz had come into popularity at the royal court of Vienna in the 1780s. Shortly thereafter it had been adopted by Marie Antoinette and become associated in the public mind with the scandals of Versailles. No decent woman, it was said, would whirl about to such spirited music, her bodice visibly rising and falling, her powder rivuleted by perspiration. But then the French throne had toppled. The excesses of the Jacobins had turned the sympathies of the British aristocracy in favor of the increasingly decapitated French nobility. And in the wake of these feelings, the waltz had crossed the channel and been taken up by the British royalty.

The traversing of the Atlantic took little longer than the channel crossing. Carolinian plantation owners, as willing to adopt British fashion as they had once been to shed British rule, were the first leaders of New World society to whirl with the waltz. Soon patrician Virginia, main line Philadelphia, and Back Bay Boston itself were all daringly atwirl.

So while Mercy Stockwell and her girlfriends locked the doors to their boudoirs to practice the waltz step, Everett Stockwell and his peers assured one another that their children would never indulge in so disgraceful a pastime as dancing the waltz. Knowing how strongly her father felt, Mercy had never even dared suggest that a waltz be played at her wedding, although all of her own friends gathered to celebrate her marriage would treasure it above any other hospitality.

Margaret was aware of this, and since the ruthlessness of Horace toward her had made her less afraid of the displeasure of her husband, Everett, she had decided that this last time under her parents' roof, Mercy should have her heart's desire. The orchestra had been told to play a waltz.

As the music gathered a momentum that could not be stopped, as the dancers started to whirl—faster, and then faster still—Margaret discreetly departed the scene before her husband could descend on her with his protests and demands for an explanation. Her flight took her out behind the stables. It was here, in a hidden glen roofed over by the full-leafed branches of oak trees, that Margaret came upon Horace with the Armbruster girl from the estate next to Riverview.

Horace had lured Priscilla Armbruster there some twenty minutes before his mother's appearance. "I will show you the prettiest bird you have ever seen," he had promised her.

Priscilla was some four years younger than Horace and, in his opinion, not very bright. She was, he knew, quite flattered by the attention of a boy on the verge of young manhood and a mighty Stockwell to boot. And despite her tender years, she had pronounced breasts that Horace lusted to fondle.

"Where is the bird?" she asked innocently when Horace pulled her to a halt in the glen.

"Here." He took her small hand and pressed it to his groin.

"Don't do that!" Priscilla pulled her hand away.

"Why not? You like me, don't you?"

"Well, yes. But—"

"When a girl likes a fellow, she kisses him." Horace stepped in to her to claim the kiss.

Priscilla was confused. She was very flattered to have Horace pay attention to her at all. At the same time, she was shaken by the bad thing he had done when he tried to put her hand on the forbidden place. Still, he was treating her like an older girl, and older girls did sometimes allow a kiss if they really liked the boy. She kissed Horace.

Halfway through the kiss, his hands moved to her bosom. He squeezed her breasts and started to unbutton her bodice.

"Stop that." Priscilla struggled to pull away.

Stronger than she was, Horace held her in place and continued the unbuttoning process. "Quit wriggling," he told her. "If you don't do what I say, I'll tell everybody you let me do it to you."

"Do it? Do what?" Priscilla was truly innocent, truly bewildered.

"What the bull does to the cow." Horace slid his hand inside her opened gown, found her nipple, and pinched it cruelly.

"Ow!" Despite the pain and the forced intimate contact, Priscilla was most of all disturbed by his words. "But I never, Horace!" she protested. "I never would! You go to hell for that. You burn through eternity. I wouldn't!"

"That doesn't matter." The sight of her naked breast, the feel of her soft flesh, aroused Horace and made him even more ruthless. "If you don't do what I want, then I'll tell everybody you laid with me. You'll be ruined. No man will ever marry you because you're spoiled. Your father will cast you out of his house."

"Please, Horace!" Priscilla was really frightened now. She sensed that Horace was fully capable of carrying through on his threat. "I'm a good girl. Don't make me—"

In response, Horace squeezed both her naked breasts hard. "You'd better do what I want!" he told her. He unbuttoned his pants and placed his erection in her unwilling hand.

Tears running down her cheeks, Priscilla Armbruster began to masturbate Horace. She was still at it, his threats to tell all the boys that she had lain with him ringing in her ears, when Margaret Stockwell appeared.

"Your mother!" Priscilla saw her first. She released Horace and, small, child breasts bobbling nakedly, flung herself toward the bushes and began to retch.

Bypassing her son, Margaret went to her. Priscilla, still gagging a little, was sobbing. Margaret comforted her. "It's all right. There now." Margaret's hands moved to cover the child's bosom. She quickly buttoned the bodice of the dress.

Horace looked on scowling, frustrated, unsympathetic.

"If my fa-fa-father finds out!" The Armbruster girl was on the edge of hysteria. "He—he—he'll make me leave his house."

"There, there. Nobody is going to find out anything."

"I wouldn't—I wouldn't have done it, ma'am. I swear I wouldn't. Only Horace said he'd tell everybody I was a bad girl who—who did it all."

"It's all right." Margaret rocked her in her arms. "Horace won't tell anybody anything. Will you, Horace?"

"Why should I?" He shrugged. "You're the adult, Mother. It's your duty to tell her parents, not mine."

"I'll do no such thing," Margaret reassured Priscilla. "Now pull yourself together, my child, and wipe your eyes. Then go back to the wedding and don't worry. You made a mistake. That's all. You made a mistake, and you won't do it again."

"Tell her, Mother." Horace allowed a small, mean flicker of amusement in his tone. "Tell her about mistakes. You know all about that, don't you, Mother?"

Margaret waited to answer him until after the Armbruster girl had left. "Yes, Horace," she said then. "I know about mistakes. But you weren't making any mistake, were you, Horace? You were taking advantage of a child four years younger than yourself by frightening her with threats just so she would relieve you of your lust."

"Ahh, yes, Mother. My lust. Well, I won't deny it. It's in my blood, I suppose. You know about that, too, don't you, Mother. You understand lust."

"Yes," Margaret admitted wearily. "I understand lust. What I don't understand is willful cruelty. That's what I don't understand about you, Horace: cruelty."

"Cruelty? Why, that's easy to understand, Mother. I'm

213

a monster. I'm the monster that you and Uncle Roger made me."

He left Margaret there defeated, despairing, and despite her good sense, believing him. Yes, Horace was a monster. It must have been she who had turned him into one.

Horace's character established, it was refined by the passing of the years. He no longer tried to force his lust on the maidens of the Hudson River Valley estates. Instead, he sought his pleasure in the bedchambers of serving girls, seduced the daughters of the Riverview sharecroppers, or bought sex in the bawdy houses on the side streets between the wharves of Manhattan and Bowling Green.

He rounded out his womanizing with other vices, most notably gambling and boozing. His eyes sunk deep beyond his youth, and the notes he signed at the gaming tables were far in excess of his allowance. By his early twenties he had established a reputation as a wastrel, a rakehell, and a sot.

His parents reacted to his excesses in different ways. Horace's mother blamed herself. During the seven years between Mercy's wedding and the wedding of her younger daughter, Deborah, Margaret deteriorated from an active matron in her prime to a weary old woman, nagged by shame and hopelessness. With the passing years, each new dereliction by her son etched harridan lines onto Margaret's once smooth round face.

Everett Stockwell, dried stringbean of a man that he had always been, regarded Horace's depradations with surprising tolerance. He spoke of a young man's right to "sow his wild oats," and there was a hint of envy and almost grudging admiration in his permissiveness. It was as if Horace's self-indulgence was some kind of reward justified by his father's own straitlaced devotion to the business of amassing the Stockwell fortune.

This fortune, to Everett, was an end in itself. With both his daughters married now and gone from Riverview, he turned to his son to perpetuate both the estate and the Stockwell wealth. Turning a blind eye to Horace's gambling and a deaf ear to the stories of his drunken debauches, he took his son into the business with him.

To the astonishment of everyone save father and son, Horace took to the mercantile world like a carp to fresh pond rills. He asked the obvious, innocent questions to be expected of a tyro, but he comprehended the answers quickly—and in all their ramifications—and very soon was putting the theory he had mastered into everyday action. From the first, Everett bragged about his son to his peers in the commodities exchange.

"Three days ago my Horace was harborside signing for futures on Indies salt to the tune of twenty thousand Dutch Sint Maarten guilders."

"You gave that boy authority to spend such a large sum?" Everett's business acquaintance, having heard tales of Horace's gambling losses, was disapproving.

"No." Everett laughed. "That was the beauty of it. He had no such authority. He took it on himself. If the price of salt slid, I'd have disowned the venture. Horace knew that. Either he'd be chastised for exceeding his authority, or we would reap a profit. As it turned out, the profit was considerable—just as Horace knew it would be."

"Knew?" The commodities broker snorted. "Guessed, you mean."

"I mean knew. Horace knew." Everett was stubborn. "He talked to sailors in with molasses from Jamaica and learned of storms breaking up trade to the south off the Windwards. Hurricanes and the like. A daisy chain, one after the other. Half the ships from Sint Maarten headed surely for the bottom to salt the briny. That's how Horace understood what he heard. And in fact, less than half the salt got through for payment on delivery at the preestablished price he bought at and sold the very same day for three times as much. The boy's a natural businessman." Everett puffed out his chest. "It's in the blood."

Proud as he was of his son's acumen, Everett did not always see eye to eye with him. "Buy low, sell high," had been one of the earliest lessons he'd tried to impress on his son, but a year later, when it came to the actual selling, Horace argued with him. "It's higher than you

215

bought," he said, "but it will go much, much higher still."

They were discussing the lots between Fraunces Tavern and Trinity Churchyard that Everett had bought many years before. Now they were worth tenfold what he had paid for them, and Everett had decided to sell and take his profit. "I will come out with triple the worth of Riverview itself," he told his son.

"That," Horace told his father, his own cocksure insolence gilding the traditional arrogance of youth, "is but a drop in the rain barrel compared to what that land will be worth as Port New York expands with future commercial development."

"New York will not expand, my boy," Everett assured his son. "Its limits have been reached. Already it runs a poor second to Boston in tons shipped. And with the opening of the western territories in Buffalo and Ohio and so forth, the shipping trade is already shifting to Quebec and to the southern access ports like New Orleans and Baltimore. Overland costs to Port New York are prohibitive. It's that simple. We have the Hudson River trade to Albany, and it is secure, but that is all we have or shall have. New York's destiny as far as shipping is concerned has been reached. Commercial real estate for warehousing with dock access has peaked, and now is the time to sell." And so Everett had sold.

Horace's last words to his father on the subject had been prescient. "The sale will make you very wealthy, Father. But if you had held the land, we Stockwells would one day be the richest family east of the Mississippi River."

He was right. The value of the land his father sold would come to be measured not in millions, but in billions of dollars. Feet would be measured not by the square, but by the cube, and with each towering skyscraper that climbed to the sun, the worth of the lot at its base would burgeon by trigonometric progression. A great opportunity had indeed been lost to the Stockwells.

Lady Luck, however, had an even greater one in store for them. As astute as Horace was in business, it was because she—Lady Luck—was his mistress that he came to lay the real foundation for the Stockwell fortune. Yes, his father was rich, but Horace would establish an empire of family wealth beyond Everett's dreams. And he would do this not because he was a skilled businessman—which he was—but because he was lucky.

Quite often, however, during those early years in business with his father. Horace was not lucky at the gaming tables he visited with increasing frequency. Astute as he was in business, he was profligate with cards and dice and the wheels of misfortune. He drank heavily when he gambled, and this neither helped his judgment nor restrained his recklessness. When he lost heavily, he would but drink more and then go to some local fleshpot to blot out his losses with orgies of debauchery. On those rare occasions when he won at the gaming tables, he celebrated in similar fashion.

One morning, red of eye and trembly of hand, Horace came to Margaret's sewing room. She was very surprised to see him. Indeed, she rarely saw either Horace or her husband. Everett customarily ignored her; her son, once her tormentor, never hesitating to use her, nor to abuse her, had with maturity granted her the relief of neglect.

Now that relief was abruptly withdrawn. Horace had a problem. His mother, he had decided, harking back to the methods that had stood him in such good stead through his adolescence, would be privileged to solve it.

"I have overextended myself," he told her bluntly. "It is an embarrassment. I do not wish Father to know. I do not wish his good opinion of me to be shaken by some youthful escapade."

"You are past the age when your escapades can be considered youthful," Margaret pointed out wearily.

"Shall we talk about your escapades when you were past your youth, then, Mother?"

"No." Margaret had no heart for the confrontation. She had no strength to deal with her son. Of late, with her daughters gone, her life had seemed emptier and emptier to her, less and less worth the living. As if in response to this, her body had grown weak. She had spells of lassitude, which the doctor ascribed to a clogging of her veins. The cold packs he had prescribed to stir the blood had not helped. Her pulses, too, turned sluggish and—seemingly—with each quarter she aged a year or more. Margaret was not well, and she did not care. "What is it that you want, Horace?" she asked, desiring only to be left alone to her lethargy.

"I have overextended myself. I need money."

"I have no money. You know that. Your father has relieved me of the household accounts."

"But you have jewelry." Horace's innate cruelty expressed itself. "Perhaps even gifts from your dead lover."

"Nothing. He gave me no gifts. Only the gift of love, the gift of himself."

"Touching. Very touching, Mother. But it doesn't solve my problem. Ungenerous as the late Colonel Stockwell may have been, you do have some jewelry, whatever the source."

"Only what your father gave me."

"That will do. Let me see it."

Not caring about the jewels, but deploring the loveless and wicked man her son had become, Margaret fetched her jewel box. She opened it. She watched as Horace pawed through it, selecting four of the most valuable pieces, among them a ruby pendant passed down to her by her mother. It caused a pang, but she did not plead with him to pass it by. She would give him no excuse to once again express his scorn. She watched him pocket the pendant. And when Horace was finally gone, Margaret waited in vain for the vise squeezing her chest to loosen.

After leaving his mother, Horace had one of the Riverview coaches take him into Manhattan. Here he sought out a pawnbroker who relieved him of the jewelry. In exchange, Horace received money to pay off his more pressing debts and to stake himself to a night of baccarat.

It was a rare night, successful beyond any he had known heretofore. Consistently the cards turned to his advantage. With each successful turn of the pasteboards, Horace celebrated with a brandy. He became quite drunk as the evening progressed, but this in no way interfered with his luck. What it did do was raise his body heat to a lust that made him more and more impatient for the excesses of the brothel as player after player was forced to retire from the baccarat table. As Horace accepted the last note from the last player, all he could think of was female flesh and his pressing need to immerse himself in it. Under this pressure, he made an appointment to meet with the last and largest loser some hours hence and receive settlement for what was owing to him.

Horace hurried off to his favorite fleshpot—one known among the sailors for the unusually sadomasochistic quality of the experience it offered. Wielding the birch enhanced Horace's lust. Sometimes, particularly when he was drunk, he would be carried away, and the most hardened among the brothel's harlots might turn squeamish and reluctant to service him.

This evening he picked one of the newest of the bawds, a German girl, young and blond and virginal looking. Her fear at his gusto with the birch aroused him to the fullest. Her face streaked with tears, her expression most pitiable, she was suffering his lust to the extreme when they were abruptly interrupted.

It was a messenger from Riverview, sent by Horace's father. His mother had been stricken. The doctor said that it was her heart and that her hours were numbered. Everett wished his son to return to Riverview and his mother's bedside immediately.

Horace stared drunkenly at the messenger. He looked down at the German strumpet, striated by the birch, tremblingly agape. He took a long, deep suck from the brandy flagon. "You couldn't find me," Horace told the messenger before turning his back on him.

"Begging your pardon, Mr. Horace?" The footman who had ridden his horse to a froth to deliver the message did not know what to make of this reaction.

"I was not to be found." Horace's voice was very soft. "Do you understand me, imbecile?" He fished out some gold coins from his trousers hanging off the bedpost and handed them to the footman. "You will tell my father that you looked everywhere—everywhere!—but to no avail. I could not be located."

Horace turned back to the blonde as the footman hurriedly departed. He picked up the birch and flexed it. The interruption had cooled his ardor, but that would soon be rectified. Even as the young German whore's eyes widened with fear at the whistling of the rod, he felt his lust reassert itself.

He had all but forgotten the message by the time his lust was spent at the bawdy house. His brain muddled by a long evening of consistent tippling, he nevertheless remembered to keep his appointment with the man who had lost so heavily to him at baccarat. Befuddled as he was by drink, squinting at the handful of notes the loser had signed, Horace realized that there was a considerable sum involved.

The man, younger than Horace, quite pale since he had sobered up and realized the extent of his losses, came from a family that valued honor above all. It was unthinkable to him to renege on a gambling debt. Thus he was waiting in his office for Horace at the appointed hour, his safe opened, his ledger spread, his assets ready to be examined and totaled and, to the extent that they were owing, transferred to Horace.

"They do not cover the debt." Never too drunk to audit accurately, Horace totaled the result and found it wanting.

"If you will extend the time, I will go to the bank and borrow the difference."

"You have property, then, on which to borrow?"

"I have my good name, sir."

"And little knowledge of the banking industry," Horace opined dryly. "Have you nothing else but that, then?" He glanced toward the strongbox. It was open. A thick sheaf of stock certificates was still inside it. "What is that?" Horace demanded, suspicious that the debtor might be holding out on him.

"Ditch-digging stock. Worthless. I would not take advantage of you, sir, by passing it off as otherwise."

"Ditch-digging stock?"

"Clinton's Folly." The young man was truly trying to be honest with Horace. "DeWitt is a friend of the family. We bought stock in his company purely out of friendship.

It cost little and is worth less. Indeed, with the latest re-
fusal by the Congress in Washington to fund his project,
added to the denial by the legislature in Albany to approve it, this stock in his company is worth nothing at
all.''

Horace picked up the sheaf of stock and examined it.
''Erie Canal Dredging and Construction Company.'' He
read the gilt-edged lettering aloud. ''Well, worthless or
not, sign it over to me anyway,'' he said. ''I won it fair
and square.''

You couldn't even call it a hunch, Horace's descendants would admit later. It was sheer blind luck. It was
the sort of luck upon which all the great fortunes of New
York State rest—the Rockefellers, the Vanderbilts, the
Harrimans.

But, thanks to the Erie Canal, the Stockwell fortune
would be the greatest of them all.

Margaret was dead by the time Horace returned to Riverview.

36

''A DITCH?'' JACK HOUSTON traced the pronounced cleft
between Patrice Stockwell O'Keefe's breasts.
''You're telling me that the foundation of the Stockwell
fortune was a ditch?''

''A very important ditch.'' Patrice squirmed and covered herself with the sheet. ''A ditch three hundred sixty-
three miles long, forty feet wide, four feet deep, and filled
with water.''

She was bemused at the interest Jack took in the origins
of the Stockwell fortune. Indeed, everything about how
the family corporation was controlled and run seemed to
fascinate Jack. He was not only interested in decision

making, but how the board operated, how Stockwell shuffled paper in the commodities market, petroleum, real estate, and—especially—insurance. Patrice, basking in the emotional warmth and physical satisfactions of their affair, was flattered by his admiration for her expertise in the world of high finance. Everything, these days, was making her happy.

Even the present setting, cramped as it was, seemed idyllic to Patrice. She and Jack were crowded into one of the narrow lower bunks on her father's yacht as it rested at anchor alongside the Riverview dock on the Hudson. They had just made love, bumping their heads, scraping their legs, getting in each other's way, and laughing even as they thrilled to their mutual climax.

Outside, it was early springtime. A small scouting party of advance songbirds was flashing color amid the greening branches of the oaks and maples. Their twittering was lost to the rush of the river as the water threatened to overflow its banks. The moist earth was turning from cold to warm, and with the rhythm of the changing seasons, life was renewing itself at Riverview.

"A ditch . . ." Jack was still turning it over in his mind.

"More than that," Patrice assured him. "The Erie Canal opened up the West, although in the beginning what was thought of as 'west' was a far cry from what we consider west today. Of course, back then, west was New York beyond Albany, and Pennsylvania, maybe parts of Ohio, but certainly nothing farther than Detroit in the Michigan Territory. Its population peaked at nine thousand along about 1820."

"What did you do? Memorize the history book?" Teasing her, Jack was nevertheless impressed.

"I've always been fascinated by how my family did it."

"Just how did they do it?" Jack was genuinely interested.

"More history," Patrice warned him. "But okay. Just before and after the War of 1812, farmers in New England and New York began migrating west—first to the lands between Albany and Buffalo, then farther and farther into the heartland. The soil in the east was hard to work, rocky. Farther west it was much richer, and the yield was much greater. Word spread, and there was a major agrarian migration.''

''This was *before* the Erie Canal was built?''

''Yes. The pioneers found the soil arable beyond their dreams. Besides that, the region was rich in timberland. Also, it abounded in fur-bearing game, which was being trapped seasonally by French-Canadian trappers. Word drifted back to New England, and so the merchants migrated to the region. They organized the fur trade. They also bought up the timberlands and set up sawmills and shipped boards ready for use. Since the country was growing, timber became big business. So now this new area that they called the Far West back then was producing food and fur garments and lumber. And all these products were in such demand that a truly vicious trade war broke out among rival shipping ports from Louisiana to Quebec over marketing them. And in this competition, the port of New York City fell further and further behind.''

''Why was that?''

''Transportation costs. Roads were poor, most of them little more than mountain and forest trails. There were no railroads yet. Shipping by waterway—river and lake—was the cheapest, but New York was limited to the length of the Hudson River. Any goods it imported from beyond Albany had to be hauled overland from Lake Erie and beyond. Before the Erie Canal was built, the cost of shipping a ton of freight overland from Buffalo to New York City was twenty cents a mile.''

''And after it was built?'' Jack asked.

''Less than a penny.'' Patrice grinned. ''But twenty-five percent of that penny went to Stockwell Limited. And there were one helluva lot of pennies.''

''And all because of a blackjack game,'' Jack mused.

''Baccarat, actually. They're similar. But there was more to it than that. Horace Stockwell pushed hard for the construction of the canal.''

''There was resistance?''

''Oh, yes. The canal would make New York City supreme among seaports on the North American continent. Other harbor cities didn't look kindly on that prospect.

When DeWitt Clinton and Governor Morris went to Washington, D.C., to ask Congress to appropriate money for the construction of a waterway to connect Lake Erie to the Hudson River, the response they got was 'Drop dead, New York.' ''

"The more things change, the more they stay the same," Jack observed.

"And how. Well, Clinton began a campaign in Albany to have the New York State legislature underwrite a bond issue to be sold to private investors as a way of financing construction of the canal. He even formed an engineering company to survey a route and begin dredging, invested substantially in it himself, and persuaded friends and acquaintances to invest as well. These were the stocks that Horace Stockwell acquired. But Albany was hostile. Dig a ditch that would cost millions of dollars to help that sinkhole-on-the-sea, New York City? Float bonds for the benefit of Wall Street? No-siree-bob. They called it 'Clinton's Folly,' and when Clinton left Albany, the stock in his company was worthless."

"Obviously that changed," Jack realized. "How?"

"The Stockwells and other powerful stockholders leaned on the legislators. Some were cut in for a piece of the pie. 'Clinton's Folly' was suddenly seen to be practical, viable, forward looking. Six years after the legislators had all but ridden Clinton out of Albany on a rail, they authorized a seven-million-dollar expenditure by the state of New York to build the canal. The contract was let to the Erie Canal Dredging and Construction Company. And overnight, from a corporate entity without assets, it became a going concern. There were subcontracts to be let, land to be bought, deals to be made. Horace Stockwell was there every step of the way."

"And so he got rich." Jack shook his head in wonder. "That simple."

"Not quite. Horace was really very shrewd. He had already bought up land cheap along the proposed route, and when the time came he sold it back to New York State for many times what he'd paid. He saw from the very beginning how important the canal would be to the future of New York City. Furthermore, long before Erie was

224

completed, he began buying midwest farm- and timber-land. He even built lumber mills. His investments around Detroit—less than fifty thousand dollars—were sold by Stockwell Industries at the beginning of the Japanese invasion of the auto industry in the mid-1970s for over six billion dollars. But then, of course, there was some luck in that, too.''

"What sort of luck?'' Jack asked.

"He bought timberlands because of the early 1800s' building boom, but that was nothing compared to the value of timber later when they started to build the railroads. Wooden freight cars, wooden carriages, wooden railroad ties—the demand sent the price of lumber skyrocketing.''

"Lucky,'' Jack agreed.

"Oh, yes,'' Patrice continued. "In more ways than one. The farmland he bought was later found to be rich in iron and copper. He encouraged immigration of cheap labor to work these mines. He built foundries where iron stoves were manufactured for the kitchens of America and Europe. And those stoves were shipped via the Erie Canal at a penny a ton in enough bulk so that the quarter-cent that came back to Stockwell Limited totaled millions of dollars annually.''

"He profited on both the manufacturing and the shipping,'' Jack realized.

"Not only that. Long after Horace Stockwell's death, those same Stockwell foundries were in place to provide prebuilt components for Henry Ford's assembly line. Before the Japanese, Stockwell had a thirty percent market share among parts suppliers of the 'big three' auto makers.''

"And so the largest fortune in the East was really earned in the West,'' Jack realized, then grinned his calculatedly boyish grin. "For a passionate lady, you sure are one helluva knowledgeable businesswoman.''

"Don't be chauvinistic.''

"In the sack I'm always chauvinistic.''

"Betty Friedan, forgive me.'' Patrice raised the sheet high, an invitation for Jack to rejoin her.

* * *

225

A long time later, after they had finished making love a second time, Jack returned to the topic of Stockwell Industries. "My background's so different from yours," he told Patrice. "I'm really in awe of the world of high finance you take for granted. The workings of the Stockwell board, for instance. That intrigues me."

"Haven't you ever asked Buffy about it?" Immediately, Patrice could have bitten off her tongue. She wasn't a hardened husband stealer by any means, but she did know enough not to mention her lover's wife when they lay side by side naked between the sheets together. "Sorry," she added quickly.

"It's all right. Anyway, Buffy never will talk about Stockwell business with me. I think she still suspects me of having married her to get my hooks into the Stockwell fortune. She acts like the board is the National Security Council and all its documents are top secret or something."

"Hardly that." Patrice was amused. "I take papers home with me all the time. More often than not they're just lying around my apartment."

Including the reinsurance stuff? Jack wondered, but didn't ask aloud. Instead, he approached his objective obliquely. He was silent a moment and then—seemingly—changed the subject. "It's really not so smart our making love up here at Riverview," he said. "I'm always nervous."

"I can understand that, darling," Patrice replied, remembering that Buffy, too, resided at Riverview.

"I wish I'd kept my place on Riverside Drive. Then I could invite you to spend the night there with me."

"Yes. That would be lovely." Patrice took the bait. "But why can't we spend the night at my apartment?"

"The one on Sutton Place." Jack grinned. "I remember. Sounds great. Pick a night."

"How about Wednesday?"

"How about tomorrow?" Jack countered.

Patrice's heart leaped at his eagerness. "All right. Tomorrow, then."

"What time?"

"Well, I have a board meeting." Patrice told Jack what

226

he already knew. "But it should be over by five. Say six o'clock?"

"Swell. Only—" Jack scowled as if it had just occurred to him. "I'll be through with my business at four. Damn! I wish I did still have my apartment. Then at least I could take a shower before you got there."

"I'll give you the key to my place," Patrice offered. "You can go there early and shower up a storm."

Bingo! "That would be great." Jack's eyes adored her. "Only you won't get it back. I'm warning you. You'll never know which night you'll find me waiting in your bed."

"Promises, promises." Patrice laughed, delighted. "If I'd only known that all it took was a shower and a key to hook you." She kissed him.

Jack kissed back fiercely, taking her breath away. Then, with a show of reluctance that was partly genuine, he glanced at his watch. "Oops! Tempis done fugited faster than I realized. I've got to get dressed and get into town. I've got an appointment."

"I've got to get cracking, too."

Ten minutes later they emerged on the deck of the yacht. Before they started up the hillside to the garage where their cars were, Jack took Patrice in his arms and kissed her thoroughly. It was the kind of kiss that left no doubt as to the nature of the tryst to which it was writing an exclamation point.

Unbeknownst to Patrice and Jack, the kiss was seen. Out for a rare early-morning walk, Buffy found herself observing it. Her husband and Patrice! It hurt her much more deeply than she had ever admitted to herself it might. Although she might joke about it, she had never truly believed that her young husband was a gigolo. The pain drove her back into the house.

Buffy went to her room, where she brooded. Then, as was her nature, she made herself stop brooding and acted. Picking up the telephone receiver, she dialed long distance. After a moment, a Texas twang crackled in her ear: "Grebbs Refinery. Can I help y'all?"

"I would like to speak to Mr. Jimbo Grebbs, please," Buffy said.

37

JACK HOUSTON TOOK a cab from Grand Central. On Broadway, just above Houston Street, it got stuck in a massive traffic jam precipitated by a burst sewer main. Deciding to walk the rest of the way, he paid off the driver and climbed out of the taxi.

Cutting east to get away from the carbon monoxide fumes, he found himself heading downtown through Little Italy to get to Chinatown and his appointment with the Don. Strolling through a heady miasma of garlic, oregano, and marinara fumes, he was at the mercy of his salivary glands.

On the northern edge of Chinatown, just below Canal Street, before the switchover from pasta to dim sung could detour his dilating nostrils into one of the fragrant Cantonese restaurants, Jack came to the ancient building housing the Sun Kai Don Noodle Company. He climbed a narrow staircase to the second floor and knocked on a door of old-fashioned frosted glass. The Don called to him to come right on in.

"Back here, old buddy."

Jack followed the voice to a kitchen behind the noodle company offices.

"Just putting on the feedbag, boy. Care to join me?"

It had been a long, hungry walk. Little Italy, Chinatown. "Thanks, yes." Jack accepted.

"Chicken steaks and twice-fried beans," Sun Kai Don told him. "Good-old-boy Tex-Mex country food. Put hair on your chest."

Jack had no trouble believing that a little while later when the Don handed him a plate so laced with red-hot chili powder that his eyes started to water before he took his first forkful. Sun Kai Don passed him a bottle of tequila with a wink. "Cool it down with this," was his advice.

They ate in silence for a few minutes. Then Sun Kai

Don got down to business. "Now how 'bout that list of companies Stockwell's buying policies from?" he asked. "You goin' to come through with that, boy?"

"No problem. I'll have it for you Monday."

"Good. Now, plus the reinsurance operation, we know there are five Stockwell insurance companies sellin' direct. Four we're familiar with. But there's a fifth one, a small one, that's new to us. What can you tell me 'bout that, old buddy?" He mentioned the name of Max Tyler's company. "Is it into smoke premiums, too?"

"It underwrites fire and theft. But it's also into straight life, annuities, and even health," Jack told him. "Its focus is on selling all kinds of insurance to the gay community."

"And it's tied in to Stockwell?" Sun Kai was surprised.

"Well, in a way it is, and in a way it isn't. Max Tyler is a Stockwell cousin. He started the company with Stockwell money he inherited. He's on the board, and he consults with Stockwell about insurance matters affecting his company, besides having a voice in other Stockwell insurance matters. But at the same time he holds his firm independent of the Stockwell holding company that controls the other Stockwell insurance interests."

"Reckon we won't meddle with Tyler's operation, then," Sun Kai Don decided. "If we ever shot down the one insurance company made its reputation fair dealin' the gay community, we'd have all kinds of problems we don't rightly need. Gays and lesbians and civil libertarians all coming down on us like so many sun-baked adobe bricks. No, sir. We don't need that."

" 'Shot down'?" Jack picked up on the two words. "Does that mean we will be shooting down the other four companies—the ones under Stockwell control that underwrite directly?"

"That and more, boy. We aren't aiming small, you know. The Stockwell insurers and the reinsurers—those are our targets." The Don smiled a down-home smile, his angled eyes crinkling. "In our opinion Stockwell Industries is a downright monopolistic organization, and it is sure enough in the public interest to break down the structure and maybe redistribute some of the assets and some of the ongoing operations along with them."

Jack stared at him. He was sitting in a Chinese noodle company eating Tex-Mex food with a man his grandfather believed to be a Mafia don. And this Chinese man with the southwestern drawl was belting tequila and licking salt from the heel of his hand and telling him—what? "Are you suggesting a corporate takeover?" Jack asked disbelievingly.

"Friendly, boy. And by no means the whole shebang." The Don dipped a tortilla chip in guacamole. "You know," he mused, "Stockwell is diversified as all get-out. Six months ago it broke down roughly five ways to twenty percent petroleum, twenty percent cultural investments, twenty percent real estate, twenty percent banking and brokerage, and twenty percent insurance. Today that twenty percent insurance is creeping up towards a third of the total Stockwell operation. Now that is what you might call a significant increase."

"Arbitrage?" Jack was still stunned.

"In a way, old buddy. That'll be the means if we get off the ground. It depends on you. Things are moving very fast. We need to know just where Stockwell's shopping to expand its reinsurance operation."

"It figures they're shifting over to insurance," Jack realized, dazzled by the magnitude of what the Don was planning. "They can't get their crude refined. So they've got petrodollars to spend."

"So we hear, Jack. And we also hear there's a young Stockwell name of Peter who's buying up fire policies in high-roller reinsurance batches like a kid with a sweet tooth discovered a sale on jelly beans. Right greedy boy, that Peter Stockwell. And his greed makes that insurance third of Stockwell vulnerable as hell. You get us those names, Jack, and we start selling that smoky paper to him. And there will soon come a time, old buddy, when we will do a friendly Teddy Turner number on the holding company behind that Stockwell insurance that should give us fifty-one percent control of one-third of Stockwell Industries."

"Just how are you going to do that?" Impressed as he was, Jack was still skeptical.

"New York State law, boy. That's how." Sun Kai Don poured Jack another tequila and pushed it toward him.

"Could you be more specific?"

"All righty. Now those four Stockwell companies are heavy into inner-city fire insurance. You bring me those names, and they'll tell me where this Peter does his shopping. Hell, the insurance business isn't that big. He's dealing with a broker peddling blocks of policies for reinsurance that he himself is maybe picking up from eight other brokers. And the buying patterns—where and who from—why, boy, they repeat themselves."

"So you've got the list. What then?"

"Why, then we start feeding policies into those companies knowing they'll be funneled to Stockwell. Pretty soon, that Peter, he'll be buying nigh all his paper from us without ever realizing it. And you know what, Jack? Those buildings he'll be insurin'—they'll be the very ones the owners have contracted out to be torched."

"You mean arson?" Despite himself, Jack was shocked.

"It's progress, boy. Move out the slums. Move in the condos. Anyway, that has nothing to do with us. Whether we buy the paper or not, they'll be torched. Believe me. It's the profit system. They stand there rotting, nobody makes a silver dollar. They burn, there's cartwheels for the landlord, the real estate people, the building contractors, even the city of New York, which gets itself a new batch of taxable high-rent high rises."

"But what about the people who live there? Don't they lose their homes? Where are they supposed to live?"

"Life isn't fair, boy. Your namesake Jack Kennedy said that. Anyway, the arson isn't our end. The insurance is."

"And you'll funnel the insurance on these buildings that are being torched to Stockwell. But part of the game is that they resell it. They won't be holding the paper. I don't get it. What kind of lever does that give you for a takeover?"

"New York State law, boy. Remember, I mentioned that. This property is in New York State. And that means that the one who held the policy thirty days prior to the fire destroying it is the one responsible for paying up. Make a note of that, old buddy. Not the original insurer. Not the one holding the paper the day of the fire. The one who took it over thirty days prior to the blaze is the one that pays. That's the New York State grace period."

"I think I'm beginning to understand," Jack said slowly. "If you can control the flow of paper Peter Stockwell buys, then you can make sure Stockwell is the insurer who has to pay up when the buildings are torched."

"That's right, Jack. And we can do it in bulk. So much bulk that we shake the financial structure of the holding company behind those four Stockwell insurance companies and of the one behind the reinsurance program Peter Stockwell runs. The stock in those holding companies is going to nosedive. And just when it hits bottom, boy, we buy."

"And you really think we'll end up with a third of Stockwell Industries?"

"I can't promise a third, boy. But I can promise you that if you stick with us, we'll end up with a place on that board equal to the one your wife has."

"That's exactly what I want out of this," Jack said. Buffy's face! He could just see Buffy's face! "I want to be that new face on the board."

"You come through for us, boy, and we'll guarantee you can be our man on the Stockwell board."

"But can it really work?" Jack asked, ignoring the words "our man." "I mean, there's a helluva lot of financial clout behind Stockwell. If it was brought to bear, they could stop us cold from taking over anything."

"It's timing, boy. And knowledge. That adds up to power. We'll know what's going to happen. They won't. They'll have too many balls—too much investment capital—in the air to be able to react spontaneously when they start tumblin'. By the time they realize it's brandin' time, the iron'll already be sizzlin' up their butts."

"Graphic." Jack couldn't help grinning. The words seemed so incongruous from this man who looked like he should be quoting Confucius to his grandchildren.

"The mob is connected around the world, right?"

"Yep."

"In Greece?"

"Sure."

"And it puts the snatch on people?"

"You've been reading too much Damon Runyon, old buddy. But that's right, too. There's revenue in ransom."

"All right, then." Jack took a deep breath. "You know about the Zelig Meyerling kidnapping. Do you know if the mob is involved with it?"

"The papers are laying it at the Arabs' door." Sun Kai Don shrugged. "What makes you think different?"

"I don't, necessarily. It's only one possibility. But it is one that the family's concerned about."

"The family you and me are about to hornswoggle? Why should you care about their problem?" the Don asked.

"Zelig's wife is a friend of mine."

The Don raised one thin Oriental eyebrow.

"Not like that. Really a friend. I'd like to help her out if I could. I mean, if you know anything—"

The Don interrupted, "I stay in business by making it my business not to meddle in my partners' business, old buddy. It guarantees a long life without holes where your guts should be."

"Couldn't you just sort of ask around among your contacts in Greece?" Jack pushed it.

"I don't ask around. You have questions for these people, you have to go to Greece yourself."

"If I did . . ." Jack spoke slowly. It was the first time the idea had occurred to him. "—And these people weren't involved themselves . . . would they maybe have the contacts to point me towards the ones who are responsible?"

"You'd have to ask them that. Maybe they would, and maybe they wouldn't. And if they did know, or find out, maybe they'd tell you, and maybe they wouldn't tell you."

"But you will put me in touch with them?"

"Oh, sure, old buddy. We're partners, aren't we? One hand washing the other and like that? You bring me that list we talked about, and I'll give you a name in Athens can maybe be of help to you."

"Thanks." Jack's mind was racing. He knew from Patrice that on Crete Holly and James were just sitting around waiting with no leads at all. Maybe he could get some information to set a rescue of Zelig Meyerling into motion. Maybe with this contact through the Don, he just could do that.

38

"POOR HOLLY. THIS really is a bad time for you."
Winifred Fitzsimmmons's high piping voice startled Holly. She had not heard Winifred approaching. Holly had taken this solitary walk along the Crete mountain path in an effort to calm nerves rubbed raw by waiting. If something doesn't happen soon, she had realized, I will scream out loud. And once I start to scream, I will not be able to stop. Why don't the kidnappers at least contact us and say what it is they want? Day after day the question went unanswered. And so Holly hiked the mountain seeking physical release from the unending tension.

"Winifred." She hid her annoyance; she had wanted to be alone. "I didn't hear you coming."

"Really? And I am such an elephant when it comes to the great outdoors." Winifred's voice was lilting and chirpy, a breath of heather fresh from Sussex.

It made Holly smile despite herself. Immediately, however, the smile vanished. Sussex was a long way off. This was Crete. There was no heather, but rather a harsher beauty of gnarled olive trees bowering against the sun, creating pockets of green-and-silver mystery in the shadows of still frosty crags. The mists were not soft English mists, but the crueler ones of Greek legend, of forests peopled with satyrs and witness to rapine, of mountain-

234

tops where lusty gods proclaimed carnality and slew at will.

Holly shuddered. And what of Zelig? his carnality? Was he alive? Or had he, too, been slain . . . at will?

"I didn't mean to intrude." Once again Winifred's treble broke the timeless silence. "If you'd rather be alone . . ."

Her tone, so obviously fearing rejection, claimed Holly's attention. Pale as ivory and tremulously English, Winifred did indeed seem pathetically vulnerable in this severe Cretan setting. Yet Holly was suspicious.

"It's all right." She didn't turn Winifred away, but she was cautious. "I was just taking a breather before the last lap." Her upward gesture indicated the unseen peak of the low mountain she had been climbing. "What brings you up here?" she asked.

"I had to get away from Lisa." Winifred sat down next to Holly on the wild grass, leaning her back against the same tree trunk. "She's having the beastlies."

"Uncle James is very concerned about her."

"Lisa doesn't want his concern. She wants his acceptance. For what she is, don't you know."

After considering, Holly replied, "That's hard for Uncle James. Any deviation from heterosexuality is difficult for him."

"And you, Holly?" The wide sapphire eyes looked at her directly. "Have you finally reached a point in your life where you can deal with it?"

"I could always deal with it," Holly snapped, then relented, allowing concern for Winifred to soften her voice. "I was naive back in Sussex, Winifred. I didn't know that you wanted me that way. I thought we were friends."

"It was one of the happiest times in my life," Winifred remembered softly. "I miss it so."

"Well, it's over," Holly said flatly. "And you know that I only considered you a friend—nothing more."

"Lisa doesn't believe that. She's driving me crazy with her jealousy."

"You never should have told her about us. Not," Holly added hastily, "that there was ever anything to tell. We were friends, that was all."

"Was it?" Winifred's intensity grew. "We embraced, we kissed."

"That doesn't make me a lesbian," Holly closed her eyes and counted to ten, trying to keep the anger out of her voice. "I hug my women friends. We kiss. It doesn't mean anything."

"Why do you lie to yourself, Holly? Even Lisa thinks you're—"

"Lisa is very mixed up," Holly reminded Winifred.

"She thinks I'm getting involved with you all over again. She's very jealous of you."

"But it's not true," Holly protested, wanting this young woman and her problems to go away.

"It could be." Still sitting beside her on the grass, Winifred twisted her upper body to face Holly. She put her hands on Holly's shoulders. "If it were up to me, it would be."

"Stop it, Winifred." Holly's voice was cold.

"Don't deny what we feel for each other!" First Winifred's voice broke, and then her control. She pulled Holly to her and tried to kiss her forcibly.

"Damn you, Winifred!" Holly pulled away and slapped the younger Englishwoman hard across the face. Even as the slap reddened Winifred's cheek, Holly regretted it. She did not want to hurt Winifred. These two young women obviously needed her help, her understanding. Holly rose quickly and plunged among the olive trees, fleeing up the trail.

Behind her, Winifred lay crumpled and sobbing on the rich, moist mountain earth of pitiless Crete.

That night, dinner at the Papatestus villa was served outdoors on the patio. Winifred was not present. Lisa, with a sharp side glance at Holly, said that her friend wasn't feeling well. Just before coffee and brandy was served, Lisa excused herself and left.

James watched her go with concerned eyes. "Do you think she's losing more weight?" he asked Holly in a low voice. "I wish she would eat more."

Holly squeezed his hand reassuringly under the table.

"Sis does look thin." Michael, spending the weekend,

echoed his father's concern. "Don't you think so?" He turned to Louise for confirmation.

Louise shrugged. Privately she was skeptical of Michael's concern for his sister. She didn't trust the young congressman. There was always something about the way he looked at her that made her press her knees tightly together. And his touch—even a simple handshake—made her skin crawl.

"We are all of us under a lot of tension," Spiro Papatestus observed. "Most of all Holly, of course."

Xanthos nodded his head and said nothing. There was always some question as to whether his English was up to following the nuances of a conversation in that language. Usually his friend Clint provided clarification, but the young man wasn't present tonight. A few hours before dinner he had announced that he was driving into Iraklion to see an Altman flick the university film society was screening.

"I thought surely we'd have heard from the kidnappers by now." James frowned. "What can be their point in abducting Zelig if they don't contact us with demands?" He did not say that it was understandable if Zelig was dead. He didn't want to upset Holly further. Still, it was what James couldn't help thinking.

Nor could the others. It made them all uncomfortable. In an effort to shift the focus, Louise made herself turn to Michael. "Tell us, Congressman," she said, "have the experts any new theories about who might be involved in the abduction?"

"There is," Michael replied reluctantly, "one new theory they're postulating."

"Yes?" Holly was instantly alert.

Now Michael appeared very unhappy indeed. "It concerns the—umm—Brewster woman," he said in a low voice. He was very careful to look at neither Holly nor his father.

"What?" James stared at his son. "What is it you're saying, Michael?"

"Or not saying?" Holly asked softly.

Michael took a deep breath. "The Brewster woman has a pretty shady past," he reminded them. "Always she

237

has involved herself with men of power, manipulating them, making fools of them."

"Thank you, Michael." James regarded his son dryly.

"I'm sorry, Dad." Having gone this far, Michael decided to continue. "Women who are attracted to power generally want it for themselves. They've been known to act to get it. Vanessa Brewster may have been the one who fingered Zelig for the kidnappers. Anyway, that's the latest hypothesis our I-spy boys are kicking around."

"Ridiculous!" James bellowed.

"But how would she have—?" Holly reacted simultaneously with James.

Spiro, Louise, and Xanthos were observing the interaction uncomfortably. There was so much raw emotion beneath the still-civilized surface of the discussion.

"Somehow the kidnappers knew where Zelig would be." Michael spelled out the reasons for the suspicion. "The only others who knew were Zelig himself and Vanessa Brewster. It's not unreasonable, given her history, to suspect her of setting him up."

"That's absurd." James's voice was icy. "If Vanessa was involved, why would she draw attention to herself by contacting Holly and revealing her affair with Zelig?"

"I don't know," Holly said slowly. "She could have done that to throw the investigation off track. In case we found out anyway."

"That's insane." James kept control. "I know Vanessa better than any of you. She may be many things, but she's not involved with terrorists."

"Dad . . ." Michael felt he had to say it. "If you know Vanessa Brewster so well, then why were you so surprised and hurt when you found out she'd gone to bed with another man? I love you, Dad, but when it comes to women—"

"That will be just about enough, Michael!" James interrupted his son sharply.

There was an awkward silence. Holly was thinking to herself that it just might be true. Vanessa might have seduced Zelig in the service of his abductors. She understood that the idea was very painful for James, that he couldn't deal with it. After all, who should understand how James felt better than she? Still, painful as it might be for James, Holly couldn't ignore the fact that it was a real possibility.

The silence was broken by the arrival of the liveried footman, who had glided onto the patio from the villa.

He said something to Louise in Greek. Spiro started to translate, but Louise stopped him. "I understand," she said. "There's a phone call for you, Holly."

Holly turned quite pale. Could this be the contact from the kidnappers for which she had been so impatiently waiting? Jumping up from the chair, she followed the footman back into the villa.

He showed her where the phone was lying off the hook on an onyx table. Holly picked it up. "Hello?"

"Holly." A female voice. "This is Carrie. Carrie Tyler."

"Carrie? What on earth—"

"Listen very carefully, Holly. First I want you to know that I'm not directly involved in what I'm about to tell you. I'm only a go-between."

"What do you mean? A go-between for who? For what? Does this have to do with Zelig?"

"Please, Holly. Just listen. I don't have much time. It's very complicated. I am mixed up with a man in a crazy kind of way. Not what you might think, probably, but I don't have time to go into that." Carrie was speaking very rapidly. "What you should know is that he's part of the group that's holding Zelig."

"Zelig's alive!" A surge of relief swept over Holly.

"Yes. Zelig is alive. My friend guarantees it. He wants to set up a meeting to discuss the terms of his release."

"What sort of terms?"

"They involve an exchange for Arab freedom fighters held in Israel."

"And if the terms are met, they'll let Zelig go?" Holly's heart was beating wildly.

"Yes. Now listen, Holly. He will come to you at Louise's villa to discuss the demands and any arrangements that are to be made. Meanwhile, I will remain with his confederates, a voluntary hostage until his safe return." Carrie sounded frightened. "I want you to know that. His safe passage in and out of the villa must be guaranteed. My own safety depends on it."

"When? When will he come here?"

"If you agree to the conditions of the meeting, I'll get back to you and set the time."

"I do agree if such a meeting can lead to Zelig's safe return. But it's not in my power to guarantee the demands will be met. I don't have the power—I mean, Arabs held in Israel—" Holly's mind was racing ahead; she was floundering.

"Holly, listen to me. To these people, as a Stockwell you can do anything. They believe Israel will do whatever America and the Stockwells want them to do. This is not a point to argue. I'm telling you this so you'll know what will be expected of you."

"But who are these people, Carrie? The last I knew you were with Greenpeace. It can't be Greenpeace."

"Of course not." Carrie was momentarily amused at the idea of straight-arrow Greenpeace being suspected of participation in such an outlandish venture.

"How can you be mixed up with some Arab terrorist group, Carrie? Who are they?" Holly demanded a second time.

"They call themselves 'Jihad of Allah.' "

" 'Jihad' means holy war," Holly remembered. "But this man, Carrie—the one you're involved with. Who is he?"

"Yusuf al-Bekka. His name is Yusuf al-Bekka." All sound was momentarily muffled in Holly's ear as Carrie covered the mouthpiece. Then, abruptly, she spoke again. "I have to hang up now, Holly. I'll contact you soon." This time the phone really did go dead.

Holly stood dazed for a moment, holding the receiver. Yusuf al-Bekka. The name still echoed hopefully in her ear. Yusuf al-Bekka guaranteed that Zelig was alive!

39

ZELIG MEYERLING WASN'T about to die. From the first he
had realized that. While his value to his abductors alive
was surely negotiable, dead it was zilch. He was safe
enough as a hostage, ill fed, ill housed, and bored, even
roughly treated, although not tortured—unless you
counted the self-abuse of idle lust.

Zelig found his sexual arousal under such conditions
more humorous than awesome. It betrayed a side of his
nature that while trumpeted by the all-intrusive media,
he nevertheless usually managed to keep in check. Only
private circumstances relaxed the reins. The boredom of
the blindfold, he supposed, qualified as a private circumstance. Well, it was boring propped up here on a dirt floor
against a baked clay wall for unseeing hours on end. Not
a glimmer of light and only the inside of his head on which
to focus. Naturally, sooner or later his attention would
stray to the erotic.

He thought of Holly. Their love was deep and real.
Damn! he missed her! Also, he felt guilty. That was
strange because Zelig did not believe in guilt. He considered it unproductive, never deserved, always a negative
force. To stray is human, so why feel guilty?

He had been without Holly for eight weeks. A woman
had come along and made herself available, and since his
wife was absent, and so deprived of nothing, he had sex
with the woman. There was no love, only a briefly shared
passion, and surely there was no loss to Holly in the
doing. A man can't be expected to store up semen like a
miser hoarding gold against a rainy day.

So there should be no guilt, Zelig reasoned with himself. But there was retribution. But why? Why—under the
blindfold Zelig raised his eyes heavenward—am I being
punished this way?

Because you made an error; he answered himself. You
weren't careful. You knew there must be surveillance.

And yet, like some Swiss schoolboy marching behind his erection, you followed your putz to Mata Hari.

Mata Hari?

Well, why not. She had been there, Vanessa Brewster, by the side of the road where he must pass and few others did. An unlikely place to hitchhike. For who else could she have been waiting? And then the come-on. Unmistakable. Body language. Which is how he, the renowned Zelig Meyerling, set himself up for the big Plaka snatch.

Had Vanessa Brewster fingered him? Had the mighty Meyerling fallen into the oldest pubic trap of all? Had she, without his noticing, put a candle in the window of her room in the Plaka signaling her confederates that the patsy was on the way down, sated with sex and ready for kidnapping?

It was dark when he'd left her. He'd come down the stairs and out onto the eight-inch-wide sidewalk of the Plaka. He'd walked past the small church with the dig exposing the relics in back of it. A spotlight illuminated a weathered madonna, but all around it was blackness. And from the blackness came hands and arms, a cloth over his face, the smell of chloroform, the bump drag into the car, and then motion and still more blackness.

Zelig awakened to it, the blackness and the sense of motion—smoother now, out of Athens, on a highway somewhere, he supposed. His eyes were taped shut with the blindfold. His hands were tied behind his back.

"What do you want?" It was all he could think of to say, each word an individual clot of fur between his tongue and the roof of his mouth.

"Why, the whole ball of wax, Dr. Meyerling. What else?" The chuckle was soft, brief.

"You would be wise to let me go." My God! Zelig thought to himself. Who is writing my dialogue? I have seen too many bad movies.

"Kill you." A second voice. "That is what would be wise. Kill you and so one less Yankee manipulator screwing the world."

"Goose and golden eggs," the first voice chided. "Killing time is all the time. First let's squeeze and see how

242

bad they want this pimple back. Graves, why, they're always waiting."

Zelig was not fearless. He didn't want to die. His stomach lurched when the second voice mentioned killing. But now, and not just because of what the first man said, he realized that whatever the eventual outcome, he was not in any imminent danger of losing his life. He was a hostage, and that meant there was something they wanted in exchange for him. If they were going to kill him, he would be dead by now. Since he wasn't, his chances of remaining alive were probably not that bad at all.

"I will squeeze, just as you advise." The second man had more to say. "Here is a squeeze." Two large fingers pinched Zelig's nose and twisted painfully.

"Hey now." The hand was forcibly removed. "No point in damaging the merchandise. Decrease the value, you know."

Something about the voice caught Zelig's attention even as he was blinking back tears of pain. The second man, while speaking English, was obviously a native Greek. Zelig, during the years he had spent overcoming his own Swiss accent, had made himself into something of an expert on the speech origins that revealed themselves when English was spoken. It was a game he played with himself. He was even able to distinguish regional speech patterns.

Yes, the second speaker, the more hostile one, came from the Peloponnesus. There was the softness of unripe olives in his vowel-stressed English.

Blindfolded, aware that someday any clue he might offer as to who his captors were might have value, Zelig concentrated on narrowing it down more. Yes, there was a quite familiar lilt to the first man's speech pattern. It was American. It was midwestern.

An urban American midwestern black man. Zelig was sure. And his partner a Greek from south of Napleon. So the gang that had abducted him was international. That, Zelig reflected, could be both good and bad. Good because such a gang would have more savvy, more sophistication, not be so likely to kill out of rage and frustration. The downside was that they would be better at what they were about, more demanding, harder to manipulate as any deal-making process moved forward.

He was, Zelig realized, in the hands of an eclectic if ill-matched group: a black American; a southern Greek; and, quite likely, Vanessa Brewster, a globetrotting Circe given to seducing Stockwell men.

Weeks later, still blindfolded, bound and cramped, Zelig Meyerling could no longer find it in himself to be grateful just to be alive. What he wanted was to be free. What was taking so long? Surely the ransom message must have been delivered by now. Surely the demands would be met. He was, after all, Zelig Meyerling. What could his captors be demanding in exchange as important as Zelig Meyerling?

The answer was unexpected.

He learned it by accident. One day, quite by chance, he overheard two of his captors discussing his situation. They had parked themselves outside the door to the basement room where they were holding him and propped the door ajar to air out the chamber. Their voices were low, but not so low that their words were not discernible to him.

"I don't see how it would alter the result if he were dead." The Peloponnesian whom Zelig had identified earlier was speaking.

"And they call Africans savages." The other man was the American black.

"I don't see the point. We could really squeeze the Americans if we wanted to. But as things stand now, they don't even know we have him."

"It's no good squeezing the U.S. Whatever the Reagan administration agreed to, they'd just unagree to as soon as they got the dude back."

"Then why did we bother to kidnap him in the first place?" asked the Greek from the south.

"Time. He's the man, and so he gives us time."

"And you think time will turn the trick?" The Greek was skeptical.

"No way they can resolve it while we've got him. NATO's on hold. Nukes are on hold. Papandreou gets to hear the other side. The Greek public gets to be reminded of how the CIA pushed the colonels. Dig it. Just holding the cat and letting them guess—that's a weapon. That's a way of delaying any decision. And the longer it's put off, the likelier it gets the Greek people will insist their government stand up against American pressure to move in on Greek turf.''

NATO and nukes! Zelig scowled to himself. He might have known. So that's who had him. Far left internationalist antinuke peace activists who stood tall in Greece. Compared to them, the Socialist Papandreou was the center. Damn! And they were probably right, too.

Zelig spent the next two days brooding over it. During that time, there were no more voices. The Greek brought his food. The other man, the black American, Zelig realized, must not be there. But then he was back.

By then Zelig had embarked on a project. It had to do with the blindfold. He'd been forced to wear it ever since the day they'd abducted him. With his hands tied behind his back except for when they brought him food, which one of them always stayed to watch him eat, there didn't seem much he could do about it. Then one night (or was it day?), lying on the hard cot they'd provided him, he discovered that maybe there was something that could be done about the blindfold.

At the head of the cot there was a metal rail. At first Zelig, bumping his head on it one out of three times, had cursed it. Then he had learned to live with it. One night, feeling its roughness against the back of his neck, he had shifted automatically. It was an adjustment he had made many times. Only this time something clicked in his mind. For just an instant the adhesive tape holding the blindfold in place had snagged on whatever that roughness was.

Searching with the nape of his neck, he located the roughness again. He worked it against the collar of his shirt until the collar folded in on itself and he could feel the roughness against the skin of his neck. Cautiously, he rolled back and forth over it. Flaking. Rusted, probably. And—yes!—a part of the jaggedness was sharp-edged.

It took half a dozen attempts before Zelig was able to position the lip of the adhesive holding the blindfold over the jagged sharpness. Then, gritting his teeth, he pressed down and jerked sideways. There was the sharp sound of a small rip being made.

Zelig repeated the motion. It didn't work. He tried again. Three attempts later, there was another small rip. Altogether it took him many hours to complete the task. There was no way of keeping track of them. And all the time Zelig had to keep listening to make sure one of his guards didn't come in and catch him at it.

In the end, he succeeded. Enough of the tape was torn at the back of his neck to give him the play he needed to move the blindfold up and down his forehead by rubbing against the bedrail. He experimented with that for a long time.

He wanted to be able to see, but he didn't want his captors to know he could see. If they knew, they'd retape the blindfold. So Zelig worked painstakingly until he had it just where he wanted it.

Zelig's belief was that to someone looking at him, the blindfold would still seem to be in place. His eyes were covered. But by tilting his head just a little, a limited field of vision was available to him. Experimenting with that, too, Zelig was able to angle his neck to see the floor, the walls, the ceiling. He could see his tray of food, and the basement window set high in the wall. And, finally, he could see the face of his captor when he brought in his tray of food.

At first it was the Greek. He was tall, dark, with an impressive mustache and a predatory nose. But then one night the other man brought Zelig's supper.

Yes. He'd been right. The man was black. His clothes were American—blue jeans and a denim shirt and Nike sneakers. And his face . . .

Zelig gasped. He knew the man. He'd seen him before. It took him a moment to realize where.

Of course! The Papatestus villa. He'd never met him, but he'd seen him there. He was the companion of that young Greek with whom Spiro and Louise were so friendly. Clint. That was his name. Clint something.

Zelig's mind raced. It figured. It was this Clint who had fingered him. He must have been tracking Zelig's movements every step of the way. Why, even his being at the Papatestus villa must have been deliberate, a part of the plan to abduct Zelig.

But how had Clint managed to insinuate himself into Spiro Papatestus's household? Spiro, after all, was very security conscious, very careful. Suddenly Zelig had another thought. If this Clint was involved, what about his friend? What about that Xanthos who was so friendly with Spiro and Louise? Had Xanthos only been used by this Clint, or—

Or was Xanthos Konstatin in on the kidnapping, too?

BOOK FOUR

40

THE ADVENT OF springtime was a call to arms for Berkley, the Riverview butler. A traditional major domo in a traditional household, he regarded it as a season when the forces—his household staff—of good—cleanliness and order—did battle with evil—dirt, dust, grime, and disorder. He marshaled his infantry with mops and brooms and dustpans, lined up his artillery—high-powered vacuum cleaners, woodstripping and scraping machines, floor waxers—made sure all the watches were synchronized, and selected the D-Day and H-Hour for his all-out assault.

War against the encroachments of daily living is, of course, far different in a mansion such as Riverview than in a suburban split-level, or an urban apartment. There are mahogany newels to be repolished, priceless Persian staircase runners to be lifted, cleaned, and then nailed back down over spotless treads with just the right tension ensured so that they will neither slide nor split underfoot. Silver must be shined, draperies taken down, hand-cleaned, examined for fraying, and rehung. Woods must be oiled, porcelain sponged, precious metals buffed. Works of art must be dusted with meticulous care, antique knicknacks must be gone over groove by groove, dimple by dimple. Leatherbound books must be examined, sent out for rebinding if necessary, and their gold-embossed titles must be polished by fingertip. Louis XIV claw feet and Duncan Phyfe joinings and baroque curlicues must all be liberated from dust. And so forth and so forth. . . .

No inspector general of Her Majesty's Royal Navy would approach his appraisal of spit and polish as critically as Berkley would judge the end result of the spring cleaning of Riverview. And because they knew this, the preceding days were a time of abject terror for downstairs and upstairs maids, footmen and furnacemen, valets and kitchen staff. Quiet and decorum, as always, prevailed among the servants of Riverview, but beneath it there was a fearful turmoil that something might interfere with Mr. Berkley's schedule.

Berkley had most carefully planned the upstairs cleaning for a time when all those who occupied quarters there would be out. Mr. James, Miss Holly, and most recently Mr. Houston were all abroad, so that simplified matters. He picked a day when Miss Patrice was taking Master Nicholas into the city to see the Easter show at Radio City Music Hall and Mrs. Houston was in Texas on business. Only—wouldn't you just know it—Mrs. Houston came back early and unexpectedly and—impossible!—with a guest. They went straight to her suite of rooms on the second floor of the main house precisely twenty minutes before the spring cleaning of Mrs. Houston's apartment was due to begin. The housekeeper in charge of the platoon assigned to Mrs. Houston's rooms immediately went to Berkley to report this unforeseen interference with his careful schedule.

The news brought a black thundercloud to Berkley's usually unexpressive visage. For once a genuine annoyance crept into his habitually neutral voice. "We must hope for a speedy departure," he declared. "Meanwhile it must be designated a no-man's-land."

"Your pardon, Mr. Berkley, sir," the housekeeper said respectfully. "But what of the noise we'll be makin'? Will it not disturb Mrs. Houston and her—ahh—guest?"

The "ahh" drew an eye cold as ice down on the hapless woman. Mr. Berkley did not stand for gossip of the masters and mistresses of Riverview by the staff he ruled. Not even a raised eyebrow was permitted, and an "ahh" such as the housekeeper's was completely beyond the pale. Under his gaze she quivered and feared—with good reason—for her job.

"You will all be as quiet as possible," Berkley told the assembled staff. "But we will do what we must do."

"Shall we vacuum the adjoining rooms, then, Mr. Berkley? And what of the floor scraping?"

"We will do what we must do." That was Berkley's final word.

"Jumpin' Jehosophat! What the hell was that?" Jimbo Grebbs, stripped down to his shorts and walking toward the bed, reacted to the sudden sound of the floor scraper going into action in the room adjacent to Buffy's.

"Spring cleaning." Forewarned, Buffy was calm. She had known today was the day, forgotten, and was now reminded by the noise of the floor scraper. "Just ignore it."

"Sure. Less noisy than an earthquake, right? I'll just pay it no mind and go on about my business."

"Our business," Buffy corrected Jimbo. She regarded him with smoldering, dark violet eyes. A tough, macho hunk of beef, she thought to herself. Even his substantial belly had more gristle than fat. A large man, tall and rangy as his home state of Texas, a shucksy outdoorsy image, and yet—those small, shrewd eyes gave the lie to the country-boy cheeks and the bourbon-red nose. There was more to this plowboy than his cornball jokes and his tummy and the lust distending his shorts. "The oil business."

"Pumpin' and barrelin' and refinin'." Jimbo grinned and pulled the sheet aside. He looked down at Buffy in a gossamer green nightgown diaphanous as cellophane. "You are one fine figure of a woman," he told her.

"Thank you." Buffy's long eyelashes stroked her flushed cheeks in response to the compliment. Her slender, well-manicured fingers played with the thick, blue-black curls of her hair tumbling over her bare shoulders.

Both gestures seemed to point down toward the rise of her smooth, full, classically sculpted breasts. She shifted position, bending a knee, drawing attention to the curve of her womanly hips and the long shapeliness of her legs.

"One helluva fine figure of a woman," Jimbo repeated.

Buffy smiled her feline smile and let the impression work its full effect. Then, just as she knew he was about to reach for her, to kneel on the edge of the bed, she spoke again. "I can have the crude moving into your refineries in three days," she told him. "The railroads are all lined up and ready to cooperate. Will that be all right?"

"The sooner the oil flows, the better," Jimbo assured her. His hand moved to trace the line downward between her hipbone and her belly.

"Of course Halsey will be furious." She slid over to make room for Jimbo beside her in the bed. "He thinks his deal with the Libyans will be our only alternative, and so we'll have to turn to him, accept whatever terms he's negotiated, and let him pocket whatever his cut is for bringing Qaddafi the business."

"And all the time I'll be refinin' oil another fellow thought he had the corner on." Jimbo kissed her. His mouth enveloped hers, warm, possessive, tongue probing. When the kiss was over, his large nose plunged into the perfumed valley dividing her breasts.

The high-pitched thump of a hammer striking tile pierced the sound of the floor scraper from the bathroom next door. Jimbo's head shot up from Buffy's ample bosom, his wide mouth twisted into a snarl. "Now that is plumb distractin'!" he complained.

"Don't be so skittish." Buffy's sharp fingernails explored the jungle matting his barrel chest.

"Hell, woman, why wouldn't I be skittish? Last time I was in this house I had your hubby comin' down on me like a privy wall of bricks."

"Well, you don't have to worry." Her lips moved from the erogenous zone of his ear to the erogenous zone of his neck. "Jack won't interrupt us this time. He's not even in the country."

"Where is he?" Somewhat reassured, Jimbo began toying with Buffy's breasts once again.

"He wouldn't tell me where he was going, and he thinks I don't know. But this travel agent called to confirm his reservation. He's gone to Greece. That doesn't surprise me. Jack's always had a sort of letch for Holly Meyerling, and that's where she is." Reacting to Jimbo's caresses, Buffy raked his chest and belly lightly with her long nails. She found his penis, hard and ready, and encircled it with her fist. "What I like best about the oil business," she said softly, "is the drilling."

41

"ZE-LIG MEY-ER-LING." WANTING to be sure he was understood, Jack Houston repeated the name for his Greek contact slowly, syllable by syllable.

"Quite so, Mr. Houston." The man was amused. "I am fluent in English, and I am familiar with both the name and the situation."

Jack reddened. It was the Don's fault. He had told Jack that the meeting had been arranged for a restaurant in the Plaka in Athens, and that all he had to do was sit at a certain table at a certain hour on a certain evening, order a Greek salad and souvlaki and a carafe of retsina to wash it down, and the man he was to meet would find him. When he sat down across the table from him, Jack was to speak the name of Zelig Meyerling as a sort of password, and the man's response would establish that contact had been made. Since it was Athens, Jack had expected that the man would be Greek. The dark, curly black beard and swarthy complexion had seemed to confirm the expectation. Nor had the fisherman's cap and dark gray, rough wool sweater led him to anticipate a response in Cambridge-accented English.

"I'm sorry," Jack said. "I didn't expect—"

The man's smile was amused. "Do you like Greek salad?" he asked. He didn't wait for an answer. "Feta cheese." He shuddered. "Drowned in olive oil. It has turned the national complexion into one giant pitted gully."

"I assumed that most Greek people like it."

"Perhaps." The man shrugged. "I wouldn't know. I am not Greek. I am Italian."

At last, a Mafioso. Jack was sure of it. "Sicilian?" he hazarded.

"No. Venetian."

"From Venice. I see. How long have you been in Greece?" Jack asked politely.

"Eight hundred years."

Jack choked on the retsina. "Eight hundred years?"

"Yes. We came to conquer. We stayed to propagate. It was the biggest mistake my family ever made. The food does not get any better."

"No. I suppose not." Jack paused. "About Zelig Meyerling—"

"Sun Kai Don speaks well of you." The Venetian ignored the opening. "He thinks we will all profit greatly, thanks to the information you have supplied."

Just before he left New York, Jack had copied from the pages Patrice kept at home the list of insurance carriers from whom Stockwell was buying up policies and given it to the Don. It figured that Sun Kai Don had needed financing for the project. Jack wasn't surprised that the Greeks had a piece of the action. The Feta Connection. He smiled to himself.

Aloud, Jack repeated his question, this time more bluntly. "Do your people have Zelig Meyerling?" he asked.

"Perhaps." The Venetian poured a small amount of retsina from the carafe into a glass, tasted it, and grimaced. He signaled the waiter. "Chianti," he ordered. "And perhaps not." He completed his answer to Jack Houston.

"Just what does that mean?"

"It means that many people are interested in the question of just who is holding Zelig Meyerling hostage. Spiro

Papatestus, for instance. A very, very important man, and a relative of the Stockwell family as well. Do you know him?''

"Yes."

"Then you know that he would very much like to secure Zelig's release."

Jack restrained his irritation. "Of course he would."

"Enough, do you think, to make certain concessions?" The Venetian sipped the chianti and smiled.

"What do you mean?"

"Have you visited Piraeus since coming to Athens, Mr. Houston?"

"What?" Jack was having trouble following.

"Piraeus. It is Greece's largest seaport. Very close to Athens. Its docking area is the busiest in southern Europe. The ships of Mr. Papatestus load and unload there all the time. He has, as you know, many, many ships. So it is natural that he owns many, many warehouses in Piraeus. The combination gives him considerable control—complete, in a practical sense—over the docks of Piraeus."

"Yes? So?"

"The longshoremen on those docks are not unionized, Mr. Houston. Several times attempts have been made to form a union, but Mr. Papatestus has always squelched them. With strongarm men, goons and scabs and such." The Venetian laughed. "On more than one occasion, we have been the subcontractor providing the antiunion longshoremen involved."

"Just what are you getting at?" Jack demanded.

"Our conscience bothers us. We don't want to be scabs any longer. We want to atone for our sins. We want to unionize those docks. Mr. Papatestus can make that possible."

Jack's mind raced. He was not naive. He had, in his younger days, worked on the docks in Brooklyn. The graft could be considerable. Shape-ups with the men kicking back in order to work—and the union handing out the work slips. Breakage, spillage, and pilferage adding up to 10 percent of everything loaded or unloaded. Even a looksee at delivery schedules signaling which trucks to hijack and when. A mob running the union in the major port of Greece was good for millions—a month, not a year.

"I can't talk to Mr. Papatestus about a union," Jack told him, "until I'm sure you can deliver Zelig. Now do you have him or don't you?"

"We do not ourselves have him," the Venetian admitted.

"We're wasting each other's time." Jack signaled the waiter for a check.

"But we know who does."

"And?" Jack waved the waiter away.

"We have to find out where he's being held."

"Can you do that?"

"Yes." The Venetian was sure. "We have contacts."

"And then what?"

"Then we take Mr. Meyerling away from his captors."

"Alive?"

"There are no guarantees. We will do our best. But before we do anything, Mr. Houston, you must speak to Mr. Papatestus and get his agreement to our unionizing the Piraeus docks. Tell him he would never have to worry about labor trouble again." The Venetian folded his hands. "In the end it would cost him less our way."

"I'll talk to him. I can't promise he'll agree." Again Jack signaled for the waiter. This time he had his wallet out, ready to pay the check.

"You see, Mr. Houston." The Venetian indicated the uneaten food on Jack's plate. "Your dinner was not very good."

Jack shrugged.

"I was right about Greek food, was I not? The decent Greek chefs go to America and open diners. That's why. The outer limits of the culinary imagination of those who are left behind are defined by feta cheese." The Venetian stood and bowed slightly. "I will make inquiries and contact you, Mr. Houston. And you—"

"I'll talk to Spiro Papatestus," Jack promised.

Spiro Papatestus, however, was not available when Jack called the villa in Crete. He had gone to Malta for meetings first with Terry Waite and then with certain PLO splinter group leaders with whom he sometimes did business. Spiro was trying to get a line on the group calling itself Jihad of Allah that had contacted Holly with hostage demands regarding Zelig. He was, Louise told Jack, expected back sometime in the next few days.

After Louise hung up from Jack's call, she rejoined Holly, James, and Michael in the library of the villa. This was the night that Yusuf al-Bekka was coming to discuss the details of Jihad of Allah's terms for Zelig's release. Awaiting him, Holly was beginning to feel the strain. The blond delicacy of her face had turned almost haggard. As Louise reentered, Holly was trying to focus on the conversation between Michael and James.

"I checked out Jidah of Allah thoroughly, Dad," Michael was saying. "Neither the CIA, nor the NSC, nor the State Department, nor anybody else involved with our intelligence apparatus has ever heard of it."

"If it's new," James hypothesized, "it may have been formed in response to an action by Halsey De Vilbiss. He convinced Spiro he had board authorization for a deal to have Stockwell oil refined in Libya, although in fact the board had said no to the scheme. Spiro subsequently met with the Libyan oil minister in Malta to arrange terms. This meeting coincided with Zelig's arrival in Greece. Doubtless it seemed to certain Arab groups that there must be a connection."

"Suppose that's true," Holly said slowly. "What does it mean?"

"There are anti-Qaddafi groups that don't want to see Libyan refineries activated. They don't want to see the Libyan economy bolstered. They want things to get worse so they can bring down Qaddafi. They want to see a climate created for revolution."

"Doesn't the United States want that, too?" Louise was confused.

"Oh, yes." James looked at Michael. "We help those groups. We give them money. We see that they can buy arms. Isn't that right, Congressman?"

"It's in our national interest," Michael admitted.

"Are you saying that this Jihad of Allah took money provided by the United States to bring down Qaddafi and used it to organize a plot to take Zelig hostage?'' Holly was outraged.

"Except that the United States never heard of Jihad of Allah,'' Michael reminded her.

"These Arab splinter groups come up with new names all the time. It's quite possible we funded them without even knowing it,'' James interjected. "And we have to take administration denials with a grain of salt, Michael. If they did learn that funding had somehow fallen into the hands of the group that abducted Zelig, they would never admit it.''

"Why not?'' Holly demanded.

"Because,'' Michael told her reluctantly, "such an admission would destroy our credibility and ultimately our influence in the Mideast.'' He turned to his father. "But you're running amok with this, Dad. What makes you think—''

Michael cut himself off as a servant entered, looked at Louise, and nodded.

"Yusuf al-Bekka has arrived,'' Louise told Holly.

Holly stood up. She was very pale. The muscles in her neck stood out, and her mouth was a thin line. She faced the doorway as the servant stood aside to allow Yusuf al-Bekka to enter.

All were struck by his youth and by his physical slightness. Slender, not tall, his boyish appearance was not what they expected. Only the intensity of his dark eyes as they moved from Louise to Holly and back identified him as a zealot.

"Which of you,'' he asked, "is Mrs. Meyerling?'' His English was halting but distinct. He wore a Berber-style turban with the Western jeans and denim work shirt favored by Moroccan university students.

"I am.'' Holly stepped forward. "How is my husband?'' she demanded.

"He is unharmed.'' Yusuf was deliberately ominous. "For the present.'' He reached into his pocket and took out two folded sheets of closely typewritten paper. "This is a list of freedom fighters held by the Israeli government. There are thirty-seven of them. When they are released, we will let Zelig Meyerling go.''

"Ridiculous!' It was Michael who reacted. "We can't force the Israeli government to take such an action."

"You are a member of the United States Congress," Yusuf reminded him. "The Stockwell family controls a vast amount of your nation's wealth. Zelig Meyerling is both a member of the Stockwell family and an agent of the United States government. The American administration will listen to the Stockwells, and the Israelis will agree to our terms if they are told to by the Americans. It will not be the first time, nor the last, that the United States leans on one of its satellites to further its own interests. The demands will be met within one week's time, or Zelig Meyerling will be executed."

"Please—" Holly turned from Yusuf's implacable adolescent face to her uncle and cousin. "Use your influence," she pleaded. "Talk to the administration. Make them talk to the Israelis. At least try. It's Zelig's life." She broke down, sobbing.

"Let me get this straight." Michael addressed Yusuf as James tried to comfort Holly. "You won't release Zelig until *after* the Israelis release these terrorists you say they're holding."

"Freedom fighters." Yusuf corrected him with a petulant scowl. "Yes. Those are the terms."

"Then what guarantee do we have that you'll release him at all? As a matter of fact," Michael added suddenly, "what proof do we have that you even have Zelig Meyerling? You've shown us nothing. No picture. No article of clothing. Nothing."

"Doubt my word if you want." Yusuf shrugged. "In one week we will send you an ear. Only it will be the ear of a dead man."

"You pig!" Michael exploded.

"And now you will give me a thrashing, perhaps?" Yusuf laughed in his face. "A Western thrashing for an Arab wog?"

"No." Michael was furious. "But perhaps we'll just send *your* ear back to your Jihad of Allah instead of you."

"You dare not," Yusuf sneered. "If I should not return, why, then Carrie Tyler will be forfeit. Don't forget that."

259

Michael took a deep breath. "Proof," he demanded. "What proof do you have that this Jihad of Allah really is holding Zelig Meyerling?"

"None." It was a new voice, and they all turned toward it. Spiro Papatestus stood in the doorway. "None at all. And I will tell you why. The Jihad of Allah does not have Zelig Meyerling for the simple reason that it does not exist. This man is a fraud."

"You sentence Zelig Meyerling to death with such talk," Yusuf responded.

"Nonsense. I have just returned from a meeting with Terry Waite and the representatives of several Arab groups. They all assure me that the Jihad of Allah does not exist. None have ever heard of you. You are a free agent, unaffiliated, trying to capitalize on a serious situation which was not of your making. You no more have Zelig Meyerling in your custody than the Boy Scouts of Greece do." Spiro Papatestus looked at Yusuf from shrewd, aging Macedonian eyes that saw right through him.

Yusuf was not intimidated. He took three long steps and stood nose to nose with Spiro. It was a bold gesture somewhat undermined by the fact that he was a head shorter and had to crane his neck to look up into the seamed visage of the Greek tycoon. For a brief second the effect was humorous. Then—suddenly—it wasn't funny anymore.

A long, sharp Moroccan dagger with a jeweled handle appeared from inside Yusuf's denim shirt. He pressed the tip against the pulse of the neck just below Spiro's left ear. "You were right," he said. "I do not have Zelig Meyerling. I was holding no hostage at all. But"—he smiled grimly—"I am now."

And while the others watched, stunned and horrified, Yusuf al-Bekka prodded Spiro Papatestus with the knife at his throat out of the room and out of the house.

As the captor and his hostage were exiting, in an upstairs room of the villa with a balcony looking out over the mountains of Crete toward the beach of Komo, Lisa Stockwell and Winifred Fitzsimmons were continuing a violent argument. It had begun earlier and escalated rapidly.

"You never got over her." Lisa had started it. "I can see it in your eyes every time she's in the room."

"That Yank imagination of yours is working overtime." Winifred's denial lacked conviction.

"Your great cow eyes go all soft." Paper thin, Lisa's figure seemed to slice through the air with her nervous pacing.

"I'm so dreadfully sorry my eyes offend you."

"They do when you look at Holly. You don't look at me that way. Once you did, but no more."

"Holly's presence has nothing to do with it." Tense with the argument, Winifred's long fingers squeezed at the tousle of her red hair. "You were carrying on about her long before she even got here. You just can't stand it that I ever had a relationship with anybody else, ever cared for another person."

"That doesn't explain why you're withdrawing from me more and more since she came."

"If I am, it's because of your bloody American possessiveness. Being loved is never enough. You Yanks always have to own people, too."

"That's right. Insult my country." Lisa's glare was accusing. "But it doesn't change anything. You lust after Holly, and you pull away from me."

"I don't." Weariness deepened Winifred's normally high voice.

"Liar!" The longer it went on, the more Lisa worked herself up. Her anger stoked some inner fire that was consuming her. "Liar! Liar! Liar!"

"Very well, then, I do. I lust after Holly. Are you satisfied now?"

"You admit it, then?"

"I admit it." Winifred had no more stomach left for denials. The truth was, of course, a lot more complex than the confession: "I lust after Holly."

"I knew it!" If it was possible to look anguished and triumphant at the same time, that defined the fire in Lisa's eyes. "And that's why you've been rejecting me."

"I haven't been rejecting you, Lisa," Winifred protested. "In point of fact, I love you."

"You love me, and you lust for Holly. Neat."

"It happens, ducks. I'm sorry. But it does."

"Stuff it, Winifred! Why don't you just leave me and go off with Holly? She rejected you. That's why, isn't it?" The more acute jealousy is, the more perceptive. "You came on to Holly, and she rejected you, and so now you're making do with me."

"I'm not making do." Despite everything, Winifred still found tenderness within herself for Lisa. "I love you." She seized Lisa by the shoulders. They felt thin, fragile in her grip. "Would I put up with you, with all of this, with all that other hell that you've put me through these past two years, if I didn't love you?"

"You love me, but you've got the hots for cousin Holly!" Lisa was deliberately vulgar. "Only Goldilocks doesn't swing that way. Too bad for you, Winnie."

"Please, can't we stop now? If we go on, we're just going to bloody each other up more."

"Screw you, you Highland bitch!" Lisa swept up her handbag from an end table and marched into the bathroom. The door slammed behind her resoundingly.

Winifred stared at the door for a moment. Then she sank down on the bed, sitting on the edge, her shoulders sagging forward, her red hair tumbling to her lap. She felt completely drained of energy. It had been a mistake to confess to Lisa that she was still attracted to Holly. There was no way Lisa could understand that. Just as there was no way she could understand that Winifred really did love her despite those feelings.

There was a good deal more than jealousy involved. Lisa was too fragile. She didn't have the strength to deal with any but the most straightforward emotions. Her need for love was all-consuming. To allow for deviation would have been to deny it. And now, Winifred knew, Lisa was deeply wounded.

For Lisa such a wound pointed only one direction: self-destruction.

* * *

Winifred made herself sit up straight. She looked at the door through which Lisa had fled. She called her name. "Lisa." And then again, louder. "Lisa!"

There was no answer. Winifred got up and went to the door. She tried the knob. It was locked from the other side. "Lisa. Open the door."

Even as she realized that Lisa would neither answer nor comply, Winifred moved to act. She crossed to the night table where her own pocketbook was lying, opened it, and fished out a nail file. She went back to the bathroom door and inserted the file in the keyhole. Forcing herself to patience, she worked it back and forth until she heard the click for which she had been listening. The bathroom door swung open.

Lisa was seated on the edge of the Carrera tile bathtub. The toilet seat was down. On top of it was an open packet of white powder and a bathroom tumbler with a little water into which the powder had been mixed. Alongside was a short length of rubber tubing. She was holding a hypodermic up to the light and squeezing it gently, measuring.

"Damn it, no!"

Winifred descended on her, grabbing Lisa's slender wrist and twisting until the hypodermic clattered to the mosaic floor. She poured the contents of the tumbler into the sink and turned on the tap. She picked up the rubber tubing and the packet of powder, raised the toilet seat, dropped both into the toilet and flushed several times in a row. Then she turned to Lisa.

"You promised," Winifred said. "After the last time, you promised."

"Leave me alone, damn you!"

"Lisa, you're going to kill yourself."

"What do you care? Go chase your blond obsession. Leave me alone."

"Damn it, Lisa, I care! All that horrible time weaning you away from the bloody stuff. And almost three months you've been clean now. Wherever did you get it, anyway? Why are you so self-destructive?"

"Leave me alone!" Lisa shouted.

Winifred took a deep breath. It was no use talking to her now. That was obvious. She checked Lisa's bag to make sure she'd gotten it all. Then she did as Lisa asked. She left her sitting there alone.

Upset, wondering if it would ever end, acknowledging to herself that whatever she might feel for Holly, she really did love Lisa and could not stand the idea of her plunging back into the drug world that had so nearly destroyed her in the past and could so easily destroy her now, Winifred walked through the bedroom and went out on the balcony. The air was cool, and she hugged herself against it. Overhead, the timeless stars of Crete blazed down in all their glory. The scene before Winifred was lit brightly. She looked at the oceans in the distance, the cliffs of Matala, the moon-white beaches of Komo. Her eyes traced the twisting snake of road crawling up the mountain. She looked at the high redstone wall surrounding the Papatestus property. And then her eye was caught by a glint on the path running between the fig trees from the patio of the house to one of the gates in the wall.

It flashed again. Winifred squinted. She could make it out now. It was a blade, poised, its sharp tip red with blood. Now it moved like a streak of light, and her eyes followed the carmined point as it slashed once again toward its target.

And in that instant she realized the target was a human being!

42

THE FIRST TIME, Spiro had not seen the blade coming. Only the coincidence of Yusuf having at that very moment tripped over the root of a fig tree in the dark had saved the Berber youth from the death the full force of the stab would have brought if it had struck home. As it was, the tip of the knife had glanced off Yusuf's shoulder, drawn blood, but not done any real harm. Now, Spiro saw the second thrust slashing toward his captor even as Yusuf straightened up from stumbling.

Spiro felt himself shoved aside violently as Yusuf dived out of range in the other direction. He was free now, Spiro realized, Yusuf's knife no longer at his throat. His first impulse was to bolt. But he was no coward, so he restrained himself and faded back into the bushes, awaiting an opportunity to help whoever had saved him from his abductor.

The second thrust of the blade had missed the Moroccan youth completely. It was the pause Yusuf needed. His own knife, no longer at Spiro's throat, was ready now. He could defend himself. Crouching in the shadows of the bushes, his features not discernible, Spiro's rescuer slashed once more. Poised now, Yusuf slid smoothly to one side and parried. He held the ornate, jeweled hilt of his dagger underhanded, like a street fighter. His feint was a sidewise move ready to rip upward if flesh was pierced.

There were loud sounds as Yusuf's opponent scrambled backward into the bushes. Yusuf plunged in after him, his knife describing a lethal advance arc. Cautiously, Spiro followed.

Both antagonists had now emerged on a square of manicured lawn fringed by sculptured hedges. One hand held wide for balance, Yusuf was closing in. His adversary was hampered by the tall pyramid-shaped hedge at his back. The Moroccan's movements, graceful and structured as a ballerina's, attested that he was no novice to the art of knife fighting. By contrast, his opponent in the shadow of the pyramid hedge gave an impression of being lumbering and clumsy. As he jumped away from Yusuf, his shoulder still hid his face from Spiro's view.

His back was to Spiro as he turned to face Yusuf. He was in a crouch, and his movements were crablike. His stance seemed to offer twice as large a target as did Yusuf's small and slender figure with its gliding, quicksilver movements. Nevertheless, he was more agile than he looked. So far, Yusuf's blade had not even scratched him.

Now Yusuf moved to attack with some urgency. He

had lost his hostage. It was imperative that he dispose of his foe and make his escape before Papatestus could alert his security guards. Smoothly closing in on his opponent, he moved his whole body like a rapier wielded by an expert swordman, his dagger its gleaming, deadly point.

Spiro gasped as his rescuer ducked under Yusuf's blade and at the same time flung his own knife into the bushes. He seized the youth's arm with both hands. And with the same seemingly clumsy movement, he sank his teeth into the wrist of the hand holding the Moroccan kris.

In vain, Yusuf struggled to switch hands. The dagger escaped his fingers. Immediately his opponent kicked it away and released him. He stepped back and loosed an uppercut that seemed to come up all the way from the ground. It caught Yusuf flush on the jaw. He dropped like a felled tree. The victor stepped over his body, picked up both knives, and turned around.

For the first time, Spiro saw his face. He gasped. The man who had rescued him was Xanthos Konstantin.

Within moments others arrived on the scene. They found Spiro hugging Xanthos and thanking him effusively in Greek. He only stopped when Louise arrived and embraced her husband.

"You're all right!" she exulted.

"Thanks to Xanthos." Spiro told her what had happened.

"Oh, Xanthos!" Louise hugged him. "How did you know?"

"I am coming from garage. Parking car. I see fellow, knife, Spiro. I follow, come up behind with knife, stab. But careful, because no good he stab Spiro first. After that is nothing."

"Nothing!" Louise and Spiro both hugged him now. Xanthos had risked his life to save Spiro. He was not just a sex partner, but a true friend. The three of them, their arms around each other, walked toward Xanthos's cottage.

43

"WHEN IT COMES to inner-city real estate, the entire fire insurance business is too close to arson." Max Tyler did not hesitate to agree with the Reverend Malcolm Darrow Cabot.

They were seated across from each other in deep leather armchairs sipping vintage sherry in the vestry of the Gotham Memorial Church. The hubbub of the Upper West Side of Manhattan was shut out by ivy-covered stone walls and mahogany wood paneling. The chamber, dim even though the Flemish tapestries had not been drawn over the high, vaulted windows, had been designed for religious meditation. To Max, however, it reflected the traditional wealth that had created Gotham Memorial.

The wealth had been that of Jonathan Braithwaite Stockwell, a forebear of the modern Stockwells. Toward the end of the nineteenth century, he had engaged the world's foremost religious architects to design and build a grand nondenominational Protestant cathedral, and he had provided an endowment in perpetuity to maintain it. Decreeing that the Stockwell family itself should have no influence over the affairs of the church, he had created a board of trustees to be composed of philanthropists and scholars who were charged with running the church and hiring a minister and whatever assistants were needed.

Reverend Malcolm Darrow Cabot had been that minister for more than twenty-five years. He was an informal, shaggy man, deliberately awkward in a way that invariably put others at their ease. Even those among his wealthiest parishioners who most deplored his reformist principles could not help liking him. Indeed, by the sheer weight of his personality, Sunday after Sunday he mounted the pulpit in opposition to those views most widely held by the Stockwells and their peers.

Despite this, Gotham Memorial was widely thought of as "the Stockwell church," and the Reverend Cabot felt strongly that what the Stockwells did reflected on his ministry. In the past this feeling had pushed him to speak out from his pulpit against the pro-Vietnam policies of Governor Matthew Adams Stockwell and to declare Gotham Memorial a sanctuary for draft resisters. Ever since he had been regarded by most of the Stockwells as a loose cannon. Their disapproval of him, however, was mixed with both respect and fear.

Max Tyler, a Stockwell by heritage, if not by name, knew this history well. Thus he had responded to Reverend Cabot's request that he call on him with some trepidation as well as curiosity. And, despite his agreement with what the minister had to say, the trepidation lingered. In his experience on the Stockwell board, social concerns and business expediencies were never anything but antagonistic.

"A delegation of my fellow clergymen has been to see me," was the way the Reverend Cabot had begun. "They represent the less privileged areas of our—umm—apple. They were mostly black and Hispanic, but there were also rabbis from the Lower East Side and Brooklyn among them, as well as the priests of blue-collar Irish and Italian flocks in Queens. They are very concerned over the torching of buildings in low-income areas and the addition to the homeless population on our streets because of it. I sympathized with their concern, but why, I asked them, have you come to me? Can you guess their answer, Max?"

Max Tyler smiled and said nothing. Knowing when not to respond was a knack that had stood him in good stead while successfully building his own modest insurance company.

"Their answer was 'insurance,' " the Reverend Cabot told him. "They sniffed out the fact that where there's smoke, there's fire, and where there's fire, there's fire insurance. People think clergyman are naive about how money makes the world go 'round, but they're wrong. These are shrewd cookies. It didn't take them long to pin down that the first step to the profits of gentrification in our fair city is arson, and that fire insurance is what pays the phoenix to rise from the ashes. As to why they came to me—well, Max, when they checked, they found that a great deal of that fire insurance was being sold by Stockwell subsidiaries, and a great deal more was passing through Stockwell in reinsurance investment blocks."

"Stockwell isn't alone in its involvement."

"Of course not, Max. The policies pass through many hands. My fellow clergymen determined that. They know that the pass-along is what guarantees the high profits. They can read the interest rates as well as the next fellow. But they have also learned that Stockwell is holding the policies on a disproportionate number of torched properties at the very time they go up in smoke. In effect, they're financing the arson. The reaction of my fellow clergymen is a mixture of anger and impotence. They feel overawed by Stockwell power. And so they came to me."

"And you called me. But why?" Max asked. "Why me? With the exception of Halsey De Vilbiss, you have much closer ties with everybody else on the board than with me. You've always been close to the Stockwell family. You're closer than I am, even if I am related. So why me?"

"One of the ministers in the delegation was Father Walter Paley. He thought you might be sympathetic. He seemed to think you have more of a social conscience than the others on the board."

Max nodded. He knew Father Paley. He had gained some notoriety by being one of the first Catholic clergymen to hold services for gays. Max hadn't gone to the services. He wasn't Catholic, and he wasn't religious. But because his insurance company had been formed with the avowed purpose of serving the gay community, he had been asked to serve on a committee concerned with that community. Reverend Paley had also been a member of the committee.

"I suppose I do," Max conceded.

"Is their perception right, Max? That's why I've come to you. I want to be sure my fellow clergy aren't letting their emotions run away with them. Just how close is the relationship between Stockwell and inner city arson?"

"Too close." That was when Max Tyler had admitted that he had thought from the start that fire insurance was being used as a scam that led to arson.

"In that case, the outrage of my fellow ministers is a rebuke to Gotham Memorial and to me personally. We have to put our heads together, Max, and figure out a way to stop this insurance business."

"Easier said than done. It's very profitable. The board voted for it almost unanimously. I was the only one against it."

"Then we must change their minds."

"You could speak out against it from the pulpit," Max suggested.

"I'd rather not. For one thing, it might tie the church into the whole sleazy business in the public mind. Certainly it would remind people of Gotham's ties to the Stockwells. Some people could even read it as the church being financed by the profits from ghetto arson. And for another thing, I don't know how effective it would be. I used to speak out against the Vietnam War every Sunday, but the Stockwells on the whole—including the governor—went right on supporting it, and the war didn't end for a very long time."

"I don't see how you're going to change their minds," Max said.

"I'm not sure myself. I was hoping you might give me some insight into their thinking. Who, for instance, do you think might be most swayed by conscience?"

"Patrice," Max replied. "But she's sort of stuck with a decision in favor of expanding into reinsurance that was originally made by James. I don't think she'll go against her father's wishes."

"James is a hardheaded businessman," the Reverend Cabot observed, "but on the other hand, I've never known him to be unscrupulous. And he is concerned about the good name of Stockwell."

"If it comes to that," Max granted, "so is David Lewis. He may only have married into the family, but he's always very concerned about its public image."

"I can talk to James and to David," Reverend Cabot decided. "A little gentle persuasion, and who knows? Along with you, Max, they could supply half the votes to end the practice. Now what about the others? What about Peter Stockwell? He bears the name, after all. Don't you think young Peter will be concerned about its being tarnished?"

"No." Max was positive. "This insurance business has been Peter's baby from the start. He fought for it, and its success proves him right. No way will Peter back off now, no matter what the effect on the good name of Stockwell."

"I see. Buffy, then? Or this De Vilbiss fellow?"

"Buffy is firmly for profit. Plus she might actually *enjoy* seeing the Stockwell name dragged through the mud. There's always been antipathy between her and the family."

"And De Vilbiss?"

"He couldn't care less about the family image. All he cares about is that the insurance project is bringing in top revenue. He'll back up Peter all the way."

"Then even if I sway James and David, the most I can hope for is to split the board," Reverend Cabot realized. He poured another glass of sherry for Max and for himself. The wine glowed a burnished gold in the dying Manhattan sunlight tiptoeing the dust motes from the upper arches of the vestry windows. "What will the effect of that be, Max?"

"It won't stop the insurance operation," Max told him. "It won't change anything."

44

"IT DIDN'T CHANGE anything." Carrie Tyler was defending herself to her sister, Beth. "And it didn't really do any harm. It was just a dumb idea that failed."

"I don't see how you can say that. Look at what you put Holly through."

Once again the twins were lying out on the deck of the

Greenpeace sloop sunning themselves. The ship was lying off Crete. In the distance, the tips of the green-and-white mountains punctured the blue silk of the Mediterranean sky.

"I'm sorry about Holly. But what else can she expect, marrying an establishment mouthpiece like Zelig Meyerling?" Carrie removed the bra to her bikini and arched her naked breasts to the sun.

Beth frowned. Since when had Carrie started spouting phrases like "established mouthpiece"? "She was really concerned about your welfare." Beth rolled the top of her one-piece swimsuit down to the waist and continued, "She was afraid that if they held Yusuf, then the Jihad of Allah might really do something terrible to you."

"Except there was no Jihad of Allah." Carrie suppressed a giggle. Beth, she knew, would not appreciate it. "Yusuf made it up."

"He may have made it up, but you're the one who called Holly," Beth reminded her. "It was a really crummy thing to do. And you're the one who said the Jihad would hold you hostage against his safe return. How could you lend yourself to that, Carrie? Were you that infatuated with him?"

"Oh, I was really hooked on him all right." Carrie turned over on her stomach. "Kind of funny when you think of it. I mean, we never actually did anything."

"You never made love?" Knowing her sister, Beth was skeptical.

"Nope. It was against his religion. Whatever else, there was nothing hypocritical about Yusuf. He was a fundamentalist Muslim who really practiced what he preached. No sex. No booze. No drugs. At least the Zelig stunt was exciting. And it wasn't as if we actually kidnapped anyone. All Yusuf was doing was pretending we had Zelig in order to fool the American government so it would pressure the Israelis to release Arab political prisoners."

"Arab terrorists, you mean!"

"To Yusuf they're freedom fighters. And I was in a state." Carrie tried to make Beth understand how it had been. "Yusuf had dropped all my coke and hash and grass over the side. He had me going cold turkey. Plus no al-

reenpeace sloop sunning themselves. The ship was lying
ff Crete. In the distance, the tips of the green-and-white
mountains punctured the blue silk of the Mediterranean
sky.

"I'm sorry about Holly. But what else can she expect,
marrying an establishment mouthpiece like Zelig Meyerling?" Carrie removed the bra to her bikini and arched
her naked breasts to the sun.

Beth frowned. Since when had Carrie started spouting
phrases like "established mouthpiece"? "She was really
concerned about your welfare." Beth rolled the top of her
one-piece swimsuit down to the waist and continued,
"She was afraid that if they held Yusuf, then the Jihad of
Allah might really do something terrible to you."

"Except there was no Jihad of Allah." Carrie suppressed a giggle. Beth, she knew, would not appreciate
it. "Yusuf made it up."

"He may have made it up, but you're the one who
called Holly," Beth reminded her. "It was a really crummy
thing to do. And you're the one who said the Jihad would
hold you hostage against his safe return. How could you
lend yourself to that, Carrie? Were you that infatuated
with him?"

"Oh, I was really hooked on him all right." Carrie
turned over on her stomach. "Kind of funny when you
think of it. I mean, we never actually did anything."

"You never made love?" Knowing her sister, Beth was
skeptical.

"Nope. It was against his religion. Whatever else, there
was nothing hypocritical about Yusuf. He was a fundamentalist Muslim who really practiced what he preached.
No sex. No booze. No drugs. At least the Zelig stunt was
exciting. And it wasn't as if we actually kidnapped anyone. All Yusuf was doing was pretending we had Zelig in
order to fool the American government so it would pres-
ure the Israelis to release Arab political prisoners."

"Arab terrorists, you mean!"

"To Yusuf they're freedom fighters. And I was in a
ate." Carrie tried to make Beth understand how it had
en. "Yusuf had dropped all my coke and hash and grass
er the side. He had me going cold turkey. Plus no al-

great deal of that fire insurance was being sold by Stockwell subsidiaries, and a great deal more was passing
through Stockwell in reinsurance investment blocks."

"Stockwell isn't alone in its involvement."

"Of course not, Max. The policies pass through many
hands. My fellow clergymen determined that. They know
that the pass-along is what guarantees the high profits.
They can read the interest rates as well as the next fellow.
But they have also learned that Stockwell is holding the
policies on a disproportionate number of torched properties at the very time they go up in smoke. In effect, they're
financing the arson. The reaction of my fellow clergymen
is a mixture of anger and impotence. They feel overawed
by Stockwell power. And so they came to me."

"And you called me. But why?" Max asked. "Why
me? With the exception of Halsey De Vilbiss, you have
much closer ties with everybody else on the board than
with me. You've always been close to the Stockwell family. You're closer than I am, even if I am related. So why
me?"

"One of the ministers in the delegation was Father
Walter Paley. He thought you might be sympathetic. He
seemed to think you have more of a social conscience than
the others on the board."

Max nodded. He knew Father Paley. He had gained
some notoriety by being one of the first Catholic clergymen to hold services for gays. Max hadn't gone to the
services. He wasn't Catholic, and he wasn't religious. But
because his insurance company had been formed with the
avowed purpose of serving the gay community, he had
been asked to serve on a committee concerned with that
community. Reverend Paley had also been a member of
the committee.

"I suppose I do," Max conceded.

"Is their perception right, Max? That's why I've come
to you. I want to be sure my fellow clergy aren't letting
their emotions run away with them. Just how close is the
relationship between Stockwell and inner city arson?"

"Too close." That was when Max Tyler had admitted
that he had thought from the start that fire insurance was
being used as a scam that led to arson.

"In that case, the outrage of my fellow ministers is a rebuke to Gotham Memorial and to me personally. We have to put our heads together, Max, and figure out a way to stop this insurance business."

"Easier said than done. It's very profitable. The board voted for it almost unanimously. I was the only one against it."

"Then we must change their minds."

"You could speak out against it from the pulpit," Max suggested.

"I'd rather not. For one thing, it might tie the church into the whole sleazy business in the public mind. Certainly it would remind people of Gotham's ties to the Stockwells. Some people could even read it as the church being financed by the profits from ghetto arson. And for another thing, I don't know how effective it would be. I used to speak out against the Vietnam War every Sunday, but the Stockwells on the whole—including the governor—went right on supporting it, and the war didn't end for a very long time."

"I don't see how you're going to change their minds," Max said.

"I'm not sure myself. I was hoping you might give me some insight into their thinking. Who, for instance, do you think might be most swayed by conscience?"

"Patrice," Max replied. "But she's sort of stuck with a decision in favor of expanding into reinsurance that was originally made by James. I don't think she'll go against her father's wishes."

"James is a hardheaded businessman," the Reverend Cabot observed, "but on the other hand, I've never known him to be unscrupulous. And he is concerned about the good name of Stockwell."

"If it comes to that," Max granted, "so is David Lewis. He may only have married into the family, but he's always very concerned about its public image."

"I can talk to James and to David," Reverend Cabot decided. "A little gentle persuasion, and who knows? Along with you, Max, they could supply half the votes to end the practice. Now what about the others? What about Peter Stockwell? He bears the name, after all. Don't you

270

think young Peter will be concerned about its nished?"

"No." Max was positive. "This insurance busi been Peter's baby from the start. He fought for it, success proves him right. No way will Peter back o no matter what the effect on the good name of well."

"I see. Buffy, then? Or this De Vilbiss fellow?"

"Buffy is firmly for profit. Plus she might actually e seeing the Stockwell name dragged through the m There's always been antipathy between her and the fa ily."

"And De Vilbiss?"

"He couldn't care less about the family image. All he cares about is that the insurance project is bringing in top revenue. He'll back up Peter all the way."

"Then even if I sway James and David, the most I can hope for is to split the board," Reverend Cabot realized. He poured another glass of sherry for Max and for himself. The wine glowed a burnished gold in the dying Manhattan sunlight tiptoeing the dust motes from the upper arches of the vestry windows. "What will the effect of that be, Max?"

"It won't stop the insurance operation," Max told him "It won't change anything."

44

"IT DIDN'T CHANGE anything." Carrie Tyler fending herself to her sister, Beth. "And really do any harm. It was just a dumb idea that

"I don't see how you can say that. Look at put Holly through."

Once again the twins were lying out on the

272

cohol and no balling. I was really mixed up, Bethie. I don't remember any of it too clearly. I think I had it in my head that if I went along with him, he'd be so grateful that at least he'd go to bed with me."

"Well, he won't go to bed with you now. He's in a Greek jail, and you're lucky you're not there with him."

"Kidnapping Spiro wasn't part of the plan. I think he just did it on the spur of the moment. Poor Yusuf."

"Poor Yusuf," Beth echoed ironically. "It will be a long time before they let him out of prison. Spiro Papatestus will make sure of that."

"You're so smug." Carrie spoke more sadly than harshly. "As if people should always pay for their mistakes or some universal balance sheet will be out of whack. I don't just mean about Yusuf. I mean with me, too. You add up people's mistakes, and you never forgive them."

Beth was taken by surprise. She sat up and looked hard at her twin from her almond-shaped eyes. "You mean what happened with Deke," she realized. "Well, I can't really forget, but I do forgive you, Carrie. But I—well, I understand how it happened. I mean, I think I've learned that people are human. That bit about the balance sheet, it used to be true. But it isn't anymore. Anybody can make a mistake, act on impulse, do something—something sexual, particularly—that they're ashamed of later. I know that now."

Carrie turned on her side and shaded her own hazel eyes with her hand to return Beth's gaze. "You're talking about yourself, sis," she realized slowly. "You hopped into bed with somebody on impulse, and now you're feeling guilty."

A flush suffused Beth's face from her neck to the hairline of her apricot tresses. "The thing I hate most about being a twin," she said, "is the lack of privacy. Damn it, Carrie, you always could see right into me."

"Who?" Carrie hid her amusement. She had lost count of the men she herself had slept with, and now here was Beth agonizing over one slip. "Who is it you're so sorry you balled? Come on, sis. Tell me. You'll feel better. I won't tell anybody."

"Michael," Beth confessed in a very low voice.

"Michael Stockwell? Our very own congressman? Well, I'll be damned. Welcome to the club, Bethie. Just how did the beast seduce you?"

"He didn't. It was the other way around."

"Well, good for you, Bethie. There's hope for the old prude yet. Pretty soon you'll be swinging with the best of us."

"Oh, no, I won't. You see, Carrie, there is a balance sheet. At least for me there is. Michael was a really bad mistake. I used him. And now it looks like I'm going to pay."

"Pay how?"

"I'm late."

"Late?"

"With my period," Beth explained.

"Oh, Christ." Carrie laughed without humor. "Wouldn't you know it? I take more chances than a free-fall sky diver, and I've never been caught. You slip once, and it's Mother's Day. Just how late are you?"

"I've missed one period."

"Have you been to a doctor yet?"

"No. I'm still hoping I'll come around."

"Well, it's not the end of the world. If you are, we'll just have it taken care of."

"You mean an abortion." Beth sighed deeply. "I don't know, Carrie. I haven't made up my mind about that yet."

"You're not seriously thinking the stud congressman will do the honorable thing? Because if you are—"

"No." Beth interrupted. "Even if Michael had a sudden change of character, I wouldn't marry him. I don't even much like him, let alone love him."

"Yes. Well, I've slept with a few I could say that about myself." Carrie thought a minute. "But if not Michael, and not an abortion, then that leaves unmarried motherhood. Is that what you're saying, Bethie?"

"I don't really know what I'm saying. Right now I'm just waiting and hoping I won't have to make a decision."

"Well, don't wait too long," Carrie cautioned her.

"I won't." Beth's sigh was heartfelt as she lay back

down on the deck and turned her face to the sun once again.

The sun turned Beth's face red. Not as red, however, as it would have been had she known that her conversation with Carrie had been overheard by Deke Wells in the galley just below the deck on which they were lying. Deke had opened the porthole to air out the galley at precisely the point in their conversation where Beth had confessed to Carrie that she'd had sex with Michael.

There was no way Deke could have made himself stop listening after that. What he heard disturbed him deeply. By the time he finally closed the porthole and went back to cleaning the galley, his face was contorted with emotion. But what emotion? Shock? Pain? Jealousy? Bitterness? Anger?

At that moment, Deke himself could not have said.

45

SPIRO PAPATESTUS'S FACE was turning red with rage as he listened to Jack Houston speak. "You are sure," he said, restraining himself, "these people are reliable?"

"I believe they are." Jack had been completely unprepared for the fury of Spiro's reaction. Startling as was the disclosure he had just passed on to him, it was by no means the most important part of what Jack had to tell Spiro.

They were seated on a bench in Athens's National Garden, across from Syntagma Square. Not too far away, Hadrian's Arch looked down on them, its weather-worn facade like a reflection of the cruelty that had taken possession of Spiro's rugged features. Around their feet scampered a dozen cats or more, trying periodically to steal the breadcrumbs from the duck whose terrain it was and who pecked at them viciously, chasing them away with ferocious quackings. The quacks and the meows provided a disconcerting counterpoint to their conversation.

Jack had explained to Spiro that the people claiming to have a line on Zelig Meyerling's abduction were criminals who wanted to unionize the docks. Jack's connection—a Venetian—had spelled out their terms for locating Zelig and engineering his rescue. Spiro's reaction to this news was positive. Logrolling came as easily to him as falling off one, and if these people really could produce Zelig, he assured Jack, then he would work out the details of a company union with them.

Privately, Spiro considered it no sacrifice. With the Socialist Papandreou in power, it was only a matter of time before he would have to allow the unionizing of his dock loading operations anyway. Just as well to have a union that would keep things in line for a payoff that was agreed to in advance. It was neater that way, and in the long run it would cost no more than having hundreds of nonunion longshoremen running around with pillage under their peacoats.

That agreed, Jack passed along to Spiro the Venetian's latest revelations. His people had determined that the group holding Zelig, while basically Greek, was affiliated with groups sympathetic to their aims in other countries. These aims were twofold: to force the Papandreou government to expel NATO from Greece and to ensure that no nuclear plants were built on the Greek isles. All those directly involved in the kidnapping were Greek save one, a black American. He was one of the two men, according to the Venetian, who had set up the kidnapping of Zelig Meyerling by infiltrating the Papatestus villa on Crete in advance of Zelig's arrival. The two men were Clint Anderson and Xanthos Konstantin.

"Xanthos saved my life." Spiro's fury was slow building.

"For his own purposes. That was his reason for cultivating your friendship from the very beginning."

"My poor Louise."

"I beg your pardon?" Jack wasn't sure he had heard right.

"Nothing." Spiro was not about to explain how his wife had been used. It was too degrading. She would be desolate. All that the three of them had done was permissible in the name of passion. None of it was tolerable for political purposes.

Spiro said nothing more. They sat silently, Hadrian's Arch looking down on them, the cats scampering at their feet, the duck quacking violently to guard its turf against the feline forays. The fierce rage that had taken possession of his craggy, lined face wiped away the civilized facade Spiro had so carefully cultivated over the years. What was left was basic Macedonian, pure savage, Alexander the Great and his father Philip in all their vengeful glory. What was left was the undisguised and unvarnished will to murder.

I will kill him, Spiro was thinking. I will go back to Crete, and I will kill him. I will kill Xanthos Konstantin!

Xanthos and Louise were lying side by side on chaise longues on the patio of the villa, sipping chilled retsina and soaking up sunshine, when James Stockwell came upon them. Regarding their firmly developed, deeply tanned bodies, James thought to himself that the ancient Greek sculptors were right: when it comes to form, the standard is always set by youth. In truth, Louise in a particularly revealing bikini, and Xanthos in latex so skimpy as to be little more than a closely molded jockstrap, might well have been lifted from some erotic bas relief girding a temple at Delphi or Knossos.

"Join us," Louise invited, patting the vacant chaise on her other side.

"Thanks, no. I was looking for Lisa."

"Is going that way." Xanthos gestured toward a path that led between a lemon grove and a stand of fig trees. "With lady English."

"Winifred was with her?" James frowned. He had hoped to have a talk with Lisa alone. He wanted—tactfully—to convey to her his feeling that her relationship with her English friend was perhaps not working out well, that perhaps she should give some thought to terminating it.

"I think Winifred was going in to Ag Alini to buy a pair of sandals," Louise told him. "Lisa was walking down to the road with her to catch the bus. But it wasn't decided if she was going with her."

"Well, if she didn't go, maybe I can intercept her walking back." James brightened. "Thanks." He set off down the path.

It was fragrant with citrus blossoms, a lazy, tangy, sun-warmed aroma. James plucked a fig or two—sugar sweet in contrast to the smell of lemons—and crunched the small, tasty seeds between his strong white teeth. He walked all the way to the road without meeting Lisa. There was no one standing by the side of the road. He glanced at his watch. The bus to Ag Alini would have come and gone by now. Both girls must have taken it. James shrugged and started back up the path.

He had retraced his steps perhaps a quarter of a mile when he heard the soft rush of water. He hadn't noticed the noise—a cool, liquid whispering over small rocks—when he'd come down the path. Curious, James left the path and followed the sound through the lemon trees to a small, graded brook. On impulse, he sat down on the bank and took off his shoes and socks and rolled up his slacks. Grinning, he waded into the brook.

Holding his shoes and socks high, he sloshed downstream. After about fifty feet, the brook turned sharply, and James climbed up the embankment there. He scrambled up to find a gently banked slope of high grasses ringed by more lemon trees. Barefoot, he made his way toward the grove, when a soft, rather high-pitched trill of laughter caught his attention.

The laughter came from an area off to his left. James turned his head. There was a small clearing there between where the grass thinned out and the lemon trees. Stretched out were two figures, embracing, entwined. At first James could not focus. The sun was in his eyes, reflecting off the tall grass, making the air shimmer. Then he made the figures out. It was Lisa and Winifred.

Both young women were wearing shorts. Both had laid

aside their halters. Winifred was palming Lisa's small breasts, and her fingers were splayed out around her thin torso almost as if to protect the ribs showing through the translucent skin. Lisa's slender face with its pronounced cheekbones was cushioned on Winifred's generous bosom, her lips toying with the half-dollar-sized pink aureole around one of Winifred's nipples, her hand buried deep below the waistband of Winifred's shorts. It was Winifred's laugh, high and excited as she squirmed, which James had heard. Now they were kissing.

James stopped short, his gasp cutting his chest like a knife. His daughter's name was expelled from his lips before he could stop it. "Lisa!"

Winifred reacted first. Jumping to her feet, she folded her arms to cover her nudity. She bent and groped in the grass for her halter. Welling tears magnified her sapphire eyes. "Mister Stockwell!" Embarrassment robbed her of further words.

"How dare you spy on me, Daddy!" Now Lisa reacted, slipping on her halter and straining her arms behind her to fasten the clasp in back.

"I wasn't—" James stood there, a figure both tragic and comic, immobilized by shock, his socks and shoes held high and to one side like an offering.

"It's disgusting of you!" Lisa was outraged. "Truly disgusting!"

"Wait, Lisa. Your father isn't—" Winifred tried to calm Lisa down.

"Please!" James got hold of himself. "I don't need your help to talk to my daughter."

"Don't you dare talk to her in that tone of—"

"It's all right. I understand. I should go now. Really. You two have things to— I should go." Red-faced and disconcerted, Winifred left them.

"You have no right to drive her away!" Lisa scrambled to her feet and started to follow Winifred.

James grabbed her, his hands easily circling both upper arms, and stopped her from leaving. "She's no good for you." He found himself stammering, groping for words, not sure himself just what it was he was trying to say. "It's her fault that you—she's—she's not normal."

"Damn you!" Lisa's lip curled, turning her face into an expression of savage fury. "What do you mean, 'not normal'? What does that make me, then?"

"You're young. You don't know what you're—"

"Stop it, Daddy! Whatever Winifred is, I am, too! We're lesbians. Why won't you just accept that? We aren't ashamed of it. I'm not ashamed of it."

"No." James shook his head, not accepting his daughter's words. "You're just young. You don't understand what she has gotten you involved—"

"I am a lesbian, Daddy! Winifred didn't make me one. I am one. You know that. I've always been one. I have problems, but being a lesbian isn't one of them. That is your problem, Daddy, not mine. If you can't solve it, if that means you don't want me for your daughter, so be it. I am a lesbian. Do you understand? A lesbian."

Staring at Lisa, James for the first time made himself face up to the full meaning of what her sexual preference meant. His daughter was attracted not to men, but to other women. Nothing could stop him from feeling the way he did now. He was filled with shame.

46

HORACE STOCKWELL WAS not an admirable character, but he was a fascinating one. Piecing together the story of his life from his son's manuscripts and the various documents, records, and diaries at her disposal was an intriguing process that could claim Holly's attention for hours at a time. Working on the history was the only thing that could truly distract her as she sat day after day at the villa on Crete and waited for some word of Zelig. As Horace Stockwell's adult life took on added dimensions of outrageousness bordering on horror, Holly found that he grew in interest in much the same way that Dr. Jekyll only really locked in the reader when he turned into Mr. Hyde. Wimps, Holly reflected wryly, no matter how intrinsically good, are never as interesting as villains, no matter how pervasively evil.

The record did indeed indicate that pure evil had a firm grip on Horace Stockwell after the death in 1810 of his mother. Horace was thirty-two years old then, and Riverview was without a mistress. It was time, he and his father agreed, for Horace to take a wife.

Like many libertines of his era, Horace wanted a spouse who was pure and innocent as well as comely. His eye fell on Henrietta van Cortlandt, whose father was one of the less notable cousins of the distinguished New York Dutch family. She had not much in the way of a dowry, but the Stockwell wealth was such that this was of little concern to Horace and she did bring with her an illustrious name, as well as those other qualities that Horace desired in a wife.

Strangely enough, Horace, who was the farthest thing from a man of sentiment, fancied himself in love with Henrietta before he married her. At seventeen, she was fifteen years younger than he, a slender, coltish beauty with auburn hair, pale skin, and the perpetually startled air of a doe poised for flight. Her timidity, verging on meekness, promised submissiveness. It was not this, however, that attracted Horace as much as the fact that he found Henrietta's aura of purity overwhelmingly arousing.

During the months before their wedding, he paid many visits to the brothels behind Bowling Green and acted out with harlot surrogates the violent destruction of Henrietta's innocence. He fantasized their wedding night and the brutal acts he would perform to reduce Henrietta to the slut he knew his mother to have been. Henrietta would be revealed, like all women, to be a vessel of seduction cloaked in virtue.

Henrietta van Cortlandt, young and inexperienced, knew that it would hurt, but she was unprepared for the pain that accompanied Horace's lovemaking. Her screams endeared her to Horace, but not because he felt any great sympathy, as Henrietta assumed. Rather, her suffering, combined with her youth, kept his lust at fever pitch. It was only when her cries turned to whimpers that his interest waned.

Horace's interest in his young wife waned more as the marriage bed transported Henrietta from adolescence to womanhood. Happily for Henrietta, Horace spent more and more of his evenings in New York City, away from Riverview. He resumed his old habits: drinking, gambling, and carousing in the brothels, where his taste for young girls and wielding the birch became well known.

His sexual interest in Henrietta revived, however, when, early in 1812, she became pregnant. Her pregnant condition made her more vulnerable, and this rearoused Horace. The more obviously Henrietta blossomed with child, the more pleasure he took in ravishing her. True, her innocence was gone, but now there was a new tenderness of flesh to be brutalized in ways sure to make the tears run down Henrietta's cheeks. For a while, Horace stayed home nights and forsook the brothels.

The child, a son, was born in July of 1812, a month after the United States declared war on Great Britain. He was named George Cortlandt Stockwell after George Washington and his mother's family. After a brief smile of satisfaction, Horace ignored the infant, his attention focused on the delay the war was inflicting on his Erie Canal project. The war dragged on inconclusively for two years, with neither side achieving its objectives. Finally, on December 24, 1814, a peace treaty was signed at Ghent in Belgium, which virtually left things as they had been before the war started. It was more than two weeks, however, before news of the treaty reached the shores of the United States. Thus it was that on January 8, 1815, two weeks after the treaty was signed, General Andrew Jackson fought a great battle at New Orleans with heavy loss of life on both sides and achieved the famous victory that created the illusion—perpetuated in the history books— that the United States had somehow "won" the War of 1812.

Horace was celebrating this victory with a pair of

frightened, nubile Creole twins and a "Lou'sana lash"—a blacksnake whip favored by overseers on delta plantations—when news was brought to him that his wife had been delivered of a second child. "Male or female?" Horace inquired.

"A girl," he was told.

"Then the birth is of no consequence," he responded, turning back to the unhappy twins and cracking the whip to signal them to turn up their bare bottoms for his sadistic pleasure.

Peace brought prosperity to Horace, and the death of his father, Everett Stockwell, in 1817 consolidated his fortune. Ignoring his family, he divided his time between expanding his western holdings and indulging his vices. He was forty years old in 1818 when his third and last child, Charles, was born, but Horace's entry into middle age in no way curbed his excesses. If anything, his obsession for youth and variety in sex partners deepened with the years. He spent less and less time at Riverview.

In the early 1820s, years of bordello living had left their mark. The doctor gave Horace a choice between reforming or an early death. Shaken, he began spending time at home. No longer frequenting brothels, Horace was forced to settle for sex with nonprofessionals. If this included an occasional kitchen maid, or the young daughter of a Hudson Valley sharecropper, in addition to his wife, it was nevertheless a far cry from his former erotic activities.

With millions of dollars pouring in from his Erie Canal and westward investments, gambling, too, lost its hold on him. He did, however, cling to his remaining vice, drinking, and his frequent rampages under the influence of brandy were deeply etched in the memory of all three of his children. George Cortlandt Stockwell, the eldest, was the most scarred by these late-night carousals, and the violent scenes that so often took place between husband and wife.

When George was fifteen years old, Henrietta became ill with a mysterious ailment that dragged on for a year. Since it wouldn't have been seemly to show discontent to the Riverview servants, and since Horace waved away her illness as "female trouble," Henrietta expressed her complaints solely to her children. As the oldest, George was the one made most aware that her body was racked more and more by a variety of symptoms that frequently confined her to her bed.

There was swelling of the stomach, and unexplained lesions of the skin, along with a rash that came and went. She was extremely nervous, and erratic poundings of her pulses and unexplained palpitations filled her with anxiety. In the grip of these symptoms, Henrietta's children, particularly her eldest, were her only comfort. But she could not bring herself to speak even to George of the final symptom, the one that finally drove her to the doctor in defiance of Horace's pooh-poohing.

"Why did you go against my wishes?" Horace demanded upon her return, too far into the brandy bottle on this particular afternoon to care that George was witness to the scene.

"A sore, a chancre," she blurted out. "The swelling was fierce and filled with pus. I was afraid." She lowered her eyes and raised them again, indicating without further words the location of the sore.

Horace poured brandy into a tankard and drained it off as if it were merely ale. "All women are unclean," he snarled.

George was mystified. Why was his father so angry? Why was his mother shaking so?

"It is you who are unclean!" Henrietta's outburst broke a lifetime of deferential habit. "I have syphilis, and the doctor says that I have caught it from you. Syphilis!"

"Be quiet!" Horace's slap ensured compliance with his request.

Watching, George did not really understand. Nor did he know what to do. But when he grew older, he did come to understand. And he also decided what he must do.

He wrote a book.

47

HOLLY INTERRUPTED HER reading of George Cortlandt Stockwell's faded manuscript when Lisa barged into the library of the villa on Crete. Breathing quickly, her eyes not quite focused and her face contorted with anger, Lisa stormed over to the table where Holly was seated.

"I have something to say—to say to you—you, Holly." Her words were expelled staccato, verbal hiccups. "I want you to stay—I want you to leave Winifred alone."

"What do you mean? I haven't been bothering Winifred." Recognizing the state Lisa was in, Holly kept her voice free of resentment.

"You know what I— You sashay around trying to— You come on to her, and—you deliberately—" Lisa began to shake violently, uncontrollably, clenching her teeth to keep them from chattering.

Alarmed, Holly went to her. "Sit down." She took Lisa's trembling arm. The skin was ice cold to the touch. She led her to a divan and sat her down. "I'm not interested in coming between you and Winifred." Holly patted the long, narrow hand.

"Winifred and I have a—have a relationship and—and—and you're intruding on—" Her voice faded out; her pale blue eyes darted wildly in a vain search for words.

"You're mistaken, Lisa. You're upset, and you're not seeing things clearly. I'm not attracted to women."

"Then why—why do you—you come on to her?"

"But I don't, Lisa. Truly I don't."

"She wants—wants you. She told—told me so. She wouldn't go on being—being attracted if you didn't respond."

"I don't respond. I won't. I'll be more careful. I promise. But you are exaggerating things, Lisa. Winifred really cares for you."

As Holly spoke Lisa subsided, slumping far down on

the divan. A moment later her tremors ceased, and her thin face smoothed to a sort of calmness. The lids of her eyes grew heavy as her pale lashes fluttered to her cheek. She seemed to be having a hard time staying awake. The transition was surprisingly abrupt, and Holly did not know what to make of it. Still, it seemed better that Lisa should rest than that her agitation should continue. So Holly simply sat with her hands folded and watched Lisa nodding off.

They were seated like that, side by side, Lisa slumped low, when Winifred entered. Because of their positions, she saw Holly before she saw Lisa. "Holly!" She spoke spontaneously. "We have to talk about what happened between us in the woods the other day."

Lisa sat up and, turning to Winifred, she caught the full impact of the English girl's infatuated expression as she looked at Holly. Lisa's laugh was as humorless as a burst from a machine gun.

"Oh, Lisa. There you are." Winifred tried to brazen it through. "I was looking for you, ducks."

"I'll bet you were!" Lisa stood up. Her voice was ominously calm now, her words unhurried, the stammer absent. "But what for, Winifred? To tell me 'what happened in the woods the other day' between you and Holly?" She quoted Winifred's words back at her. "I think it would be better if you two discussed that by yourselves first and got your story straight." Lisa started for the door.

"Lisa, don't be silly." Holly tried to stop her.

"Bitch!" Lisa wheeled, and the word came out as a shriek. "I believed you, and all the time you've been meeting her behind my back!"

"It wasn't like—" It was too late. Lisa had left the room.

"She's bloody zonked," Winifred told Holly. "Out of her cranium."

"Did you tell her you were attracted to me?" Holly demanded.

"Yes." Winifred blushed. "I just got tired of denying it, and Lisa didn't believe my denials anyway."

"I don't care." Holly was furious. "I don't need this.

I have more troubles than I can handle. You talk to her, Winifred. You make her see that whatever may be in your head, I'm not a party to it.''

"Talk to her?'' Winifred laughed. "I wish it was that bloody simple. Have you ever tried talking to a junkie, Holly?''

"A junkie?'' Holly stared at her. "You mean heroin?''

"When she can get it. Coke or hash when she can't.''

"How long has this been going on?''

"Two years that I know. She was much worse when I first met her. But then, in the beginning, when things were really good between us, she tapered off. I had her practically kicking it, until she heard you were coming here. You see, I'd told Lisa about you before I even knew you two were related. I had no way of knowing she'd become even more obsessed with my attraction to you than I am.''

"But shouldn't she be getting help?'' Holly asked.

"She was. In Paris, I got her into a treatment program. I moved in with her to make sure she stayed clean. I held her hand through the sweats and the nightmares and the screaming mimis. I've done what I can, and I'll go on doing it. Regardless of how I feel about you, Holly, I would never let Lisa go down the drain.''

"Then you really do care about her,'' Holly realized.

"On the mark.'' Winifred smiled a cool, compassionate, peculiarly British smile. "It really is possible to love two people at once, you know.'' She sighed. "I'd better go run her down now before she OD's or something.'' Winifred left.

Shaken by what she had heard, Holly went out on the terrace and stared at the sunset. Lisa a drug addict; Winifred standing firm between her and self-destruction. There was always more to things than appeared on the surface. Winifred could behave like a love-struck schoolgirl toward her and at the same time shoulder the responsibility of Lisa's salvation. Yes, people were a lot more complex than their morality.

The setting sun was spectacular, burnishing the green-and-white mountains to pearl and amber and drenching the sea with shimmering gold. Small rainbows jumped from silver leaf to silver leaf in the olive grove. Just beyond, an afterglow polished lemons in the soft breeze. The lushness of Crete seemed tangibly emotional at twilight.

A car pulled into the driveway beside the terrace, the squeal of its brakes breaking the spell. Spiro Papatestus got out, looking hurried and—even at this distance—angry. "Hello, Spiro," Holly hailed him.

"Hello, Holly." For Spiro, who was always quite courteous, the greeting was minimal. "Have you seen Louise?"

"I saw her walking that way about half an hour ago." Holly pointed in the direction of the cottage shared by Xanthos and Clint.

Spiro's face darkened. He immediately hurried down the path Holly had indicated, the path that would lead him to the cottage. He was sure he would find his wife there. His wife and her treacherous lover, Xanthos Konstantin!

48

PERHAPS TWENTY MINUTES before Spiro's return, Louise and Xanthos had gone hand in hand to the cottage. Once life had seemed complex, happiness elusive to Louise. Xanthos, with his youth and energy and straightforward lust, and her wise and understanding husband, Spiro, had changed all that. Life was now simple, physical, free of vexing thought; happiness was as elemental as the sex act itself. Without shame, without guilt, Louise lived in the moment, on the nerve ends of her desires, letting her flesh dictate her actions, questioning neither her needs nor their satisfaction.

It was not just physical. Xanthos freed her emotions as

well. In his arms she felt not only passion but love. When Louise gave herself up to him, she felt not only erotically possessed, but truly cherished. She also felt secure. Nothing she did, or didn't do, would be judged, looked down on, found wanting. Degradation was not possible between them. Every sort of desire was permissible, every appetite acceptable. How wonderful for a woman to be able to tell her lover, "I want you now!" and to whisper in his ear with no concern for taboo words just how she wanted him, and just what she wanted him to do, and just what she was burning to do to him.

Louise had whispered such words in Xanthos's ear as they entered the cottage. He had laughed his rich, mellifluous laugh and kissed her. And then he had responded. "Is good what you want. But I am massaging you?" he inquired, his large sun-browned hand moving to the back of her neck and kneading it gently. "Or you are massaging me?"

"Both." Louise's hazel eyes smoldered. Taking a jar of fragrant tiger balm from a cabinet, she led Xanthos to the bedroom. "First you, then me," she told him.

Louise knelt on the bed, one knee on either side of his muscular thighs. She unbuttoned the cotton shirt he was wearing, bending over to kiss each of the nipples on his chest by turn, tickling them with her tongue. Xanthos's muscles rippled in response, and her excitement grew. She removed his shirt and then carefully took off his sandals. After unzipping his jeans, he wriggled free of them with her help.

Dipping the tips of the fingers of one hand in the fragrant tiger balm, Louise began to massage Xanthos. She spread the ointment over his back and shoulders, then rubbed it into his well-muscled flesh. Her fingertips tingled sensually when he reacted with sighs of pleasure and small writhings. The writhings became more pronounced as Louise worked her way down. Xanthos's hips rolled sensually from side to side as she rubbed the small of his back. She paused before moving on to his bottom.

Her exertions had made her perspire. She pulled off her sundress now and tossed the top of her bikini to one side. Hands splayed wide over Xanthos's buttocks now,

Louise leaned hard on them, rubbing in the tiger balm with her palms. The sinews there flexed under these ministrations. Xanthos's thighs parted.

"Oh, no," Louise teased him. "Not yet. This is a massage. First I have to do you, and then you me, and then, well, maybe."

"Maybe? Maybe I am falling asleep by then."

"Oh, I don't think so." She applied the balm to the backs of his thighs and rubbed it on. Then she smacked his sturdy bottom with the flat of her hand. "You can turn over now," she told him.

When he complied, Louise laughed. "Oh, my," she said. "Oh, my my."

"What do you think? Is human you play with, not statue."

"The massage is supposed to *relax* you."

"I am relaxed. He is tense. Massage him."

"Don't rush." Deliberately ignoring his erection, Louise repositioned herself and applied the tiger balm to Xanthos's chest and belly, finishing with his thighs. Then she kissed him quickly on the lips. "Now you do me," she said, removing her bikini bottoms.

Xanthos sat up and looked down at her. Her deep hazel eyes, sparkling with mischievous desire, met his. Her nipples had hardened, her long, red-gold hair fanned out over her full breasts wildly, a peek-a-boo mantle. He reached out with both hands and squeezed her bosom gently, lovingly. "Massage first," he conceded. "But not lasting too long."

"No," Louise agreed murmuring, "Not too long." She stretched out on her stomach and closed her eyes, the long lashes shadowing her cheeks. "Please, darling, not too long." Louise gave herself up to the exquisite sensations of the tiger balm and Xanthos's clever, loving hands.

Her skin felt like velvet to her as Xanthos stroked in the ointment. When she turned over at his urging, his touch turned the tips of her breasts to blazing matches. Her hips rolled voluptuously, her tongue circled her lips, her back began to arch.

"I want you," Louise moaned. Her hand fluttered to

290

the back of his neck and pulled his face down to hers. The kiss was urgent.

When it was over, Xanthos laid the tiger balm on the nightstand. "Is here for you." He displayed himself to her. "However you are wanting."

"Lie back." Louise was feverish with excitement. She studied his body and then his face as Xanthos stretched out. Sitting on her haunches, her heels digging into the softness of her bottom, she drank him in with her eyes, forcing herself to take her time, commanding leisure all the while that passion made her pulses pound with impatience.

He followed her perusal of his naked form with laughing eyes.

Her glance lingered on his penis, which rose like some erotic totem from the curly jungle of his groin. She swung over Xanthos and sank down, impaling herself to the hilt.

"Oh, God!" She was filled with him—not just physically but emotionally, and in her mind as well. "Do it, my love!" she gasped, rocking back and forth, twisting down hard in small, delicious circles.

"Is happening." Xanthos cupped her panting breasts and thumbed the hard nipples. He rose up against her, abrupt and hard at first and then more slowly, circling deeply and counter to her movements.

"Ahh!" Louise fell forward, her hair tumbling over his face, and kissed him deeply, clinging as he entered and reentered her with long, clever, corkscrewing strokes.

She dug her nails into his shoulders. She leaned back and down hard, drawing him in to the fullest. She flung her head back, and her eyes shot open at the approach of their mutual climax. They opened wide and looked straight ahead.

There, behind Xanthos, in back of his pillowed head, stood Spiro, her husband.

"Hello, darling," she greeted him breathlessly.

Spiro did not answer. Instead, he took a quick, long step forward which placed him directly beside the pillow on which Xanthos's head rested. Taking a revolver from his pocket, he pressed the muzzle to Xanthos's temple.

Louise's scream drowned out the sound of the hammer clicking back.

Even as she screamed, Louise's hand moved, slapping the muzzle away from Xanthos's temple and knocking the gun out of Spiro's hand altogether. As it hit the floor with its hammer cocked, the gun fired.

As Spiro shrank back with the loud retort of the gun, fearful that his wife might have been injured by the wild shot, Louise, mistaking the movement for an effort to retrieve the weapon, lunged toward her husband with hands formed into claws, bent on preventing him from murdering her lover. The movement dislodged her from her erotic impalement as it roused Xanthos from the lethargy of fear that had seized him when the revolver went off.

Slowly, still in a sort of trance of terror, Xanthos slid out from under Louise as she struggled with her husband. When they slipped lingeringly to the floor, grappling, he reflexively gathered up his clothes and sidled toward the door. En route he spied Spiro's revolver lying on the floor. He stooped and picked it up, his movements still lethargic. Then, suddenly, Xanthos bolted from the cottage as Spiro overcame his wife and thrust her from him. He was out the door only a moment or two behind Xanthos. "Guards!" he bellowed. It was crucial that the security guards be alerted before Xanthos could make his escape.

The response was prompt. Spiro had not stinted on safety for his villa. The security staff was professional, always on the alert, trained to react quickly in emergency situations. They sprang into action now. Spotlights came alive all along the walls defining the perimeters of the estate. Armed sentinels fell into position, Ouzi submachine guns held at the ready. Large police dogs and their handlers began to sweep the grounds, moving inward from the perimeters toward the villa. The crackle of walkie-talkies solicited an accounting of the safety of staff and guests and family.

While all this was falling into place, a siren, sounding from the gatehouse at the main driveway to the estate, roused Holly from her perusal of the Riverview papers. When she went out on the patio to see what was happening, the twilight that had been fading into dusk the last time she noticed had given way to night. Because it was cloudy, and the moon and stars overhead were obscured, the searchlights swooping over the grounds seemed doubly ominous.

"What is happening?" Startled by the busy scene unfolding before her, Holly spoke aloud.

The last thing she expected was an answer. Nevertheless, she got one. A voice from the shadows to one side of where she was standing, but very close at hand, replied: "They look to find me."

Holly wheeled toward the voice just as Xanthos took a small step forward. It was measured so that she could see Spiro's gun pointing at her while he would still not be visible to anybody else. "Coming here, please." He gestured with the gun.

"What—"

"Moving quickly, please. Is no time for talking." He took Holly's arm and propelled her into the darkness around the side of the villa. The searchlights did not penetrate behind the shrubbery there. As they moved, Xanthos pressed the gun into her ribs. The pressure both quieted Holly and made her afraid. Obviously Xanthos was desperate. She could feel his tension as he prodded her in the direction of the garages. They had almost reached that destination when they heard the growl. A Doberman emerged from the lemon grove where it met the gardens. Reining in the guard dog, its handler immediately spoke into his walkie-talkie, relaying Xanthos's position to the other security guards.

The response was very quick. The spotlights were redirected, lighting up the entire area demarcated by the lemon grove, the garden, the villa, and the garages. There were sounds of running as reinforcements converged on the site. Xanthos, pushing Holly ahead of him into one of the pools of light, held Spiro's revolver high and pointed it at the side of her head. "Leaving!" he announced loudly. "Car and not interfering, please. Quickly. Otherwise I am blowing off lady's head."

Spiro arrived on the scene just in time to hear this. He cursed himself for having let Xanthos slip through his fingers at the cottage. He would have liked nothing so much as to direct his men to open fire on this renegade who had deceived his wife and betrayed them so despicably. But he dared not risk Holly's life.

"We'll give you what you want," he snarled in Greek. "Just release Mrs. Meyerling."

"I would never be so foolish." Xanthos answered him in Greek as well. "You will provide me with a car immediately, and I will leave with her as my hostage. It is the only way I can be sure you will not interfere with my escape."

More words were exchanged, with Spiro playing for time so that his men might get into position to follow Xanthos when he left. Finally, however, there was no choice but for him to agree to the conditions. The Mercedes sports coupe was brought to Xanthos, he and Holly got into it, and the security force stood aside while the gates were opened and he was permitted to leave.

Once they were on the road, Holly's mind began to race. The Mercedes was barreling at top speed, forcing Xanthos to keep both hands on the wheel to navigate the maniacal curves and hairpin turns of the Crete mountain roads. The revolver was in his lap, clenched between his thighs. Its metal gleamed in the dull greenish glow from the dashboard.

Holly's eyes darted to it. Did she dare to make a grab for the gun? If there was a struggle, Xanthos would surely not be able to keep control of the car. No. Even if she succeeded in seizing the weapon, the chances of hurtling over the side of the unrailed road into the abyss below were too great.

"Not even thinking it." Xanthos had seen her eyes move in the light from the dashboard. "Killing you surely, and if not, dying together."

"You're well away now. Why don't you just stop the car and let me out?"

"And give up bargaining chip Mrs. Zelig Meyerling along with Dr. Meyerling? Not so foolish."

"You're with the gang who abducted my husband?" Holly's heart pounded.

"Not denying." Xanthos shrugged. "Is no point."

"Is Zelig alive? Is he all right?"

"Is living. Is coming to no harm. Also you. We are soon making demands, perhaps. Is by now long enough Premier Papandreou sweats, wondering." Xanthos looked in the rearview mirror. He cursed aloud, harshly, in Greek.

"What is it?"

"Spiro people following." Xanthos floored the gas pedal and whipped around a curve, tires screeching.

Holly twisted around in her seat. She counted three sets of headlights negotiating the turn behind them before Xanthos took a hairpin turn on two wheels and they were lost to view. Now the Mercedes was barreling down the mountain at top speed toward a fork in the road. Unexpectedly, Xanthos veered to the right at the fork, taking the road that led back up the mountain toward the ridged center of Crete, rather than the connecting road to the shore highway with its choice of many routes. "Is calling ahead police blockading," he muttered. "Is trying to herd us that direction."

Whether he was right or wrong, looking down over the side of the road they were now climbing, Holly saw the three pursuit cars all take the other road at the fork. Xanthos had shaken them. "Where will you take me now?" she asked him.

"Long way. Other side of mountains. Field. Airplane. Flying to Greece, safety."

Safety, Holly thought. Safety for whom? True, she would probably get to see Zelig, but still—

Still, Holly was now herself a hostage.

BOOK FIVE

49

After finishing a frankfurter from a vendor on the street, the Reverend Cabot crossed over and entered the Stockwell Building. He took the elevator to the twenty-seventh floor where the executive offices of Stockwell Industries were located and where a meeting of the board that he had arranged to attend was being held.

First he had to navigate the twenty-seventh floor's opulent reception room. Murals by Gilbert Stuart framed by oiled mahogany walls, discreetly fading handmade tapestries, and twin dull patinated bronze plaques, an unobtrusive carpet from the Far East by way of Britain and modest Walloon hand-loomed curtains, deep, overstuffed fauteuils from Provence and a Louis XIV escritoire serving as a reception desk lent the room an aura of respectability, aristocratic wealth, and sedate charm. On other floors, where Stockwell business was actually conducted, there was glitter, even opulence, computerized glitz, and revived art deco, indirect lighting designed for upwardly mobile and bushy-tailed young executives who never squinted, never blinked, and surely never questioned the directives received from the twenty-seventh floor.

Ambling up to the receptionist, rumpled and friendly,

Reverend Cabot wondered to himself if he shouldn't perhaps have worn his turnaround collar. Prick a conscience or two, perhaps. Ah, well, too late now.

The receptionist's voice was modulated, welcoming, but not particularly friendly. Her smile let the Reverend Cabot know that he was expected, but not enthusiastically. "The board is in session," she informed him. "Mr. Lewis asks if you'll be good enough to have a seat until they take up the matter which concerns you."

So much for the power of the pulpit. The Reverend Cabot sank onto an antique armchair that was the financial district equivalent of a warm bath. He reached for the newspaper on the pocked pecan antique table in front of him. *The Wall Street Journal*. So what else is new?

How long, O Lord, he wondered, before I will be summoned?

In the conference room, seated in straight-backed Duncan Phyfe chairs around the two-hundred-year-old oval oak table, five members of the board of Stockwell Industries regarded the sixth.

David Lewis was saying, "Stockwell crude is now stockpiled to the limit with no prospect of refining. To sell it unrefined would be to accept a large loss. To go on pumping oil out of the ground under such circumstances—producing and selling at a loss, that is—would be foolhardy. We have reached the point where this board must decide to cap our wells."

"Causing large-scale unemployment in western New York State," Max Tyler pointed out.

"That can't be helped."

"Let's stick to our concerns," Peter interjected dryly. "I agree with Uncle David. We have to cut our losses."

"But we can refine." It was the moment for which Halsey De Vilbiss had been waiting. At long last the board would be forced to accede to his plans. "The Libyans will cut a deal. Spiro Papatestus has ships standing by to transport the crude, and he's ready to guarantee later transportation of the petroleum from Libya to whatever European markets we specify." Halsey did not mention the "honest broker" fee the Libyans were paying him.

298

"Twice the board told you not to pursue that initiative." Max Tyler was furious.

"Zelig," Patrice reminded De Vilbiss, arranging the silk bow at her throat. "The decision was not to do any business with Libya because Qaddafi might be involved with his abductors."

"That has been ruled out," Halsey assured the board. "Spiro Papatestus has established through his sources in the Mideast that Qaddafi isn't involved."

"That's true." David Lewis confirmed it.

"Will you go along with this, Patrice?" Max asked her.

"No." Patrice's small chin stuck out over her bow. "I won't."

"I will," Peter offered.

"And I," David Lewis added. "The Stockwell oil division has a responsibility to its stockholders."

"Then it's decided." Halsey was quietly jubilant. "I can set the wheels in motion."

"I wouldn't do that." Buffy spoke for the first time. "If you do, you will make both Qaddafi and Spiro Papatestus very angry. Spiro's ships will stand empty waiting for Stockwell crude, and Qaddafi's refineries will gather dust."

"Mrs. Houston—" Halsey De Vilbiss took a breath so deep with apprehension and outrage that it mottled his California tan.

"Stockwell crude has already left its storage tanks," Buffy told him calmly. "It's on its way to Jimbo Grebbs's refineries in Texas. Upstate New York can keep right on pumping. The tanks can handle the crude because it will just be passing through. That should make you happy, Max. No layoffs."

"How?" David Lewis stared at Buffy.

"A lady never tells." She smiled sweetly.

Of course, if Buffy really was a lady, Patrice reflected, Qaddafi would be getting ready to wash his feet in Stockwell crude. Patrice did not, however, make that observation aloud. Instead, she turned to David Lewis. "It seems our oil problems are settled," she said. "Shouldn't we ask the Reverend Cabot to step in now? I think we've kept him waiting long enough."

"I don't know why we have to waste time with him at all," Peter grumbled. "The church is the church, and business is business."

David Lewis spoke to his nephew. "Someday, with maturity, you will understand why things are not so clear-cut." He buzzed to signal the receptionist to bring in the Reverend Cabot.

As the Reverend Cabot entered the boardroom, the only really friendly faces he saw were those of Max Tyler and Patrice O'Keefe. The previous evening the reverend had spoken long distance to James Stockwell on Crete, appealing to his well-known social responsibility and explaining how Stockwell insurance was promoting inner-city arson. James had promised him that his daughter would vote with Max to end the program. Now Reverend Stockwell was hoping to be able to persuade the rest of the board to do the same.

In stony silence, the board heard his explanation of what was happening and his plea to end it. When he finished speaking, David Lewis told Reverend Cabot bluntly that in his view Gotham Memorial and its pastor had no business meddling in the practices of Stockwell Industries. "Just as the founder of the church intended that the Stockwells should have no say in its running," David Lewis declared, "he also intended that its minister should not meddle in the activities of the firm." There were murmurs of agreement from Peter Stockwell, Halsey De Vilbiss, and Buffy Houston.

"I see my ministerial obligations somewhat differently." The Reverend Cabot smoothed a wrinkle in his trousers that immediately reasserted itself. "With no other alternative, I'll be forced to speak out from the pulpit on this matter."

"Are you threatening us, Reverend Cabot?" David Lewis's face was a thundercloud.

"No, no. Of course not. I am only telling you that as minister of Gotham Memorial, I feel it must be made clear that the church disassociates itself from business ventures which increase suffering in the world."

"Meaning Stockwell's insurance practices?"

"Not if they were terminated. I mean, I could hardly

use them as an example then." Not just the Reverend Cabot's eyes but his whole face had seemed to twinkle.

Furious, David Lewis launched into a diatribe in which the phrase "moral blackmail" recurred often. In the end, however, he surrendered. "My concern for the family name," he announced, "forces me to conclude that this board should phase out the insurance program."

Not one of the other three board members was similarly moved. Halsey De Vilbiss was the first to react. Having lost out on the oil deal, he had no intention of sacrificing the profits from the insurance venture as well. "My obligation is to Sarah Stockwell's business interests. Your objections present no conflict with them," he told Reverend Cabot.

Peter Stockwell also stonewalled the minister. "It's a new day, Reverend." He was barely polite. "You can nail up all the demands you want on the door to this boardroom. Our religion is making money, and sinners or not, threats of denunciation and retribution from your pulpit won't put a stop to business as usual."

Buffy was amused. "Embarrass the family, Reverend Cabot? When will you give this sermon? I want to be sure to be there."

Max Tyler and Patrice and even David Lewis next tried to sway their fellow board members, but to no avail. In the end, the twinkle was wiped from the Reverend Cabot's face, and he left the boardroom with a parting promise that his would not be the only pulpit to denounce Stockwell and other insurers who fomented inner-city arson. Waiting for the elevator, the Reverend Malcolm Darrow Cabot acknowledged to himself that he had failed.

The reverend was a modern minister. He didn't believe in miracles. If someone had said to him at that moment, as he stood in front of the bank of elevators in the waiting room of the executive offices of the Stockwell Building, "The Lord moves in mysterious ways his wonders to perform," he would have been skeptical. No matter the justness of the cause, providence did not usually tinker to change defeat into victory.

That, however, was just what happened. Behind him, in the boardroom, the telephone rang. Frowning, David

Lewis picked it up and reminded the switchboard operator that he had asked her to hold all calls. She responded with a name that made him roll his eyes and hand the phone to Halsey de Vilbiss.

"Hello?" De Vilbiss spoke into the phone. "Oh, hello, Mrs. Tyler."

"Insurance, Mr. De Vilbiss. Insurance." The aging voice of Mrs. Sarah Stockwell Tyler was loud enough for the other members of the board to hear it. "Now, if you have acted like a southern California lawyer on this matter, Mr. De Vilbiss, then you must change your position. You see, I have had a call from my nephew James, and we are agreed that there must be no tarnishing of the good name of Stockwell. . . ."

50

"STOCKWELL." THE WAY that Xanthos pronounced the name, it came out "Zdork-wheel." He regarded Holly resentfully. "Is name symbolizing arrogance to Greek people. How are you understanding? You are born into wealth and power of Stockwell family. You are marrying diplomat playing ball with colonels. Party of your grandfather is voting aid to these villains. Is in your blood, duplicity."

"You speak about duplicity? After the way you wormed your way into the Papatestus household."

They were in the mountains north of Athens on the last leg of a week-long journey. First they had driven to central Crete, where they had waited two days in a barn for a small airplane that flew them to the Greek mainland. Here they had lain over at a safe house south of Napleon in the Peloponnesus until another car was delivered to Xanthos. They had gone to a second safe house near Egio, and now they were on their way from the Argolid to their final destination.

During this time, Holly had lost her fear of Xanthos. She realized that he would not harm her gratuitously. Sometimes, as they were doing now, they even argued politics. Their discussion ended as Xanthos stopped the car and considered the terrain. For some time they had been following a dirt road through a dense woodland. As the road descended, it had been losing definition, its surface washed away by recent rains. Finally it petered out to rocks and mud. Xanthos motioned with the gun for Holly to exit the car. They would have to walk from here.

She slid out. Taking her arm firmly, he guided her down the mountainside. It was dusk, and after they had walked for about an hour, it was night. Trees over their heads blotted out the sky. Xanthos had taken a flashlight from the glove compartment of the car, and they walked, slipping and sliding, in the pitch-black countryside, Holly following the beam until they reached the floor of the valley and the terrain leveled off. They emerged from a pine grove, and in the star glow from the suddenly revealed sky, Holly saw a small house of wood and stucco. They started for it, but when they reached the front steps, Xanthos halted abruptly.

"Is not right." For the first time in a long while, the muzzle of the revolver prodded Holly's ribs.

"I don't understand. What's the matter?"

"No guard." Slowly, he propelled her ahead of him up the porch stairs to the front door of the house. "Is something happening here. . . ."

Some two hours before Xanthos's arrival with Holly, something had indeed happened at the house where Xanthos's confederates were holding Zelig Meyerling hostage. The sound of loud, excited voices in the room next to the one in which he was being held had aroused Zelig from his sleep. The voices were in Greek, which Zelig spoke haltingly but could understand quite well. He was able to make out their voices fairly clearly. The American black man had been arrested. Zelig listened carefully. Yes. Clint whatever-his-name-was had returned to the Papatestus villa to find Xanthos gone and the Greek national security police waiting for him. Another member of the gang had seen Clint in handcuffs being placed aboard a government plane at the Iraklion airport. But wait, there was more. Zelig strained to hear. Xanthos Konstantin had also been unmasked as a member of the conspiracy, but he had successfully made his escape. He had taken a hostage. Another hostage.

A moment later Zelig learned that the hostage was Holly.

No! Inside his head the word was a prolonged moan. Not Holly! With a sick lurching of his stomach, Zelig was immediately more fearful for her than he had ever been for himself.

Before he could think further, the mustached southern Greek, the one who tended toward brutality, and his confederate entered Zelig's room. If Clint had been caught and Xanthos was on the run, there was a strong probability their organization had been infiltrated and their cover blown as well. It would only be a matter of time before the premises were raided. They must take their prisoner and move on quickly.

None too gently, they drew Zelig to his feet and propelled him toward the door. His hands were still bound behind his back, and the blindfold was still in place. They were unaware that Zelig had managed to loosen it so that by tilting his head a certain way he had some vision.

He tilted his head now, focusing on the long center hallway of the house as they half carried, half pushed him down it. They dropped him in a heap where the hallway met the foyer by the front door, before they went back to get the knapsacks containing their belongings. He was alone and considering what to do. Should he run now? From under the blindfold, his gaze fell on the front door. He blinked and focused again on the same spot. The door was opening.

The figures that slipped in and positioned themselves in the shadows of the unlit foyer were murky. Zelig's heart pounded. Obviously a rescue effort was being attempted. Once Zelig had been present when the CIA ran the numbers, and the computer came up with a 76 percent probability of hostage blood flowing whenever force was used in a rescue attempt. Now Zelig wished he had not committed that statistic to memory.

Coming back down the hallway now, halfway to Zelig, one of the two Greeks also noticed movement in the foyer. Immediately he pulled the automatic from his belt as his partner raised the submachine gun he was carrying. Hands still bound behind his back, Zelig flung himself flat on the floor with his head under a small rough wooden telephone table.

The first shot was unbelievably loud, the chorus that followed a cacophony. From the first the Greeks were out-gunned. Perceiving this, they retreated back down the long hall, their weapons still spewing bullets more or less at random. The rescuers followed, pursuing the Greeks out the back door of the house and across a yard to the woods.

"Let them go," directed one who seemed to be in charge. "We are not police."

Inside, in the hallway, Zelig at last dared to raise his head. The small foyer was acrid with gunsmoke. In the confined area, the cloud was as heavy as the stench. Eyes smarting with tears under the blindfold, he angled his head to peer through the haze and looming above him saw Jack Houston.

Jack knelt beside him and removed the blindfold. He cut away the rope tying Zelig's hands behind his back and helped him to his feet.

"Holly." Zelig's voice shook with concern. "She's been taken hostage. Have you had any word?"

"Yes." Jack nodded grimly. "Xanthos is on his way here with her. My friends here"—he indicated those with him—"have contacts who have been following Xanthos's progress since he left Crete. Now will be the hardest part for you, Zelig. We have to get in position. We have to be quiet. We have to wait."

And so they waited. . . .

Now the waiting was at an end. As Xanthos and Holly reached the top of the porch steps, he reached around her and turned the doorknob. The front door swung open easily. The inside hallway was dark. He nudged Holly to precede him inside.

They had gone only a couple of feet when Xanthos stopped her. It was too quiet. Something was definitely wrong. Instinct told him to get out with his prisoner while he could. Holding on to Holly's arm, squinting into the darkness, he started to move backward.

It was too late. There was a sudden quick movement behind Xanthos. A flashlight glared blindingly. The butt end of a revolver swung surely from the darkness and collided crunchingly with the back of his head. Simultaneously, Holly was grabbed and pulled to one side. If Xanthos's reflex had been to pull the trigger of the gun he was holding on her, the bullet would at worst have grazed her.

But he didn't pull the trigger. It had all happened too fast. Xanthos simply crumpled to the floor, and the gun went spiraling off into the darkness.

The lights went on, blinding Holly. The arms that had grabbed her still held her. She realized they were familiar before she was able to focus well enough to recognize the face.

"Jack!" she exclaimed.

He grinned, hugged her, and released her. Beside him a bearded man wearing the peacoat of a Piraeus dockworker bent over Xanthos to make sure he was really unconscious. He was.

Holly's next thought was of her husband. "Zelig?"

"Waiting inside. Against his will, I might add," Jack told her. "But he's had a rough time and was in no shape for this."

"He's alive, then." Good news; nevertheless, Holly was anxious. "But is he all right?"

"Are you all right?" Zelig burst in then, as worried about her as she was about him.

Holly's heart lurched. All the long months of worry! Her eyes spilled over at the sight of her husband. She stepped into his embrace fervently and clung to him.

"I was so worried!" His voice was a quavery croak in her ear.

"I've been beside myself!"

"When I heard you'd been seized—"

"Day after day without word—"

"I was so afraid that—"

"He's not dead! He's not dead! All I could do was keep telling myself that!"

"Oh, my darling!"

"Oh, Zelig!"

Embarrassed, Jack turned away from the reunited couple. He looked down at Xanthos's unconscious body. "He is going to have one helluva headache when he comes to," he remarked.

"Well"—in Zelig's arms, Holly remembered how Xanthos had deceived Spiro and Louise—"he deserves it."

She snuggled against her husband. His ordeal had left its mark. Deep shadows smudged his warm brown eyes. His face was unshaven and gaunt. His waistline had narrowed considerably. "You've lost weight," she murmured.

"Only in the stomach." Zelig's lips were against her ears, whispering. "Not where it counts." There was a slight stirring against her thigh.

Yes, Holly thought, Xanthos deserves what he gets for deceiving Spiro and Louise. But they weren't the only ones who had been deceived. Again there was that hardening pressure against her leg. "I've missed you so," Zelig whispered. "I want you. Only you."

"Do you?" Holly took a quick step backward. "Do you, darling?" She was remembering, in sharp focus now, Vanessa Brewster and Zelig's affair with her. "*Only* me?" And then Holly did something so out of character that it was difficult for Zelig to believe it was really happening.

She slapped her husband full in the face.

51

Xanthos inhabited the mind of Louise Papatestus as fully as once he had possessed her body. All the time he was using me, Louise thought, unable to banish the hurt. Just using me. The words played and replayed through her brain like a stuck phonograph record.

At first when Spiro had explained to her about Xanthos, she had refused to believe him. She thought that something must have snapped inside Spiro, that perhaps he had been jealous all along but repressing it, and now all that jealousy had burst murderously forth. How else explain the gun? There had been murder on his face. How else explain that? If she had not slapped his hand away, Xanthos would be dead right now. Yes, Spiro was insanely jealous. That's what it had to have been.

Only slowly did Louise come to accept the truth. Xanthos had fled. He was holding Holly hostage. Clint had been arrested. The newspapers and the television were full of stories of the men and the kidnapping.

Finally Louise had to listen to Spiro. She had to believe him. She had to acknowledge to herself that Xanthos had been using her from the first.

But he had made her feel so—so like a woman. He had liberated her. She had come alive in his arms. Apparently it had all been a betrayal, a huge joke, but even so Louise could not deny how Xanthos had made her feel. Alive! Yes, alive!

And now it was over. He was gone. He had used her, and he was gone. She would never feel alive again. She would never be alive again. And so—

Louise emptied all the pills from the different bottles out onto the tabletop, and, scooping them up in small handfuls, she swallowed them.

A short while before they found Louise, Holly emerged from the house into the patio of the villa and found James sitting there. He was staring out over the mountains toward the shoreline digs of Knossos. His expression was profoundly sad.

"Hello, Uncle James." She bent and kissed his cheek.

"Oh." Deep in thought, he was mildly startled. "Good afternoon, Holly. Why aren't you busy packing?"

"Stockwell overefficiency. I'm all finished and ready to go as soon as Zelig and Michael get back from that meeting at the embassy in Athens."

"What time does your plane leave?"

"Ten tonight. Nonstop from Iraklion. Zelig pulled strings to arrange that. Jack is going with us. I wish you'd change your mind and come, too."

"Thanks, no. I have concerns here on Crete." James hadn't meant to sigh, but he did.

"I'll miss you." Holly took his hand and pressed it to her cheek. "I've never really thanked you, Uncle James, for everything you've done. I don't know how I'd have gotten through this ordeal without you."

"Well." He managed a smile. "You are my favorite niece. I'm glad it worked out all right and you have your husband back safely."

"Will you ever be able to forgive Zelig, Uncle James? For Vanessa, I mean?"

"I don't really blame Zelig. It takes two, you know, and both of them adults with consciences of their own." James regarded her empathetically. "But how about you, Holly? Have you forgiven him?"

"No." Holly's lips compressed tightly. "I haven't."

"And will you?" Looking at his niece, James already knew the answer.

"I don't think so, Uncle James. It's not something that can be forgotten so easily."

"I wonder"—James sighed unintentionally again—"how we got to be such an unforgiving and hard-nosed bunch, we Stockwells. Bred in the bone, I suppose."

"We're not all like that. Look at the governor. No, Uncle James, it's not really genetic. It's you and me." Holly shrugged. "We can't help ourselves. People are always falling short of the standards we set for them, and the real problem, I suppose, is that we're too rigid to forgive them."

"I suppose." James thought of Vanessa. He could take one of the cars. He could drive down to Knossos. He could be there in twenty minutes. He could take her in his arms and— But he wouldn't. He knew he wouldn't. There would always by the image of her making love to Zelig. "But we are who we are; we behave as we must behave."

"If you feel that way," Holly responded, "then what's the point of staying behind here on Crete? Why don't you fly home with us tonight?"

"Lisa." His voice was full of pain. "I'm very concerned about Lisa."

"Oh, Uncle James. I know."

"I knew about her and Winifred, you see, but I didn't really believe it. I didn't believe that a child of mine could be changed from a decent young girl into a deviate."

"Lisa's not a deviate, Uncle James."

"She's been warped." James was not hearing Holly's words. "Her normal sexual desires have been twisted. I blame Winifred Fitzsimmons for that. Somehow she influenced my daughter, and now Lisa calls herself a lesbian. Winifred Fitzsimmons is ruining Lisa's life."

"That's not fair, Uncle James. Winifred didn't turn Lisa into a lesbian. She didn't force Lisa into the relationship. Lisa entered into it willingly. It's the way she feels."

"I cannot believe that."

"Listen to me, Uncle James. Please. I love you. You know that. I want to help you. You must hear the truth about Lisa. Don't say anything. Don't protest. Just listen."

Jolted by his niece's intensity, James nodded. "All right, Holly. I'll listen."

"With or without Winifred, Lisa *is* a lesbian. You've known that for some time. Now you must accept it. It's not the end of the world. It's not a perversity, and it's not an illness. *That* is not Lisa's problem." Holly's words were ominous.

"No? Then what is?"

"This is going to hurt you, Uncle James," Holly cautioned.

310

"What do you mean? What are you trying to say?"

"It's drugs, Uncle James." Holly felt awful, but he had to be made aware. He had to understand that there are far worse things in the world than one's daughter being gay. "Lisa has a drug problem."

"A drug problem? What do you mean? How long? How serious?"

Holly told him everything she had learned. "Lisa had already been shooting heroin for almost a year when she and Winifred first met in Paris," she began. Holly went on to describe how Winifred had gotten Lisa into a drug rehabilitation program, how she had stuck by her through the horrors of withdrawal, how Lisa had been clean for two months when they came to Crete, and how she had just recently had a relapse and started using drugs again.

"If not for Winifred"—Holly did not mean to be overly dramatic, but she had to make sure James understood just how serious the situation was—"Lisa might well be dead of an overdose by now." The horror in her uncle's eyes told Holly that he recognized the truth in her words. "Their love—Lisa and Winifred's—no matter how imperfect it may be, no matter the problems they have with each other, no matter how society—good people like you, Uncle James—denigrates it, represents Lisa's best chance for survival. Winifred isn't just Lisa's lover. She's also the best friend that Lisa has."

There was a long silence after Holly stopped speaking. James was very shaken. "I see," he said finally.

"Don't take it away from her, Uncle James. Don't put any more strain on their relationship."

"I won't," James agreed. "I won't interfere."

Relationships, he thought to himself, are difficult enough without that.

52

"RELATIONSHIPS IMPOSE OBLIGATIONS," Deke Wells began stiffly, self-consciously. "People have the right to expect certain things from other people when they have a relationship. That's why I want to marry you."

Openmouthed, Beth Tyler stared at Deke in silence. This is so sudden, she wanted to say, but she didn't. In truth, she could not think of *what* to say. "I didn't know we still had a relationship," she blurted out finally. "Let alone one that imposed an obligation to get married."

They were standing at the rail of the afterdeck of the Greenpeace sloop looking out toward the open sea. Its blue green merged with the multicolored hues of a horizon bathed with gold by the setting sun. The breeze was strong, lifting Beth's long hair in a red-gold cloud that mingled with the colors of the sky.

"I care about you," Deke told her, reaching for her hand. "I know you have a problem. You don't have to face it alone."

Beth was bewildered. "What problem?"

"I overheard you telling Carrie about Michael." Deke had trouble keeping the anger out of his voice. "I know you're pregnant."

"So you're going to be noble and make an honest woman of me," Beth said, reacting to the tone of his voice. "Is that it? Marry me because I'm pregnant, even though the child isn't yours?"

"Well, yes."

It was a rare moment for Beth. For once in her life she felt more like Carrie than like herself. "You jerk!" she said to Deke.

"What did you—"

"I'm not pregnant. You're off the hook."

"You're not pregnant?" Deke suddenly felt foolish.

"No. I was late. That's all. So you can take your nobility and stuff it.'' Beth leaned away from him, toward the railing.

''Do you mind telling me just why you're so mad?'' Deke demanded, grabbing her shoulders to make her face him.

Beth met his gaze with level, steady eyes. ''First *you* tell me why all the time we've been together you never mentioned anything about marriage, but after we break up and you think I'm pregnant by another man, you climb on your white horse and come galloping up with an offer of orange blossoms.''

''I thought you were too committed to Greenpeace to get married. That's why I never mentioned it before.''

''But then you took pity on a fallen woman.'' Beth was ironic. ''You really are a jerk.'' Beth turned her back on him.

Deke thought about it. ''You're still mad because of that time with Carrie,'' he said slowly. ''That's it, isn't it?''

''No. That isn't it.'' Beth did not turn around to look at him. ''You want to know what I'm mad about? I'm mad because I went to bed with Michael to get even with you. I'm mad because you made me so jealous, you and Carrie, that I made myself do that even though I didn't really want to.''

''Then you're mad at yourself,'' Deke realized. ''Not me.''

''Ooh!'' Beth ground her teeth and turned to face him. ''Noble and filled with insight, too. God, I hate you!''

''Enough to marry me?'' Deke's grin was tentative, his eyes pleading, hopeful.

Beth twirled around, sending locks of golden-red hair whipping her face. ''Never!''

''Do you have to be so indecisive?''

''I loathe you!'' Despite her words, the hint of a smile tugged at the corners of Beth's mouth.

''We'll work it out.''

''Why would you still want to marry me anyway?'' Beth asked sarcastically, lifting an eyebrow. ''I'm not even pregnant.''

''We can fix that.'' Deke said solemnly.

Beth laughed. "You're impossible!"

"Sure. So what do you say? You want to get married?"

"No."

"Okay, then." Deke compromised. "You want to get engaged?"

"No."

"Well, what do you want?"

Beth surprised Deke then by leaning close and whispering in his ear. Slowly, a grin spread over his face. He nodded. Then, jostling each other, they went down the steps to the cabin they had once shared.

They were careful to lock the door behind them so that Carrie would not interrupt their lovemaking.

53

A WEEK LATER, in Yonkers, Jack Houston faced his grandfather from the foot of the nursing home bed. The old man was glum. He looked at Jack from eyes rheumy with disappointment.

"You blew it, boy. Had to go traipsing off to Europe playing Don Juan Coyote, and while you were gone, the deal went in the toilet."

Jack sighed. "I know, Grandpa."

"Outfoxed by the clergy, boy; done in by the cloth."

"I'm sorry."

"You're a real putz, boy. You threw away the opportunity of a lifetime. We could have had those Stockwells by the short hairs. And now—well, you know what you got, boy?"

"Not much, Grandpa."

"Zilch. And you know why, boy?"

"I think I do, Grandpa."

But the old man was not to be stopped. "You didn't

look to the fine-tuning, boy. That's why. The Don's people were floating paper according to what you told them,
Jackie. They consulted with the torches and identified the
property that was going to burn. Then they bought up all
the policies covering that property. And then they turned
around all ready to resell those policies to Stockwell, and
whaddaya know? Stockwell isn't buying. Some sky pilot
jerked their leash, and they are out of the insurance business. Now, when those fires break out, the investors the
Don lined up on your say-so are the insurers who will
have to pay."

"Why do I have to sit here and listen to what I already
know, Grandpa?"

"That's the trouble with you kids. You always think
you know everything." The old man went off on a five-
minute tirade regarding youth's lack of respect for the
wisdom of age in today's society. Then he returned to his
topic. "So the upshot is this, boy. The Don has to use his
investors' money to buy off the torchers so they don't—
repeat, don't!—burn down these slums. Now how about
that, boy?"

"Well, the Reverend Cabot's happy."

"Damn bleeding heart!"

"So are the people who live there, I guess. Or they
would be if they knew." Jack offered his grandfather a
silver lining.

"Well, screw them!" It was refused. "What I'm telling
you, boy, is that not only did the Don's investors get no
return on their money, they actually lost a substantial
amount of their capital buying off the torches."

Jack shrugged. "They'll make it back on cocaine."

"They'll take it out of your hide, boy. You listen good
now. The people pissed at you believe devoutly in violence." The old man's eyeballs danced, at first slowly,
then in a quick conga. "Cement overcoats, meat hooks,
lopped-off ears and fishes in the mouth, bodies in pieces,
torsos in the trunks of cars, sudden explosions and stran-
gler's cords and slim toledo blades, broken bones and
crushed kidneys and—"

"Enough, Grandpa."

"You get the picture, Jackie?" The old man's pleasures

were few. Now he licked his lips, enjoying himself. "To these people you are now sewage. Disposable sewage. The Don called before, and that's what he said. 'Tell your grandson, Jack Houston, he is disposable sewage.' Those were his exact words."

Jack spread his hands in an attempt to appear casual. Actually, he was very worried. He already knew what his grandfather was warning him about. The danger was very real. But what could he do? "I'll keep a low profile, Grandpa," he promised.

"You'd best do a damn sight more than that, boy. You'd best make tracks. And fast."

"Make tracks, grandpa? But where would I go?"

"If I were you, boy, I'd go over the ocean and beyond. Yessir, boy. Over the sea."

"Yes. Well . . ." Jack stood up. "Visiting hours are just about over, Grandpa, and right now I think I'll just go home."

"To the ends of the earth, Jackie. Don't wait. Go now."

"I am, Grandpa. I'm going."

For the moment, however, Jack Houston was only going home to Riverview.

54

HOLLY WAS PERCHED on the window seat of her study above the Riverview library when she saw Jack's BMW pull into the garage. On impulse, she threw on a cotton jacket over the sapphire-blue silk shirt she was wearing with linen slacks and clattered down the spiral staircase and out one of the French doors to intercept him. "Hey, stranger." Holly's greeting caught him exiting the garage in the late spring twilight. "It's the happy hour. Come have a cocktail with me."

"You're on." Jack followed her back up to the studio, admiring once again her long, slender body, her graceful carriage. From the window seat she'd just been occupying, he observed Holly as she did things with gin and vermouth, olives and ice. "How is everything going?" he asked.

"Lousy." Holly grimaced. "And you?"

"I don't want to talk about it."

They grinned at each other. Holly handed him a martini, and they clicked glasses. "Here's to not talking about it, then." Holly raised her thin-stemmed crystal wineglass to the rays of the setting sun and took a deep sip.

They were silent for a long, companionable moment. Then Jack spoke. "How's Zelig?" he inquired.

"You're talking about it," she reproached him.

"No, I'm not. I'm only inquiring about your husband."

Holly's face settled into a grim frown. "He's in Washington," she said tersely.

"Well, at least he's not in the hands of terrorists," Jack quipped.

"Terrorists, bureaucrats." Holly shrugged. "Anything to distract himself from home and hearth."

"Is that why you slapped Zelig?" Jack was curious. He had been too polite to ask any questions the night of the rescue. But now he sensed that Holly might want to talk about it. "Because he was easily distracted?"

"I slapped him because I found out he slept with another woman when we'd only been married eight weeks." She freshened up Jack's martini and then her own from the pitcher. "You know how that makes you feel? Foolish. That's how. You feel foolish."

"Oh, yeah." Jack thought of Buffy and grimaced. "I know. Along with a lot of other things, you certainly do feel foolish."

"Mostly that's how you feel." Holly's blue eyes looked directly into his. "You remember how faithful you've been, how you pushed down your own desires. So there you were denying yourself, and all the while your spouse was having a ball. You really do feel like a fool."

"Well, the nice things about *uncommitted* sins is that

you almost always get a second chance," Jack told her mildly.

"Do you?" Holly set here glass down and joined him on the window seat. Her next words were soft. "Do I, Jack? That night you were up here, the night we first heard Zelig was being held hostage, that night you acted like you wanted me."

"I did," Jack leaned forward to take her hand.

"And now?" Holly whispered, gazing into his hypnotic blue eyes. "Do you still want me, Jack?"

They kissed then, deeply, tenderly, until Holly pulled away. "I wanted you that night, Jack," she admitted tremulously. "I want you now."

In one swift movement Jack took her in his arms. His hands slid inside the silk shirt. Her breasts were warm, her body trembling. Standing, Jack drew Holly to her feet.

Slender and lissome, Holly's body melted into Jack's. His hands grazed her back, circled her waist, pulled her closer.

"I want you, now." His voice was husky. He cupped her trembling buttocks in his strong hands, raising her against him. He looked down at Holly's face.

It was streaked with tears.

"What's the matter?" Jack was startled by the sight.

"Nothing. I'm sorry. Nothing. Really. Don't stop. Make love to me, Jack." Her voice degenerated into quavering, and his name came out with a sob.

"Holly, baby. What is it?" Jack pulled away and looked down at her, genuinely concerned.

"Nothing. Everything. Oh, dammit, don't look at me. Just do it and don't look at me."

"Holly, I can't make love to you while you're having a crying jag."

"Why not?" Her sobbing voice was almost a wail.

"Holly. Holly." He pulled her close again and encircled her in his arms. He felt her warm tears flow over his chest. "I'm your friend, Holly. Your good buddy, remember? Go ahead and cry, baby. Go right on and cry it all out."

"If you were—were my friend," she hiccuped, "you'd make—make love to me."

"No, I wouldn't. That's not what you want. Not really. Be honest. You want Zelig, not me."

"I don't! I don't!" She pounded his shoulders with small fists and then started to cry all over again.

"Sure you do. But even if you didn't, Holly, I couldn't make love to you now. I have this idiosyncrasy, you see. I can't make love to any woman while she's sobbing her heart out. That goes double if the woman is a friend. How could I take advantage of a friend that way?"

"We are friends, aren't we?" She sniffled and accepted the handkerchief he fished out of the pocket of his pants for her. Then she sighed as she looked up at him. "I guess you're right. What man in his right mind would want to make love to a wretch like me?"

"I would. But not tonight. Tonight you need a friend more than a lover, and maybe I do, too. So what say I take my pal Holly out to dinner?"

"Dinner?" Holly looked at him wanly.

"Sure. I know this little place overlooking the Hudson that has the best brook trout in New York State. I'm hungry. Aren't you?"

"Well . . . yes. Yes, I am. Actually, I'm famished." She blushed to realize it was absolutely true.

"Then wash the tears off your face and let's go."

When Holly emerged from the bathroom, her sleek blond hair was tied back with a white ribbon, and her eyes were only slightly red. Jack greeted her with a grin. "Absolutely the best-looking woman I never made love to," he told her.

"A dubious distinction for which you can probably thank my husband," she told him wryly.

"Thank you, Zelig Meyerling."

"Damn you, Zelig Meyerling, you mean." Holly took Jack's hand in hers with a sigh and led him down the circular staircase.

55

WHEN HOLLY RETURNED from dinner with Jack, she found she was still too keyed up to sleep. She went back to her studio and mulled over the events of the evening. Thinking about them, however, just made her feel foolish and angry all over again. She loved Zelig, and she knew that he loved her. But could she ever trust him again?

Finally, she turned to her researches to get her mind off Zelig's perfidy. She was almost finished now with her checking and rechecking of the part of Riverview history that was covered in the unpublished satiric novel by George Cortlandt Stockwell. The point had been reached where it merged with the real-life records of the tragic fire that destroyed the first Riverview mansion.

With painstaking thoroughness, Holly now went over the events leading up to that fire. . . .

Horace Stockwell, founder of the Stockwell fortune, dominated these events. It was not surprising that to George, the eldest son, Horace was as fascinating as he was frightening. This fascination increased as the boy grew into manhood. The fear, at no small psychological cost to George, was internalized. By such mechanisms are writers molded.

The first impetus for George's writing came with the death of his mother in 1829 when George was seventeen years old. Henrietta van Cortlandt Stockwell was herself only in her mid-thirties when she died of the syphilis she had contracted from her husband. From the first the doctor classified her illness as "tertiary, cardiovascular in nature with fairly rapid deterioration of the thoracic portion of the aorta." The prognosis was negative. This form of the disease was inevitably fatal.

Painful as her ordeal was, Henrietta's mind was clear right up to the moment of her death. This differed from the course the disease took with Horace. In his case it was the brain that was affected, and the deterioration was both prolonged and subtle. Because Horace was sarcastic by habit and bitter by nature, the effects were not immediately evident, and his symptoms were obscured from his children.

Their concern focused on the year-long ordeal leading up to their mother's death. To Horace, Henrietta's agony was an irritant. He did nothing to hide his impatience with his wife's suffering. His father's attitude marked the beginning of the very real loathing that George later expressed toward Horace in his writing.

"Mother is suffering!" George, on the brink of tears, would plead with his father to summon the doctor to administer an opiate to ease Henrietta's pain.

"Malingering. It's the way of women, my boy. They whine and they complain at discomforts of which no man would take any notice."

"She's very ill!"

"Woman trouble. If you were more mature, Georgie, you would disregard it."

"How can you be so callous?"

"Callous?" Horace was irritated, his response cold. "Your concern is weakness, George. It is"—the fatherly coup de grace—"unmanly."

Horace repeated this verdict to George on the night following Henrietta's death. She had been laid out in an ornate casket in Riverview's front parlor. As was the custom, despite the wasting effects of the disease on her body, the coffin was open. All three children had been brought in by Horace to view their mother's remains. His youngest son, Charles, who was eleven years old, and his daughter, Elizabeth, age fourteen, had managed to restrain their tears at the sight of their mother's pitiful corpse. George, although the eldest, had not.

"Unmanly." This time Horace's judgment was final. George would never measure up to what a father had a right to expect of his first born son. "Unmanly."

Horace's contempt of his son grew when George reached the age where he was expected to take his place in the Stockwell business. From the first, George showed absolutely no aptitude for mercantile pursuits. The extent of Horace's western investments confused him. The meticulous tracking of shipping through the Erie Canal and the computing of Stockwell's percentage of the fees collected bored him. George neither had a head for real estate, commodities investments, nor the firm's most recent import-export ventures. And when his father took him on a tour of the mills and foundries he owned on the far side of Lake Erie, George expressed shock at the deplorable conditions of the workers employed there.

With that, Horace gave up on his eldest son. Later—a calculated rebuke—Horace brought Charles into the business. Charles, barely sixteen years old at this time, had a methodical mind, and he showed strong apititude for both investment and management. Thereafter, Horace would take a malicious sort of delight at the dinner table in contrasting young Charles's talents with George's failings.

Not surprisingly, George absented himself from Riverview and his father to seek approval elsewhere. He found it with an older Catskill neighbor. This gentleman was illustrious, kindly, interested in George, and encouraging of his talents. His name was Washington Irving.

Irving had just returned to the Hudson River Valley after seventeen years in Europe. With his tales of Ichabod Crane and Rip Van Winkle, he had immortalized the Catskill region of the Hudson River Valley and established himself as the foremost American fiction writer of the period. George Cortlandt Stockwell could not believe his good fortune that so notable a man of letters should take an interest in him.

Horace was contemptuous of his son's relationship with the author. "A scribbler of fairy tales for children," was his sneering categorization of Irving. "Neither merchant nor soldier, neither man of affairs nor man of action. But then why should I be surprised, George, that so thin-blooded a son as you should model yourself after such a person?" This had been Horace's reaction upon discovering that George had literary aspirations of his own.

Irving, however, was encouraging. Although occupied

with finishing *The Alhambra*, his own book on legendary Moorish Spain, he encouraged George to keep a journal that would eventually be the basis for the novel Holly was reading. He taught George techniques of character, description, and plot transition, as well as how to build drama and suspense.

From the first, George's theme was the Riverview environment. Not just the land and the wealth, but the way they were acquired. His father was a central character. Even as he was rewriting his notes with Irving's guidance, George was observing Horace's increasing alienation and downspiraling deterioration.

The process speeded up after Elizabeth married a southerner, Thomas Cole, in 1834 and departed Riverview for her new husband's tobacco plantation in the Carolinas. With his daughter gone and no other female member of his family in residence at Riverview, there were no restraints on Horace's self-indulgence. The syphilis had by now progressed to the point where its rotting of his brain was giving him severe headaches. He fought these constantly with brandy.

George was Horace's primary target in his alcoholic rages. His brother, Charles, despite his youth, was virtually running the Stockwell business now and was only at Riverview on occasional weekends. George, never able to handle his father's excesses as well as Charles did, retreated more and more into his writing. Still, his father's attacks on him were the least of it. Far worse were Horace's drunken carousings and his diatribes against his dead mother and his dead wife and the entire species of woman in general. These tirades went beyond drunkenness to a sick sort of misogyny bordering on madness.

Impotent from syphilis, Horace sought sexual pleasures primarily from female pain, measurable by his warped brain in terms of the ingenuity of the new torments he devised and of the whimpers, cries, and screams they could provoke. The plaintive cries of the wretched scullery maid dispelled any sympathy George might have left for his father.

George shut out the cries with work. He had amassed three volumes of notes by 1836, and in that year he began to write the novel itself. The work went quickly, and by the following year he had a first draft to show Washington Irving. The eminent author took time out from working on *The Adventures of Captain Bonneville* to critique George's work. His main criticisms concerned the brutality of the main character and the bitterness that pervaded the novel. Irving suggested that George rewrite the work and temper it with humor and satire..

Following Irving's advice, George discovered wellsprings of irony within himself. The knack to skewer with a quip, a description, a fillip of plot, came naturally to him. And applying his intellectual abilities this way brought his hatred of his father under a semblance of control. If George still had no pity for Horace, he was nevertheless gaining the understanding that underlies all successful irony.

Inevitably, Horace became aware that George was not merely "scribbling" but was working on a substantive literary project. In a rare sober and rational instance, he was curious about it. "You have no experience, Georgie. What can you possibly write about?"

"Not much, Father. Not much."

"You don't drink. You don't gamble. You don't avail yourself of women."

"I'm well aware of my sins of omission, Father."

"Show me your chicken scratchings," Horace suggested.

"I think not, Father. They wouldn't really interest you."

"If your writings are so dull, why do you go to such pains to keep them under lock and key?"

"It's late, Father." George evaded the question. "Time to go to bed."

"Don't you condescend to me, boy!" Horace roared. "Don't you ever think you can manipulate me. That's a woman's trick," he muttered, and then raised his voice again. "You're womanly, Georgie; you disgust me!"

George was silent.

"What you need is a good thrashing. A birching." The thought distracted Horace. "Have to see to the horses," he mumbled. The horses were in the stables. The scullery maid was lodged above their stalls. Horace left to fetch her.

That was one of the last coherent conversations that George had with his father. Over the next year, the pace of Horace's deterioration increased. He drank more, spewed out his venom irrationally, and behaved with increasing brutality. And, although George didn't realize it until that tragic night in 1838, Horace also became obsessed with his son's "scribblings."

George had been out that night, dining with Washington Irving. He returned to Riverview late. Exiting the barn after stabling his horse, he spied the light of a flickering candle in an upstairs window. The window looked out from the study where George did his writing. It was always kept locked. George had locked it himself that night before leaving. He reached into his pocket. The key was still there. Apprehensive, George hurried in to investigate.

It was as he feared. The lock had been smashed, the doorjamb pried with an andiron. Horace was seated at the writing desk with George's manuscript spread out in front of him. Intent on the close-writ parchment, his face was a study in barely suppressed rage. When he looked up and saw George, the rage exploded.

"You miserable scribbling whelp!" Horace raised the candle holder high to regard his son. "You liar!"

"No lies there, Father." George moved forward to reclaim his manuscript.

"All lies! All!" Horace moved quickly backward, out of George's reach. "You libel your blood! You insult your flesh! You malign your father! Liar! Liar!" He was quite crazed now, still managing to evade George, clutching the manuscript in one hand, the candleholder in the other. "Woman spawn!" Spittle hung from his lips. "Female filth!"

"Calm yourself, Father!" Again George reached to reclaim his manuscript. "And give that back to me."

"Never! This manure must be destroyed!" And with those words Horace raised the pages of the manuscript to meet the flame of the candle.

"No!" The hand George flung out to reclaim his manuscript knocked it from his father's grasp. It fell to the floor in its binder.

Horace stooped with the candle, still determined to burn the manuscript. George knocked the candle from his father's hand, and it landed behind Horace. Unnoticed, the flame rose to ignite the tail of the older man's silk cutaway jacket.

Their shadows danced in the flickering light. Bent on destruction, Horace's ravings spewed forth with increasing intensity. Reading his son's exposé had pushed Horace over the brink to which his syphilis had carried him. Pure madness and hatred bubbled from his lips now. His curses were aimed not just at George, but at his mother, his wife, and—by name—even at the poor scullery maid who had submitted to his whippings. The novel had been a mirror held up to Horace, to his life, and what he saw was—quite simply—intolerable.

Now George spied the live flame licking up one side of his father's cutaway coat in back. Alarmed, he made a move to smother it. Horace, misunderstanding the movement, swept up the candle holder from the floor, the flame still alive in it, and swung it full force at the son he thought was about to attack him. The heavy pewter caught George flush on the cheek and sent him reeling backward, stunned.

As George staggered, Horace felt the heat of the fire engulfing his clothing. He screamed and flung the candle from him. As he twisted vainly to try to cope with the flames writhing over his back, the candle ignited the dimity curtains tied back from the windows. Flames wreathed Horace's body. Recovering from the blow his father had struck him, George once again tried to come to his aid. He flung himself over Horace, trying to smother the fire.

Horace grappled insanely, propelling them into the blazing curtains. Flailing wildly, he pulled the curtains down and the heavy oaken cornice from which they were suspended as well. The cornice struck George on the head, knocking him unconscious.

It also knocked from the wall a large decorative pewter tray that had been presented to Horace's uncle, Colonel

Roger Stockwell, by Paul Revere. Horace's mother had treasured that memento and had hung it here when the chamber had been her sewing room. Now the tray landed on top of the manuscript on the floor, forming a shield against the flames. Because of it, the manuscript was one of the few things at Riverview to survive the conflagration that followed.

Neither father nor son survived it. Horace Stockwell was burned alive, his mad screams fanning the flames. George, who never recovered consciousness, was also consumed by the blaze. Indeed, both men were dead before the fire spread beyond the confines of the study to the rest of Riverview. Spreading rapidly, the blaze was unstoppable by the time the servants realized there was a fire. It was all they could do to get out alive themselves. Most of them lost what few possessions they had as the mansion burned.

Watching the inferno from the barn, the eyes of the Riverview scullery maid were wide with awe—and strangely content.

The day after the fire, George's brother, Charles, was summoned to Riverview. It was he who confirmed that the two blackened corpses were those of his father and brother. And it was he who found the charred but virtually intact manuscript of the novel written by George Cortlandt Stockwell.

Charles brought the manuscript back to his office in Manhattan with him after the double funeral. It was a while before he could bring himself to read it. When he did, his grief over his brother's death was compounded by a dilemma.

The work was not only a damning indictment of his father but also satirized his forebears. It detailed suicide, adultery, womanizing, perversion, gambling, and business manipulation—all of it reflecting poorly on the Stockwell family. The manuscript could embarrass the Stockwells for many generations to come. Its contents must never be made available to the world at large.

Yet Charles could not bring himself to destroy it. The work had been the focus of his poor dead brother's life, his major accomplishment. To destroy it would be to deny that George had lived at all. Finally Charles sat down and wrote a letter to his sister, Elizabeth Stockwell Cole, in South Carolina. He explained that the manuscript he was sending her had been written by George, that it was an indictment of their father and of other of their forebears, and advised Elizabeth that for her own peace of mind it would be best if she did not read it. He asked her to hide it in some safe place removed from prying eyes.

"Despite its potential for embarrassment," Charles wrote, "it should be preserved. It is a part of our family heritage. It should not be lost. A hundred years from now—two hundred, who knows?—some Stockwell may have the perspective to find in George's work the truth about events best forgotten for now. Let us at least hope so. . . ."

Do I have that perspective? Holly wondered now in the midnight of her Riverview studio as she closed the book on Horace and his writer son, George Cortlandt Stockwell. All this time it has lain in a trunk in Mildred Peckinpaugh's basement waiting to be read. To be judged?

No, Holly decided. Not to be judged. People were too complex back then to be judged. And, she supposed, they still are.

56

PEOPLE WERE MORE than complicated, they were unexpected. The insight came to Jack Houston at an awkward moment. He had boarded James's yacht at the Riverview dock on the Hudson River intending to deal with a delicate situation. He was, however, greeted by a sight that made it necessary to postpone his intentions.

328

Patrice O'Keefe, deliciously naked except for a large, black velvet bow tied around her neck in the fashion usually associated with posh Fifth Avenue packaging of imported Belgian chocolates, greeted him. "Happy birthday." Patrice held her arms wide to greet him, her brown eyes smoldering behind tortoiseshell-rimmed eyeglasses, her wavy chestnut hair splayed artistically over the white pillow on the bunk where she had positioned herself to greet Jack.

"It's not my birthday." Jack had smiled tentatively down at her petite, curvaceous, inviting body.

"I know." She laughed and batted her eyes, laid aside her glasses and wriggled. "It's mine."

"I'm sorry." Jack was embarrassed. I didn't know. You never told—"

"That's all right." Patrice squirmed again. "But I want my present."

Jack undressed. Yes, people were unexpected. To most people Patrice personified the image of the new corporate woman, serge-suited with muted stripes, shrewd-eyed behind businesslike glasses, a hardball player with the bows of her blouses her only concession to femininity. It was the picture of Patrice that had emerged from the piece *Fortune* had done on her a year or so earlier, it was accurate and, in its way, definitive of her public personality.

Patrice's private persona, however, was quite another matter. With Jack, she left not just her composure but her maturity at the door. Her lovemaking was as abandoned as her body was compact. It was hard to believe that this small, passionate young woman with her hands clasped around his neck and her legs locked around his waist as she propelled him backward in a way that made him bounce from one wall to the other as they made athletic, energetic, demanding, laughter-laced love was the same person who had taken the Madison Avenue advertising world by storm and then moved so competently into the elitist realm of Wall Street high finance.

Finally, breathless, they fell onto one of the bunks where, somewhat more slowly and savoringly, they concluded their wild copulation. A while later, Patrice stretched voluptuously. "Happy birthday to me," she purred.

"Happy birthday, Patrice." Jack kissed her gently. Sex had not only been fun, it had been easy. Now came the hard part. "Listen," he said, "there's something I have to tell you."

"Oh-oh. Sounds ominous." Patrice clasped her hands between her still gasping breasts.

"I have to go away, Patrice."

"What do you mean? You just came back. Greece, remember?"

"I know. But it can't be helped. I have to leave again." Jack pulled up the sheet to cover his body.

Patrice was hurt by his modesty. "Are you in some kind of trouble?"

"Yes. I am. The kind that makes it imperative that I leave the country—and fast."

"What is it? What's happened?"

"It's too involved to go into, Patrice. Just take my word for it. It's a case of I have to go, or else."

"I'll go with you." She took his hand in hers and pressed it to her breast.

"I couldn't let you do that. Your whole life is here. Your career. Everything."

"I don't care about that." Patrice clung to him, seeking the reassurance of his flesh with the length of her body. "I'll go with you if you want me to."

"You're a woman of substance, Patrice. You can't throw it all up. You'd hate yourself if you did. You'd hate me. I could never let you do it."

"You don't want me to go with you." Patrice's soft body stiffened, and she withdrew slightly. "That's really it, isn't it?" There was more fatalism than surprise in her voice. You knew you were setting yourself up for this moment, girl. You knew it.

"It's for the best." Jack winced at his own hypocrisy as he uttered his next words. "I am married, after all."

Oh, yes. Both ears and the tail. Well, if you persist in chasing after the same old toreador, lady, what do you expect? Sooner or later, you had to get gored.

Patrice managed what she would have been devastated

to hear described as a brave smile. "Well," she said, "when ya gotta go, ya gotta go."

"I don't have to go quite yet," Jack told her, feeling guilty. "We could celebrate your birthday again."

"Sure. That would be nice." Patrice pulled the sheet off both of them. "Let's relight the candles on the cake."

Happy birthday, Patrice. She smiled up at him and fluffed up the black velvet bow above her plump naked breasts. Happy birthday to you.

Patrice would have enjoyed the second time more if only she hadn't been hurting quite so much. . . .

57

"POOR PATRICE." THERE was not quite as much malice in Buffy's voice as Jack might have expected. "Whenever our eyes would meet at board meetings she'd look so guilty, and now here she is getting the short end of the stick again."

"I don't think she'd appreciate your sympathy." Jack responded to his wife dryly.

They were in the suite of upstairs rooms they still ostensibly shared at Riverview, although it had been some time since they had slept together there. Buffy had returned from the city looking smart and urban in an understated, form-fitting gray suit with small, genuine gold buttons designed especially for her by Claude Montana. As she was removing her matching gold choker, she had heard noises from the wardrobe room. Investigating, she'd found her husband Jack tossing clothes into a large suitcase. He'd told her he was going away on an extended trip, and that was when Buffy had made the remark about Patrice.

331

"Even so," Buffy answered Jack, "Patrice will doubtless miss you very much."

"Which is a damn sight more than you can say." Since he hadn't made up his mind yet exactly where he was going, Jack was having a hard time deciding whether to pack light or heavy clothes.

"Well, darling, since you haven't been around very much, what with Greece and Patrice and all, you can hardly be surprised at that." Buffy perched on the arm of a chair upholstered in white kid, her body automatically arranging itself to best advantage.

"I'm not surprised. It's what I've come to expect from our marriage."

"Oh, now don't be bitter, Jack. Not now when you're leaving for—just where is it you said you were going, anyway?"

"I didn't say. I haven't made up my mind yet."

"I see." Buffy shifted position, casually displaying a length of shapely, silken leg. "And how long will you be gone?"

"I don't know." Jack laid a pair of Rugby shorts atop a ski sweater in the suitcase.

"How very mysterious. It almost sounds as if you were running away from something." Taking a cigarette holder from her purse, Buffy inserted a Galoise in the end of it.

Disapprovingly, Jack took time out from his packing to light the cigarette for her. "Do the warnings of the American Cancer Society mean nothing to you?" he asked.

"Of course they do. I'm a generous contributor." Buffy blew a cloud of smoke at him. "But then as you know, consistency has never been one of my virtues."

"Your many virtues."

"Ahh, darling, sarcasm was never intended for use by people in glass houses." Buffy reached out and patted his cheek. "But you haven't answered me. Why the hurried departure?"

"Business." Jack did not expound on the answer. He packed thermal socks and beach sandals.

"The insurance business, darling?"

Startled, Jack stared at her. "Buffy," he said with

grudging admiration, "you never cease to amaze me. How did you find out?"

"The New York State Regulatory Board. I've been at a hearing all day along with Peter Stockwell. Topic: inner-city arson. Conclusion: Stockwell Limited is spanky clean. But the people we didn't buy from, darling, they have real trouble. Now why, we asked ourselves, would they take the trouble to acquire so much hot paper with the obvious intention of unloading it on us? Well, there could be only one answer, darling: arbitrage—a takeover in the making. But they would have had to have inside information to do that. Plus they needed a tie to the arsonists. Now I thought about the sudden reigniting of your passion for Patrice, coincidental with her replacing her father on the Stockwell board, and I put two and two together. Of course I wasn't sure until just now when I found you getting ready to skip the country."

"I suppose you'll tell the others." Jack was thinking of Patrice. She would be terribly hurt if she discovered how he'd used her.

"The other board members, you mean? Peter and the rest?" Buffy shrugged. "No, why should I tell them? They'd probably think I put you up to it."

"Why should they think that?"

"Well, Patrice might want to believe it just because she wouldn't want to think you could be such a bastard all on your own." Buffy thoughtfully tapped the ash from her cigarette holder into a Spode ashtray. "You must have involved yourself with some very rough boys," she said. "And now I suppose they're out for your hide."

"That's about the size of it." Jack packed a heavy wool shirt and a pair of latex bathing trunks.

"And so you have to get out of the country fast."

"Yes." He wrapped a snorkel mask in a woolen scarf and tucked it in a side pocket of the bag.

"You look like you're packing for a trip to Siberia by way of the Riviera."

"Yeah. Well. Maybe." Jack was noncommittal.

"Do you really think these people are out to hurt you?"

"Well, I don't think they're into painless death."

"Jack, you're frightening me." Buffy stubbed out her cigarette. Her violet eyes were wide with concern.

"You were right before." He studied her face and then spoke slowly. "Consistency isn't one of your virtues."

"Despite our marital conflicts, I really don't want you to come to any harm."

"Well, that makes two of us. But don't feel too badly, Buffy. You can always go to Texas for consolation."

"That's all over."

"Don't tell me Jimbo Grebbs wasn't as self-advertised."

"I got what I wanted from him." Buffy said it straight out. "So there was no reason to go on."

"And he got what he wanted from you."

"And Patrice got what she wanted from you."

"And everybody's happy!" Jack flung some suntan lotion in the suitcase beside a pair of fur-lined gloves.

"I'm not happy." Buffy's voice was very small. "I'm miserable. I miss you, Jack."

"Damn it, Buffy, don't do this to me. Not again."

"I can't help it. I love you."

"So much that you can't stay away from other men."

"You weren't faithful, either," Buffy reminded him.

"I would have been. If you had been satisfied with just me, I would have been faithful. Damn it, Buffy, why couldn't you have been satisfied?"

"For how long?" Buffy stood up and started to pace, arms folded, hugging herself to herself. "For how long, Jack, before you took a good look at me and it really—really!—dawned on you that I am seventeen years older than you are? How long, Jack, before you begin to see the wrinkles, the flab, the weariness?"

"So far I haven't spotted any of those things. Not the wrinkles. Not the flab. And weariness? You've got more energy than a troop of Brownies jogging to the soda shop. . . . Wait a minute! Wait a minute!" Jack stopped short. "How did I let you sidetrack me like that? Next you'll be convincing me that you cheat on me with other men—with Jimbo Grebbs, that Texas pile of—because you're afraid if you don't, I'll think you're getting old and

334

won't want you anymore. Jesus, Buffy, how do you do this to me? How do I always let you?"

"It's true, though. You do find me more attractive when other men are attracted to me."

"I do not!" Jack denied it. "And I am not concerned about your goddamn age. I love you, dammit. That's the hell of it. With everything, it always comes back to that. I love you."

"Well, I love you, too." Buffy's voice was unusually shaky. "I really do, darling."

Buffy's admission took the wind out of Jack's sails. He could only stare at her.

"If you have to leave the country, leave with me, darling. Please. Please, can't we go together?"

"Where?" Jack was still looking at her. God how he loved her. God how he hated her. This woman would drive him crazy. She really would. "Where would we go?"

"I have this little hideaway in the Caribbean," Buffy told him. "It's the one thing I came away with from my first marriage—before the governor." She removed the fur-lined gloves, the thermal socks, and the ski sweater from Jack's suitcase. "It's a beach house on a bluff overlooking the water on the French side of St. Martin." She went to her bureau in their wardrobe room, opened a drawer, and took out a terrycloth beach robe and a bikini. "It's very private, and we can just lie out on the beach naked and make love in the sun." She arranged her things in the suitcase beside Jack's. "What do you say, darling?"

"It will never last. It will only be a matter of time before we start going at each other again. Someone will come along, and you'll make a pass at them—or I will. We're just not monogamous people, Buffy. Let's face it."

"Of course not, darling," she murmured, kissing him then, knowing full well that after the kiss—and not very long after—he would agree. "Of course we're not monogamous. But we do have so much fun trying to be. Don't we?"

58

"I WILL NEVER be anything but monogamous again."
Although the words were spoken aloud, Louise Papatestus was making the promise to herself rather than to her husband. "I'm not cut out for promiscuity. I really did want to kill myself. I meant to take enough pills to die."

"An overdose of birth control pills mixed with Maalox is not a very efficient way of going about it." Spiro patted her hand fondly and beamed at her from his leathery Macedonian face.

"That's not fair. I took other pills, too."

"True. Tranquilizers and barbiturates—but not enough to kill you. And oh, yes, that laxative."

"God, I was sick!" Louise shuddered. "The price I paid for thinking I was suited to the swinging life-style. Well, I'm just not built for it."

"You most certainly are built for it, my dear," Spiro disagreed. "Indeed, few women are constructed by providence in a manner so harmoniously in tune with the swinging life-style as you."

"I was humiliated." Why couldn't Spiro understand? "I wanted to die. Do you call that in tune?"

"We were speaking of your qualifications," Spiro reminded her. "Not your reaction to being deceived. It was to be expected that that would be violent. You are a very proud woman, and Xanthos injured your pride." They were seated on the terrace dawdling over thimblefuls of bitter Greek coffee sweetened with ouzo. "Shall I ring for more?" Spiro suggested.

"To stave off the late-afternoon breeze. Yes. That would be very nice." Louise sighed, frustrated at her inability to get through to her husband. "Yes," she admitted. "My pride was injured. What woman wouldn't feel that way? Xanthos used me and—quite simply—I felt so abused that I wanted to die."

"It's true." Spiro nodded his thanks to the servant who had brought it and poured more coffee from the samovar for Louise and himself. "Xanthos used you sexually for his own ends." He added the ouzo. "But we used him as well. Didn't we?"

Louise sipped the hot brew and approved. As always, the mixture was perfect. It was one of Spiro's many endearing talents. "I suppose we did," she conceded unwillingly. "But that part of it was really only because I wanted to give you pleasure."

"Was it?" One of Spiro's bushy eyebrows arched toward his silver hairline. "Not to give *you* pleasure, my dear?"

Louise felt defensive. "Well, I was already having my pleasure with Xanthos before he moved into the cottage." The memory made Louise feel humiliated again.

"Exactly so. And then, in collusion with me, you brought him here and made love with him in front of me for my pleasure. And didn't my pleasure give you pleasure, Louise? Didn't it make lovemaking with Xanthos that much more pleasurable for you because I was watching? And wasn't that using him, Louise?"

"It's all so confusing. I didn't calculate before I did any of the things I did. I just did them, reacted, behaved according to my feelings." Louise was pleading for understanding.

Spiro did not notice. "Feelings. Ah, yes. Believe me, Louise, feelings can be a far greater erotic exploiter than politics will ever be. Be honest with yourself, my beloved. You used Xanthos just as he used you. Each of you had different motives, that's all."

"He aroused my passion!" Louise's outburst was bitter, the more so because Spiro was so insensitive to how deep the hurt went. "I thought I aroused his. But I didn't."

"Of course you did. A man can't fake that. There are times when a woman can, but a man really can't."

"But what was he feeling?" It was the question Louise had asked herself over and over since her suicide attempt. She could not come up with a satisfactory answer.

"What were you?" Spiro was relentless. "What were

337

you feeling that time when I first joined you?" he asked softly. "Be honest with yourself, Louise."

"Lust." She shuddered with self-disgust. "Sheer animal lust."

"And whatever emotions you had for Xanthos, or for me, took second place to satisfying that lust. That's so, isn't it?"

"Yes." Louise felt defeated once again by Spiro. "That's so. Xanthos turned me on, but my lust had a life of its own."

"And it still does, my dear. Xanthos may be in jail where he deserves to be, but that is no reason why you and I should not go on just as before, indulging our pleasures, finding what joys are available to us."

Louise became aware that her head had been aching with confusion for some time. "I certainly seem to have come a very long way in a very short while," she reflected sadly. Only yesterday she had been shy of men and afraid of sex. And now— She considered what Spiro had just said. "I'm not sure I understand what you mean," she hedged, not wanting to face the facts her husband was spelling out for her. "Are you suggesting . . . ?"

The question hung between them. Spiro answered it with a nod. "The world," he said, "is full of Xanthoses."

"Oh, surely not." The horror Louise felt went deeper than her words could possibly convey.

"Oh, surely yes. Trust me, Louise," he told her. "In this I am right."

Louise stared at her husband. She had always trusted him to take care of her. What had happened was one thing. She had slipped into the affair with Xanthos, one licentiousness easily following another, with a sort of emotional logic that had carried her along. However it might have looked to an uninvolved observer, to Louise the progression had been easy, natural, almost—well—innocent. But to do what Spiro was now suggesting! To plan in advance to find some man, some stranger, and to engage him in a ménage à trois to satisfy her husband's voyeurism! No matter if she was being inconsistent, the idea truly horrified Louise. "But where would we ever—" She didn't finish the sentence. What did it matter where?

"I should not think we would have to look far." Spiro nodded his head toward a car as it pulled up the driveway and stopped beside the villa's garages. A man got out and started walking toward them. "Here comes, perhaps, a likely candidate."

"Oh, no!" Louise stared with distaste at the man approaching them.

"Well, don't you two look serious." Congressman Michael Stockwell walked straight up to them and sat down at their table. "What can you be talking about?"

Louise did not hear Spiro's answer. The fact that he had suggested Michael Stockwell went beyond irony for her. Michael, with his macho come-on, had long represented to Louise all that she loathed most about men. He was the high school boy in the back of the car with his hand inside her bra. He was all the men who had pawed her during her years as a model. He was all the mixed-up and twisted men that Xanthos, with his straightforward lovemaking, had been the antithesis of for Louise. What Spiro was suggesting was not possible.

It was more than that. Ignoring their chatter, Louise made herself face it. It was not just Michael. Who the man was didn't matter. Spiro's kindness to her didn't matter. All the things—the emotional and sensual liberation—that she had gained from their marriage didn't matter. Once it had, but not any more.

In a very short time Louise had experienced ecstasy, and she had plunged into hell, and these experiences had changed her. The repression that had held her in its grip for so long had been banished, but she no longer felt a need to replace it with promiscuity. She had attained womanhood and with it the strength to make her own emotional, romantic, and erotic choices. Her husband would no longer make them for her. She would no longer allow Spiro to prod her, no matter how gently, into actions, involvements, affairs. From here on, she would be her own woman.

Louise sighed. The next thought was not so much a decision as a recognition. Her marriage to Spiro must end.

59

E ARLY THE NEXT morning, James Linstone Stockwell was standing in the front driveway to the villa with Winifred Fitzsimmons. They were surrounded by Winifred's and Lisa's luggage. Lisa had gone around back to the garage to fetch the rental car that the two young women would drop off at the Iraklion airport before catching their plane to Athens where they would pick up their connecting flight to Paris.

"Winifred," James said. "I'd like to ask you a favor."

Winifred regarded Lisa's father warily. From the first, James had barely concealed his belief that *she* was responsible for Lisa turning to homosexuality. Following the day when James had stumbled on them in the woods, he had been less than civil to Winifred. Even if that had been not quite so evident lately, Winifred could hardly be blamed for being leery of James.

"And what would that be, Mr. Stockwell?" she responded.

"Write to me when you have a chance. Let me know how Lisa is coming along."

"But why?" asked the young Englishwoman. "Surely Lisa will be writing to you herself."

"I'd like to hear from you. I really would."

"I don't quite understand." Winifred spoke her mind. "I didn't think you approved of our relationship."

"I didn't. But now—well, try to understand, Winifred. I'm fifty-three years old, and I come from a conservative tradition. Given my background, the kindest view I could be expected to take would be to label . . . female homosexuality as a sickness. It's not easy for a man like me to come to grips with this, especially when it involves his daughter."

"I suppose not." Winifred was not very sympathetic.

"If you're a logical person, and I am, then you think in terms of cause and effect. Why has my daughter turned out this way? And following that logic, you fall into assigning blame."

"Not everybody does. Some people find the charity to withhold judgment. Others seek understanding. Loving people simply accept."

"That's what I'm trying very hard to do now, Winifred." James was earnest. "You see, I do love my daughter very much."

"And so you are trying to forgive her sin." Winifred reverted to sarcasam.

"It's not my primary concern anymore. Truly it isn't. I've gone beyond that. It's Lisa's health I'm worried about now—both mental and physical. This addiction business."

"You know about that?" Winifred was surprised.

"Holly told me. She said that you told her."

"Yes. Of course. I should have realized she'd tell you."

"How bad is it?" There was anxiety in James's voice as he asked the question.

"At the moment quite bad. It was worse two years ago, though. I think Lisa will improve once we return to Paris and she settles back into the treatment program. There's peer support there, and she seems to react very positively to that."

"Is there anything I can do?"

"Be loving. Supportive. And the most difficult thing of all: Allow Lisa her independence, her right of choice."

"I think I approve her choice."

"Do you now?" Winifred was amused. "Do you mean that if your daughter had to go and disgrace the Stockwells of Riverview with another female, then I'm not the worst British butch she might have chosen?"

James looked at Winifred steadily, refusing to be intimidated. "I won't lie to you," he told her. "I'd rather Lisa preferred men. But I don't think she could have chosen any man more to my liking than you are."

Winifred was still digesting that as Lisa pulled the car up in front of them. James helped the two girls load the baggage into the trunk. Then Winifred got behind the wheel while he and Lisa said their good-byes.

As Lisa walked around the car to get in the other side, Winifred called to James: "Oh, Mr. Stockwell."

"Yes." He bent down to her open window.

"I think perhaps that you are a very nice man," Winifred told him. "And you're not half so bloody conservative as you think you are."

"Well, thank you."

"And I will write. Keep you posted as to how Lisa's coming along and all that."

"Thanks again. I really do appreciate that."

"Good-bye to you, then, James Stockwell." Winifred kissed Lisa's father full on the lips. She put the car into gear and headed it toward the main gate.

Lisa stared at Winifred in astonishment all the way down the mountainside.

Perhaps I'm not. Winifred's words nagged at James the rest of that morning. Perhaps I'm not so bloody conservative as I think I am. Scuttling an uptight righteousness is a small price to pay for holding on to a daughter's love. Face it. I'm too dogmatic altogether. Maybe all these years I've had it wrong. Maybe virtue is its own punishment, and the righteous man is the lonely man. Well, dammit, I don't want to be alone.

"I don't want to be alone." That afternoon, James drove to Kommos, scrambled down the dusty slope of the digs, confronted Vanessa, who was as dusty as the slope and perspiring and freckly in the hot sun to boot, and greeted her with that admission.

"A man like you would never have to be," Vanessa told him calmly. She held her blouse away from her substantial bosom and fanned air down the front of it between her heavy breasts. "Lots of women would be glad to be with you, James. You're very attractive, you know."

"I don't want other women. I want you."

"I want you, too, James. Very much. But I am what I am."

"I love what you are."

"Highly sexed."

"I know. That's what I love best."

342

"I'll always want you more than any other man. But if you're not available—"

"I'll be available. I'll make sure of that," he promised her.

Vanessa couldn't help smiling. "Then there hasn't been some great revelation from up high prompting you to forswear your jealous nature?"

"Well, no." James had to admit it. "The idea of you in another man's arms drives me up the wall."

"Then what's changed?"

"I'd rather risk a jealous rage than be without you."

"I see." Vanessa considered it. "Well," she said, "I suppose that is progress of a sort."

"Sure." James grinned at her. "Progress is always incremental. One day at a time."

"I can't promise you fidelity," Vanessa warned.

"And I can't promise you I won't kill the man—or you—or both of you."

Vanessa grinned back at him. "Ah, James, you're much too civilized for that. Violence just isn't in your nature."

"That I will change. It's a promise." James put his arms around her ample body in its rumpled khaki skirt and blouse and kissed her. "Step out on me, and I'll be more violent than you ever dreamed was possible."

"Really? Well," Vanessa told him, "that's a challenge I don't think I can refuse."

"In that case," James suggested, "is there some four-thousand-year-old tomb around here that's empty where we can go and make love?"

60

"I UNDERSTAND THAT James has decided to stay on in Crete." The Riverview dining room was too large

343

for just two people. The length of the table made it necessary for Zelig to raise his voice. The additional decibels caused a slight echo.

"So I've heard." The cold tone of Holly's reply discouraged the topic.

Their being served dinner alone together in the main hall was accidental. With James on Crete, Jack and Buffy having just taken everybody by surprise by leaving together for parts unrevealed, Patrice back in her Sutton Place apartment, and Nicholas in bed already after his early supper, Holly had assumed she would eat alone. But here was Zelig back from Washington without having notified anybody he was coming, and so, of course, there had been nothing for it but to have the servants set another place for her husband—if only for the sake of appearances.

"This is really quite tasty." Zelig dropped the topic of James and returned to his chateaubriand.

"Cook will be pleased that you are pleased." Hauteur became Holly as it did few women. It complemented her aristocratic features. It was a mood that sculpted her beauty to the fineness that had made him so eager to marry her in the first place. Her modulated Bryn Mawr voice vibrated ever so slightly in the large room as she spoke.

"But I have probably eaten too much of it." Zelig elevated his hooded eyes from the Dresden china and silverplate. He pushed away from the table and patted his stomach. Already he had gained back the weight he lost. Washington food, he supposed. "Why don't we take our coffee and whatever in the drawing room?" he suggested. "It's cozier there."

"I'm not sure I want to be cozy." Holly didn't actually say "with you," but her meaning was clear.

"Even polite hostilities are best contained in more intimate surroundings," Zelig told her. "Believe me. I know. After all, I am a diplomat."

"You are a diplomat," Holly repeated a short while later when they were seated across a coffee table from each other in armchairs in the smaller and more intimate east wing drawing room. "But are you declassified?"

344

Zelig's smile was amused. "I didn't know you cared."

"I am as curious as the next citizen of the United States about such matters, even if I am your wife."

"Well, then—officially, there was no declassification because none was necessary, since my mission was not classified in the first place."

"Well," Holly observed. "It's easy to see you've been debriefed, anyway."

"Oh, yes." Zelig inhaled the bouquet from the brandy snifter. "This is special," he commented.

"Grandpa laid it away sometime in the late fifties. I believe it was a gift from De Gaulle." Holly sipped. "You were going to tell me about your unclassified mission," she prompted Zelig.

"Not much to tell, really. The Reagan administration sent me to Greece for three purposes. The first was to give unofficial assurances regarding American aid so long as Greece's NATO commitments were honored. The second was to offer certain concessions from the American business sector in return for an expansion of the American military presence in Greece. The third was to arrange with Spiro and other Greek industrialists for the setting up of nuclear plants in Greece and for the shipment of fuel for those plants through Greek ports such as Piraeus."

"And were you successful?"

"Neither Haig nor Weinberger thinks that I was"—Zelig stopped short.

"Ahem." Berkley's clearing of his throat from the doorway apologized for the interruption. "Colby has returned from the airport, Dr. Meyerling," he informed Zelig. "He asks what you would like him to do with—"

"Have him bring it in here if you will, Berkley," Zelig told him.

"Very well, sir." The butler withdrew.

"What's that all about?" Holly wanted to know.

"A gift for Nicholas. I thought we should have a look at it before he sees it."

"He's probably asleep by now." Despite the hurt she was nurturing, Holly was touched. "It was nice of you to think of him, Zelig."

"Nicholas is your son. I'm your husband. I want us to

have a good relationship even if you and I, at the moment, don't."

"What did you get for him? Why did it have to be picked up at the airport?"

"Because it came from Switzerland. It's a—"

Zelig was interrupted by the entrance of the chauffeur. He was holding something in his arms. Holly took one look at it and clapped her hands. "Oh, Zelig!" she exclaimed. "How adorable! Nicholas will love it."

"Where shall I put him, Dr. Meyerling?" Colby asked.

"Her." Zelig corrected him.

"Give her to me, Colby," Holly requested.

The chauffeur handed the squirming puppy to Holly, bowed, and left.

"Precious!" Holly was smitten. "Wherever did you find her?"

"Switzerland. I told you. She's a Bernese mountain dog. I had one myself when I was a little boy growing up in Berne."

"Is she a sort of St. Bernard?" Holly cuddled the puppy against her cheek.

"Not really. Smaller, for one thing. She'll grow large, but not quite that large. These dogs are bred to haul milk carts up and down the hills in the villages. Also as companions and guard dogs—herd dogs, really—for little children. They're very gentle, but very protective as well."

"She has such beautiful markings."

"That's because she was bred from champions. The markings are what make Bernese mountain dogs special. See, long, curly black hair covering the body, white paws with golden-brown stockings, a white tip at the very end of the tail, a white diamond at the nape of the neck, a brown-and-white mask, perfectly symmetrical, with a thin white stripe separating the brown framing the eyes of the pandalike face—such markings are the standard for the breed. She has them because her parents were both top-ranked show dogs in Switzerland."

"What's her name?" Holly wrinkled her nose as the puppy licked her face from chin to forehead with a long pink tongue.

346

"Reine Alpen Lucerne the third." Zelig smiled. "A big mouthful for a puppy, but she'll grow into it."

"A big mouthful for Nicholas, you mean. I think we'd better shorten it to Lucy for him."

"Very well, then. Lucy it is."

Holly stroked the puppy, which burrowed between her breasts. Her face was flushed and had softened with pleasure, her haughty demeanor dispelled by the ball of fur wriggling against her.

"I should have sent for two," Zelig observed. "One for Nicholas and one for you."

"I do love her," Holly admitted. But then she remembered that she was still furious with Zelig and why. "I'm sure that Nicholas will be very pleased." Her tone recovered some of its distance and coldness.

Zelig winced. It was so damn hard. At first he had told himself that the interlude with Vanessa was totally without importance and that Holly must surely see that once her anger abated. But then he had faced the fact that the hurt he had inflicted on her was deep, and that it was this hurt, and not Holly's anger, which must somehow be dispelled. The realization brought him face to face—perhaps for the first time in his life where women were concerned—with his own guilt. Now Zelig was learning that acknowledging guilt was one thing, while dealing with it, atoning, was something quite different.

"I would very much like to please you, too," he responded tentatively to Holly. "Isn't there some way we can patch things up?"

"Like Uncle James and Vanessa, you mean?" Holly stroked the soft fur.

"Have they reconciled?" Zelig was surprised. "I hadn't heard about that. Only that James was staying on in Crete."

"He's staying indefinitely," Holly told him. "He's living with Vanessa."

"I'm glad."

Holly looked down at the puppy. "Uncle James has forgiven her."

"Good," Zelig approved.

"Is it?" The puppy whined softly.

"In these liberated times scarlet letters are supposed to be erasable, aren't they?"

" 'These liberated times'!" Holly scowled and shushed the puppy. "The modern catch phrase by which the guilty excuse themselves."

"I'm not excusing myself, Holly." Zelig was earnest. "Still, if James can find forgiveness in his heart for Vanessa, then might there not be some way you, too . . . ?"

"James was not married for only eight weeks!" Holly cried. "He and Vanessa were not married at all." The puppy's squirming was detracting from her righteousness. Holly set Lucy down on the Flemish carpet. "James was not stuck at home nursing a sick child while his brand-new mate wrote off his marriage vows."

"It was so damn casual," Zelig told her. How many times since Greece had he spoken these words to Holly? But he didn't know what else to say. "It meant nothing."

"That does not make me feel any better." Holly frowned at Lucy sniffing the oiled mahogany claw foot of a Chippendale chair.

Zelig sighed. "You know," he said, "I have learned one very important thing from my associations in the White House over the years."

"And what's that?"

"When it's necessary to move with all deliberate speed to take the household pet out." Zelig swept up the puppy and walked from the drawing room to the parlor and through the French doors to the Riverview garden.

Laughing in spite of herself, Holly followed. She watched as Zelig set Lucy down on the ground. The puppy yelped gratefully and made a beeline for the nearest clump of trees.

"You see," Zelig told her. "You have to forgive me. You are in my debt. I have saved your carpet."

"Berkley is in your debt. The cleaning of soiled carpets is his domain."

"If you don't forgive me, I will send the puppy back to Switzerland."

"Nicholas would hate you," Holly assured him.

"Nicholas hasn't seen Lucy yet. He would never know."

"You can't joke your way back into my good graces. You can't charm me. Even taken as I am with Lucy, you can't buy me with a puppy, either."

"Then what can I do to make things right between us?" Zelig spread his hands. "Holly—Holly, my darling—I do so want to make it up to you."

"For a start, you might try groveling."

"Unseemly."

"Well, if you're not truly contrite—" Holly wheeled around and almost tripped on Lucy running in circles around her feet.

"I am contrite," Zelig protested. "But when a man with a paunch gets down on his knees, he looks ridiculous. Couldn't I just apologize?"

Holly looked down at Lucy. The puppy cocked her head at her as if asking the question herself. "Well," Holly conceded. "I suppose that would be a start."

"I am truly sorry."

Zelig's brown eyes held hers. Holly searched his for signs of—of what? True repentance? Guilt? She wasn't sure. The puppy yelped to attract Holly's attention. When she had it, she wagged her tail approvingly.

"You trained her to do that!" Holly accused Zelig.

"I never set eyes on this alpine mongrel before tonight. I swear it."

The dog responded to Zelig's voice by going to him and lying down with her head across his foot.

"Liar." Holly did something she almost never did. She giggled.

"I love you," Zelig said then.

"I love you, too," Holly blurted out.

The puppy looked up reproachfully as Zelig moved his foot to cross over to Holly. "God, how I love you!" He took her in his arms, holding her close.

"Zelig, I—"

He kissed her. "I have hurt you," he murmured, holding her tight. "I know that, my darling. I'll make it up to you. I promise."

"Oh, Zelig! I was so sure of you. And now—"

"It will never happen again. I swear it." Zelig was truly contrite.

"But how can I be sure?" Holly asked with the honesty that was characteristic of her.

"Never again, my darling. Believe me. I love you so much. Please." His words came out slowly, solemnly. "I will never hurt you again if you will only forgive me. Just please forgive me." Zelig meant it as sincerely as he had ever meant anything in his life.

"I forgive you." Holly wanted so very much to believe that he would never betray her again. In time, she told herself. In time, I will.

The puppy stood in front of them with her head cocked and her tail wagging her entire round, furry back end. Holly turned her face up to be kissed again. This second kiss was longer, filled with love as the first one had been, but with the beginnings of passion as well.

"Let's go inside." Zelig's arm encircled her waist.

"Yes, please. Let's."

Zelig led Holly back through the French doors. Lucy followed at their heels, bouncing and tumbling. Inside they kissed again—a long kiss, deep and loving and filled with promise for the night ahead—while the puppy raced in circles around the Flemish carpet.

They had just parted and were standing circumspectly, arm in arm, watching the excited puppy with amused eyes, when Berkley appeared once again. "A telephone call for you, Dr. Meyerling," the butler announced.

"Tell whoever it is that Dr. Meyerling has already retired," Holly told Berkley.

"For the rest of the year," Zelig added.

"It's the White House, sir. I'm sorry."

"Go ahead," she sighed.

"I'll take it in here," Zelig told the butler, his voice resigned.

"Very good, sir." Berkley left.

Zelig picked up the phone. "Zelig Meyerling here," he said. "Hello, Jim. How is the president?"

Holly perched on the arm of the Chippendale chair and looked at Zelig with soft and loving eyes.

"He does? . . . Another mission. But I've only just returned, Jim. . . . To where? Yes, well, of course that is very interesting. Most provocative. Most. Even so . . . By personal request of the president. Yes. I understand. But listen, Jim, can't my country find someone else to need? . . . Who? Well, what's Oliver up to these days? . . . He's involved, too, is he? I know. I know. The national interest. Well, let me discuss it with my wife." Zelig covered the mouthpiece quickly as Holly reacted.

"Another mission!" She stuck out her tongue at him. "What do you think of that, Lucy?" she asked the puppy as it continued running around in happy circles.

The reply was a surprisingly deep bark for a puppy.

"Lucy says that you'd do better asking me in the morning," Holly told Zelig.

The receiver was still crackling in his ear. Now Zelig interrupted. "Yes, when you put it that way. Nancy. Of course. Nancy." Zelig rolled his eyes. "Yes, well, I suppose I really do have no choice if Nancy's the one who . . . All right, Jim. I'll do it. Call me back tomorrow and we'll go over the details." Zelig hung up the phone.

"You're a tower of marshmallow," Holly told him reproachfully.

"I have no choice." Zelig spread his hands. "If some cowboy fouls this one up, the repercussions could affect the prestige of the United States throughout the entire world."

"The entire world." Holly's tone was fond, loving, but ironic. "What do you think of that, Lucy?" she asked the puppy.

The answer was not what she expected.

"Uh-oh!" Zelig started to move, but he wasn't fast enough.

"And we just took her out." Holly shook her head ruefully. "There goes the Flemish carpet."

"I don't know if Riverview is ready for this cur." Zelig picked up the puppy and frowned into her happy face.

"Oh, Riverview has endured a lot worse than Lucy."

It was true. Riverview had always endured what had to be endured. The future wouldn't change that. Riverview would endure puppies and people, squabbles and scandals, financial finagling and international intrigue, just as it always had. Riverview would abide Lucy just as it abided all those who settled there. It would sit atop its verdant wooded hills overlooking the swift-moving Hudson River, and it would stand firm through all the years and all the turbulent events that swept over it. Riverview would abide, and Riverview would endure.

FROM TOKYO TO TAHITI,
SAN FRANCISCO TO SAINT TROPEZ,
SOAR TO THE GLITTERING HEIGHTS
OF FAME AND SUCCESS WITH
DAZZLING WOMEN OF WEALTH, BEAUTY,
AND POWER

In fabulous stories of romance, sparkling heroines rise to positions of unparalleled renown and power. Traveling to the most exclusive addresses in the world, FORTUNES heroines gamble with love and money in the impassioned pursuit of their goals. For in their glamorous, privileged world, the irresistibly sexy women of these stories overcome even the slickest adversaries as they forge their own destinies and realize their wildest dreams.

Capable of wielding passion and power with equal charm, FORTUNES heroines capture the hearts of readers across the country—and men around the world.

Look for the next book in the FORTUNES series, *Expensive Choices,* coming soon from Ivy Books.